# LEAGUE
## OF LIARS

ALSO BY ASTRID SCHOLTE

*The Vanishing Deep*
*Four Dead Queens*

# LEAGUE OF LIARS

## ASTRID SCHOLTE

G. P. Putnam's Sons

## G. P. Putnam's Sons

An imprint of Penguin Random House LLC, New York

First published in the United States of America by G. P. Putnam's Sons,
an imprint of Penguin Random House LLC, 2022

Library of Congress Cataloging-in-Publication Data
Names: Scholte, Astrid, author. | Title: League of liars / Astrid Scholte. | Description: New York:
G. P. Putnam's Sons, [2022] | Summary: "Four teens caught up with the illegal use of magic band together
to devise the ultimate jailbreak" —Provided by publisher. | Identifiers: LCCN 2021041667 (print) |
LCCN 2021041668 (ebook) | ISBN 9780593112373 (hardcover) | ISBN 9780593112380 (ebook) |
Subjects: CYAC: Fantasy. | Magic —Fiction. | Justice —Fiction. |
Classification: LCC PZ7.1.S336533 Le 2022 (print) | LCC PZ7.1.S336533 (ebook) |
DDC [Fic] —dc23 | LC record available at https://lccn.loc.gov/2021041667
LC ebook record available at https://lccn.loc.gov/2021041668

Book manufactured in Canada

ISBN 9780593112373 (hardcover)
1 3 5 7 9 10 8 6 4 2
ISBN 9780593463093 (international edition)
1 3 5 7 9 10 8 6 4 2
FRI

Design by Eileen Savage | Text set in Carre Noir

For everyone who needs an escape. Follow me.

If you're reading this, that means I succeeded. Or maybe I failed spectacularly and you found this on my deathbed.

Whatever happens to me, I won't apologize for what I've done. It was the only way.

The only way to set things right. And separate the truth from all the lies.

You might not believe what I'm about to tell you. But it's true. Every word.

Trust me.

# Telene Government Hierarchy

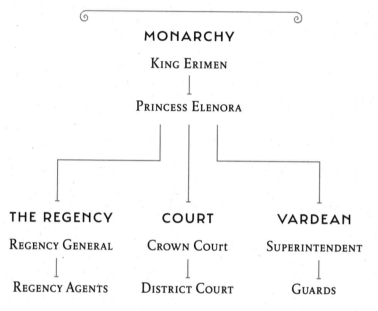

MONARCHY

KING ERIMEN

PRINCESS ELENORA

**THE REGENCY**

REGENCY GENERAL

REGENCY AGENTS

**COURT**

CROWN COURT

DISTRICT COURT

**VARDEAN**

SUPERINTENDENT

GUARDS

*By royal decree, no person shall use or attempt to use extradimensional magic lest they wish to suffer the full consequences of the law.*

—Telene Code of Conduct,
Chapter 1, Page 1

# LEAGUE OF LIARS

# CAYDER

Becoming a criminal is a choice," my father would say. "We either choose to accept the ways things are or try to force fate's hand."

Father always spoke in such definitive terms: Shadows were dangerous. Edem was illegal. And liars were cowards.

Well, then call me a coward, because some lies were necessary. Like the tiny detail of where I was working over the summer. What my father didn't know wouldn't hurt him.

Before I left the house, I checked to see if my sister had once again snuck in via the latticework outside her bedroom.

"Seriously, Leta?" I groaned at her disappointingly empty room. Apparently, I wasn't the only Broduck keeping secrets.

Over the last month, she'd been away more than she'd been home, and even Father was bound to notice her absence.

After inhaling breakfast, I joined the commuters gathered by the local trolley stop to Downtown Kardelle. Although the permacloud hung over the capital city, diffusing shadows into a safe gray, the group stood away from the buildings. Despite what Father said, shadows weren't inherently dangerous, but people instinctually shied away from what could linger within.

The 7:30 trolley announced itself by screeching around the bend. The carriage hurtled by, packed to the brim with commuters, the driver not even offering a wave of apology as he passed the stop.

It hadn't taken me long to learn the trolley never ran on schedule and I had to be thirty minutes early to arrive at work on time.

Last week marked the start of my three-month apprenticeship at Edem Legal Aid before commencing my final year at school. My mentor was none other than Graymond Toyer, the number one public defender of edem-based crimes. And an old friend of my father's. I needed Mr. Toyer's recommendation if I wanted to shorten the duration of my undergrad studies and apply to law school after two years instead of the usual four. And as my sister liked to remind me, patience wasn't one of my virtues.

That wasn't entirely true; she said I possessed *no* virtues.

I planned to eventually become a prosecutor for the Crown Court. The Crown Court was the highest court in the land and dealt with the most serious edem crimes. But studying the other side of the law would be invaluable as a prosecutor, ensuring justice prevailed for victims and their families. Families like mine.

As I glanced at my watch, something bright sparkled off the glass face.

A spot of sunshine.

Thanks to the machine in the center of the city that pumped

water into the air at the exact right temperature to generate a fog, it was rare to glimpse unobstructed sunlight. Occasionally, if the temperature unexpectedly changed, the permacloud would falter, allowing the sun to break through. With sun came the darkest shadows.

While most streets had been cleared of any substantial trees and the shadows they could cast, hundreds of lampposts lined the sidewalk to flood diffused light at nighttime. With nearly constant cloud cover during the day, the lampposts' shadows shouldn't be a concern.

But now, with the sun streaking though the cloud, the thin gray lines on the sidewalk turned black. And within the pitch-black shadow lay a shifting substance—as though something dark and simmering had been spilled onto the pavement.

*Edem.*

My first and only use of extradimensional magic was when I was ten. I'd been grounded by Father for accidentally breaking a vase—one of Mother's favorites—not long after she'd passed away. Desperate to escape my room and the oppressive manor, I'd smashed my permalamp, which kept shadows at bay. I welcomed the darkness, waiting for edem to appear. It didn't take long. An obsidian shadow trailed up my hands and wound around my arms.

"Free me," I'd commanded.

Edem allowed you to manipulate time and change your reality. My rescue was provided in the form of a ladder, plucked from yesterday, when the gardener had set up his window-cleaning equipment outside my bedroom.

While my father hadn't known I'd escaped—the ladder fading and returning to the past once I'd climbed down—he soon uncovered my crime when the Regency came knocking the very next day in full body armor, their silvery cloaks trailing behind them. The flash of silver reminded me of my mother's own cloak, and for a brief moment, I'd foolishly thought she had returned home.

The Regency were a trusted arm of the government who monitored and reported edem fluctuations to the monarchs of Telene. While the royals decreed edem law, the Regency enforced it. They tracked shifts in time and pinpointed the exact coordinates to investigate and arrest the person responsible. When they arrived at Broduck Manor that day, they quickly realized I'd been the culprit; a smoky gray design crisscrossed both my arms from where the edem had touched my skin.

Known as an *echo mark*, it indicated the use of edem. The larger the impact, the longer the mark lasted. Luckily for me, the gardener had not been on the ladder at the time it was stolen from the past and delivered into my present. Had the gardener fallen to his death, my echo mark would have been permanent. A death echo.

I hadn't touched edem since.

I glanced at the commuters around me. No one else appeared to notice the edem lying within the shadow. I planned to ignore it, until the man beside me moved into the patch of sunlight.

From behind, we could have been mistaken for one another: both in tailored suits, his hair not too dissimilar from my own structured dark brown coif. But his skin was much paler than my warm beige. I wouldn't have given him a second glance until he bent to the ground.

Surely he wasn't about to—

*"Please."* His voice was urgent as the inky shadows trickled over his skin like liquid, covering his fingers in darkness. "I can't be late. Not again. I'll lose my job. Please. *Help me.*"

Edem spread from the lamppost's shadow, across the sidewalk and into the cobblestone street. It pooled in the center of the road and began to rise into the shape of a trolley—near where a child was crossing the tracks. The trolley would run him down before he could even realize what happened!

The shadows began to solidify and turn red. Any second now, the trolley would be pulled into our reality from somewhere in the past or future. What would happen if there were people on that trolley when it disappeared? If they were now on the tracks, they could be killed when the trolley returned to its timeline.

I shoved the man away from the shadow. The shadows on the street dispersed instantly, the connection to the edem lost.

"Hey!" I gestured to the kid crossing the tracks. "You could have killed him!"

"I'm sorry!" the man cried. "Please don't tell the Regency! I was desperate!"

The trolley was always late, and yet this man was the only one who sought out edem. *He* had decided to act selfishly and damn the consequences. It was that exact kind of thoughtlessness that had killed my mother.

"I'm sorry!" the man said again.

The woman beside me had already opened a panel on the

5

nearest lamppost and pulled out a pair of shackles. She snapped them onto the man's wrists, locking him to the post before he could make a run for it.

The Regency had their own trolley line that ran throughout the city, allowing them to dispatch agents to sites of edem crimes and any attempted usage. Opening the panel alerted the Regency; it took only ten minutes for them to arrive at the scene.

Four Regency agents jumped off the small trolley in unison, their silvery cloaks falling down behind them with a *thwump*. They were dressed head to toe in a light gray, the color of Telene and the royal family—and safe shadows. Silver epaulets lined their shoulders, and rows of polished buttons ran down their front.

My mouth went dry. I was ten years old again, trying to explain to my father why the Regency were at our door. But this time, I wasn't about to be dragged from my home.

"What happened here?" one agent asked, his gravelly voice booming. His brown hair was buzzed short, and under his thick beard, his skin was pockmarked and pale.

"Please," the shackled man whimpered. "I didn't actually use edem!"

The agent turned away. "Who can explain what happened here?"

I swallowed down my fear and stepped forward. "Our trolley didn't stop," I said. "So this man attempted to find another form of transport." I nodded to the patch of sunlight that was already fading, along with the black shadow. "He nearly killed a kid who was crossing the street."

The agent moved toward me, and I forced myself not to shrink back. "And how was this disaster averted?"

"I pushed the man out of the shadow." I'd done what was expected of any citizen of Telene, and yet now, faced with the Regency, I felt like I'd made a mistake.

The agent nodded. "Well done, son. Our king thanks you for your quick thinking."

Before I could say anything further, the agents surrounded the man.

"Stop!" the man cried as they removed the shackles from the post. "I didn't do *anything!*"

I flinched as the agents shoved him into their trolley. I'd hate to see how they treated someone who had actually used edem.

The man looked back at me as the trolley departed. I swallowed down a lump in my throat.

I'd saved a boy's life, but at what cost?

I shook the thought free. The Regency *had* to be strict. It was the only way to protect our nation.

The man would have to argue his case before the court.

———

I finally arrived at Edem Legal Aid at ten a.m., my shirt and vest sticking to me like a second skin. I pushed the office door open with a little too much force. The door banged into the wall behind. Several people glanced up before seeing it was me and then returned to their typewriters.

"Whoops," I offered sheepishly.

The office clerk at the front desk furrowed his brows behind his minuscule glasses. A line of black hair ran around the back of his pale bald head, as though someone had taken a pen to it but had forgotten to color within the lines.

"You're late, boy," Olin said gruffly.

"I know, I know," I said. "A man on the street attempted to use edem, if you can believe it."

"We work at *Edem* Legal Aid," Olin said with a roll of his eyes. "I can believe it."

"Right, of course. He made me miss my trolley, and I had to run all the way to Downtown Kardelle to catch the connecting trolley to the Unbent River."

"That explains the smell." Olin wrinkled his nose.

I hoped he was kidding. Then again, I'd never even seen Olin smile, let alone make a joke.

I brushed past Olin's messy desk to reach my own by the window that overlooked the red-brown river.

"Hang on—" He held out a narrow envelope with a waxy crimson seal. "Mr. Toyer asked me to give this to you when you arrived."

The seal looked like a blot of splattered blood. A symbol of two chained hands with a bar down the middle was pressed into the wax.

The emblem of Vardean.

Vardean was Telene's only prison, where criminals from all over the nation were jailed for breaking the law, edem-related or not. While most kids would have pissed themselves over the sight of that emblem, I found it comforting.

After the Regency had discovered a naive ten-year-old had been the cause of the edem fluctuation the night I'd escaped my bedroom, I was sentenced to a year at Vardean Reform. The boarding school was attached to the prison complex and housed any edem abusers under the age of sixteen.

While my year at Vardean Reform was meant to be a punishment, I'd thrived there. It had been a relief to escape both my father and the memories of Mother back at Broduck Manor. There, I'd learned the intricacies of the law. Something to focus on—something to push the grief away. Vardean was a pillar of strength and protected the good citizens of Telene from dangerous criminals. Over that year, my appreciation of the justice system had been born. In truth, I would have stayed at Vardean for the rest of my schooling if allowed.

"What's this?" I asked Olin.

"A letter from Vardean," he replied with another roll of his eyes. "Surely you recognize the emblem from your time there?"

Disdain dripped from each word. Many people looked down upon those who'd spent time at Vardean, even if it was the school and not the prison sector. Was that why Olin was so short with me? If Graymond could look past my childhood misdemeanor, surely Olin could too.

"Mr. Toyer was called in to Vardean to process a new client over the weekend," Olin said. "He's still there."

"But we were planning to go through appeals paperwork today."

"Would you prefer to stay here?" he asked, honestly confused.

"Is that a trick question?" I grinned and snatched the envelope from his hand, then ripped it open.

*Dear Cayder,*
*Change of plans for today. Meet me at*
*Vardean prison foyer at 10 a.m.*
*Don't be late.*

*Graymond Toyer*

Not exactly illuminating, but Graymond couldn't divulge any details about his new client, in case the letter was misplaced. Confidentiality was an important part of practicing law; I knew that. And I was good at keeping secrets.

Slipped in behind the letter was a blood-red token with the prison emblem pressed onto its face. I ran my fingers across it. *A ticket to Vardean.*

"Graymond wants me to meet him there?" I'd been trying to get back to Vardean ever since I'd left. Without breaking the law, of course.

Even though my father worked at the prison as a senior district judge, he'd outright refused my suggestion of working with him over the summer. He'd forbidden me from pursuing a career in law, claiming he didn't want either of his children involved with Vardean. He wanted to forget what happened to Mother and refused to even mention her name.

Ever since her death, he had a single-minded focus for his job. My sister and I were merely annoyances and mouths to feed. Father thought I was spending my summer working at the Downtown Kardelle Library. Out of trouble. And, most importantly, out of his sight.

If I ran into him at Vardean, then my ruse would be exposed and he would ensure my apprenticeship with Graymond would come to an end. Graymond had promised not to tell my father what I was up to this summer—he knew how stubborn my father could be. But I couldn't pass up the opportunity to see Graymond in his natural habitat. Perhaps I'd get to see a trial in action!

Something prickled under my shirt's crisp collar. Anxiety *and* anticipation. "It's past ten a.m.," I said.

Olin was unmoved. "Then you better get going."

"Olin, my friend, you are the master of the understatement."

He finally cracked a smile. "Good luck, Cayder."

———

Vardean was an hour away from Downtown Kardelle by suspension tramway. The gondolas were made entirely of glass so if any criminals attempted to break out, they could be easily spotted by the prison guards posted at either end. And in the hundred years of Vardean, no one had ever escaped.

I sat alone in the glass gondola as it skimmed along the ocean; my father, the lawyers, judges, jury members and prison employees would have already made the journey earlier this morning. No one else was allowed access; even prisoners' families were prohibited from visiting.

I glanced behind me to see if I could spot Broduck Manor on

the cliffs. Like most wealthy families, we lived on the coast called Sunshine Mile—named after the yellowish cliffs the homes were built on. The three stories of white stone stood out from the jagged golden rock. It looked like a beacon of hope, but it was nothing but a lie.

Broduck Manor used to be a happy home. When my mother was alive, my father had been a reasonable man and was known to smile and—sometimes—laugh. My sister and I spent our days playing inside the enclosed gardens, a sanctuary from the outside world. The house was full of warmth and love. A true *Sunshine Mile* home.

The manor had become its own kind of prison since Mother died, and Leta and I had attempted to break free in different ways. While I threw myself into my studies in hopes I could shorten my undergrad degree and apply to law school sooner, Leta had become increasingly obsessed with edem. She spent more hours out investigating superstitious stories about edem creatures than she did under Broduck Manor's ornate ceiling.

Leta claimed that our mother had also believed there was more to edem, and she wanted to prove her right. While Mother had never spoken such nonsense to me, I allowed Leta to continue her childish fantasies.

Mother used to work for the Regency and would travel to edem crime scenes to gather evidence for the court. Her last trip had been to a rural town called Ferrington, half a day's trip outside the city. While she was investigating a crime scene, a nearby farmer used edem to make it rain, conjuring a severe storm in seconds and catching my mother in the downpour. The sandy soil became a mudslide, and my mother was swept off her feet and into a ravine.

She died because one selfish man thought watering his crops was more important than the safety of those around him.

The Regency had been swift to arrest the perpetrator, and he was currently serving a fifteen-year sentence in Vardean. While the sentence wouldn't bring my mother back, at least justice had been served.

My mother's death had forever altered my course in life, but it had also given me a purpose.

The gondola rattled through the gray permacloud for a few miles before it dispersed. I sucked in a breath. I would never get used to the sight before me.

Out on the horizon, a black streak cleaved the sky in two. Like a static bolt of lightning, but where light should be, darkness reigned. Known as the veil, it was the source of edem and many kids' nightmares. A fissure between our world and another, allowing time-altering magic to seep through.

In front of the veil, a building with one central spire rose from the ocean.

*Vardean.*

Almost one hundred years ago, a ship crossed this exact section of ocean until it shuddered to a stop, the engine dying. The captain descended into the engine room to discover what had happened and found the entire room gone. Not destroyed. Gone. In its place was a black void—the veil. Returning to the deck, the captain found the other half of his boat had disappeared through the darkness, along with his crew.

The captain managed to escape on a lifeboat before the rest of the ship disappeared into the veil, never to return.

The ruling king and queen of Telene sent their top scientists to investigate the phenomenon. While one diver was near the veil, he discovered a dark substance under the shadow of a boat. He touched it, thinking the boat was leaking fuel. But when the liquid began to climb up his hand, he panicked and ordered it to go away. Misunderstanding the diver's intent, edem transported the man to another part of the ocean, hundreds of miles from his boat. The man was barely conscious when he returned back to the research base. Initially, his ranting about being magically transported out to sea was seen as delusions from exhaustion. But after some tests, the scientists discovered this liquid—edem—could manipulate time, and the consequences were always unpredictable and often disastrous.

These scientists became the Regency. At first, edem only appeared in black shadows close to the veil itself. But the more they did their tests, the more the veil grew and edem spread to Telene's shores. And while the Regency developed the permacloud to prevent dark shadows and their connection to edem, they could not control what people did inside their homes, forcing the king and queen to declare the use of edem illegal. But not everyone abided by the law. Before long, the fissure stretched up into the sky.

To this day, edem had not spread beyond Telene, but if people continued to break the law, it would eventually infect the shadows of the rest of the world. Before the veil, people moved freely between nations and shared their cultures and customs with one another. But as the veil grew, the neighboring nations shut their borders and halted any trade until edem could be brought under control. That was one reason Vardean, and the legal system, was so important.

The veil crackled behind Vardean—a sign that someone had recently used edem. I thought back to the man on the street today. Even with the threat of being arrested, people continued to risk imprisonment to change their fate. If I hadn't intervened, a boy would be dead, possibly dozens more. The Regency *had* to be strict.

The gondola descended toward Vardean and pulled to a stop. I stepped onto the station that connected to the prison via an enclosed metal bridge. A steady humming drowned out the sound of the waves, like the buzz of an engine or an overloaded lightbulb about to pop.

A young prison guard stood by the gated entrance. Unlike Regency agents, Vardean guards were employed by the prison itself. The guard wore black instead of light gray, and the only splash of color was the red Vardean emblem on her peaked cap and the piping along her collar like a plump vein. She looked like the typical guard I'd glimpsed while at Vardean Reform; the only act of rebellion was her bleached white hair, which hugged her brown face like a baby to its mother. She was pretty in the way that said she clearly couldn't care less what you thought.

"Morning," I said, flashing her my best smile.

"Stand with your legs and arms out," she commanded, her expression unmoved. I complied, and she ran a handheld metal detector over me. It made the hairs on my arms and the back of my neck stand up. Then she pulled my satchel from my shoulder and rummaged for contraband items.

She cocked a dark eyebrow. "Reason for coming to Vardean?"

I handed her my red token. "I'm with Edem Legal Aid."

"Aren't you a bit young to be an attorney?" Amusement lit her face, the apples of her cheeks lifting.

"I'm Graymond Toyer's apprentice, the number one public defender in Telene."

She laughed. "Not for long."

I blinked a few times, wondering if I'd heard her correctly.

She didn't clarify and pressed a button beside the gate. "Visitor for Graymond Toyer," she said into a mouthpiece. She inserted my token into a slot, and the gate retracted into the wall.

"You'll get the token back when you head home, Boy Wonder."

"Thank you, er . . . What's your name?"

She cut me off with a wave of a hand. "Does it matter? You won't see me again."

Why was she implying I was only here for a day?

"Well?" she asked when I didn't move. "Go on, then." She gestured toward the open gate. "Shoo."

I walked along a narrow corridor that led to a crowded room. Several passageways branched off the central foyer to courtrooms, interrogation rooms and legal offices, and the hallway to the far right led to the reform school. People bustled by with papers stacked under their arms. I recognized their expressions as the same one I wore whenever I looked in the mirror: determination.

The first time I'd entered this foyer, I was ten years old. I'd been surrounded by kids my age who'd each committed minor edem infractions. While everyone else shook with fear, a strange feeling of calm washed over me. Just as it did now. This was a place where everything made sense. This was a world where justice prevailed. This was a world I understood.

"Cayder," a low voice said from behind me.

I jumped, recognizing the voice. But it wasn't my father's scratchy growl.

"Mr. Toyer." I turned with a grin.

Graymond Toyer had warm brown skin and a neat speckled beard. His tailored royal-blue three-piece suit hung precisely on his broad shoulders, making me feel underdressed in my beige vest, white shirt and tawny pants. I would have worn my best had I known I'd end up at Vardean today.

"Sorry I'm late," I said. "There was an incident at the trolley stop. I got here as quickly as I could, Mr. Toyer."

"Not to worry, son," he said, clapping me on the back. "And I told you to call me Graymond. *Mr. Toyer* is my old man."

I nodded. I knew Graymond from when I was a kid. He was always at Broduck Manor, working with my father in his study or helping my mother in the garden. My father's parents had passed before I was born, and my mother's family lived overseas, and so Graymond became like an uncle to Leta and me. That was until my mother died. Graymond hadn't visited since. Whether something had driven a wedge between my father and him or whether my father had simply shut Graymond out like he had his own children, I wasn't sure.

"What am I doing here?" I asked. "I mean, I'm glad to be here, don't get me wrong. But . . . well, why?"

Graymond laughed and walked me to the middle of the room. Fine lines feathered out from around his mouth and brown eyes. He simply pointed upward.

Now that I was standing in the center of the room, I could see a circular opening in the stone ceiling. A metal elevator slowly descended with a *click click click*.

"I thought you might want to assist me with my new case," he said.

I bounced on the balls of my feet. "Really?"

"You've put in some solid hours back at the office doing dry paperwork, but I want you to see what the law is really about."

"Vardean." I'd always wanted to see the prison sector. As a student, it had been off-limits.

"No." Graymond frowned. "Helping our clients."

My cheeks burned; I felt like I'd failed some kind of test.

Graymond pushed the rusty elevator door open when it reached us. "Welcome to Vardean, Cayder."

The elevator rose toward the hole in the rocky ceiling, and my heart beat in time with the *click click click* of the elevator chain.

"First, I want to warn you . . ." Graymond leaned back against the elevator wall, his arms crossed. "I know that you plan to become a prosecutor once you graduate law school, but I expect you'll have an open mind as to what can land someone in here. It's easy to jump to conclusions and judge the inmates."

"Of course, sir."

He nodded, short and sharp. "Good."

The elevator entered the hole in the ceiling, and for a moment, all I could see was a bright cone of light surrounding us.

"What matters most to our clients is that we listen to the story they tell us," Graymond said. "I know you're a hard worker, Cayder, but are you a good listener?"

Unless it was having to listen to my sister and her insistent conspiracy theories about the veil, then yes. "Of course."

"*Listen*, but do not judge. Does this make sense to you?"

"Suuuure," I said, dragging out the word.

"I say listen, as their *stories* are all we have. And yes, they are simply stories. Their point of view. What they saw. What they smelled. What they heard. And what they did and didn't do. Is it fact? Is it the truth?" He paused, and I wasn't sure if he wanted me to answer. "We don't know."

"But if—"

"We don't know, Cayder. My job as a public defender is to present the case as I know it to be true. The burden of proof is on the prosecutor—they must prove beyond a reasonable doubt that my client is guilty."

"What if your client *wants* to plead guilty?"

"Interesting you should mention that." He scratched at his beard that matched his cropped silvery hair. "My new client claims that he is indeed guilty."

"And you don't believe him?"

He tilted his head side to side noncommittally. "Let's see what you think."

The elevator pulled out of the rock and into the prison sector. The building looked like a swollen birdcage, with row after row of cells lining the walls. The ceiling was made of a glass prism, refracting hundreds of beams of light, preventing any dark shadows. Vardean was the one building where you could control the presence of shadows both day and night. The only place where time couldn't be altered, or a crime committed.

While I'd witnessed the occasional fight and nightly break-downs in the dormitory, there was no comparison to the chaos unfolding before me. Criminals were screaming, crying, spitting and—from the smell of it—pissing and worse. Arms and legs reached out from the bars, desperate for contact or merely acknowledgment.

The yelling amplified as we stepped out of the elevator.

"They all have a story," Graymond said with a sweep of his arms, raising his voice over the racket. "Are you ready to listen?"

Now I understood what the guard had referred to earlier. A part of me, the sane part, wanted to walk back into the elevator and descend back to the foyer, get on the next gondola out of here and never return.

Another part—the part that longed for justice for families like my own—reveled in the sight.

My chest expanded. My head felt light and buoyant.

I was back.

# CHAPTER 2

## JEY

J ey loped through the streets, a fowl tucked under one arm and a knife clasped in the other. The fowl fluttered against his side as he fled; members of the King's Guard, who upheld the general peace of Telene, were close behind, shouting as they pursued.

"Stop now," one yelled, "and we'll only take your hands, not your head!"

"Tempting!" Jey yelled back over his shoulder.

He wound his way through the stalls of Penchant Place, which sat in the center of the overstuffed capital. The smell of coal and dust from the nearby industrial district of the Unbent River clung to the air. And not even the sweetest stolen pastry could mask the stink of too many people living in close quarters.

Jey sidled into a narrow alley away from the market and the hollers of the guards. He began questioning his choice of stolen goods as the fowl started nipping at his fingers. A bag of rice didn't bite.

The guards chased Jey through the alleyways, their continued bellowing allowing him to stay a step ahead.

"Surrender now, you scoundrel!" one shouted.

Jey was well acquainted with that voice. He'd often been chased by this guard. He liked to think of their meetings as a special kind of dance, one that he had perfected over the past five weeks. The guard was spindly, all arms and legs, but he was fast. While Jey was fit, at six foot three, he was too tall and broad to be nimble and quick. He was used to the careful precision of climbing walls and trees, not darting between narrow gaps of market stalls.

Jey could hear the guard's swift footsteps as he neared.

No matter which way Jey turned, he couldn't seem to lose him. The guard lunged, reaching for the tail of Jey's shirt.

Jey darted into another laneway, leaving the man's fist empty.

In front of him stood a stack of crates, blocking his exit. Jey cursed and glanced behind him.

The guard sneered as he drew close. "Got you!"

"Don't worry," Jey muttered to the fowl. "I've been in worse scrapes than this." He launched himself up the stone wall, the fowl's feathers flapping in his face.

"Cut it out!" Jey said. "Can't you see I'm trying to escape?"

"Stop!" the guard cried.

Once Jey landed on the ground, he kicked out behind him, toppling the crates into the guard's path.

"Ha!" Jey rejoiced. The fowl clucked in disapproval. "Don't be so persnickety," he clucked back. His mother would've approved of his word choice. She'd worked hard to ensure Jey attended Kardelle's most prestigious high school before she'd passed away.

Only when Jey reached the edge of the Unbent River did he allow himself to slow. Along the north side of the river sat an abandoned construction site, the perfect refuge. The developers had gone bankrupt before the luxury terraced houses had been completed. Now the only luxury was a tin roof and an unobstructed view of the murky brown river that looked more like sludge than water. Still, it suited Jey just fine.

"Here," Jey said, plopping the fowl into a pen he'd built from abandoned materials at the construction site. He dropped a handful of grain next to the bird. "Don't say I never gave you anything."

He sucked on his fingertips; it felt as though the fowl had nibbled them to the bone. "This is the thanks I get for saving you from becoming someone's roast dinner?"

The fowl cocked its head at Jey as though she were asking a question.

"Oh, this?" Jey glanced at the knife in his other hand. "That was all for show." He slammed the blade into his palm, and it retracted into the handle. "It's a stage prop."

When the fowl clacked, Jey added, "I need eggs. A dead fowl feeds you for a day or two. A live fowl feeds you for months, if not years." He spun the faux knife before sliding it into his belt. "Got to think bigger, mate."

When the fowl didn't stoop to eat the feed, Jey shrugged his shoulders. "Ungrateful bird."

Jey placed his tattered deck chair by the river's edge and crossed his long legs out in front of him. As the sun set, it ducked under the permacloud, turning the river amber, as though gold lined the banks. As much as he enjoyed the house now—if you could call it that—he hated to think what this place would be like in winter with no walls to protect him from the cold. But even if hunger scratched at his belly, frostbite tickled his toes and rats became his nightly bedfellows, he could never go back to his father's house.

While the Unbent River looked dirty, it was only due to the color of the soil underneath. The water itself was clean, and it had been Jey's bathing and drinking water for the four weeks he'd lived here—not in that order, of course.

Jey retrieved a bunch of torlu berries from his pocket and smiled. His favorite treat. At times like this, he would remind himself what was important. He was alive. And although he was currently alone, he was no longer lonely. And Jey knew the true meaning of loneliness.

After Jey's mother passed away from a sudden illness two years ago, he'd been sent to live with his estranged father. He'd never wanted Jey in his life, and his opinion didn't shift even when Jey was living under his roof.

Jey's parents had met through their work at the Regency. Jey's mother, Yooli, specialized in horology—the study and measurement of time. Van, Jey's father, and Yooli worked together to develop the edemmeter—a piece of equipment that registered temporal glitches and provided precise coordinates of edem usage. Before that, the Regency did randomized sweeps of neighborhoods, checking citizens for echo marks. Everyone learned to fear the drumming of the Regency's footsteps at night as they searched homes, often arresting people based on suspicion and gossip alone.

After the success of the edemmeter, Van was promoted to take over the position of the retiring Regency General, the head of edem research and the ruling monarch's top advisor. He became obsessed with his job, edem and wealth. He had grown up in a poor household, and he saw the promotion as an opportunity to ensure he would never suffer the way his parents had, unable to pay the rent one week to the next. He rarely left the Regency headquarters, not even for Jey's birth.

Yooli stayed with Van for two years before she gave up on trying to change him. Van dedicated every waking moment to "protecting Telene," and no matter how much she tried to fight for his attention, Van would not bend. His work was more important than anything else. Including Jey.

Yooli decided it was better to live in a house full of love than a house of disappointment and regret. Van didn't even bat an eyelid when Yooli announced she was leaving and taking Jey with her.

With the borders shut, Yooli could not move to be with her family in the neighboring nation of Meiyra. Instead, she applied for a teaching job at the prestigious Kardelle Academy. It wasn't a well-paying job, but it allowed Jey to attend for free. Jey often thought she'd placed his happiness above her own.

While their new home had been tiny in comparison to the house his father lived in, their world never seemed small. Each night, they would explore a different part of the city. Jey's mother would point out the constellations while they ate her homemade rolled rice bread with spiced dipping sauces, a traditional dish from Meiyra. Jey inherited her love of the outdoors and couldn't bear the thought of being contained.

Now both his parents were dead.

While Jey missed his funny and kind mother, he wasn't sure how to mourn a man he never really knew. And a man who had made no attempt to know him. It was easier to play the part of runaway.

Back when Jey was at school, he'd loved the performing arts, and he lost himself in the role of uncaring orphan. After four weeks, Jey wasn't sure if he really didn't feel anything about his father's death, or if he'd adopted his role too well.

Jey had planned to take his time eating the torlu berries, but once the first berry exploded in his mouth, he devoured the rest. He would've liked to have stolen more food, but the fowl had made that difficult. He'd have to go back into the market tomorrow for more supplies.

He knew his time was almost up; additional guards were being posted at the market as the days wore on, and Jey didn't believe in coincidences. He'd eventually have to move on to somewhere no one knew his face.

But Jey had his reasons to stay near Downtown Kardelle.

He heard a crunching noise and turned to see the fowl was eating her feed.

"See?" Jey said. "I look after you, you look after me."

He wasn't really sure what else it took for a fowl to lay eggs, but he hoped to wake to a fortuitous gift. He deserved some good fortune after everything that had happened.

Later that night, Jey huddled under the blankets he'd stolen. At nighttime, he thought about his girlfriend, Nettie. He thought about everything he'd lost when his father died. Including a future with her.

The following week, he was arrested for his father's murder.

# DEPARTMENT OF JUSTICE

## VARDEAN, TELENE

### *Arrest Report*

**Name:** Jey Bueter

**Age:** 18

**Height:** 6'3"

**Arrest location:** Penchant Place

**Edem crimes:** Suspected of killing Dr. Bueter—his father—by aging him hundreds of years

**Other crimes:** Petty theft

**Recommended sentence:** 50 years in prison

# CHAPTER 3

# CAYDER

I followed Graymond to a cell located on the eightieth floor. Graymond gestured to a prison guard to unlock the cell. Inside, the inmate sat at a table, his legs placed on the tabletop, crossed at the ankles, as though he was lounging in front of a fire. His dark hair flopped over his forehead. He'd rolled back the gray sleeves of his prison uniform and undone the buttons at the front to further display numerous dark gray echo marks that wound up from his fingers and across his chest. Underneath the marks, his skin was the color of Kardelle's sandy beaches.

I rocked back on my feet. He didn't look much older than me. And he looked familiar, although I couldn't quite place him.

"Mr. Toyer," the inmate said, but he didn't shift from his position at the table. "A pleasure to see you again. And welcome, new visitor, to my humble abode." He stretched his echo-marked arms wide.

The cell was completely unadorned aside from the table, a narrow metal bunk against the far wall, and a showerhead above a hole in the floor to act as a toilet and for drainage. It made my old dorm room look palatial in comparison. Both the table and the bunk were rectangular wooden structures that seemed to rise out of the stone floor, with no room for anything to hide underneath, including shadows.

"Cayder," Graymond said, taking his seat opposite the inmate. "This is my new client, Jey Bueter."

*Of course!* I remembered reading about the Regency General's strange death in the newspaper five weeks ago. This must be his son, although they didn't look alike; Dr. Bueter was fair with blond hair. "Aren't you my neighbor?" I asked.

"Oh?" Jey cocked his head like a bird. "You an inmate too?"

I scoffed. "No."

"That's right . . ." Graymond pulled out a file from his briefcase and placed it on the table. "Jey and his father lived a few houses from Broduck Manor. You attended the same school, although a year apart."

"*Broduck?*" Jey looked taken aback. "As in Judge Broduck?" He jerked his thumb at me. "We're letting in spies now, Mr. Toyer?"

"I'm not a spy," I said.

"Sure you are, mate," he said with a wink. "But I won't hold that against you."

"Cayder is my apprentice. He's on your side," Graymond said. "*We're* on your side. We're here to help. If you would only let me." He muttered the last part mostly to himself.

Jey leaned back and placed his hands behind his head with a sure nod. "He's a spy."

"I'm here to learn the truth," I said firmly.

"Oh yeah?" Jey said. "Well, as I told your boss when I was arrested two days ago, I did it. Case closed."

"You're guilty?" I asked.

"Of course." Jey flashed a wide grin. "I'm a thief, a liar and a killer. What do they call that?" He didn't wait for our response. "A triple threat."

I pressed my lips together. Jey wanted a reaction, but I refused to bite. I was well practiced with not taking my sister's bait over the years.

The left side of Jey's prison uniform gaped open, revealing the image of a skull over his heart, the edges blurring into fragments of bone.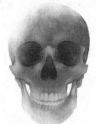

"Something got your attention?" He noticed my stare. "This one appeared the night I killed my father. Looks a lot like him. Without hair, muscle and skin, that is." He winked at me. "Or eyeballs."

*A death echo.* Clearly, Jey *had* killed his father. Why was Graymond questioning Jey's confession?

"Jey," Graymond said, shuffling some papers on the desk. "Can you please tell Cayder what happened the night your father died? I'd like him to hear the details from you so we can best put together your plea for the preliminary trial at the end of the week."

"Sure." Jey cracked his knuckles. "My father had been ordering me around all day, and I was tired of hearing his voice. So I smashed the light in his office and reached out to the edem in the dark. I ordered edem to silence him. And then"—Jey snapped his echo-marked fingers—"he aged a couple hundred years in front of my eyes. Turns out, it's hard to talk after your jaw falls off your face and turns to dust." I winced, but Jey didn't pause. "I've been living on the streets for the past five weeks, stealing whatever I needed—or wanted. My life was going along swimmingly until I was caught trying to pinch a loaf of bread. I was sent here to await my preliminary hearing. Then, enter you."

Graymond let out a deep and exhausted sigh. "Your admission matches the report from the arresting guards."

"Isn't that a good thing?" I asked. The case appeared pretty straightforward to me.

"Not when it matches *exactly*," Graymond replied, switching his attention to the inmate. "Jey, I've represented hundreds of criminals across my twenty-five years of being an edem public defender—"

"You want a medal?" Jey interrupted.

Graymond shook his head. "I've learned across the years to notice patterns and trends. Liars"—he gestured at Jey—"recount their stories perfectly. As though they've memorized the story from start to finish. However, the truth is organic. Details are remembered in bits and pieces. That's the way the mind works. One detail leads to another."

"Photographic memory." Jey tapped his temple. "I take after my father. That's why he was so good at his job."

"You're hiding something," Graymond disagreed. "And I need to know what that is so we're not surprised in court. I need to know what I'm dealing with."

Jey snorted. "You're dealing with a kid whose father couldn't have cared less about him. The man barely featured in my life, even when I slept in the room next door." He shrugged. "My world doesn't feel much different now that he's gone. And *that's* the truth."

I could somewhat relate to Jey's situation. Since my mother died, my father had retreated into his work. He was stubborn, unforgiving and hard to live with. And yet I would never want any harm to come to him. He was still my father.

"If you don't show any signs of remorse," Graymond said, "I can't ask for a reduced sentence."

Jey shrugged. "I don't care."

"Why?" Graymond asked, leaning his elbows onto the table. "You're a smart kid. Why would you want to spend the rest of your life in here?"

"Because the food's free," he said with a grin. "I don't need a trial—I did it. That's all there is to it."

"You have nothing further to say . . ." Graymond prompted, a question in the lift of his brow.

"As much as I appreciate the visit," Jey said, "I've told you everything that happened. You may leave now." He waved us away with a flourish of his hand.

Graymond begrudgingly pushed to his feet and knocked on the door to be released by the guard. I scrambled after him, not wanting to be left behind.

"What do you think Jey's hiding?" I asked once we were back in the elevator. "He has a death echo—he killed someone."

"Yes," Graymond agreed, "but why run from a crime for five

weeks only to openly admit your guilt once you're arrested for petty theft?"

"Perhaps he wants to atone for his father's murder?"

"Does Jey strike you as someone who wants to atone for anything he's done in his life?"

I couldn't help but smile. "Not really, no."

Graymond scratched at his graying beard with agitated fingers. "I wish I had the whole picture. Something about Jey's insistence on his guilt doesn't ring true. The punishment is going to be severe, considering who his father was."

I nodded. "Who's in charge of the Regency now?"

"Dr. Bueter's second-in-command."

I doubted anything would change with new leadership. The Regency had had a stronghold over Telene since the veil first appeared.

"Why don't you enter a guilty plea?" I asked. "If that's what Jey wants?"

Graymond sighed as though I didn't understand, and I didn't. "Because my job as a public defender is to ensure my clients don't end up spending their lives in here. I need something, anything, to show Jey isn't a cold-blooded killer."

"And you're sure he's not?"

Graymond was quiet for a moment.

"I'm positive that whatever happened that night, we don't know the half of it."

# CHAPTER 4

## CAYDER

My office will be your base camp for the remainder of your apprenticeship," Graymond said, opening the door to a room that was smaller than my bathroom back at Broduck Manor. Stacks of paper were piled so high that you couldn't see out the small window.

"Really?" I couldn't contain my grin.

Graymond moved aside some papers from his chair. "I want you to come to Vardean each morning from now on." He sat down heavily; he looked tired. He clearly hadn't slept much over the weekend since Jey's arrest. "I need help finding out what Jey is holding back from us before I enter his plea on Friday. Even if we enter a guilty plea, the Regency's prosecutor is likely to push for a public trial due to the high-profile nature of the case."

I made myself a space to sit on some cardboard boxes. "Why would they do that?"

"To maximize Jey's sentence," Graymond said, his brow

furrowing. "They'll want to put him on the stand and make a spectacle of the trial. Killing the general implies the Regency is now weak; they'll want to assert their power and take a strong stance on anyone who thinks of acting against them. They'll want to lock him away for life."

"How did Jey get arrested?" I asked.

"He was caught stealing a loaf of bread on Saturday. While it wasn't an edem-based crime, Jey admitted guilt over his father's murder." Graymond tapped his notes with a pen. "According to Riva, the cook, Jey was in the house when she left for the night. He's the only suspect."

"Can we trust Riva?" I asked.

He nodded. "She worked for the family for years and had nothing to gain from Dr. Bueter's death."

"Okay," I said, mulling that over. "What's your plan, then?"

"Jey says he's guilty," Graymond said, "and I don't question that. But I do question the details of the crime and what led him to it. Killing his father, then fleeing his home implies that he never planned to inherit his father's fortune, thus the crime was not motivated by money. And while Jey wasn't close with his father, that's not reason enough for murder. Why not run away and start anew?"

"Maybe he wanted revenge first?" I suggested. That was the number one reason people killed. Jey openly hated his father.

"Perhaps." Graymond pressed his lips into a thin line. "But revenge means he had malicious intent. That won't reduce his sentence." He cleared his throat. "I know you want to be a prosecutor, Cayder, but there's a difference between someone who's a danger to society and someone who made a mistake and is more of a danger to themselves. Jey is the latter."

"How can you tell?"

"From the look in Jey's eye when he speaks of his father. There's grief there. Loss. A person who is a danger to society does not care about what they did. Jey's not as good a liar as he thinks he is."

I hadn't seen anything like that when I'd been in Jey's presence. All I'd seen was brashness and bravado. At least I thought I had. I jotted down a few notes in my book.

"I don't know, Graymond. He seems pretty heartless to me."

"*Seems.*" Graymond pointed at me. "Yes. But there's something more there. And that's what we need to get to the bottom of. I will abide by Jey's wishes for a guilty plea if I need to, but I want to dig deeper first."

No doubt the prosecutor would be doing the same thing. Any secrets that Jey kept would soon surface.

"Cayder, I'm going to be frank with you." Graymond leaned forward, his face serious. "Each year, I see more and more people placed behind bars for the remainder of their lives. Each year, I see more guilty verdicts and stricter sentences for crimes that once would've resulted in a few months' imprisonment or even a fine. While my percentage of not-guilty verdicts remains at seventy percent and my appeal requests granted remains high—that doesn't change what's happening out there." He pointed to the door. "Jey is too young to spend the rest of his life in here for one mistake. That's why we have Vardean Reform. Kids learn from their mistakes without it destroying their lives. Their crimes are not marked on a permanent record. And there's a very low rate of recidivism."

I couldn't trust my voice to reply. Would my life be very different if my edem crime had become a part of me? A permanent echo mark for everyone to judge?

"That's one of the reasons I accepted your request for an apprenticeship," Graymond said.

I'd assumed it was because of the history with my family. "Thank you?"

He chuckled. "You don't need to thank me, son. You don't need my forgiveness either. You needed a second chance. As does Jey. Let's make sure he gets it, shall we?"

———

The queue to board the gondola at the end of the day moved painfully slowly. I tucked my head close to my shoulders in case my father was among the crowd. He rarely made the journey home these days, though, spending more nights at Vardean than he did in his own bed.

I looked wistfully behind me as the glass gondola departed the station with a jolt. The veil crackled in the background.

A low, rumbling laugh germinated in Graymond's chest. "Don't worry, son. Vardean will be there tomorrow."

"But the question still remains: Will you be?" a voice asked from behind me.

The guard who'd escorted me into Vardean this morning had a hand on her hip as she studied me. She'd changed out of her prison uniform into a casual yellow sundress, which contrasted against her warm brown skin. Her bleached-white hair was curled tight around her face, and her lips were painted a blood red.

"What do you think?" I asked, trying to stand tall and proud. And failing.

She tapped her chin. "You look tired but not broken. You look . . . invigorated, even." She leaned forward to study my face. "Are you *sure* you spent the entire day at Vardean?"

I smiled. "That I did."

"You are very strange, Boy Wonder. Most people want to spend their summer by the beach, not inside a ghastly prison."

"Ah," Graymond said. "It's nice to see you two together again, brings back old memories."

I raised an eyebrow at him. *"Again?"*

"That's Kema," Graymond answered. "My daughter."

"Really?" I asked. "You look so different!"

Kema tucked an errant bleached-white curl behind her ear. "Do I know you?"

"It's Cayder." I grinned. "You used to come over to Broduck Manor when I was a kid."

"Oh!" She snapped her fingers. "I remember!" She leaned forward as though she was trying to find ten-year-old Cayder behind my eyes.

I glanced at Graymond. "Why didn't you tell me Kema was working here?"

Graymond and Kema exchanged a look I didn't understand. "I wasn't sure you'd run into each other," he replied. "Sorry, son. I should have told you."

"Yes," Kema said. "You should have." She slapped me on the arm. "Good to see you, Boy Wonder."

I groaned. Looked like I wasn't ditching that nickname anytime soon.

"How have you been?" I asked.

"Over the past seven years?" She shrugged. "Good, on average."

Last time I saw Kema was before my mother died and Father retreated from the world. As kids, we'd been friends, getting up to all kinds of mischief around the manor while our parents discussed matters of the law.

"How have you been?" she asked. "How's Leta?"

It was my turn to shrug. "She's always off investigating something about the veil."

Kema laughed. "Nothing's changed, then?"

"Guess not," I said. "What do you have planned for this evening?" I'd always liked Kema, although I wasn't sure if she liked me as more than a friend.

"I'm having dinner with my girlfriend. You?"

*Ah well. It was worth a shot.*

I patted my bag that housed my notes on Jey's case. "Just some light reading."

"Are we still on for lunch this weekend?" Graymond asked his daughter.

"That depends," she said. "Will Mom be making my favorite dessert?"

"Of course," he replied. "Torlu berry pie with ice cream."

She smiled. "Then I'll be there."

Something lodged in my chest. It was such a short interaction, but the ease of it reminded me of what Leta and I had lost when Mother died.

"How long have you worked at the prison?" I asked Kema to distract myself from falling into wistful memories.

"Two years," she said. "I started working there after I graduated school."

"It can't be as bad as you make it out to be if you've lasted two years."

"It's worse," she said. A small crease appeared between her brows. "You'll see."

———

It was almost curfew by the time I reached Broduck Manor. The wrought-iron gate loomed before me, the surrounding flood lamps highlighting the intricate curls and whorls of metal that looked all too similar to the rusted metal of a prison cell.

I didn't want to cross the threshold; I hated the feeling of being lost within my own home. Homes were supposed to be full of love and laughter, not empty hallways and closed doors. My mother's presence lingered within the walls, and Leta and I were too scared to make noise and frighten the memories of her away. The house was a tomb. Somber and mournful.

But if I wasn't inside before eight p.m., I could be fined. The Regency were already swarming the streets, searching for anyone who was out at night. Five fines, and you were sent to Vardean for a year. That wasn't how I wanted to return to the prison sector.

I pushed the gates open and walked up the crushed-shell

drive that led to the manor. The three-story white stone house sat along three acres of manicured cliff-side gardens. My mother used to tend to the gardens herself, but since her death, my father employed a team of people to oversee the various greenhouses and fish-filled ponds. Keeping her garden alive was one of the kinder things he'd done after her passing.

I could imagine my mother stepping through the fog of the misting fountains, her black hair cascading down her back, a smile blessing her face.

The gardeners had all gone home for the night, and the grounds were quiet and still. Only now did I realize how I'd been affected by the stale air of Vardean. A tightness around my chest, which I'd put down to anticipation, unraveled in the evening breeze.

I pulled off my boots as soon as I opened the front doors. My father never let us wear shoes on the marble floors, and it was one thing I could never seem to defy him on.

"Leta?" I called into the empty foyer. I didn't bother asking if Father was home.

No one answered.

*This is ridiculous!* Did she plan to stay away all summer? The least she could do was tell me where she was or when she would return. Unlike Father, *I* cared. And I would've liked to tell her about Vardean—an interest we had in common. Although her curiosity lay close behind Vardean—the veil—not the prison itself.

After eating slices of roasted fowl with crispy torlu root left in the oven by the cook, I headed upstairs. Sometimes I wondered if it would have been better if Father had sold the manor after

Mother's passing. While it pained me to think of never walking these hallways again, it physically hurt to be constantly reminded of what we lost.

Once inside my room, I headed to bed. My mind had been working overtime all day; I was mentally exhausted. And yet I couldn't relax.

I turned on my side and stared at the poster hanging on the wall.

The diagram of Vardean had once hung on the back of my dorm room door. It was supposed to instill fear in its students—a representation of what their future could hold if they didn't change their ways. On my final day, I'd pulled the poster from my wall as a reminder of what I wanted to be a part of.

Justice.

Today was a massive leap toward becoming a prosecutor. By the end of the summer, I would know firsthand what it was like to be in court.

I couldn't wait for what tomorrow would bring.

VARDEAN

# CHAPTER 5

# CAYDER

I ran into Graymond at the tramway station the next morning.

"Cayder," Graymond said with a shake of my hand. "Been burning the midnight oil?"

"Huh?"

"You look like you haven't slept a wink, son." His smile faded. "No nightmares, I hope?"

"I'm not a kid anymore, Graymond. I was looking over my notes on Jey's case till late last night."

"Ah," he said. "You have a thirst for knowledge, just like your father."

I shook off the suggestion. "I couldn't figure out what Jey is hiding."

"Trust me." He nodded. "He's not telling us the whole truth."

"How do you know?" As a prosecutor, I would need to be able to expose liars in front of a jury.

"Because Jey is working hard to make it look like he's relaxed—as though he doesn't have a care in the world." The gondola pulled into the station, and Graymond and I boarded. "Do you know anyone who would be so blasé about being arrested?"

All the kids at Vardean Reform had wanted to go home as soon as they arrived at the dormitory—everyone except for me. They did everything they could to shorten their sentences.

"No, I suppose not."

"He's putting on a good show; I'll grant him that," Graymond said. "But that's all it is."

"I think you're right," I said. "Jey studied drama at school."

"You remember him?"

"No," I said. "His year had over four hundred students, but I found his picture in the school yearbook. He was president of the drama club during his senior year."

"Good find, Cayder." He clapped me on the back. "Now we need to get to the truth."

"Did you ever consider becoming a prosecutor?" I asked. "You're a good judge of character."

Graymond shook his head with a laugh. "Your father and I used to have this same conversation in law school. He would argue there's more money on the other side, which you know firsthand to be true." I nodded. Our home on Sunshine Mile was a far cry from the small apartment Graymond owned above the Edem Legal Aid offices. "But I was never driven by money. I want to help people."

"I do too," I said. "I want to bring justice to those who need it."

A cloud crossed Graymond's face. He'd also been friends with my mother.

Before I started working for Graymond, the last time I'd seen him was seven years ago at one of my mother's infamous parties. My mother loved entertaining, relishing the joy of others. Each party had its own theme.

"It's not a party unless there are costumes," she used to say. "Parties are a chance to escape the ordinary. To *be* extraordinary."

The last party before her death had been a summer-themed bash held in the depths of winter. Even though the snow had piled high against the arched windows, people arrived in swimsuits, sun hats and sandals. My mother's delighted laughter echoed throughout the manor. She requested that I wear yellow to match the ocher of my eyes. At ten years old, I'd been embarrassed to be dressed by my mother, but I couldn't say no to her—few people could. She introduced me to all her friends as her "little ray of sunshine." That night became one of my most cherished memories of her.

The party lasted into the next day, and Mother let me stay up to watch the clock strike twelve—the first time I'd seen one day become the next. A natural shift in time where today became yesterday and tomorrow became today. No edem required.

Mother died the very next week.

Graymond and I handed over our tokens at the security checkpoint.

"Let's go visit Jey this morning," Graymond said. "Hopefully he's changed his mind after another night in Vardean." He grimaced. "Most people do."

The gate retracted into the wall. We walked down the corridor, but the opening to the foyer was blocked by a guard—Kema.

She nodded to her father. "Morning, Dad." Then waggled her eyebrows at me. "Excited for your second day, Boy Wonder?"

"Of course."

She huffed a laugh. "You're still such a strange kid."

"I'm only three years younger than you," I pointed out.

"In years, maybe. But in maturity . . ." She let the sentence hang.

"Very funny," I muttered.

Graymond looked over Kema's head into the vast and empty foyer. "What's the holdup?" he asked.

"New inmate," Kema said with a nod to the elevator in the center of the room. "Yarlyn wants the foyer clear while they transfer them from the interrogation room to the top floor."

"The top floor?" I asked. "Isn't that where the class one criminals are kept?"

"Anyone responsible for multiple edem-fueled deaths or deemed the most dangerous to society." Kema glanced at her father. "Another one of your clients, Dad?"

He shook his head. "No."

"Not yet, though, right?" She grinned. "Dad gets assigned all the toughest edem cases. The ones that are held at Crown Court." I could tell she was proud of her father. I wished I felt the same about mine.

But Graymond wasn't looking at his daughter. He was watching a short woman cross the foyer toward the elevator. She wore a polished gold prison emblem on the lapel of her uniform, and a metal truncheon hung from her belt. Her sleek silvery hair fell in a blunt bob beneath her black cap.

"That's Yarlyn, the superintendent," Kema said to me. "My boss."

Yarlyn turned in a slow circle, surveying the room. Guards were posted at each opening to the foyer. The room was silent until she held a finger upward, signaling dozens of prison guards. They marched two by two toward the elevator.

"Must be a high-profile case," I whispered to Kema.

"Or someone *very* dangerous," she whispered back.

"Shhh," Graymond admonished. His breaths were coming in short puffs, his eyes wide. Sweat beaded his brow.

"What is it?" I asked.

"Cayder," Graymond said, his voice strained. "Don't do anything stupid."

"*What?* Why would I . . . ?" I glanced between the rows of guards and noticed someone moving in between them. The inmate. I twisted around Kema to take a closer look.

My mouth went dry, and a spark hit my chest like a live wire.

The girl's wrists were shackled together by heavy chains, her hands clad in gray gloves. Her brown hair was cut in a short but messy bob around her heart-shaped face. Her cheeks were flushed against her pale skin and her eyes wide as she took in her surroundings. Her brows were dark and bushy—like mine, and unfortunately, like our father's.

"*Leta?*"

No. It couldn't be. My sister was at home. She was . . . Actually, I didn't know where she was. But she wasn't a criminal. And she certainly wasn't someone who needed a prisoner's escort. This had to be some kind of mistake.

I hadn't realized Graymond had his arm on mine until I tried moving into the foyer.

"*Don't*, Cayder," he said.

"That's my sister." My voice sounded strange. Distant. "My sister!"

I wasn't sure how, but I managed to pull away from Graymond, a man who had twice my strength.

I ran across the stone floor, my footsteps like gunshots in the quiet foyer.

"*Leta!*"

The guards shifted formation, encircling her, their truncheons pointed in my direction. Were they protecting her, or me?

"Cayder?" Leta asked in surprise. Her eyes were glassy, but her jaw was set. I knew that look all too well. She was trying not to cry.

"Let her go!" I shouted.

Two strong arms circled mine, pinning them. "Don't move." It was Kema. Her breath hot against the back of my neck. I pulled against her, but she didn't budge. "Don't touch her." It wasn't a threat, but a warning.

Yarlyn stepped away from the elevator and pulled out her own truncheon. "What's this all about?" Her voice was sugary sweet but commanding. While I felt the heat of her gaze, her dark brown eyes darted around the room, perpetually alert.

"Apologies, Superintendent," Graymond said. He placed his heavy hand on my shoulder. *Stay quiet*, the gesture ordered. "This is my apprentice."

"Do you know this criminal?" Yarlyn asked me, pointing her truncheon at Leta.

*Criminal?* This was my little sister. The girl who had slept in my bed every night for a month after our mother died. The girl who named her peas and carrots before eating them.

I thought about denying it, but there was no way word wouldn't travel to my father. He would soon know we were both here.

"She's my sister."

Leta's chin wobbled, and my insides squeezed, pushing all the air from my chest.

*My little sister. In Vardean. This is a nightmare.*

"Then the prosecutor will need to question you too." Yarlyn nodded at the guards, and they shuffled Leta toward the elevator.

Kema had loosened her grip, and I approached Yarlyn. "About what? What is she charged with?"

"Leta Broduck has been charged with using edem," Yarlyn said, her voice and expression impenetrable. "She used edem to torch the town of Ferrington last night. Three hundred people were killed in the wildfire."

"What?" I asked. "No. No. No, she didn't—she couldn't. She *wouldn't.*" I tried to catch Leta's eye, but her face was downcast.

"You were with her last night?" Yarlyn asked, raising a silvery eyebrow.

"I—" I hadn't seen Leta for almost a week. I'd assumed she was out of town with some conspiracy-theorist friends. I'd had no idea she was in Ferrington—where our mother had died.

"No."

"Don't worry," Graymond said, his hand still on my shoulder. "We'll figure this out. I'll represent Leta. Everything will be fine."

"I'll set up an interview with the prosecutor," Yarlyn said. She walked away as though my entire world hadn't come crumbling down.

The guards opened the elevator door and unceremoniously shoved Leta inside. A few followed her in. The door closed, and the elevator rose. Leta kept her eyes locked on mine as she disappeared into the prison sector.

I gave her a nod.

I would do whatever it took to get her out of here.

## CHAPTER 6

# LETA

Leta's pale skin glowed in the moonlight as she crept through the high stalks of the torlu fields. She pocketed the bolt cutters she'd used to sever the electricity to the farm's flood lamps and enjoyed the cool shadows that washed over her skin like a gentle caress. She'd chosen a farm on the outskirts of Ferrington, far from the main street, where the entire town had gathered for the evening. It was a sweltering summer night, and the flood lamps had made her shirt and pants stick to her skin. Not anymore.

Unlike most people, Leta longed for shadows. Ever since she was a child, she'd had an affinity for the darkness. She liked that anything could be out there, a whole world full of possibilities hidden from sight. And one of those possibilities was why she was in Ferrington.

Ferrington was a small rural region around three hundred miles from Downtown Kardelle, near the easternmost point of the nation. Not long after edem had first been detected, a group of farmers emigrated from the agricultural nation of Delften to plant crops and rear livestock. Ferrington was known for its mineral-rich soils, a positive side effect of edem. Crops flourished, the torlu berry in particular. Used in jams, jellies, fermented tonics and even vitamin supplements, torlu berries had become Telene's principal agricultural export. But in the last few years, other nations had retracted their trade deals and refused all immigration requests until the Regency stopped the spread of edem.

In the hundred years since the veil had been discovered, many people had fled Telene, searching for safer shores. The monarchs had provided monetary incentive for people to stay. In turn, they'd nearly bankrupted the government.

Some people, veil worshippers, believed the only solution was to master the use of edem for industry and the economy. But the monarchs refused to put society at risk and allow the veil to grow.

Leta believed edem could be better understood. Ever since her mother had died, she'd taken it upon herself to know everything about the time-altering substance. And while the Regency worried itself only over what edem could do and its consequences, Leta wanted to know more about where it came from.

At school, Leta had been taught that the veil was like a tear in the world's surface and what lay beneath was edem. That never made much sense to her; there had to be more to the veil than a liquidy pool. When her teachers provided no satisfying answers, it further fueled Leta's fascination.

Leta's father often blamed her veil obsession on her mother. And it was true, like her mother's, Leta's mind never yielded. Her mother had curated a library full of books on edem theory. At night, Leta used to ask her mother to throw a blanket over the permalamp and read myths of the veil to her. Her mother would oblige, teaching her that darkness itself was nothing to fear and that edem was not as dangerous as everyone believed. She taught Leta that edem was trying to help by carrying out the wishes of the person who wielded it, and that we needed to learn how to master it rather than outright condemn it. Although she never allowed her daughter to touch edem, she merely helped Leta to be at peace with its presence.

As Leta walked through the fields, she thought about her mother's final moments. Had she walked this exact path? What had she been thinking of before she died? Did she have a moment of clarity, or was she terrified of what was to come? And would she be happy knowing Leta had continued her investigations?

These stories, or conspiracies—as Cayder liked to refer to them—were a connection between mother and daughter that lingered in the darkness. Investigating these stories was the only way Leta knew how to keep her mother's memory alive. In the harsh daylight, the memory of her mother's face was hazy. In the dark, she could still hear her voice filling her head with dark fairy tales.

Leta first read about edem creatures in a book she'd borrowed from the school library, not from her mother's collection. When she had asked her mother about the creatures that supposedly roamed the region of Ferrington at night, her mother had said they were just another tall tale.

As Leta got older and continued her own investigations, she began to question whether these were tales at all.

Leta had never wanted to visit Ferrington. For years it hurt to even think of the place that had taken her mother's life. Then, six months ago, Leta found a piece of paper stuck in the back of one of her mother's books. The letter detailed a sighting of an edem creature by a local farmer in Ferrington that was dated mere days before her mother had died near that farm. Leta began to wonder if there was more to her mother's death.

Had she been attacked by one of these creatures that reportedly broke into homes in the middle of the night, searching for food—their hunger never satiated? What were the creatures, supposedly made of edem, looking for? Naysayers claimed the only things plaguing Ferrington were the windstorms that got trapped in the valley, not creatures from another world.

Cayder would be furious if he knew where Leta was right now, but she had to find out if there was any truth to the stories.

This time, her source was reliable.

"I'll find out the truth," Leta whispered into the black. "I promise, Mother."

With the electric buzz of the flood lamps gone, Leta could hear the swish of tails and scratching of claws as small creatures scurried through the fields. But she couldn't hear anything unusual.

*What does an edem creature sound like, anyway?* she asked herself.

In the distance, she could see a small flicker of fire in

the center of town. The town's populace had gathered for Edemmacht—a celebration commemorating when farmers from Delften first arrived in Ferrington and discovered the rich soil. The festivities mostly included torlu berry pie competitions and drinking excessive amounts of torlu tonic around a bonfire.

The fire was for ceremonial purposes only; after all, flood lamps were installed in nearly every corner of the town, and the night was already blisteringly hot. Legends stated that fire would keep the edem creatures—the hullen—away. The *hullen* was Delft for the "living dark," and while many locals thought the stories to be old superstition, others blamed any strange goings-on in the town on the edem creatures. Broken windows, frightened livestock, unexplainable noises at night. And the constant flickering of lights.

Leta was relying on the excessive drinking at Edemmacht to ensure her plan went off without a hitch. She wouldn't leave until she had her answers.

As she approached the cage she'd set up that afternoon, she saw a small blue bird sitting inside, so still, she thought the bird was already dead.

"I'm sorry," she whispered, taking the bird into her gloved hands. "I don't want to hurt you."

She'd asked around town about the stories of the hullen. Most had laughed off her questions and blamed the windstorms. But one woman had told her to head to a small bar on the main street. There she would find Ritne Arden.

Leta was not disappointed. The old farmer had been easy to

spot, a glass of torlu tonic in his hand, sitting in the corner of the brightly lit bar, his skin like old cracked leather.

"Ritne?" Leta had asked as she took the seat next to him.

The man looked up slowly from his drink, his eyes bloodshot and glassy. "You come to laugh at an old man?" He spoke with a slight Delft accent, his vowels clipped.

"No, I was told you could tell me about the—"

"Shhh." He pulled her close by the crook of her arm. "Don't say the word. It's not safe."

Leta unlatched his skeletal hands from her. "We're safe. There's no edem."

Ritne's eyes flashed about the bar. "I'm not worried about that. I'm worried about . . ." He lowered his voice to a whisper. "The Regency."

He nodded over to an agent who stood watch off to the side of the room.

"Oh?" Leta leaned forward even though Ritne's breath smelled like a vat of fermenting torlu berries and made her eyes water. "What about them?"

He smacked his chapped lips together. "Why do you want to know?"

"My mother was killed in this town seven years ago," Leta said. "I think she was out here investigating the existence of the hullen."

"Your mother worked for the Regency?"

She nodded. "If these creatures are real, why are the Regency keeping them a secret?"

"No one believes me." Ritne downed the remainder of the liquid from his glass.

"*I* believe you." Although she didn't. Not yet. She needed proof there was more to edem. More to the veil. Then her father would have to listen.

Ritne's eyes lit up. "You've seen the hullen?"

"No," Leta admitted. "But I want to." She needed to. She needed to make sense of *that* night. The truth would make up for everything else she'd done.

Ritne told her she needed to offer a sacrifice for the hullen to appear. A sacrifice of flesh, blood and bone.

That was why she was now standing in the middle of the dark, a bird in one hand, edem curling around the other.

"I'm sorry," she said again to the bird. She didn't have a weapon, but edem would take care of that. She hoped edem would make the bird's death as swift and as painless as possible.

She closed her eyes as the edem coiled around her free hand like a serpent.

*I can do this. I can do this.*

She heard the sound of an animal shrieking and a loud bang in the distance.

# DEPARTMENT OF JUSTICE

VARDEAN, TELENE

*Arrest Report*

**Name:** Leta Broduck

**Age:** 16

**Height:** 5'2"

**Arrest location:** Ferrington

**Edem crimes:** Suspected of using edem to spark a wildfire, destroying the town of Ferrington and killing hundreds

**Recommended sentence:** Life in prison

# CHAPTER 7

# CAYDER

The prosecutor interviewed me for two hours. Well, that was what he called it. It felt like *I* was on trial—all because I was Leta's brother. No matter how many times I argued that my sister would never hurt anyone, let alone an entire town, the prosecutor wouldn't listen.

"You don't know where your sister was last night?" Mr. Rolund, the prosecutor, asked. He was a lean man with a wan complexion and a wispy white mustache with twisted ends that looked like rats' tails. His movements were as frenetic.

He kept returning to that one question, as though it erased every other thing I'd said before that. As though I hadn't given years and years of proof that Leta was nothing but a good person. As though nothing I said even mattered.

I glanced at Graymond; he stood in the corner of the interrogation room. Still, silent, but imposing. I'd never appreciated his formidable presence more than I did in that moment. Knowing he would help Leta eased some of my concern. Although I wouldn't breathe easy until my sister was free.

"No. But that doesn't mean she's guilty."

"That doesn't mean that she's innocent," Mr. Rolund countered.

"Where's my father?" I asked. "He can vouch for her. Even if you don't listen to me, surely you'll listen to a senior district judge?"

The ends of Mr. Rolund's mustache twitched. "This is a class one edem murder, not a simple crime. Your father holds no sway in a Crown Court matter."

"She's only sixteen!"

"A case as serious as this," he replied, "with so many fatalities must go before the Crown Court. No matter the criminal's age. Are you sure you weren't with her last night?"

I crossed my arms over my chest. "I've answered all your questions." I knew my rights. The prosecutor couldn't hold me in here for being related to a defendant. "Let me go."

"You can talk to me now," Mr. Rolund said with a sick grin. "Or in court."

I didn't flinch. "I guess I'll see you in court."

———

"What in the burning shadows is going on?" I asked Graymond once we left the interrogation room. "How can they think my sister did this?"

Graymond's face looked drawn; his skin, sallow. "I spoke to the arresting guards while they were setting up your interview with the prosecutor. There's a lot of evidence—"

"*No.* Leta wouldn't hurt anyone."

He nodded. "Let's see what she has to say."

We took the elevator to the top floor, and my heart squeezed with every passing level. I still couldn't grasp the idea that Leta had been arrested. The screams of the inmates faded into the background as the elevator rose. My brain was awash with a hum that drowned out every other sound. A question that muted all others.

*What would I do without my sister?*

I knew it was a selfish question. What mattered most was to get her out of Vardean, not because *I* needed her, but because she didn't deserve to be here. She wasn't a criminal.

Even with her continual mysterious absences, she was the only remaining functional part of the Broduck family. And as much as I buried my head in my studies to escape reality, I couldn't escape the truth.

I needed Leta.

I couldn't imagine a world without her.

A prison guard unlocked the cell door and followed us in. Unlike when we visited Jey, we weren't allowed to be alone with her. The Regency had marked her as one of the most dangerous criminals in a decade. There hadn't been such a significant use of edem since the previous king and queen had been killed.

"Cayder!" Leta ran to me as soon as she saw me. She threw her shackled hands around my neck. She smelled like sugar and smoke.

"Stand back!" the guard shouted.

"It's fine," I said, removing her arms from my neck. *Why is she wearing gloves?* "She's not going to hurt me."

The guard grunted. "Stay on the other side of the table, Ms. Broduck."

Leta reluctantly pulled away and slumped into the chair.

"It's okay." I was unsure what else to say. I was relieved to see there wasn't a scratch on her, although the prosecutor would use that against her.

"Where's Father?" she asked. She looked like a trapped bird, her large eyes darting about, her arms twitching. Her face was pale, and her usually rounded pink cheeks were sunken. Her short brown hair was tinted gray from some kind of powder. Ash?

"I haven't seen him. I think he's still being interviewed."

Leta shifted in her chair. "He's going to kill me."

Our father was the least of our problems.

"Leta," Graymond said. "Do you remember me?"

She studied him, her dark brows furrowing. "Uncle Graymond?"

He gave her a sad smile and took the seat opposite her. I sat next to him, although my body fought me. I wanted to grab Leta's hand and run.

"I'm a defense attorney for edem-based crimes," Graymond said. "I'm going to represent you."

"Thank you." Some color returned to her cheeks.

"I'd like to start with what led to the events of last night. No detail is too small."

"I didn't do it," she said, jutting out her chin. "We should start there."

Graymond nodded and took out his notepad. "Of course."

Leta made to run her gloved hands through her hair but stopped because of the shackles.

"I was in Ferrington because—"

"*What?*" I asked. "Why were you in Ferrington, of all places?"

"I was about to tell you," she said with a huff. "If you'd listen, Cayder. You and Father *never* listen."

I pointed at her. "Don't start with me. You're in Vardean. You've been arrested for killing three hundred people!"

"I didn't do it!" She threw up her hands, the chains clanking together. A flush spread up her pale skin.

"Cayder." Graymond spoke softly, slowly. "If you can't stay calm, I'll have to ask you to leave."

"I'm not going anywhere."

"As I was saying," Leta continued, "I was in Ferrington because I was investigating creatures made of edem."

I groaned. "Seriously, Leta? *Creatures?*"

"Can you unlock these?" she asked the guard, ignoring me. "I promise you can knock me out if I so much as breathe in the wrong direction."

The guard looked her over. At five foot two, she was hardly the most imposing person in the world, although her eyes were a dark fire. He nodded and unlocked her shackles.

She ran to her bunk and pulled back a sheet, revealing some pieces of paper. She brought them over and scattered them across the table in front of us.

"What are these?" I asked. My sister was always doodling in her sketchbook, but I'd never seen her draw anything like this.

The sketches were of winged creatures with hooked horns on either side of their snub-nosed faces.

"The hullen," she said. She tapped the page. "This is what lives in Ferrington. This is what Mother was investigating for the Regency. *This* is what really killed her."

"What are you talking about?" I asked. "She was interviewing the citizens about an edem crime. It was an accident."

She narrowed her eyes. "Are you sure about that?"

I was ten years old when Mother died; she'd never shared her work with me. Although it appeared she'd shared more with Leta. I hadn't been interested in edem or the veil at the time.

"Did Mother tell you about the hullen before she died?" I asked.

Leta chewed on her bottom lip. "Not exactly. I found a report of them in one of her books. I went to Ferrington to find out more about these creatures. They've been haunting the town for years, breaking into houses at night, shattering windows and climbing over rooftops."

"The Regency have investigated those stories," I said. "Ferrington is known for their destructive storms and nothing more."

"That's a cover-up," Leta said. "There are no windstorms."

"You saw these creatures in Ferrington?" Graymond asked. Leta shook her head slowly. "Then how do you know they exist?"

"I can't tell you that," she said, setting her jaw.

"Why not?" I asked.

"It doesn't matter where I got the information," she said. "What matters is that the information is accurate."

I rolled my eyes. "You get your information from conspiracy theorists."

"Not this time," she replied.

"You used to believe that the veil was like a mirror and that another version of ourselves lived on the other side. You believed that for a year when we were kids!"

"This is different."

"How?" I demanded.

"It just is!"

That argument would hardly hold up in court.

"So, what?" I asked, looking at her sketches. "Your drawings are supposed to be proof that these things exist?"

"This is proof that I didn't start the fire," she said. "*They* did."

I squeezed my eyes shut. She'd allowed this ridiculous obsession to get her arrested. For what?

"I'm afraid this won't be considered proof," Graymond said calmly. "Everyone at the Edemmacht celebration perished that night." Graymond leaned forward. "You were found alive where the fire started."

Leta placed her hands on the table. "I was trying to find out if the hullen existed, that's all. I didn't burn down the town. The hullen are to blame. They've been trying to destroy Ferrington for years."

"But you didn't see them?" Graymond asked. "Did you see anyone else out there that night?"

"No," she said. "I stayed clear of the festival, as I didn't want anyone knowing what I was doing."

I sank into my chair with a sigh.

"Leta," Graymond said, "can you please remove your gloves?"

"My gloves?" she asked, leaning away from the table. "Why?"

"Please," Graymond insisted.

Leta glanced at me. "I'm sorry, Cayder."

"Sorry about what?" I asked.

She tucked her chin to her chest. "It's not what you think. Please remember that."

"What are you talking about?"

She removed her gloves one at a time. I felt my insides hollow out.

Her hands were covered in detailed gray marks. The pattern looked like bones, as though the flesh and muscle had fallen away.

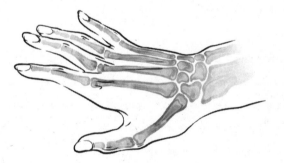

"*No,*" I whispered.

Leta had a death echo. The permanent mark of a killer.

# CHAPTER 8

# CAYDER

I was numb. My sister had killed someone. The evidence was clear as a shadow in sunlight.

She'd killed all those people in Ferrington, and it wouldn't matter if it was an accident. She would spend the rest of her life in Vardean.

I stared motionless at the table as Graymond probed her for more information about what had happened. The details didn't really matter. Like Jey, Leta would be condemned by the jury the moment they saw her death echo.

I barely heard my sister claim the death echo was from killing a bird and not a person. And Graymond's response that there had never been any record of such a mark from killing an animal. He tried to convince her to take responsibility for her actions, as that *might* lessen her sentence, but Leta refused to budge. She claimed the edem creatures had created the fire, although she hadn't seen them do so and couldn't explain how.

The entire time, I could feel her eyes on me, but I couldn't lift my head. Despite our differences, we'd vowed to be there for each other after Mother's death. Now Leta was slipping through my fingers.

A spark of fury burned within me. She knew the risks of going to Ferrington. She knew she was breaking the law. Now we would both pay the consequences.

I felt like something had struck me in the back and lodged within my ribs.

She'd betrayed us both.

———

"Cayder?" Graymond asked. "Did you hear what I said?"

I glanced up from my makeshift chair of boxes in Graymond's office.

"What?" I asked.

I'd been staring vacantly at the Regency report on Leta's case for over an hour, unable to venture past page one.

*Three hundred people. Dead.*

Even though I'd seen the death echo on my sister's hands, I couldn't believe she was responsible.

A frown pulled at Graymond's mouth. "I said you should go home. You need to take some time to process what's happened. Don't worry about your sister right now; take care of yourself. I'll look after everything here."

*"Don't worry about my sister?"* I repeated. "She's going to rot in this place!" I threw my hands in the air, scattering the pages of the report across the cramped office.

Graymond's eyes turned steely. "She *won't*, I promise you."

"She was found in the only unburnt section of the field." Apparently, I *had* absorbed some information from the report. "She tampered with a flood lamp. She was outside her home after curfew. And that death echo on her hands . . ."

"I know it doesn't look good now, son. Rest assured, we'll get to the bottom of this. I promise Leta won't spend the rest of her life in here."

"But you can't promise she won't spend some of her life here, can you?"

I knew it was unfair to put this on Graymond. He hadn't seen my sister or me since Mother died. He didn't owe us anything.

Graymond stood, and I found myself standing along with him. "I promise you that I will do my best to free her from this place."

I nodded because I had to. I had to believe in him. Or I would break.

"Okay," I said, heading toward the door. "I'll see you tomorrow."

Graymond ran his hand over his cropped hair. "Take the week off."

"I can't do that." If Leta couldn't take the week off, then neither would I.

He nodded in understanding. I was sure he wouldn't leave if Kema were the one behind bars.

"I'll be here tomorrow," I assured him.

I'd just reached out to open the office door when it flung inward. I jumped back to avoid being smacked in the face.

My father flew at me. He was a large man, his black hair clipped close to his pale and freckled skin. He pushed me up against the wall. While he wasn't as tall as I was, he was broader and had more weight behind him.

"How dare you!" he snarled into my face. His blue eyes were a sea of storms. "You were supposed to look after her! You were supposed to steer clear of this place! I only ever asked you to do one thing, and you failed!"

"Let . . . go . . ." My hands flapped helplessly against his grip.

"Alain!" Graymond attempted to prize my father off me. "Release him!"

My father whirled on Graymond. I let out a gasp and sagged onto my knees. My father was an irate man, but he'd never raised a hand against me or my sister.

"How could you?" My father pointed at Graymond. His face was so red and blustering that he could barely get the words out.

"I accepted Cayder's application because I thought it would help mend the rift between us, Alain. Your issues are with me. Not your son!"

"My issues are with you both! Cayder knew I wanted him to have nothing to do with Vardean. He knew I wanted my children far from this place." He spun back around to me. "Edem took my wife, and now look at what you've done!"

"What *I've* done?" I was still doubled over, but I glanced up at that. "It's because of you that Leta was in Ferrington in the first place. It's because of you that she seeks out these ridiculous conspiracies. The hole in her heart isn't simply because of Mother's death. It's because you abandoned us!"

"You were supposed to look after her!" he seethed.

I laughed, but it came out like a wheeze. "Have you ever tried telling Leta what she can and cannot do?"

He scoffed. "All my trials have been put on hold until after Leta's arraignment. Do you think I'll be allowed to retain my judgeship if my own daughter is found guilty of murder?"

"Really?" I fumed. "That's what you're worried about right now? Your job? This is Leta's life! This is our family!"

"I know," he said simply.

All the energy drained from my father's body, and he sank onto one of Graymond's boxes, burying his face in his hands. I thought he might cry, but my father *never* cried.

"I've taken on Leta's case," Graymond said, placing a hand on my father's shoulder. "I will do everything I can to ensure she goes free."

"The jury will see her death echo and convict before you even open your mouth," he said.

"Trust me," Graymond said. "I've had tougher cases."

We both wanted to believe him, but we knew it was a lie.

———

Even though I'd agreed to leave Vardean for the day, it didn't mean I was leaving Leta's case behind. Graymond allowed me to take the Regency report while he and father talked through Leta's plea options.

I shared the gondola with a few prison employees back to Downtown Kardelle Station. They sat as far away from me as possible, as though my sister's imprisonment were a condition that could be caught. Word had spread quickly through Vardean and would soon spread to Kardelle, not only via the whisper network but newspaper reports. Most journalists cared more about being the first to break a story than reporting the truth. On the Sunshine Mile, and among "high society" like the circles my father ran in, your worth was only as good as your name. And the Broducks' was now forever tainted.

It reminded me of when I'd first returned from Vardean Reform. My childhood friends refused to see me. Whether it was their parents' choice or theirs, I never found out. For a while, I'd thought Kema had stopped visiting because of me. My best friend, Narena Lunita, had been my only constant. Her mother worked at the *Telene Herald*, and she was one of the few journalists who cared about truth over gossip.

I'd read the entire Regency report three times before the gondola reached the station. So far, nothing I'd read would help Leta go free. The only seed of doubt I hoped to germinate was the bonfire at the Edemmacht celebration. Although the reports stated the fire started near where an unconscious Leta was found, I hoped there was something else there. Something that managed to spread a bonfire into a blaze that ripped through the town in one evening.

While Leta was stuck telling the same story, I needed a new angle. And there was only one other person who knew more about the veil than my sister. That was Narena.

I ran from Downtown Kardelle Station to the State Library. The imposing white marble building sat in the exact center of the city, close to Penchant Place and across from the gondola station. Before the veil, knowledge and progress had been Telene's focus. The first buildings that were built were the library, town hall, university and banks. Afterward, the government switched to the preservation of what we already had. While other nations continued to advance in all areas of technology, Telene focused only on what reduced shadows and edem. Lighting solutions were Telene's main industry, but that wasn't of value to the other nations, not unless edem spread to their shores. And the Regency did everything to ensure that would not happen.

Narena spent her lunchtimes on the library steps while she worked for her father, the head librarian, over summer break. I spotted her sitting on the stone stairs, her eyes closed and face tilted back, trying to catch the heat from the diffused sunlight subtly casting her amber skin with a warm glow. Her long black hair almost touched the step behind her.

"Narena!" I shouted as I wound my way through the crowd.

Her eyes opened, and she smiled, dimples appearing on either side of her cheeks. "Cayder! What are you doing here?"

"Did you know?" I asked as I reached her, my chest heaving in short gasps.

She blinked, smile and dimples fading. "Know what?"

"About Leta! Did you know she was in Ferrington last night? Did you know she was arrested?"

"What?" Narena leaped up. "What are you talking about?"

"She didn't tell you?" I studied her face for the truth. While Narena was my best friend, she'd bonded with Leta over her theories of the veil. "She didn't tell you her plan?"

"Her plan to do what?" She grabbed my shoulders. "Cayder, you're scaring me."

I buckled, sitting down heavily on the stairs. Narena sat beside me.

"Leta was found in what remains of Ferrington this morning. The entire town was incinerated overnight. They think Leta is responsible." I ran my hands over my face.

"Ferrington?" Her eyebrows pinched together. "The town where your mother died?"

"You don't know anything about it?"

She chewed on her bottom lip. "No, Cayder. She didn't tell me anything about Ferrington. I knew a few things, but I didn't—"

I held up a hand. "Tell me what you know."

She avoided my gaze when she replied. "I knew she had met someone new—a new source, although she wouldn't say who they were."

Leta had claimed her source was telling the truth, but what if they put her up to this? My sister was easily influenced when it came to stories about the veil and edem.

Where was this informant now? Had they perished in the fire, or were they out there somewhere, happy Leta had taken the fall for the crime?

This could help our case. We didn't have to prove Leta innocent, just prove there was reasonable doubt that the echo marks weren't from starting the fire. This informant *could* be that reason.

"Cayder." Narena put her hand over mine. "You're shaking. Have you eaten anything today?"

I ran my hands through my hair. "I can't eat. I can't even think clearly."

She gave me a gentle smile. "Eating can help with that." She grabbed her bag and pulled me upright. "Let's go."

"But your job at the library—"

"My father will understand."

———

Narena took me to a Meiyran restaurant not far from the library. She claimed it wasn't as good as her mother's cooking, but they made a great long-fish fry. I couldn't tell; I didn't taste a single spoonful, my focus miles away. But Narena refused to talk until I finished my plate.

Narena had a habit of wanting to rescue wounded animals and nurture them back to health. A rabbit with a broken leg, a mouse caught in a trap. Sometimes I wondered if the only reason she'd stayed by my side after I was sent to Vardean Reform was because she saw me the same way.

*Broken.*

Afterward, we headed to a student pub called the Belch Echoes, around the corner from the Telene School of Law. The old narrow three-story building was nestled in between two abandoned storefronts with faded FOR LEASE signs hanging in the windows. Unless you were in the business of making lights or providing valuable resources like food, your business was destined to fail. And most of Telene's taxes went toward the Regency.

Narena had purchased three fermented torlu tonics, two for me. She balanced them in her hands as we climbed to the top floor. The pub survived off the thirst of students and thus didn't mind an underage patron or two. The pub's ceiling bowed and the stairwells swayed, yet there was something appealing about it. A reminder of a bygone era—when times were simpler and *edem* was a word no one had ever heard of.

"Drink," she said, placing two of the glasses in front of me. "It will settle your nerves."

Normally I wasn't a fan of alcohol, but the hard look in Narena's eye prevented me from questioning her methods. I took a sip. It fizzled on my tongue and warmed my chest. It tasted more of bubbles than the sweet berry it was made from.

"Now," Narena said. *"Talk."*

I told her everything that had happened today. The story sounded like some kind of ridiculous nightmare, without the punch line of me waking up to find out it was all a dream. I showed her Leta's arrest report.

Narena pulled out her notepad and pencil. "When was the last time you saw Leta?" she asked. "Did she say how a creature of edem could even start a fire? What was she trying to prove out there, anyway?" She sounded exactly like her journalist mother.

"Hold up," I said. "Is this an interview?"

She gave me a sheepish grin. "Of course not." She put her notepad down. "Sorry."

"It's okay. I was hoping that you might have heard of the hullen from your mother?"

Narena shrugged. "Stories about creatures crawling out of the veil is an old superstition, which the Regency has debunked over and over. There's never been any proof of anything other than edem coming through the veil."

"Did Leta ever tell you she believes our mother was killed by these creatures?"

Narena tapped her pencil against her notepad. "Leta had a different theory about the veil and edem every week. But I don't remember her saying anything like that. I would have told you if she had."

"We need to find this informant," I said. "They're our only lead."

"I can ask my mother about known conspiracy theorists," she said. "See if any of them have spoken with Leta recently."

"She didn't tell you anything else about this source?" I asked. "She mentioned that they were different."

"No. Only that they were going to lead her to the truth." Narena tilted her head. "She wouldn't tell you who they were?"

"No."

"Another secret," Narena said with a thoughtful nod.

Turned out, Leta was secretive about a lot of things.

"Do you think this person set her up to take the fall?" Narena asked. "What about her echo mark?"

"I don't know," I said honestly. "But I can't imagine Leta ever hurting anyone. Can you?"

"Of course not. But why would she cover for this source?"

"You tell me. I don't understand the minds of women."

Narena rolled her eyes. "You don't understand the mind of your sister."

Fair point. "Do you?"

She thought it over for a while, running her finger around the rim of the glass. The ringing sound echoed through the small pub.

"Well?" I asked.

"Let me get you a list of names," she said. "We'll figure out what secrets she's hiding."

—————

I wasn't surprised to find the house empty when I arrived at Broduck Manor; I hadn't expected Father to come home.

As I climbed the marble stairs to my bedroom, I tried to imagine what life would be like if I were left alone in this house full of memories and grief, but the mere thought of it was suffocating. I couldn't lose another family member.

Being born less than a year apart meant Leta and I had been inseparable as children. Aside from Narena and Kema, I hadn't had many friends, even before my year at Vardean Reform. Leta and I had always understood one another. Then Mother died, and we started veering in different directions.

When I returned from Vardean Reform, we'd tried to return to our old ways. After being alone with Father, Leta wanted to be free from Broduck Manor. She'd become obsessed with the belief that there was more to edem. For an entire year, she dressed in black, saying it made her feel closer to the veil and to Mother. She believed she was continuing Mother's investigations.

We fought constantly. I told her she was being childish and that Mother was a scientist who never believed in silly veil superstitions. I wanted Leta to let go of her obsession, as it was preventing her from moving on from her grief. I knew if she held on to it too tightly, it would be her downfall.

I hated that I was right.

After a few years of trying to control Leta, I gave up. I let her do whatever she wanted. I let her slip away at nighttime to meet up with veil worshippers, knowing she was breaking curfew. I let her keep her secrets. Trying to get her to change just pushed her further away. If I wanted her in my life, I needed to accept her for who she was, and accept our differences. And I had accepted that we would never be as close as we once were. All the while, I worried about my studies and getting into law school. I worried about myself.

Father was right. It was my fault she now sat in a cell. I was her older brother; I was supposed to protect her. But I'd given up on her and let her obsessions become all-consuming.

Leta may have pushed me away, but I didn't stop her.

Now I might lose her forever.

# CHAPTER 9

# JEY

J ey awoke to silence. With little to do between mealtimes, he'd decided to nap between lunch and dinner. In the few days he'd been in prison, he soon realized Vardean was not known for the quiet. People were always yelling or shouting or banging against the bars. Especially Jey's neighbor, who only stopped bellowing his innocence after losing his voice. Since Jey's arrest over the weekend, he'd gotten used to the ruckus—it was a nice change from living on his own by the Unbent River. Silence troubled him.

The only time the inmates were quiet was when something attracted their interest.

*A new prisoner, perhaps?*

Jey approached his cell's bars and attempted to look down into the cavern below, but he couldn't see anything but the rocky landing. Then he heard the screech of the elevator door closing.

He started counting as the mechanical whine hummed throughout the cavern. It took four seconds to travel between each floor and three hundred and twenty seconds to rattle past Jey's cell on the eightieth floor.

He caught a glimpse of a girl's pale face.

*Leta Broduck*—Cayder's sister.

He'd heard of the latest arrival at lunchtime. Word spread like a disease, from cell to cell and level to level. She'd likely be returning to her cell on the top floor after a new round of interrogations. She must have claimed to be innocent. Only the innocent were questioned over and over. Those who fessed up to their crimes, like Jey, were left to their cells until their arraignment. Aside from Mr. Toyer, who continued to visit every day in hopes Jey would change his story.

Jey returned to his bunk. He wasn't set to see his lawyer again until tomorrow. But he was tired of all the questions. Jey was fairly certain Mr. Toyer didn't believe him, which annoyed Jey, as that meant he was a bad liar. He couldn't take the risk of being found innocent. He couldn't risk going to trial.

It was time to change tactics.

———

Vardean didn't segregate inmates based on age or gender, but on level of crime. The only other form of segregation was at mealtimes. While Vardean stretched high into the sky, the singular food hall was located on the ground floor, above the prison's foyer. To ease congestion, prisoners were given scheduled mealtimes, when they would eat with inmates of a similar age, regardless of whether or not they had committed an edem crime. While

Jey was eighteen and technically an adult, he still ate with the juvenile inmates.

At seven p.m., Jey's cell door opened automatically. As he passed his neighbor's cell, the old man held out his time-withered hands.

"I'm innocent!" the man cried, his voice barely above a whisper.

"You and every other person in here, mate," Jey muttered. Although perhaps the old man spoke the truth. It was impossible to tell; even the guilty pleaded innocence, as it was their only chance for freedom.

Other juvenile inmates were released from their cells and headed toward the stairs like well-trained rats. Jey took two stairs at a time, eagerness coursing through his body. He'd never been good at sitting still or being cooped up inside. His long legs begged for freedom—more so than his mind. Jey knew that the physical restraint, not the mental shackles, would be the end of him in this place. He longed for a wall to scale or a mountain to climb.

He had to get out of here.

"Did you see the new prisoner?" Bren asked as he sidled in next to Jey.

Bren was seventeen and his cell was located on level fifty. He had been arrested along with the notorious Brotherhood of the Veil, named after an underground club and gambling ring that used edem to fight one another. Bren had only been fifteen when he'd been caught up in the Brotherhood's promises of wealth, power and infamy. And while the infamy proved true—the entire club had been shut down and arrested two months ago—they never made good on their promises of wealth or power.

While Jey had only met Bren over the weekend, they had bonded over their love of cheese and fluffy white bread—a luxury they might never taste again inside the walls of Vardean.

"Only a glimpse," Jey admitted.

As Bren tried to keep pace with Jey, sweat dotted his cool brown skin.

"Did you hear what she did?" He didn't wait for Jey to respond. "She killed three hundred people in one night!"

"Allegedly," Jey said.

"Right." Bren snorted. "Like I *allegedly* joined the Brotherhood of the Veil because I thought they were a band."

Jey slowed. "Is that what your lawyer wants you to say?"

Bren sucked his lips together, and his mouth disappeared into his face. "Yeah."

"You're best to stick with the truth," Jey said, knowing he was being a hypocrite. "You didn't know the Brotherhood used edem to fight each other. Tell the jury you signed up to be a part of a fight club, not to use edem."

Bren's chin trembled, and Jey worried he was going to cry. Showing fear was the worst thing you could do in this place. Everyone had to wear a mask. Jey most of all.

He patted Bren on the back. "You'll be fine, mate. Your arrest was for being involved in an illegal club. You didn't use edem, and you have no echo mark." Bren's hearing started in two days, and the fear was palpable on his friend's face. "You'll be fine," Jey repeated. But Bren wasn't listening. His hands were shaking, his eyes searching the room.

The food hall was a narrow room with low rafters. The lights flickered from the proximity to the tear in the veil, as though the dimension on the other side wished it always to be dark, but there were enough lights on the ceilings and walls to ensure there weren't any shadows for edem to linger within. Four long wooden blocks ran the length of the room, acting as tables, and a buffet sat along the back wall near the kitchen.

Jey let Bren approach the buffet first. He hoped food would help settle Bren's nerves for his upcoming trial. Jey, on the other hand, hadn't come for the food. Not today.

"Afternoon, Ryge," Jey said, nodding to an inmate serving dinner. The middle-aged man looked like he hadn't eaten anything for months; the lines of his pale face were steep cliffs and valleys.

"Jey, my man," Ryge said with a smile. Jey had a habit of making friends wherever he went, a skill he was hoping to utilize to his advantage. "How are you doing today?"

"Can't complain," Jey said with a grin. "Can't complain."

"You're the only one who doesn't. *Here*—" Ryge held out two slices of boiled fowl meat.

Jey thought of his old friend. He'd decided to let the bird go free the day before he'd been arrested. "I don't eat meat. What else you got?"

"Oh! Sorry." Ryge slopped some stewed vegetables onto Jey's tray instead. "An extra helping."

Jey saluted. "A true hero, Ryge." He grabbed a stale bread roll from the basket, but before he moved on, he asked, "Do you have anything to help cut the bread?" He waved the bread roll in the air.

Ryge halted, the ladle of stew frozen in his hand. "What did you say?"

"I'd like something to spread some torlu jelly onto my roll. You know these rolls taste like rocks."

Ryge shook his head. "Nah, you don't want that."

Jey grinned his usual easy grin. "I think you'll find that I do."

"Are you sure?" Ryge leaned over the counter, his eyes darting to the prison guards who stood watch by the entranceway.

"I'm sure." Jey gave a resolute nod. He placed a small seed from a torlu berry on the counter. While the seed wasn't worth anything now, a torlu tree bearing fruit would be highly valuable for Ryge. He could run this entire prison with his own source of torlu tonic.

"Come on!" an inmate called from behind. "What's the holdup?"

Ryge swept the seed off the counter. "Sorry, Jey. You'll have to use your hands. As you know, knives are banned in Vardean. You can clean up with this—" He gave Jey a folded napkin.

Jey let out a loud, disappointed sigh. "Just when I cleaned my nails." He took the napkin from Ryge and slipped it onto his tray. "Thanks anyway, mate."

The inmate gave him a knowing look and said, "Take care of yourself, man."

"I always do."

Bren had taken a seat closest to the guards standing watch.

Bren didn't trust the other inmates, especially those who used edem. Aside from Jey, of course.

Jey ignored Bren's confused look as he walked right by him. Instead, he approached the far end of the food hall and joined a table of inmates, plopping his tray down noisily.

"What a beautiful day," Jey said, squeezing himself in between a boy with suntanned arms the size of Jey's head and one of the boy's friends.

When no one at the table said anything, Jey continued, "The sun's out, the birds are singing and the water's just fine. You should jump on in." He took a big bite of his roll and forced himself to swallow the rocky mouthful.

*Burning shadows,* he thought. How he missed fluffy bread.

"Are you lost?" the inmate with the bulging arms asked. Jey knew—as he'd witnessed during a breakfast brawl yesterday—that this inmate had a bad temper. He also happened to be the head of the Brotherhood of the Veil. Even without looking, Jey knew Bren's eyes were on him.

*Why not feed two fowls with one bag of seed?* Jey thought. Bren deserved retribution.

"Lost?" Jey shook his head. "I'm right where I want to be." He smiled. "With you."

"Walk away now, while you still can, *father killer.*"

*Ah. Looks like I'm not the only one keeping tabs on the other inmates.* "Or what?" Jey asked good-naturedly.

The inmate jolted to his feet, moving faster than humanly possible. Jey had learned from Bren that the Brotherhood's leader's muscles were permanently affected by using edem on himself to move around a boxing ring. His gray jumpsuit was torn off at the shoulders, his muscular arms covered in gray echo marks that looked like veins.

While Jey kept fit running from the Regency agents at Penchant Place, this guy was clearly stronger. A lot stronger. Not to mention faster.

"Okay," Jey said, glancing up at the boy's face. "You're going to stand—interesting." He scratched his chin. "What happens next?"

Big Arms scrunched his nose as though he smelled something unpleasant. "You're lucky we're not alone."

Jey considered the prison guards by the entrance. He had yet to garner their attention. Meanwhile, Bren watched on with concerned eyes.

*Well, that won't do.*

"Lucky?" Jey stood as well; he was at least a head taller. "We're in Vardean. I think our luck ran out, mate."

Big Arms' face pinched in confusion. "What's wrong with you? You got a death wish?"

"Not really, no," Jey said frankly. "In fact, I'd really like to get out of Vardean. How about you, fellas? Any dreams beyond this place? Someone to love and hold on the outside, waiting for your return?" He puckered his lips and batted his eyelashes.

"You won't survive the rest of the week." Big Arms clenched his fists, but he didn't advance. He didn't want to upset the guards and end up in solitary confinement.

The guards were now watching, primed for action, yet they hadn't shifted from their spot by the entrance.

"Is that a promise, or"—Jey twirled his hands—"a prediction?"

"Shut up," Big Arms said. "Or I'll make it a promise."

Jey leaned over him, using his father's inherited height to his advantage. "I don't think you have the guts to *do* anything. Not here."

Big Arms gestured to the inmates sitting at the table. "Have you lost your mind? Don't you know who we are?"

"I simply sat at your table, and *you're* the one who lost it. I was looking for a change of scenery. Gets a bit boring in here. Am I right, folks?" Jey glanced around at the rest of the Brotherhood, but they were all watching with dumbstruck expressions.

*No help there.*

Jey sighed and sat back down.

"Who else thinks I should leave?" Jey asked. The inmates stared at him blankly. A few looked to Big Arms for guidance. "No one? *Good.* I look forward to our mealtimes together. Just so you know, I like to be romanced. Sonnets are good. Extra food?" Jey leaned over and grabbed a bread roll from another inmate's tray. "Even better."

"What are you doing?" Big Arms fumed, his skin blazing red.

Jey twisted around. "I'm laying down the law. That's what this"—he gestured between them—"is all about, right? A show of dominance. Well, I'm pretty sure I won. This is my table now. *My* crew."

Jey continued chewing on his bread roll until a thick arm went around his neck.

*Finally,* Jey thought as he was hauled off his seat.

The first punch hit Jey in the stomach. He doubled over, the last chunk of roll flying from his mouth and onto the floor.

The food hall went quiet before it erupted in jeers. The inmates scrambled from their seats to get closer to the action, circling the fight and blocking the guards from intervening.

Big Arms cocked back his fist and struck Jey in the left eye. Jey staggered toward the table, falling into his food tray. He picked up the tray and then slammed it into Big Arms' face, all the while saying a sad goodbye to his delicious vegetable stew.

Jey could hear the guards yelling over the commotion and pulling the crowd away one by one to reach the fight.

They wouldn't be quick enough.

Big Arms knocked Jey to the ground and pinned him to the floor with one foot on his chest. His nose looked broken from Jey's attack—he grinned maniacally. "You deserve this, you great big fu—"

But Jey didn't let him finish. "And you deserve this—" He shoved the knife that was hidden in the napkin into the side of Big Arms' leg.

This was no prop knife.

Big Arms' eyes went wide. He stumbled backward. Darkness pooled under the leg of his gray jumpsuit.

A guard with bleached-blond hair that contrasted with her brown skin yanked Jey from the ground and grabbed the knife from his hand. Jey let it go easily. He didn't need the knife any longer.

The deed was done.

# CHAPTER 10

# CAYDER

Graymond glanced up from his desk, a haunted expression on his face, when I entered his office the next day.

"Cayder," he said. "How are you holding up?"

"I'm all right. Did you even go home last night?"

Graymond sighed and stretched in his chair; his shirt looked rumpled. "I wanted to stay with your father."

"Did you find out anything more from Leta?"

He shook his head. "She's adamant about these creatures. She believes they started the fire."

"She's lying."

His jaw snapped shut halfway through a yawn. "How do you know?"

I placed a piece of paper on his desk. "This is a list of every known veil conspiracy theorist that the *Telene Herald* has spoken to over the years. I believe one of these names holds the truth to that night in Ferrington."

"Explain this to me as though I'm a child." Graymond rubbed his temples. "A *tired* child."

I couldn't help but laugh. "I spoke to my friend Narena, and she said Leta was meeting up with a secret informant. I bet that the real culprit is right here." I tapped the list. "We have to work out which one spoke to my sister and encouraged her to go to Ferrington."

"I don't know, Cayder," Graymond said. "Just because Leta didn't tell you about her source doesn't mean they are involved."

My sister wasn't a killer. This *had* to be the answer. "There's only one way to find out."

"All right, but if you want to—" A bell chimed from behind Graymond. He turned to a slot in the wall, and a rolled piece of paper fell out. Graymond groaned, his eyes darting across the page as he read.

"What is it?" I asked.

"That little—*urgh!*" Graymond stood, the piece of paper crumpling in his hands.

"What's wrong?"

*"Jey."* He muttered a curse under his breath. "He got into a fight and stabbed another inmate."

"He *what*?" Even though Jey had been arrested for his father's murder, it was hard to picture him assaulting someone. Using edem meant you could commit a crime without getting your hands dirty. Jey didn't strike me as someone with a taste for violence. "What happened?"

"I don't know; I need to speak with the superintendent. Jey's now in solitary confinement on the top floor, which means I won't be able to speak to him for a few days. The superintendent believes he's more of a risk than initially thought." Graymond looked up at the ceiling. "Why would he do this?"

I shrugged. "He let his temper get the better of him."

Graymond glanced at me. "Jey isn't a fool." He started pacing behind his desk, his broad shoulders stooping with each advancing stride. "There's more to this, I know it. I need to convince the superintendent to let me speak with him." He jerked his chin toward the door. "You go talk to Leta. See if there's anything to your theory.

"Don't these kids want to be helped?" he muttered as he left the office.

Leta was drawing when I entered her cell. Dozens of papers littered the floor. At first, I couldn't make out what the pictures were.

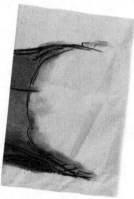

Until I realized each sheet made up a piece of the same image. A giant winged creature stared up at me. I shivered.

"The hullen," Leta said, sitting back on her heels. She had her gloves on, and the fingertips were smudged with charcoal, which she'd also smeared across her forehead. The jagged line between her brows made it look as though she were cracking in two.

"Leta," I said.

She glanced up. "Where's Uncle Graymond?"

It was strange hearing that name after so many years. I was transported back to a time when Leta, Kema and I would play hide-and-seek while our parents discussed boring topics like politics and the state of Telene's economy. Leta would want to hide in Father's office, knowing if she got caught, we'd both be grounded.

I would try to talk her out of it, but I couldn't control her. Not even back then. And so Kema and I would be forced to end the game and play something else. Leta would go off and sulk, feeling left out.

"He's busy," I said. "It's time for a Broduck sibling chat."

We took our seats at the table.

"How are you?" I asked.

"Just peachy," she replied with a fake smile.

"Leta, it's just you and me now—"

"And that guy." She pointed to the guard in the corner.

"Drop the act."

"What act?" Her doe-like eyes were wide.

"That you're not terrified to be in here. And tell me the truth about Ferrington. Tell me what really happened."

She nodded to the drawings behind her. "That's all you need to know."

"I don't believe you."

She frowned. "Why is it so hard for people like you to believe there is something more than edem in this world? Something more to the veil."

"People like me?" I countered.

"Skeptics. Mother believed. She had an open mind. You're too much like Father. You need proof—evidence—to believe in something."

"I'm not getting into a debate with you over these creatures. I need you to tell me who put you up to this."

"No one," she said. "I've been researching the veil my entire life. You know that."

"Do you want to live the rest of your life behind bars?"

Her thick dark brows pulled together. "Of course I don't."

"Then why won't you help me and Graymond?" I asked. "We need something—*anything*—to assist in your case. Anything that will make the jury doubt you're guilty." I glanced at her gloves.

She noticed my focus and pulled her sleeves down. "I've already told you and Graymond everything I know. I sacrificed the bird using edem, and the world went dark. I woke up to the Regency telling me I'd burned down the entire town. But I didn't do it."

"How do you know it was these creatures that burned down the town and not someone else?"

"Because no one else was out there with me."

"No one?" I placed my list in front of her.

She raised an eyebrow. "What's this?"

"Every veil worshipper and conspiracy theorist that the *Telene*

*Herald* has either interviewed or been contacted by over the past fifty years."

I watched her scan the list, waiting to see if she lingered on any name more than another.

"And . . . why?" She hadn't given anything away.

"You don't know any of these people?" I asked.

"Sure." She shrugged. "I've met with some of them in the past."

"Did you see any of them recently?"

Leta slid the piece of paper back over to me. "What are you on about, Cayder? You're not usually so ambiguous."

"I spoke to Narena yesterday," I said. "I know that you have a new source you were meeting up with."

Two pink spots flushed across Leta's fair and freckled skin. "So?"

"I believe this new source made you go to Ferrington. I believe they started the fire, and for some reason, you're covering for them."

She shook her head, and the short strands of her hair flicked about. "No. That's not true. It was my idea to go to Ferrington to find out the truth. And I was there. Alone."

"How can I believe you?" I asked. "When you've been hiding secrets from me this entire time?"

She leaned forward, grabbing my hands in hers. "Because I'm your sister."

"Then tell me the truth, *sister*. Why do you have an echo mark on your hands if you didn't start the fire? If you didn't kill anyone."

"I told you." She pulled away. "It was the bird. Can't you just believe me? Why do you always need proof?"

I let out a heated breath before responding. "I do believe you, Let. But without evidence, the jury won't. We need more than some silly superstition."

"Then I'm doomed."

"I don't believe that. We can get you out of this mess. Please, tell me what really happened."

"I'm not a violent person." Her chin wobbled.

"I know you're not." The back of my eyes stung. "Of course. I know that."

Tears welled in her eyes and spilled over. "I hate that all those people are dead because of me. I hate it, Cayder. But I can't rewrite the past. Not even edem can."

I couldn't breathe. "Are you saying you *did* start the fire?"

"No," she said. "The hullen. They started the fire. But if I hadn't been there. If I hadn't summoned them . . ."

Again with the creatures. "Leta—"

"*They* did this, Cayder. I need you to believe me. *Please*, believe me." She wiped her tears with her gloved hands, streaking charcoal down her cheeks.

How could I? She spoke of creatures whose existence was as tangible as shadows themselves. And her hands . . .

"I offered them the life of a bird, but they took mine instead." She choked on her tears. "They took mine instead."

She placed her forehead on her arms and wept.

# CHAPTER II

# LETA

The rest of the week moved slowly, as though being close to the veil played with the passage of time. Only mealtimes signified the lapsing of days; the illuminated glass ceiling ensured that darkness never seeped into Leta's cell. As a class one criminal, Leta was not allowed to eat meals with other inmates, and food was slipped through the slot in the door.

The only time she saw another human being was when Graymond and Cayder came to visit. Even though her father was a judge, he wasn't permitted in the prison sector. The superintendent couldn't show any preferential treatment to Leta's case. She was lucky Cayder was allowed.

Each time her brother visited, he would try to force her to say something that wasn't true. To blame someone else or dismiss the idea of the hullen altogether.

Despite the growing distance between them over the years, she loved her brother. She hated seeing him hurt and knowing she was the one causing the pain. But she shared Cayder's resolve, the stubbornness they got from their father. She wouldn't falter.

On Friday morning, Leta prepared for her arraignment. A tiny scratched mirror above her sink aided in her fruitless endeavor to tame her thick, short hair into some semblance of order. Trying to fix her pallid complexion was a futile effort; the lack of sleep had taken its toll. She would have loved a touch of powder and a dark lipstick. Although she supposed it was best she didn't look too put together for the hearing. She should look like she was miserable. And she was.

Leta's prison uniform hugged her rounded hips in a way that would have made her self-conscious a few years ago, but she'd learned to love her body and the soft curves she'd inherited from her mother as much as she loved Delft pastries. In particular the deebule, a fried ball of dough filled with torlu jam and a healthy coating of powdered sugar.

Leta couldn't think about torlu berries without being reminded of the fields in Ferrington and all the innocent people who had perished in the fires. Perhaps she should plead guilty in the arraignment as Graymond wanted.

If she hadn't been there that night, they would all still be alive.

Graymond had advised her not to speak of the hullen. With the echo mark on her hands visible for the jury to see, it was best she took responsibility for the fires and showed remorse, in hopes of a lesser sentence with a manslaughter charge. If she pleaded not guilty, the jury could still vote to convict, and then she would be facing a murder charge and life in prison.

Even though Leta had no evidence of the hullen, even though

she hadn't seen the creatures with her own eyes, she *knew* they were real. They *had* to be real. What was the alternative? That she *was* guilty?

She shivered as though a shadow had been cast over her.

Why couldn't she remember that night? Was it possible that in her attempt to sacrifice the bird, she *had* created the fire? Were all those people's deaths on her hands?

She shook her head. She couldn't think that way. She had to stick to her truth. It was all she had left.

Leta pulled a sketch of a flower from the pages on the floor and folded it into a small square to place inside her inmate jumpsuit. The drawing was of a blooming heart—a heart-shaped flower, and her mother's favorite. The flower was rare outside the nation of Delften due to the sandier soil in Telene. And yet Leta's mother had managed to grow a patch of blooming hearts in the front garden, the bulbs a gift from Leta's grandmother back in Delften. Looking at those flowers outside her bedroom window had always given Leta strength. She hoped the drawing of the flower would do the same for her now.

The prison guard unlocked her door and let Graymond and Cayder in to escort her to the courthouse. Cayder was dressed in a dark blue three-piece suit she'd never seen before. His brown hair was brushed back off his forehead, making his amber eyes stand out.

He looked like he was going to be sick.

"How are you feeling this morning, Leta?" Graymond asked.

Leta pulled at her jumpsuit's sleeves, wishing she could also be wearing her finest. "I'm all right."

Truth was, she hadn't slept a wink the night before. While she didn't cry herself to sleep anymore, she hated nighttime. The hardest hours were between two and six a.m., when fatigue weakened the rage of the inmates and a stillness settled over the prison. Only then would Leta hear the footsteps of the ever-present guards as silence rose from the dark like the moon in the night sky.

Even though there were no shadows in Vardean, Leta imagined the worst in the quiet. She imagined the hullen seeping through the walls of her cell, not bound by physical limitations. When she closed her eyes, she imagined them creeping closer, hovering above her bunk, ready to finish off the job they'd started in Ferrington.

———

The Crown Courtroom was located below the foyer. A disk of glowing diffused light hung from the ceiling to prevent any shadows. Two tables were arranged at the front of the room, facing an ornate iron balcony. Graymond led Leta and her brother to the tables and nodded for them to take a seat.

A young man with deep brown skin and thick black hair sat behind a typewriter below the balcony. A stenographer. One stray lock curled over his forehead, toward his large round glasses. Leta's fingers twitched for a pencil and paper, wishing to capture his likeness. He caught her eye, then quickly glanced away.

He was afraid of her.

She swallowed down her self-pity. There wasn't time.

"The Crown Judge will sit there," Graymond whispered, pointing at a seat at the edge of the balcony.

"What about the jury?" she asked.

Graymond gestured behind them. "There isn't a jury present for plea hearings. Just the prosecutor and the judge."

"My father?"

He shook his head. "In Crown Court arraignments, no one outside the immediate proceedings is allowed to sit in."

Leta hadn't often looked for her father's support, but she had imagined him sitting behind her during her hearing.

"How many people make up the jury?" she asked. "If we go to trial?"

"Twelve," he replied.

Twelve strangers would decide the rest of her life.

She shivered, her hand finding the folded drawing of the flower tucked inside her jumpsuit, near her heart.

"It's going to be all right," Cayder said. It was the first thing he'd said to her all morning. His voice didn't hold his usual conviction.

Leta hated that she had ruined this moment for him; he'd wanted to see the inside of a courtroom ever since he'd been sent to Vardean Reform. She had ruined both their lives. Gossip was a form of currency in the city of Kardelle. Committing a crime and being suspected of a crime were one and the same, and both would land you in Vardean. If you were related to a convicted criminal, then you too must be dangerous, and avoided.

Leta's insatiable nature had led to the downfall of the entire Broduck family. And yet Leta would not yield.

"This is your last chance to change your mind," Graymond said. His face held much concern, and his brows pulled together. Leta noticed his graying beard was less neat than at the beginning of the week. "If you plead guilty, we can skip the pain of a trial and see what deal can be made."

"A deal where I spend most, but not all, of my life in prison?" she clarified.

Graymond closed his eyes for a brief moment. "It puts the power back in our hands," he said, "and out of the jury's."

Leta nodded. She couldn't feel anything below her neck. "And if I plead *not guilty*?"

"As I've said before . . ." He bowed his head to meet her eyes. "I don't advise you to do so. With the backlog of trials, it could be months before your court date. And the evidence is unlikely to work in your favor—I cannot guarantee you a not-guilty verdict."

"*Months* we can spend to find out the truth," Cayder interjected. "Months to strengthen Leta's case."

The two men exchanged a heated look. Clearly, Cayder was not on board with the guilty plea. And although Leta didn't want her life to be turned inside out for a trial, she couldn't admit to a crime she hadn't—as far as she was aware—committed.

"I understand," Leta said.

"Please remember that a trial for a crime of such a nature will be long and arduous—for everyone involved," Graymond said. "Every aspect of your life will be pulled apart by the prosecutor."

"You flatter me, Graymond," a pale man with a white mustache said, striding to the platform. He took his chair at the other table. Leta recognized him as the prosecutor who had questioned her upon her arrival at Vardean.

He grinned at Leta, deep grooves appearing on either side of his mouth.

"Mr. Rolund," Graymond said curtly.

Cayder reached under the table and squeezed Leta's hand. "Whatever you decide, I'll stand beside you."

That was what Leta was afraid of. As much as she wanted him with her, she was worried what the trial would uncover.

"All rise for the Honorable Judge Dancy," a court clerk announced from the back of the room.

Leta scrambled to her feet. She wished she'd asked her father about legal proceedings or listened more to her brother over the years. She knew nothing about what to expect aside from what Graymond had told her.

Judge Dancy was an elegant woman with russet-brown skin and tight silvery curls. She wore a flowing gray robe—the color to represent that justice was impartial. Her slight frame reminded Leta of an old torlu tree that could break in a strong wind. Her cane clipped across the wooden floor as she approached her seat; the head of the cane was a bronze bird in flight.

"Sit," Judge Dancy commanded as she took her place, her voice anything but fragile.

Leta had barely touched the chair before the judge launched into her speech.

"Ms. Broduck, you have been charged with starting an

edem-fueled wildfire that caused the destruction of the town of Ferrington, killing three hundred townsfolk. How do you plead?"

The stenographer's rapid-fire typing echoed throughout the court. Leta glanced at Cayder. She'd thought the prosecutor and Graymond would speak their case before she had to say anything. Wasn't that what happened in hearings?

"Ms. Broduck, how do you plead?" Judge Dancy prompted, her eyes inscrutable.

Leta tangled her fingers together. "While I was in Ferrington that night, I didn't—"

Judge Dancy cut her off with a wave. "Now is not the time for explanations. We need your plea only."

Graymond gave her an encouraging nod. She knew what she should do. What would cause less pain to her family and allow her to make a deal with the prosecutor. She knew what was right.

"Not guilty," Leta said.

Whether or not that was what Judge Dancy hoped to hear, she gave nothing away. "Hmmm," the judge murmured.

Cayder squeezed her hand again.

"Considering the severity of this case," Mr. Rolund said, "and significant loss of life, the Regency asks the Crown Court to fast-track the trial to Monday."

*This Monday?* Leta thought. *That's too soon!*

"Your Honor," Graymond said, standing alongside his opponent. "Monday does not give the defense enough time to prepare for the trial. Ms. Broduck was only arrested on Tuesday. This time frame is highly unusual."

"The girl is dangerous, Your Honor," Mr. Rolund said, his eyes cutting to her and away again.

As the stenographer typed his words, it felt as though the statement were being carved into stone with each loud tap.

*The girl is dangerous.*

Cayder's grip on Leta's hand turned painful. Leta glanced at her brother, but his eyes were focused on Mr. Rolund. She could see the tension in his posture and the hatred in his eyes.

"Ms. Broduck has yet to be found guilty of such a crime," Graymond reminded the judge. "I ask that you give us the necessary time to prepare our case as you would for any other defendant."

"Ms. Broduck isn't any other defendant," Mr. Rolund stated. "She is a danger to the community."

Leta felt small and insignificant. They spoke about her as though she weren't sitting beside them. As though she were already condemned.

Gossip was fact. Truth was irrelevant.

"Pardon me, Your Honor," Cayder said, letting go of Leta's hand to rise. "My sister is already in Vardean. What possible threat can she pose?"

"You would say that about your own sister," Mr. Rolund replied with a sneer. "I urge the judge to dismiss Cayder Broduck from this courtroom, as anything he says is biased."

"Then *you* should be dismissed," Cayder threw back. "As everything you say is biased. You don't care about the truth, only that someone takes the fall!"

"Enough!" Judge Dancy said, her gavel slamming onto the

podium, causing the stenographer sitting beneath her to jump. "I will dismiss you both if you don't settle down."

"Apologies, Your Honor." Cayder took his seat. Leta wasn't used to seeing her brother so agitated. He was the sort of person who was always in control. Leta had been the troublemaker in the family.

"I agree that this is an unusual case," Judge Dancy said with a nod. "Therefore, we must adapt to the circumstances presented to us. Three hundred people died on Monday night. Their families deserve answers and swift justice. We cannot delay." Judge Dancy looked at Leta for a long moment. Leta wished she could disappear. "However, I do acknowledge Mr. Toyer's concerns. I therefore grant you till next Friday before we begin the trial. Then the jury will decide the truth."

*The jury will decide the truth?* Leta thought.

The truth was the truth. Who was the jury to decide what really happened, when none of them were there that night?

"Thank you, Your Honor," Graymond said.

Leta swallowed down her tears. They wouldn't do her any good.

# CHAPTER 12

# CAYDER

Father was awaiting our return in Graymond's office. He looked like he'd aged ten years overnight, his usually warm beige skin pale and his eyes bloodshot.

"Well?" he asked without preamble.

"Not guilty," Graymond said wearily, hanging his suit jacket on the coat hanger by the door.

"Good for her," Father said. "Broducks don't back down from a fight."

"The trial begins next Friday," I said, slumping onto my makeshift chair of boxes. "We only have a week to prepare."

Father balked at that. "Is that some kind of joke?"

Graymond patted my father's shoulder as he sat down at his desk. "I'm afraid not, Alain. Leta's case has been fast-tracked at the Regency's request. Judge Dancy wants a resolution as swiftly as possible. The newspapers will be all over this. Everyone will want Leta to pay for the lives lost, and the Regency will take heat for not preventing such a crime. The prosecutor is out for blood."

"Then we have to work quickly," I said. "I'll speak to everyone on my list over the weekend. I'll find out who put her up to this."

Graymond rubbed the bridge of his nose. "That is a tenuous plan. If no one admits to being there with Leta, we have nothing. We are better spending our time elsewhere."

"The Regency have nothing but circumstantial evidence," I said. "Just because she was there that night doesn't mean she did it."

"Her hands, Cayder," Graymond reminded me. "They speak more than any other piece of evidence will. And her claims that the echo marks appeared after killing the bird are weak, at best."

"Then it's hopeless!"

"No," Graymond said. "It's never hopeless. Not until the final verdict. The case could go on for weeks. We have time to find new evidence."

"What's your plan?" my father asked. The strength of his gaze and words weighed heavily in the room. My father didn't speak often—when he did, you listened.

"We put everyone who's ever known Leta on the stand," Graymond said. "We prove that she is a good person who would never want to hurt anyone. As a public defender, I cannot lie. I cannot claim someone else started this fire"—he glanced at me—"but I can redirect the jury's thoughts. I can cast doubt on the prosecutor's claims." He flicked through his notes. "Our best course of action is to plant a seed about the bonfire spreading through the town, overcoming Leta with smoke and causing her to pass out. That would explain her fragmented memory."

III

"What about the fact that she was found in the only area not touched by fire?" I asked.

"We won't be able to account for everything," he admitted. "Alain, will you take the stand?"

"Of course," he said gruffly. He turned toward the door, swaying on his feet. For the first time in my life, I worried about him. He'd always seemed so strong and larger than life. Now he looked like a stone wall about to crumble.

"Father?" I asked. "I'm so sorry. I know that I should have—"

"Your apologies are useless to me," he said, not turning around. "Help your sister go free, or the Broduck family is done."

———

Over the weekend, Narena and I tracked down every single conspiracy theorist on our list. While many had spoken with Leta over the years, no one admitted to recently speaking with her or traveling with her to Ferrington. And with the newspapers splashing Leta's face on the front page, calling her the most dangerous criminal in Telene's history, they weren't about to now. Leta's name was forever tainted, just like the echo mark marred her skin.

Narena told me the *Telene Herald* had sources inside Vardean, and I wished I knew their names so I could have a nice little chat . . .

But Narena said there was no way her mother could reveal their sources without losing her job. I couldn't ask her to do that. I didn't want to bring down another family in the pursuit to save mine.

On Monday morning, Graymond and I created a list of all the witnesses who could attest to Leta's good character. We had to disclose our list to the prosecutor that night in preparation for the trial on Friday. So far, we had myself, Father and Narena on the list. While some conspiracy theorists over the weekend had said they would vouch for Leta, I didn't trust them to take the stand without twisting the trial to their own agenda. They desired the spotlight more than wanting to help Leta go free.

Graymond said it would be better if I didn't take the stand, as the prosecutor would try to use my time at Vardean Reform against me. I agreed, but our witness list was pathetically short. I didn't know any of her friends from school, and to be honest, I wasn't sure if she had any. For the past few years, I'd assumed she spent her days investigating ridiculous theories with like-minded peers. But what if I was wrong? What if she was out there alone all this time?

A knock interrupted our planning.

"Dad." Kema nodded to Graymond. "The superintendent needs you in her office."

"What about?" he asked, looking up from his papers. He looked as tired as I felt, the brown of his skin darker under his eyes.

Kema shrugged. "I'm a lowly guard. Yarlyn says jump, and I ask how high." She sent me an apologetic grin.

"It's probably an update on Jey's solitary confinement," Graymond said with a nod to me. "I'll be back shortly."

I'd completely forgotten about Jey; his case held little importance now.

Kema hovered in the doorway; she pulled on the brim of her cap. "I'm so sorry about having to restrain you the other day, Cayder," she said. "I hope you know that I was—"

"Just doing your job."

"No!" She rushed to my side, her brown eyes fierce. "I didn't want you to get arrested too! People have been thrown in here for less."

"All I did was defend my sister."

"I know." She bobbed her head in understanding. "And I would have done the same, but you have much more of a chance of helping her out here than up there." She pointed to the prison sector that hung like a giant gavel above us, poised to fall.

"Thank you, Kema. It helps having a friend on the inside."

She laughed, a short, relieved sound. "You're not locked in here."

I clasped my hands together until they turned white. "It feels that way. If Leta doesn't go free . . ." Father was right. Our family was over.

"You have to think positively," she said. "My father will do his best, and I promise to keep an eye out for her while she's here. Nothing bad is going to happen—" She grimaced apologetically. "I mean, nothing *worse* is going to happen. Chin up, Boy Wonder."

———

When Graymond returned to his office two hours later, he was flustered. His shirt was untucked on one side, and his tie askew.

"What did the superintendent want?" I asked.

"I need to—" He glanced around the room. "I need to send a letter back to the office. I need help on—"

"I can help." I approached his desk. "What do you need?"

"No, Cayder. You can't help me with this." He shuffled through his drawers, looking for something. "Where did I put that pen?"

"Here—" I grabbed it from his front pocket and held it out to him.

"Oh," he said, not looking me in the eyes. "Thank you."

Something was wrong. "What is it?"

He was silent for a moment. "I need someone to take over your sister's case."

"What?" I flinched. "What are you talking about?"

He collapsed into his chair, covering his eyes with his hand. "I've been assigned to take over an existing case." He shook his head. "I can't handle both—it's not fair to either client. The cases are both too complex."

I crossed my arms over my chest. "Then get someone else to take on this new case."

Graymond lowered his hand; his eyes were rimmed red. "I can't, Cayder. I have to. I've been appointed by the Crown Court."

"Leta is going to trial at Crown Court."

"This is a higher priority. I'm sorry, but—"

"You're sorry?" I couldn't believe what I was hearing. "You promised me you would do everything you could to ensure Leta wouldn't spend her life here!"

"I'll get my best lawyer to—"

"*You're* the best!" I snapped. "Tell this other client that you won't represent them. You *can't.* You told me I could trust you."

Graymond took in a deep breath and let it out slowly. "I'm sorry, son. This is out of my control. One of the disadvantages of being a public defender is that you always have more cases than you can handle. I need someone to sit in on the pretrial disclosure tonight. That's when the prosecutor provides the list of all the witnesses. We need to be prepared for whoever might take the stand. And as much as I'd like to be, I can't be in two places at once."

I wouldn't allow him to abandon Leta. He had promised to look after her. We needed him. *She* needed him.

"Who's your other client?" I asked. "Why are they more important than my sister's freedom? My family, *Uncle Graymond.*"

Leta wasn't any other client. We'd meant something to him, once.

Graymond glanced away. "I can't tell you that."

"Now you don't trust me?"

"This isn't about you, or Leta." His face was drawn, remorseful. "I'm sorry, Cayder. My hands are tied."

"So, what?" Anger stretched like a caged animal inside me, bursting to be free. "You get some second-rate lawyer to get up to speed in four days and start Leta's trial on Friday? You know that's a terrible idea! You're condemning my sister to life in prison!"

"Please, Cayder." Graymond let out a sorrowful groan. "Don't make this harder than it has to be."

"Let me talk to your other client. Let me explain why they can't have you." Surely they would understand if I told them the situation we were in?

His face crumpled. "I *can't.*"

I paced inside the cramped office, but there wasn't enough room to walk off my fury.

"What other case could possibly be more important than Leta's?" I asked. "You heard the judge; this is a rare case. Leta needs *you!*"

My father had abandoned both my sister and me after our mother had died, and Graymond had only returned to our lives to leave us once again.

"I know this is difficult to understand—" he began.

"I understand"—my voice was flat—"that everything you've taught me about being a public defender is a lie. You don't care about helping people. You don't care about my family. You only care about yourself."

"That's enough, son." Graymond stood. "I'm still your boss. And this is a lesson you must learn in life—not everything will go your way. You have to learn to twist and turn when need be."

I barked out a laugh. "My mother died when I was ten years old. I spent a year in Vardean Reform. My father is never at home. And my only family is at risk of being locked away for good. I know what it feels like to take a punch. Now I need someone to help me fight back."

I struggled to control my breathing, my gasps rasping in my ears.

Graymond raked his hands through his cropped graying hair. "The only way I can possibly continue with Leta's case is if I were to get some help with my new case. But—"

"I'll do it. Whatever it takes. You name it."

"I know you will, son." Graymond pulled at the tie around his neck as though it was too tight. "But this is an extremely delicate case. Even more so than your sister's."

"Who's your client?" I demanded again.

Graymond closed his eyes. I thought I'd lost him. I thought he was about to order me out of his office. But then he opened his eyes, his jaw set, his shoulders squared. "You cannot speak a word of what I'm about to tell you to anyone, you understand? Not even your sister. No one is allowed to know about this. *I* didn't even know until today."

I *didn't* understand. But if it meant Graymond staying on my sister's case, then I would do whatever it took. "I promise."

"Good," Graymond said. He grabbed his jacket by the door. "Then let's go visit the princess."

I blinked. "I'm sorry, *who*?"

"The princess of Telene," Graymond repeated.

Perhaps Graymond needed a break. He wasn't making any sense. "Why would we visit the princess?"

"She's my new client," he said.

"Client?" I repeated.

"She killed her brother."

I stared at him uncomprehendingly. "Her brother? That means she . . ."

He nodded.

"She killed the king."

## CHAPTER 13

# PRINCESS ELENORA

Six weeks before her imprisonment, Princess Elenora donned her finest dress of ruby-red silk with a high crystal-encrusted neckline before heading out her bedroom door and shuffling down the palace halls, her shoes in her hands.

She was late. She was always running late.

Elenora had the habit of getting caught up in whatever she was doing: walking the perimeter of the castle isle, dreaming of the day she could leave; reading a book in the castle library, learning about the world outside; or gazing out the castle's tallest spire to glimpse the boats heading to the mainland, wishing she were aboard.

All activities led to Elenora wanting more than the small craggy isle the royal castle was built on and the polished blue stone walls that surrounded her. She'd often grumbled about the kings and queens of old and their poor decision to build the castle on an isolated island instead of on the mainland. Although she knew it was for her safety—for the only method of transport to the castle was by boat, and the waters were watched by the King's Guard at all hours of the day and night. Only those granted access by the king were allowed to set foot on the isle. Which made for very boring birthday parties. For once, Elenora would have liked to have a guest who wasn't paid to be there.

Elenora quickly laced up her shoes in the middle of the corridor. Her brother, Erimen, would be disappointed at her tardiness. And she hated disappointing him—not because he was the king, but because he was her brother. Today was an important day for him.

A member of the king's staff spotted Elenora as she scrambled toward the chamber of government.

"Elle!" Simone whispered. Simone had deep brown skin and shiny dark hair. She usually sported a genuine smile, but not today. "You're late!"

"I know, I know." Elenora brushed past Simone.

"Wait!" Simone held out a mask with twisted horns, covered in brilliant lumanite gemstones. "You forgot this."

Elenora let out a well-worn sigh.

She hated wearing the mask. Not only was it heavy, but she could barely breathe through it, and it made her skin itchy and hot when she wore it for too long. Wearing the mask in public was a royal tradition that Elenora wished her brother would abolish. The reflective masks had originally been crafted for kings and queens not only to signal their authority, but to ward off the dark. The glittering gemstones would pick up the smallest fraction of light and reflect it around the room, protecting the royals from edem. Wearing the masks in all public outings meant that no one, aside from their own staff, knew the royals' faces.

Although Elenora hadn't left the isle since she was twelve, she still had to wear her mother's mask when visitors came to the palace. Erimen refused to eliminate the custom. He had only been sixteen when he was crowned and liked the connection to their late parents, who had died five years ago.

The royal family had traveled to the mainland to celebrate Elenora's twelfth birthday. A grand celebration had been planned for the entire city to attend in Elenora's favorite part of Kardelle—the Royal Gardens.

The crowds waved their gray flags—the official color of Telene—as the royal family traveled down the main street via a slow-moving trolley. The plan had been to end the parade at the gardens, where an expertly trained orchestra was poised to welcome them, along with tables upon tables of every kind of food Elenora could imagine.

The trolley had traveled halfway to its destination when the surrounding flood lamps sparked to life due to low light. Normally, the lights switching on during an overcast day would not cause any harm. But someone had tampered with the wiring, and the normal diffused halo was a sharp triangle of light, beaming onto the trolley and surrounding street.

The crowd scattered, frightened of the pitch-black shadows that appeared around them, were cast *by* them. Around fifty rebels dressed in black, veil worshippers, leaned down to touch the edem shifting in the shadows.

Twelve-year-old Elenora had never seen anyone use edem; she watched in awe as the inky shadows spread up from the ground and covered the rebels.

"Control," the rebels all said in unison.

Edem rolled out onto the cobblestoned street. The King's Guard shifted to protect the royal family. The edem congealed in the center of the street and rose like an onyx moon.

The king and queen pushed Elenora and Erimen to the back of the trolley and away from the bubble of edem, which was sure to burst.

Later in court, the rebels denied they'd planned to hurt anyone. They merely wanted to prove to the king and queen that edem could be controlled. That it could be contained and could be useful for Telene—a resource, not a virus that needed to be eradicated.

But their plan backfired.

Too many rebels tried to control edem at the same time. The bubble shuddered, not knowing whose mind to follow. Then, like a firework, it exploded. Shards of shattered cobblestones flew out in all directions.

The king and queen, and ten of their guard, were struck by flying fragments of stone. Elenora and her brother were protected by an upturned trolley seat but trapped beneath it. People screamed so loudly, Elenora couldn't hear her parents' final words to her. They watched in horror as their parents bled out in front of them, their faces masked from view.

The next week, sixteen-year-old Erimen was crowned and new rules were put in place to ensure the royals' safety. Barriers around the isle guaranteed that no one could enter or exit without explicit permission. Elenora was banned from visiting the mainland, and Erimen traveled only in the direst of cases.

Some nights, Elenora could still hear echoes of the explosion when she lay in bed.

Still, Elenora was desperate to be a part of the world outside. She wished for someone to know her as herself, and not "Princess Elenora of Telene." She wished for a life beyond the isle. She wished to throw away that cursed mask and never have to wear it again. But she would not dishonor her parents' memory and their traditions any more than Erimen would.

Elenora took a deep breath and begrudgingly placed the heavy mask over her face before stepping into the royal chamber. The rough material scratched at her skin, and her breath echoed in her ears, making everything seem dramatic, as though each breath were a lament.

Erimen sat at the head of a long wooden table, his face hidden behind a sparkling wolflike mask. Tufts of his red hair stuck out from underneath.

Elenora bowed to her brother before taking a seat beside him.

Woven tapestries hung from each section of the hexagonal room, in between luminous glass columns. Five of the six tapestries represented the different senses, with a depiction of the king and queen seeing, tasting, smelling, hearing and touching all that Telene had to offer. One tapestry showed the masked king and queen peering across the jagged coastline to the ocean, another had them drinking goblets of fizzing torlu tonic, the third detailed the couple lifting a flower to their masked faces, the fourth depicted the king and queen listening to an orchestra, and the fifth showed the royals shaking hands with their people. The final tapestry depicted the king and queen gazing into the veil, their reflections distorted and slightly demonic.

Edem was the sixth sense.

At the start of each season, the Regency reported the stability of the veil to the royals. How much had it grown? Were there any hot spots of edem usage across the nation? How many people were detained in Vardean per month? What was the most common edem crime?

Based on today's learnings, her brother would adjust his plans. He might send more agents to monitor specific regions at nightfall or increase the severity of fines for any attempted use of edem. Even with the permacloud in place, neither the Regency nor the king could control what happened inside people's homes.

The Regency General's mouth twitched, as though he wished to mention Elenora's tardiness but couldn't. Between the two men lay multiple scrolls with colorful lines traversing the pages.

Elenora wasn't a fan of the Regency's reports. The presentations were dull and removed the human component. Most of all, she disliked the Regency General, Dr. Bueter. He was a tall man who towered over Elenora. His dull blond hair was slicked back from his forehead, which was perpetually pinched, as though simply being in the room filled him with disdain.

Elenora was fairly certain the Regency General thought she was a childish fool, a mere figurehead, but the royals were the head of the government. *They* decided Telene's future. Not the Regency.

The Regency were merely in charge of monitoring the veil and arresting edem abusers.

Dr. Bueter spoke of increased fluctuations of edem and higher arrest rates as though they were disconnected from the people of Telene. As though everyone's life was merely a number to be monitored and graphed. Elenora imagined the graph of her life as a steady and uninteresting line. It hadn't always been that way. Not when Elenora was allowed off the isle. Not when her parents were alive.

Even though Elenora was the royal spare, she was required to attend all meetings about edem and the veil. While her brother would make the decisions, it was expected that Elenora understood the plight of her people. As princess, she was tasked with hosting royal charities and events, including helping those impacted by edem accidents. But now, with the government close to bankruptcy, there was little support they could provide other than a letter of condolence.

Elenora wished there were more she could do.

"People are willing to break the law and risk imprisonment to improve their standing in life," Dr. Bueter said, his voice as haughty as his posture. He measured each word before speaking, his tone low and even. Elenora had been known to discreetly fall asleep behind her mask . . . until she started snoring. "Greed is what poses the most risk to the veil," he said.

"Greed and wanting to improve your life are not the same thing, General," Erimen disagreed. His voice was somewhat muffled by the mask. "You came from a working-class family; surely you understand the desire to improve your standing?"

"I improved my life through hard work," Dr. Bueter said. "And protecting the people of Telene, even if from themselves and their own selfish desires, does improve their standing. The most pressing matter is to reestablish trade, to break down the boundaries between nations. It's the only way for Telene to not only survive but thrive."

"I agree. But I also wonder if there isn't some kind of compromise that can be reached. If we worked out how much edem can be used without affecting the veil, perhaps we can improve the overall standard of living in Telene? It's been one hundred years, and the veil has not reached our shoreline, nor has edem spread to other nations."

Dr. Bueter lowered his fair brows. "We've only survived this long because we have a no-tolerance stance on edem usage."

"And yet Vardean is still full of people," Erimen said with a sad shake of his head. "Our method of deterrence is far from perfect. We take away people's freedom for using a resource that presents itself so easily. Telene was once a flourishing nation, but we are now stagnant. As you said, we need to reestablish international trade. We need to reestablish immigration, in both directions. While other nations have focused on technological and medical advancements, we're stuck trying to brick up a leaking dam."

"Edem is not a resource to grant people their petty wishes," Dr. Bueter said bitterly. "People cannot be allowed to use it if we ever hope to have access to the rest of the world. I implore you to focus your efforts on forcing the other nations to break down the borders as soon as possible. They are as much a problem as edem, maybe more."

*"Force?"* Erimen asked. "No. We need to meet their requirements, but we must also listen to our own people and their wants and needs."

Erimen pulled a scroll toward him. The map of Telene displayed the hot spots of edem usage dotted across the nation.

"I'll set up meetings with the mayors of each region to discuss their main concerns. See if some balance of edem usage can be reached," Erimen said.

"That would be a waste of your time." Dr. Bueter crossed his arms over his chest.

Elenora was surprised by the general's tone. Surely her brother wouldn't allow him to speak so bluntly?

"Helping Telene is never a waste of time," Erimen said. "My parents raised my sister and me to place the people's well-being above all." He glanced at Elenora. "They taught us not to fear edem, but to respect it."

Elenora reached out under the table and squeezed his hand.

"And look what happened to them," Dr. Bueter said. His tone lashed like a whip.

How dare he speak so callously about her parents! She gritted her teeth.

"We must find a solution," Erimen said, rising in his chair like the king he was. "We must find a way to help our people before we turn our focus offshore. And if edem is that solution, then we cannot shy away from it. Sometimes the forbidden fruit is the most desirable. Let's remove that temptation."

Dr. Bueter blinked as though Erimen had spoken in another language. "Your Majesty, there is no way that we can—"

"That is my order." Erimen stood, ending any debate. "Thank you, General."

Elenora found herself nodding. Perhaps there would not be as many arrests if the people were given what they wanted. Perhaps only a taste of edem was required. Perhaps that was enough.

Elenora wished *she* could have a taste of freedom. A taste of the world outside. She missed it. She missed being a part of the world rather than a prisoner of her own life.

Despite the luxuries she enjoyed, her life was not so different from that of an inmate at Vardean.

And like a criminal, she too had no chance of escaping.

# DEPARTMENT OF JUSTICE

VARDEAN, TELENE

*Arrest Report*

---

**Name:** Princess Elenora

**Age:** 17

**Height:** 5'5"

**Arrest location:** the castle isle

**Edem crimes:** Suspected of killing the king

**Recommended sentence:** Life in prison

# CHAPTER 14

# CAYDER

*The princess.* Here, in Vardean. I couldn't believe it. And although Leta was my priority, I wanted to know more about the princess's case. I *needed* to.

"Why haven't I heard about the death of the king?" I asked as we boarded the elevator to the top floor. "When did it happen?"

Graymond scrubbed his hand across his face. The whites of his eyes stood out against his skin. I felt for the man. When was the last time he left this building? Or slept?

"Four weeks ago," he said. "The Regency didn't want to incite panic, so they're keeping his vanishing under wraps until the princess is tried."

"When is her trial?"

Graymond blew out a breath. "That's the problem. It continues to be delayed while the Regency collects evidence. Her previous defense attorney recently quit, which is why the Crown Court reassigned the case to me."

"How did the king die?"

"It's curious. The Regency say he simply vanished."

"How is that possible?" I asked. "Isn't he always surrounded by his guard?"

"Most of the time." Graymond nodded. "But not when he's with his sister. The Regency found her trying to flee the castle isle on a small boat, an echo mark on her neck and no sign of the king. As you can imagine, this is an incredibly important case for the government and Telene in general."

"What does the princess claim happened to the king?"

"I don't know," Graymond said, "which is why we must speak with her."

The elevator continued to rise toward the shining glass prism ceiling. The inmates shouted at us as we passed by their cells. It was concerning how quickly I'd adapted to the ruckus and pushed it to the back of my mind.

"Don't the royals have criminal immunity?" I asked. I could have sworn I read that in one of my law books.

"Only the ruling king or queen," Graymond explained. "The princess has not been crowned. She was brought here as soon as the king disappeared."

The princess's cell was different from the others on the top floor; it was an enclosed stone box, no bars open to the landing. Did they really believe she was that dangerous?

The superintendent stood as immovable as the door she guarded. A few guards kept vigil nearby, including Kema; the remainder were posted at Jey's and Leta's cells. I caught a glimpse of Leta's face peering through the bars. Every time I saw her, my breath lodged in my throat and fury seared through my veins.

I had the strange thought of wanting to burn Vardean to the ground.

Hopefully, it wouldn't come to that. Not while Graymond remained on her case.

Kema raised an eyebrow as I walked by. How long had she known the princess was here?

The superintendent placed her hand near her truncheon as we approached. "What is *he* doing here?" She narrowed her eyes at me.

"Cayder is helping me with the pri—"

"Shhh," she admonished. "Only a few guards know. We're to keep *her* presence in Vardean quiet until the trial is over."

"Of course, Yarlyn," Graymond said wearily. "I haven't told anyone."

"Except him." She jerked her chin at me.

"My name is Cayder, in case you forgot," I said. "And I won't tell anyone."

"You're related to a criminal." She shook her head, her blunt bob of silver hair rippling around her narrow face. "You can't be trusted."

I wasn't surprised she thought that. After all, Vardean inmates were guilty until proven innocent.

Graymond took a step forward. "I can vouch for Cayder."

"You're willing to risk your job for this kid?" she asked, eyebrow raised.

He didn't hesitate. "I am."

"It's your career." She shrugged.

"Since when do you guard cells, Yarlyn?" he asked. "Isn't that below your rank?"

"I can't risk anything happening to"—she gestured to the metal door behind her—"*this* inmate while under my roof."

"Why, Yarlyn, it almost sounds as though you care," he replied with a grin.

"Hardly." She snorted. "I want to make sure the girl survives to be sentenced for her heinous crime."

"Careful," Graymond warned. "You're close to crossing the line. You're to remain impartial, Yarlyn. Not side with the Regency—or anyone."

The two of them locked eyes. Graymond was a tall man, so Yarlyn had to tilt her head to meet his gaze. Still, she didn't look any less imposing. If I were Graymond, I would've recoiled.

"Fine," she said, her voice even. "But don't expect special treatment because of who she is."

"That"—Graymond pointed at her—"is what I'm counting on."

Yarlyn took a key from a chain on her belt and unlocked the door.

The inside of the cell was a similar layout to Leta's, although there were additional bars between us and the princess. The cell's ceiling was open to the illuminated prism above. The reflective light bounced off something in the center of the bunk, playing havoc with my vision. It took me a moment to realize it was the princess's jeweled mask.

The princess was crouched on her bunk, a black-and-white dress bunched around her. She looked like a budding flower or, rather, a decaying flower. Her shining mask had horns on either side of her face; I could see her eyes were shut. Was she sleeping?

"She wouldn't take off the mask, so we let her keep it," the superintendent said with a shrug. "Thought it was safer that way."

"For whom?" I asked.

The superintendent scoffed. "She killed the king; you work it out."

"What about her dress?" Graymond asked. "Why didn't you give her a clean uniform to wear?"

"She doesn't deserve one," the superintendent replied, then turned on her heel, slamming the door shut behind us.

"Nice manners," I muttered.

"Princess Elenora," Graymond announced, approaching the internal bars. "My name is Graymond Toyer, and this is my apprentice, Cayder Broduck. I've been appointed by the Crown Court as your new public defender after your previous defense attorney stepped down." When the princess didn't reply, he added, "I'm very sorry to hear about your brother. The king was a great man and ruler."

The princess didn't shift from her bunk. Nor did she open her eyes.

"Princess?" Graymond said loud and clear, as though he worried the mask impacted her hearing.

"She's ignoring you," I whispered.

At that, the princess opened her eyes and locked on mine. They were a blue, almost-gray color, not too dissimilar from the stone walls surrounding us.

"Should we bow or something?" I asked Graymond. "Or does

the whole being arrested for murdering the king negate royal civilities?"

Graymond shot me a dark look, then moved as close to the princess as he could with the bars separating us.

"I'm here to help you, Princess. I will do everything in my power to ensure you're not found guilty. But first, I need your assistance. I need you to tell me what happened to your brother."

I had the habit of saying the wrong thing to fill in silence when nervous. I begged myself to be quiet. I was sure Graymond was doing the same.

"Princess?" Graymond asked.

After a long moment, Graymond pulled out his notebook and started reading. "The arresting agents informed me that you were found four weeks ago as you attempted to board a boat and flee the castle isle, an echo mark on your neck and no sign of your brother. In your own words, can you explain what happened that night? I'll follow up with your previous attorney to obtain their notes, but in the meantime, I need all the information I can get. Any small detail can help in our defense. Anything at all."

The princess didn't move. The only signs that she was awake were occasional blinking and the slight rise and fall of her chest.

Why wouldn't she say anything?

After a few silent minutes, Graymond's hopeful expression faltered.

"What's wrong with her?" I asked when we left the cell.

He rubbed the bridge of his nose. "She doesn't trust me. She doesn't trust anyone."

"Aside from her echo mark and fleeing the castle isle, is there any other evidence of her guilt?"

"She's the only person who would benefit from her brother's demise . . . Still"—his mouth twisted in contemplation—"I need to hear what happened. Assumptions are not reason enough to condemn someone to a life in prison, as you know."

I swallowed sharply, not needing the reminder of my sister's case. "If she *is* innocent, why won't she explain what happened? Clearly she used edem that night."

"Either someone has told her not to or she's worried opening up will bring her closer to a guilty verdict. But I'm on her side. Guilty or not." I wasn't sure if he was trying to convince himself or me.

"What can we do?" I asked, surprising myself. I'd never thought much about the monarchs of Telene. The king and the princess lived on a small isle in the middle of the harbor, out of sight and, often, mind. While the king made decisions about the law and future of Telene, the Regency were more immediate and present.

"Right now," he said, "I only know what the arresting agents have told me. Perhaps you could help me track down the previous attorney's notes? The court said they weren't filed." I nodded. "Then I'll continue to work on Leta's trial."

"Thank you!" I wanted to throw my arms around him, but I restrained myself.

"Remember," he said, pointing at me. "No one is to know about the princess being in Vardean."

"Of course." I would keep my mouth shut if it meant Graymond would stay on Leta's case. "Neither the king nor the princess has an heir. Who's in charge of Telene now?"

"The Regency. Until after the trial."

"And if the princess is found guilty?" I asked. "What then?"

"The next in line to the throne will be crowned."

I thought about the princess's eyes and how they tracked my movements. "Maybe she didn't speak to you because I was there?"

Graymond thought for a moment. "I don't think that's it," he said. "She'll open up to us. Eventually." But he didn't sound like his usual confident self.

Although her face was hidden behind a mask, I didn't think she looked weak or prone to breaking. She looked strong. Determined.

If she didn't want to talk, then I had a feeling we were in for a long wait.

# CHAPTER 15

# JEY

Jey hated solitary confinement. He missed mealtimes. He even missed the incessant wails of his old cell neighbor. While he shared the top level with two other inmates, there were empty cells between them so he could neither hear nor see who was inside. Although he knew one cell was occupied by the infamous Leta Broduck. The other was guarded both day and night.

Aside from the guards roving the top-floor landing, the only other distractions were when food was pushed through the slot in the cell door. Jey's meals were smaller than when Ryge served him down in the food hall, and he received bloody, undercooked slices of meat that made his stomach turn. But he could do nothing about it. He'd created this situation, so now he had to make the best of it.

Early Tuesday morning, Jey's cell door opened. Six days in solitude and finally someone to talk to.

"My two favorite people!" Jey exclaimed when Cayder and Mr. Toyer entered his cell. "I've been so lonely up here. I even miss my shadow." He gestured to the illuminated ceiling. "Any idea how they do that? Remove all shadows?"

Mr. Toyer sighed in response, and he took a seat at the table beside Cayder.

"I've tried getting to know my neighbors up on the top floor, but they're too far away." Jey pouted. "What can you tell me about them?" He approached the table. "Bring me news from the outside world—or at least outside this prison cell."

"Worry about yourself, Jey," Mr. Toyer said, his mouth in a firm, grim line.

Jey liked Mr. Toyer, who, so far, had put up with his antics. Had he pushed him too far?

Jey knew he could be an acquired taste. At least that was what he'd learned from his father.

Jey had not seen his father for fourteen years and had thought they had much to catch up on when they were reunited after his mother's death. He used to pepper his father with questions about his life and his work in the vain attempt to get to know the man. Jey avoided asking what his mother was like when she was younger, knowing his father would shut down completely at the mention of her name.

While Jey's father obliged his persistent questions for the first few weeks, he could tell he never fully had his father's attention. If life was a stage, which Jey liked to think it was, then Dr. Bueter's work was the main act, and his son wasn't even located inside the theater.

Jey wasn't used to sharing the spotlight; his mother had always placed him front and center in her life, but the more prominent

Jey tried to be, the more his father retreated into his work. Jey soon discovered that although Dr. Bueter was happy to take financial responsibility for his son, his commitment ended there.

The contrast between the small, warm and loving home he shared with his mother and his father's often empty manor could not have been greater. Jey was used to spirited discussions over a bowl of homemade poached long-fish and crispy noodles made of torlu root, not the awkward mealtimes of a chef-prepared meal while his father read over Regency reports, nodding every now and then to Jey's monologue.

His father was never cruel, but his casual indifference made Jey miss his mother all the more. But he didn't blame his father; they were too different, and too many years had passed where they were estranged.

Without his mother, Jey wondered if he would ever feel loved again. Then he met Nettie.

Jey had planned to leave his father's house and live with Nettie as soon as he turned eighteen, but fate had dealt him a different hand. Instead, Jey celebrated his eighteenth birthday on the streets, mere days before his arrest.

"Somebody's not in a good mood today," Jey said in a sing-song voice, crossing his ankles up on the cell table.

"Somebody stabbed another inmate and placed his entire future at risk," Mr. Toyer replied tersely.

"Who?" Jey placed both hands on his chest over the skull echo mark that was visible due to his unzipped uniform. "Me?"

Mr. Toyer shuffled some papers. "I'm not in the mood for your games, Jey."

Apparently neither was Cayder, as he hadn't uttered a word, although he watched with narrowed eyes as if he was trying to figure him out. Jey glanced away.

"Okay, so I screwed up." Jey ran a hand through his black hair, setting his angular jaw. "An inmate jumped me. I had to protect myself, or I wouldn't be here right now. And wouldn't that be a shame?"

"Where did you get the knife?" Mr. Toyer asked.

Jey shook his head. "I made it."

"You made this?" Mr. Toyer held out a photo of a bloodied kitchen knife.

"The kitchen staff didn't even clean the blood off?" Jey asked. "Well, that's just lazy."

"The blood's still on it, as it's evidence for the prosecutor. He's pushing the court to have your trial canceled."

Jey was mildly surprised, although this would work to his benefit.

"Did Big Arms die or something?" Jey had been careful not to hit any important arteries.

"*Big Arms?*" Mr. Toyer frowned. "No, your victim did not die. He's still in the infirmary."

Jey scoffed. "He was hardly a victim when he was pummeling me."

"That doesn't matter, Jey. What matters is that you're now considered a dangerous criminal—"

"Wasn't I already considered that?" Jey scratched his chin with long fingers. "I thought I'd done a pretty good job—"

"Damn it, Jey!" Mr. Toyer threw his file on the table. "I'm

trying to get you out of here, and you continue to do your best to ruin your chance of freedom. Why?"

Jey shrugged, his expression indifferent. "Freedom is over-rated. And I did kill my father, after all. I'm right where I'm meant to be."

Cayder scrunched his nose up at that.

"If you want to spend your life in here," Mr. Toyer said, "then I can't help you."

*Good.*

This was the first time his attorney looked defeated.

While Jey didn't want, or plan, to spend his life in prison, he also couldn't go to trial. He couldn't have the prosecutor delve further into the night his father died. For Mr. Toyer was right, there was much about that night that Jey was hiding from him.

He needed Mr. Toyer to give up on him, and Jey could tell he was close.

"I don't need your help," Jey said.

He couldn't have anyone find out the truth.

# CHAPTER 16

# CAYDER

As far as I was concerned, if Jey wanted to spend his life in Vardean, then he was welcome to. Having one less client to worry about would allow Graymond to focus on Leta. But I knew Graymond's mind was on the princess's case first and foremost. As frustrated as I was, I couldn't blame him. The king's disappearance was as mysterious as it was concerning.

After lunch in Graymond's office, we returned to the princess's cell. She was still sitting on her bunk when we entered; she didn't appear to have shifted since we visited yesterday.

"I want you to know," Graymond said as he approached the internal bars, "it's my job as a public defender to help you, but I also need you to help yourself. I need you to tell me what happened so we can form a plan. I know you're tired and scared. But I also know there's more to your story. There's more to every story. *Please*, Princess. Let me help you."

The princess pitched forward, like a puppet cut from its

strings. My heart lurched as she fell face-first off the bunk. The mask thudded against the stone floor but did not break.

"Guards!" Graymond shouted. "Help!"

The superintendent rushed in, saw the princess's splayed form and quickly unlocked the interior door.

"Princess!" Graymond pulled her limp body from the floor. "Are you all right?"

"She hasn't eaten or drunk anything over the past few days," Yarlyn said, her voice dispassionate.

"Can she even drink with that mask on?" I asked.

"Take her to the infirmary," Graymond ordered. "Make sure she has a private room and take that damn mask off."

I could hear her short, sharp breaths. The poor girl could hardly breathe.

*Poor girl?*

Was this all a ploy to earn our sympathy?

When Leta was twelve, she spent a month in bed, crying about a stomachache that wouldn't fade no matter what tonics she drank. I was terrified she was going to die, leaving me all alone with Father. But when the doctor visited, she claimed that Leta wasn't sick at all. She merely wanted attention. But the attention she wanted was from Father, and despite her convincing performance, he had relegated her welfare to me.

Slate-gray eyes found mine from behind the mask. Concern jolted through me. She looked weak, beaten.

Had I been wrong about her yesterday, or could the princess be playing us all for fools?

Graymond and Yarlyn propped up the princess under each

arm, but the princess couldn't find her footing. Her bare feet slipped on the dirty stone, and she slumped against Graymond. The weight of her dress attempted to drag her back to the floor. Graymond noticed and gathered the long train of material in his hands.

"Cayder," Graymond instructed. "Get the door for us."

The princess's head lolled to the side, the mask slipping. I saw a flash of smoky gray swirls across her neck.

Her echo mark.

As Graymond and Yarlyn half carried, half dragged the princess from the cell, her limp hand swept mine and pressed something into my palm. A scrap of white material from her dress.

I glanced up, aghast. The princess's eyes were open. And focused.

Once the cell was empty, I unfurled the scrap. A note written in red.

Blood?

Help me, Cayder.

The princess wanted *my* help. But why? Why wouldn't she trust Graymond? He was her best chance at freedom. And why wouldn't she speak to us? Why hand me this note instead?

I didn't have time for this. I needed to help my sister get out of here. I needed to find a reason for the jury to doubt her guilt and see past the death echo marking her hands.

And yet I couldn't stop staring at the princess's note.

"Hey, Boy Wonder." Kema entered the princess's cell. "Are you okay?"

I scrunched the material into my fist.

"I'm fine," I said. "It's just a shock to see the princess in Vardean."

Kema nodded, her lips pressed together solemnly. "You should go home."

"I've promised to help your father with the princess," I said. "It's the only way he can continue to work on Leta's case."

Kema glanced behind her to the open door and the guards lingering outside. "Is there anything I can do?"

I thought about the princess's note. While I didn't know her story yet, the princess clearly wanted to speak with me, and me alone. At this moment, I didn't care why. I needed to make it happen.

"Can you arrange a meeting with me and the princess?" I asked. "Just the two of us?"

Kema pursed her lips. "Why?"

I showed her the note.

"Is this blood? *Her* blood?" she asked, horrified, although I'm sure she'd seen worse after working two years in Vardean.

"I think so. I need your father to focus on Leta's case, and clearly the princess wants to speak with me. Will you help?"

Kema nibbled on her bottom lip. "I don't know . . . I'm one of the few guards who knows the princess is in Vardean. If anyone found out I arranged—"

"You're arranging a client to see her lawyer." I shook my head. "There's nothing wrong with that."

She grinned. "As much as you might think you are, Boy Wonder, you're not a lawyer."

"Not *yet*." When she didn't say anything further, I shrugged. "Look, I'm merely talking with her. What's the worst that could happen?"

She raised an eyebrow. "Do you want to find out?"

"Wouldn't you?"

Kema dragged her fingers through her short white locks. "Okay," she said finally. "It's not the first time I've had to keep a secret from my father."

"The princess?" I asked.

She nodded. "I've been guarding her cell since she was arrested. I've wanted to tell him about her every day. But—"

"You value your job."

"It's not that." She frowned. "There's something strange about this case."

"That's an understatement. The king disappeared without a trace."

She shook her head. "Dad's the princess's third attorney in a month. I've never seen that happen in such a short amount of time. I don't know what the princess is doing, or saying, but no one hangs around for long."

"Then it's time we find out."

———

"Just act like you're not doing anything wrong," Kema whispered to me as we approached the infirmary on the first floor.

"I'm not," I said. "I don't think . . ."

My father had never particularly liked the royals, but my mother had. She'd worshipped the royal family as though they hung the sun and the moon and were the very reason the stars glimmered at night. When the old king and queen visited Telene, she would dress me and Leta in our finest and we'd travel into the city to catch a glimpse of their masks. She believed the monarchs were something more—something out of the ordinary. And something to behold.

My father, on the other hand, hated that the royals were treated better than anyone else, especially himself, simply because of their bloodline. He couldn't understand how my mother, a Regency employee, could be so enamored with them.

"The best leadership for Telene is the Regency working in harmony with the monarchs," she would say. "If the Regency were a boat, then the monarchs are their rudder. We are nothing without them."

"Pompous figureheads," my father would snarl. "That's all the royals are. The government is almost bankrupt, and the standard of living has never been lower, leading to more people using edem," he would declare, all from within his marble-tiled dining hall. My father never understood irony.

Sometimes I wondered how my radiant mother had ever been drawn to my irritable, volatile father. Even as a child, I couldn't remember my father happy. I'd never seen the lighter side of him that my mother must have seen to want to spend her life with him.

If my mother were alive now, she would do anything to help the princess.

Inside the infirmary, curtains were hung around the beds to

create the illusion of privacy. Diffused lights dangled above each bed, ensuring no stray shadows could make it into the room.

It was easy to spot where the princess was being held. Yarlyn stood guard outside the door, her arms across her chest.

This wasn't going to be easy.

"Toyer," Yarlyn said with a nod to Kema. "What are you doing in here?" *With him* was implied.

"My father," Kema began, "*Mr.* Toyer, that is, has asked Mr. Broduck to check in on his client."

Yarlyn stared at me for a long moment. I could feel the sweat gathering between my shoulder blades.

"He was just here," she said. "Why didn't he come back himself?"

"He's busy," I interjected. "As you know, he has three cases he's working concurrently."

"One of which is your sister's." Her voice was thick with suspicion.

"I'm not doing anything wrong." And it was true. The princess asked for my help, and I was here to give it. I was officially helping Graymond, even if he didn't know it yet. "If you don't let me speak with my client"—I squared my shoulders, channeling Graymond—"then you're interfering with the law, which we can use to have the inmate's case thrown out."

Yarlyn clenched her teeth. She wanted to fight me, but she knew I was right.

"Go on, then," she said, stepping aside. "For all the good it will do you. She hasn't uttered a word in days. Not since her last attorney quit."

I gave Kema a nod of gratitude.

The princess's room was small, with no windows. A hot white light burned brightly from above; it was so bright, it stung my eyes. I blinked a few times before I could make out the shape of the bed and the princess lying on it. The bed was a simple bunk atop a wooden block, so no shadows could be cast underneath. Next to the bed were some empty glasses, which must have contained different tonics, and the princess's discarded ornate mask.

I approached cautiously. A thin sheet was brought up to the princess's chin. Her blond hair splayed about the pillow like a halo. Her skin appeared to be the color of bleached parchment paper, and just as fragile. Her lips were white, cheeks sunken.

"Princess?" I whispered softly.

Aside from the slight rise and fall of her chest, she didn't move. She must have been sleeping. I'd wait. I didn't think the princess of Telene would appreciate being woken by a stranger, even if she'd asked to speak with me.

I'd turned to walk away when cold fingers grabbed my wrist.

"Don't go," the princess whispered.

Her eyes were large and more of a dark blue than gray, like where the ocean met the veil.

"Princess Elenora." It was different with her mask removed. Intimate. "You wanted to speak with me?" I held out her note.

Her hand shook as she reached for it; evidently not everything about her illness had been a ruse.

"Thank you for coming." Her voice was soft, breathless.

"Your note made me think it was urgent." I smiled wryly. "How can I help you, Your Highness? And why don't you speak to Mr. Toyer? He's a good lawyer, the best—really. He can help you. You just need to—"

She held up her hand. "You talk too much."

"Sorry." I bowed my head.

A glimmer of a smile spread across her face, and my heart faltered. Her skin flushed pink when she smiled, as though she was coming back to life.

"I need your help," she said, the smile disappearing.

"I can't help you. Not really. But you can trust Graymond. He'll do whatever he can."

She closed her eyes for a brief moment. "Everyone who knows the truth disappears."

*Disappears? Like her brother?*

"What are you talking about?"

Her gaze locked on mine again, and I fought the urge to glance away. "I've had two defense attorneys since I've been in Vardean. I told them both the truth—I told them everything that happened that night." She blew out a breath. "Now they're gone."

"They quit," I said.

"Is that what the court told you?" The princess sat upright, keeping the sheet pulled up to her neck. "They got rid of them both because they knew the truth."

"Who's *they*?"

Her eyes darted to the door, where Yarlyn was waiting outside. "If I tell you, you have to promise not to tell your boss. He's already in danger."

What was she talking about? "If he's in danger, then I am too. You have to tell us what's going on."

"You're just a kid whose sister has been arrested for murdering three hundred people. Your word is tainted. They'll claim you're out for revenge."

I bristled. "How do you know about my sister?"

"It doesn't matter. What matters is Mr. Toyer's life. If I keep my mouth shut, if I don't tell him the truth, then no notes will be shared with the prosecutor. It's the only way to protect him."

"From who?" I pushed.

"Do you promise?" she asked, ignoring my question. "Do you promise to protect your boss?"

If Graymond was in danger by representing the princess, then I needed to know the truth. But if knowing the truth put Graymond in danger . . . then what?

I couldn't decide without knowing all the facts.

"I'll keep this between you and me," I said. *For now.*

She sighed. "Thank you, Cayder. I don't know what else to do. I don't want to be the cause of another lost life."

"Tell me what happened," I insisted. "Who are you so afraid of?"

She pulled her shoulders up toward her ears. "The Regency."

No one really liked the Regency, but they kept Telene safe. A necessary evil. "What about them?"

Her bottom lip trembled. "They made my brother disappear."

"Then Graymond will help you go free." This was a good thing; this gave Graymond enough for a plea, and he could focus his energies on Leta's case in the meantime.

She laughed cynically. "The Regency is in control of Telene now. They keep delaying my trial so the truth can't be heard, and silencing anyone else who knows what happened." She shifted on the bed. "The only reason they haven't silenced me is because the superintendent controls Vardean. For now, anyway. I have to get out of here. I have to make them pay for what they did. Everyone must know the truth."

"Truth about what?"

"I don't know, exactly," she said, slumping back against her pillows. "My brother disappeared before he could tell me what he'd uncovered. But they're lying to us. Lying to the people of Telene."

"How do you know?"

She lowered the sheet.

Her neck was adorned in gray swirls around stars as seen through a rippling lake.

"Because my brother told me before he disappeared."

I flinched back from the bed. "You killed him."

She closed her eyes for a moment. "No. I was trying to help him, but everything went wrong."

"Using edem is unpredictable," I said. "You know that." I wouldn't keep this from Graymond. Leta was innocent. He had to focus on her case, not the princess's. "You caused your brother's death. You'll be found guilty."

The princess held her pale hand to her neck as though she could make me forget what I'd seen. "You don't know what happened."

No, I didn't. Even so, I was wasting my time here. I started to leave.

She reached out for me. "*Please.* Let me explain."

What was there to explain?

"I was trying to help my brother," she said, sitting up on her knees. "He came to me, gravely wounded because of the Regency. I wanted to heal him using edem. But it was too late . . ." She hiccupped as tears ran down her face. "The Regency obliterated him! They turned him into dust."

"Then why are you the one with the echo mark?" I asked.

"Because I was trying to save him!"

"If that's true," I said, "why don't you tell Graymond that yourself?"

"You don't understand," she said, her eyes pleading. "The Regency will never allow me to take the stand. The entire trial is a sham. They keep pushing back the date in the hopes they can take over Vardean. Then they can silence me like they have everyone else."

"If I can't speak the truth to anyone," I said, "then how can I help you? Why did you even ask me here?"

"Your sister."

Something snapped within me. "What about her?"

"While I can't take the stand, *she* can. Your sister's case is sure to receive media coverage; it's the only way to expose the Regency!"

"I'm not a lawyer," I said. "And even if I was, I'm not going to risk my sister's freedom to air your political grievances with the Regency."

"My grievances are Telene's grievances." She clenched her fists. "They made the king disappear! They've taken control of the government so no one can stand opposed. No one will ever know the truth."

I leaned forward. "And what *is* the truth?"

She glanced away before replying, "My brother was poised to expose a secret about the Regency before he died. My parents, and their parents before them, had always set the laws in accordance to the Regency's advice, without question. But Erimen was different. He challenged their suggestions. He wanted to allow for a small amount of edem usage to appease the people without causing a large impact to the veil. When the Regency General stood by his opinions, my brother began his own investigation and found the reports presented to him—to us—were not accurate." Elenora's shoulders curled inward, and she wrapped her arms around herself.

"What did he uncover?" I pressed.

"I don't know!" she cried in exasperation. "He disappeared before he could tell me."

"So, what?" I asked. "You want my sister to get on the stand and risk her entire future and talk about some kind of Regency conspiracy that you don't have any evidence of?"

My sister was *in* Vardean for believing in conspiracies. I didn't care that this was the princess of Telene asking for help, I would not allow Leta to jeopardize her trial.

"I won't do it," I said. "This has nothing to do with her case."

The princess's gray eyes were like flint to start a fire. "Who do you think destroyed Ferrington?" she asked.

The room was a furnace. My vision warped, and I grabbed on to the side of the bed to stay upright.

"The Regency?" Even though I'd whispered them, the words were too loud in the small room.

The princess nodded.

"They burned Ferrington to the ground."

# CHAPTER 17

# CAYDER

*Ferrington*—the town where my mother died and where my sister had supposedly killed three hundred people.

"How do you know?" I asked, my voice a handful of gravel.

Princess Elenora inched forward on her bed, hope lighting her eyes. "My brother was not happy with the reports from the Regency and decided to meet with the mayor of each region to see what improvements could be made. First, he traveled to the Regency headquarters to see the edemmeter firsthand." She gestured below us to the Regency headquarters, in the lower levels of Vardean. "While he was there, he discovered unreported cases of edem usage in Ferrington. And the plans to torch the entire town during Edemmacht."

"Why?" The word was a wheeze, my lungs too tight to take a full breath.

"I don't know," she admitted. She placed her hand to her chest, as though her words pained her. "My brother was gravely injured when he arrived back at the castle isle. He never found out what the Regency were trying to cover up there."

"What do you want me to do?" My mouth was dry; my head pounded.

"I need you to go to Ferrington," she said. "I need you to find proof of the Regency's cover-up, and I need Leta to take the stand at her trial and tell the world what really happened to my brother. It's the only way I can get him back."

I blinked. "I'm sorry?"

She took my hand in hers. "My brother is still alive, Cayder."

"I thought you said he was obliterated?"

"*Here*, yes." Her eyes held mine with an intensity that was equal parts alluring and frightening. "But he's alive on the other side of the veil."

*Another veil superstition.*

Leta had also once believed our mother now lived on the other side of the veil, as that was where people went when they died. When their time ended in our world, it would continue on in another.

I pulled free of the princess's grasp. I hadn't believed in such childish fantasies then, and I didn't believe in them now.

But I understood the need for hope. It was an anchor against the tides of grief.

"Ferrington is gone, Princess," I said gently. Just like her brother was gone. "There's nothing left."

The princess closed her eyes. "Then your sister and I are both doomed. She can't win her case. Not against the

Regency. Not when they can manipulate the evidence to suit their agenda."

"I'm sorry, Princess."

"You're the only one who can help me," she said, tears running down her cheeks. "Mr. Toyer will be watched now that he's representing me. You're the only person I can trust in here. You're the only one who can find out the truth. The Regency must pay for what they've done."

If there was any truth to the princess's claims, then I needed to find out. As much as I wanted to run to Graymond with this information, I needed to play this safe.

"What should I be looking for?" I asked.

"You'll go?"

"I'll go." I said. "For you, and my sister."

She pushed herself up and kissed me on the cheek.

"They're hiding something," she said. "The fire was to cover their tracks. You need to find out what they were doing out there."

If there was anything left, I'd find it.

"I'll be back soon," I promised her.

———

When I returned to Graymond's office, I found him stooped over his desk.

"Where have you been?" he asked.

"With Kema." It was the truth. Mostly.

Graymond let out a mournful groan and rubbed his temples.

"Are you all right, sir?"

"Migraine," he said tightly. "An old foe that pays me a visit far too often."

"Perhaps you should head home?" He was no good to any of us while he was debilitated. "You haven't rested in days."

"Perhaps," he repeated, but made no move for the door.

I admired his determination and hated what I'd said earlier. Graymond truly cared about his clients. And I cared about him.

"Graymond?" I asked.

He raised his head slowly. "Yes?"

"I'm sorry," I said.

He nodded. "I understand, son. It's a difficult time. I don't reproach you."

I had two days to find proof of the Regency's involvement before Leta's case started on Friday, but there was one bit of information I needed before I set out for Ferrington. Unlike most of Telene, I needed evidence before believing rumors. Gossip was not fact. "What happened to the princess's two previous attorneys?"

Graymond rubbed his eyes. "They quit. It's not unusual. This place can break the strongest of people."

"Are you sure?"

Graymond blinked at me. "Why do you ask?"

"I'm just interested." If what the princess said was true, I didn't want to implicate Graymond. I knew him well enough to know that he would dive headfirst into this case if he believed the Regency was at fault. But if Graymond truly was in danger, I needed to keep him in the dark.

"You couldn't get their case files?" I asked him.

"No," he said. "The court had no record of their work. They mustn't have handed it in before they left."

That sounded suspicious to me. "Is that normal?"

"During pretrial disclosure, both parties are to present their information in hopes of a settlement," he explained. "But there was no such record for the princess's trial. I assume this is because of the sensitive nature of the case."

I wasn't so sure about that. "Can you contact her old attorneys directly and ask for them?"

He nodded. "Good idea, son. I fear I'm not at my best this afternoon."

I bounced on the balls of my feet as Graymond called the first attorney's office.

"Hello, this is Graymond Toyer from Edem Legal Aid. Can I please speak with Traxon Marks?" He frowned as he listened to the person on the other end. "Oh? I'm so sorry to hear that . . . *No*, I was not informed . . . My sincerest condolences. Thank you."

My head felt disconnected from my body as Graymond relayed the news that Traxon had passed away a few weeks ago.

"From what?" I asked.

Graymond rubbed his temples again. "It felt too callous to ask."

I swallowed sharply. The princess was right—her former attorney was dead. But was the Regency to blame?

Graymond called the princess's most recent attorney. I barely registered the words as Graymond told me that she'd resigned from her firm a few days ago and hadn't been heard from since.

The princess was telling the truth.

Before I left Vardean, I was tempted to run to Leta's cell and tell her everything I knew about the Regency's involvement, but I didn't want to get her hopes up. I wasn't sure what I'd find out in Ferrington—if anything. I still needed evidence.

I told Graymond that I would spend the next day at the legal offices of the princess's previous attorneys while he concentrated on Leta's trial. He hadn't seemed too concerned about the fate of the princess's former lawyers, or perhaps he was too unwell to react to the news. I hoped Vardean wasn't finally breaking him.

Ever since I'd learned the legal system at the reform school, I'd seen this place as a monument of hope. Where the good were set free and the bad punished.

But now I wasn't so sure what Vardean really represented and what justice even meant. For the families of those who had perished in Ferrington, justice was seeing another life—Leta's—be sacrificed. For the Regency, it was seeing Jey punished for taking their leader from them. Did I really want to be involved in that system?

The future I'd imagined for myself was slipping further and further away from reality.

Narena came over to Broduck Manor early on Wednesday morning to join me for our expedition to Ferrington. She radiated impatience; I could already see she was writing a story about the trip in her mind. But I couldn't tell her about the princess; instead, I told her I wanted to know more about the town my sister supposedly burned down before her trial started on Friday. It wasn't exactly a lie.

The first trolley to Ferrington departed at 9:30 a.m. We arrived at Kardelle Junction half an hour early, as I'd learned not to trust trolleys. We couldn't afford to miss it; the next trolley wouldn't leave for four more hours, and I couldn't wait any longer.

I needed the truth. I needed to go to Ferrington.

Kardelle Junction was the central artery for all transport around Telene, a colossal sandstone building with bright lights embedded in the ceiling like stars. My mother used to take Leta and me to Kardelle Junction to watch all the commuters coming and going.

"See?" she had said. "Life is full of unlimited possibilities." She gestured to the different passageways that led to different trolley platforms. "Every day, we make decisions. We change our future. Without the use of edem."

She tapped my nose and laughed. Meanwhile, Leta asked which trolley would take her to the veil.

Narena and I grabbed some torlu-filled deebule pastries from a cafe while we waited for our departure time. The terminal was full of people traveling in and out of the city.

Narena elbowed me. "You're uncharacteristically quiet."

I pushed the deebule around on my plate and licked the powdered sugar from my fingers. "It's been a draining week."

"It's only Wednesday." Her brows pinched together in concern. "How's Leta holding up?"

"As well as can be expected. She's happy she gets to plead her case for a jury, but I don't know that it will help . . ."

If the princess was right, then the Regency would do anything to cover up their involvement. And Leta's prosecutor represented the Regency. I hated to think what he would resort to in order to ensure she stayed behind bars.

"What does your father say?" Narena asked.

"Nothing. He hasn't been home since Leta was arrested." I poked my pastry. "I suppose he thinks that's an expression of love."

"We all show love in different ways, Cayder," she said. "I'm sure he's doing all that he can."

"Well, it's not enough." I stood, leaving my deebule pastry uneaten. My stomach twisted with anxiety. "Come on—it's nearly time to board."

The trolley to Ferrington was only four carriages linked together; the rural town hadn't exactly been a tourist hot spot. The only people who settled out there were farmers hoping to make the most of the fertile soil.

We paid the trolley conductor the cheapest fare and were ordered to sit in the last carriage. A large diffuse circular light hung from the ceiling of the trolley like a moon at nighttime. Seats were arranged around small tables to encourage travelers to buy expensive snacks that tasted like cardboard. Not that I had any intention of eating. My mind was miles away, back with Leta in her cell.

As soon as we took the far seats, Narena started unloading items from her bag onto the table. The *thump* of her heavy books brought me back to the present.

"Some light reading?" I asked with a raised brow.

"I thought I'd do some investigating of my own." She picked up a book and flipped to a page she'd marked with a ribbon decorated with Meiyran lettering. "This chapter was written by an old woman whose ancestors lived on a houseboat off the coast of Kardelle, not far from where the veil is. She claims her great-grandparents spoke of strange things happening in the water long before the veil was uncovered by the Regency a hundred years ago." She held the book open for me. On the opposite page was an image of a multilegged creature circling the bottom of a boat.

"You believe creatures existed *before* the Regency uncovered the veil?" I asked, running my fingers over the creature's rows of razor-sharp teeth. It looked strikingly similar to the drawing Leta had done of her edem creatures—the hullen.

Narena flipped to another page. "These are all stories, but I thought maybe it would be useful for Leta's trial. I'm sure I've seen this book in Leta's room before—she wouldn't be the first person to believe that there was more to the veil than edem."

I took the book from her hands. "No, but she's the first person to be arrested for burning down an entire town to prove they exist."

Narena sat back into her chair abruptly. "You don't believe she's guilty, do you?"

"I don't." I looked out the window and watched the scenery fly by, unable to face her. "But she has a death echo—I can't deny that. If we don't find anything to the contrary out in Ferrington today, then I'm afraid it doesn't matter what I think. The jury will find her guilty."

Narena didn't respond, but I could tell she agreed. A death echo worked in two ways. It marked you as a killer *and* marked the end of your own life. A life forfeited to Vardean.

I glanced back out the window and watched the city turn to forest and then the forest to desert and dust.

———

It was midday by the time we reached Ferrington. But the train did not slow; it sped past the station.

"Why didn't we stop?" I asked.

"Ferrington is still considered a crime scene," Narena said with a lift of her shoulder.

We'd come all this way. I wasn't leaving without some proof that Leta was innocent and the Regency were involved.

"We'll get off at the next station and walk back." It was the only way.

We departed the trolley at Tavitch—a small coastal town north of Ferrington and near the border of the permacloud's reach. It was strange to see patches of bright sunlight hitting the rocky cliffs and the water below. It was like our entire world was in black and white and I was seeing color for the first time. As much as I wanted to admire the red rocks and bright blue ocean, this wasn't a sightseeing trip.

It took us an hour to walk through the hills and reach our destination.

Below us lay the valley of Ferrington. The entire landscape was cinders and smoke. Every tree. Every store. Every house. Gone.

*"Burning shadows,"* Narena murmured.

I nodded in agreement. The town had been annihilated. It reminded me of what the princess had said about her brother.

*They turned him into dust.*

We walked down the hill and onto the main street, staying clear of the station. Smoke clung to the air as though the fire happened mere hours ago, and not over a week. My eyes stung and my lungs constricted.

I hated to think that my mother's and my sister's lives had both ended here.

"Come on," I said to Narena. "Let's go exonerate Leta."

# CHAPTER 18

## CAYDER

Narena and I walked down what remained of Ferrington's main street in silence. The frameworks of a few buildings still stood, as did a couple of melted lampposts, which now curled toward the ground. This wasn't the remains of a fire; this was the aftermath of an inferno. No wonder so few had survived.

And Leta.

An out-of-control bonfire could never have caused this kind of destruction. It wouldn't be difficult for the jury to believe edem was the cause of this unnatural fire. And when they saw Leta's hands, her fate would be sealed.

The town was silent—no calls from birds or footsteps from creatures. The place was truly deserted. A graveyard. I hoped we wouldn't stumble across any skeletal remains; I wasn't prepared to face the reality of the lives lost here. Just as I'd not been able to face the reality of my mother's death seven years earlier. Even though it was a closed casket at her memorial, I couldn't approach. I wanted to remember my mother as the amazing woman she was and not the broken body left behind.

We followed the map I'd taken from Leta's case file to the field where she had been found. By the time we reached what was left of the rolling orchard, my long-sleeved shirt might as well have been fused to my skin. With the permacloud trapping in the heat from the fire, the humidity was stifling. And yet it was nothing compared to what the people of Ferrington would have felt in their final moments before they died.

I coughed in sympathy, heaving from my lungs the residual smoke that permeated the air and was kicked up from the ground as we walked.

Nothing of the orchard remained. Not a single torlu tree. Even the tall poles of the flood lamps had been destroyed. If metal couldn't survive the blaze, what chance did anything else have?

Which raised the question, how had Leta? If she hadn't been the cause of the fire, if the princess was right that it had been the Regency who struck the match, then how had she survived?

"Cayder," Narena whispered. Ash clung to her black lashes and dotted her amber skin like gray freckles. "I think we should go back. There's nothing here." The enthusiasm that had lit her face this morning was washed away by the gray world in front of us. I didn't blame her for not wanting to spend any more time out here.

I nodded but said, "I need to see it."

"See what?" she asked.

I wasn't sure yet, so I didn't reply.

I continued toward the middle of what I assumed used to be the torlu fields, although nothing remained but blackened earth. My nose twitched at the heady scent of death, but I continued on.

*There*—a patch of grass. The only splash of green in this otherwise ashen world. A perfect circle.

"What is that?" Narena asked, her inquisitive nature overtaking any trepidation. She crouched to the ground and reached out but didn't touch the grass, as though it might be hot.

"That's where Leta was found unconscious," I said. "This is where she supposedly started the fire."

Narena dumped her backpack on the ground, sending a plume of ash into the air. "That can't be right."

"What?"

Narena walked the perimeter of the small circle. "If Leta started the fire, then the damage would be the worst *here*." She scraped her foot along the grass that lay next to the untouched patch. "This grass is browned, but not incinerated like the rest of the town."

I stared at her, unblinking, for a long moment. "You're saying the fire started somewhere else?"

This could be the evidence we needed! But how did that prove that the Regency were behind this? How did that help Leta?

Narena shrugged as though it were obvious. "It looks like the fire soared toward her from all angles but burned out before it could reach her. What did Leta say happened?"

"She said these edem creatures—the hullen—lit the fire after she summoned them by killing a bird with edem. She doesn't remember how it exactly happened."

"That doesn't make sense."

I grabbed a pencil from Narena's backpack and flipped to a blank page in one of her books to sketch what I saw. I couldn't imagine how scared Leta must have been, waking to find the entire town burned to a crisp and her hands covered in a death echo. She must have felt so alone.

I heard the flutter of wings, and a small blue bird landed on the green grass.

Narena and I stared at it, unable to move. The one living thing we'd seen in this entire town.

"Could that be Leta's bird?" I said. The bird she claimed she'd killed and the cause of the death echo on her hands. "How did this one bird survive when everything else is dead?"

Narena pulled a bread roll from her bag and crumbled it onto the grass. "Poor thing. It must be starving." The bird pecked at the crumbs. Narena scooped it into her hands and carefully placed it inside her bag while it was distracted by the food. "I'll set it free in Tavitch. It can't survive here. I can't believe it's survived for over a week."

I nodded, not really listening. If Leta didn't kill the bird, that means she lied about her death echo. Then what caused it?

"Cayder?" Narena asked, her voice strained. "We really should head back to Tavitch. We don't want to miss the last trolley home."

She was right. We didn't want to get stuck here overnight; it was miserable enough during the day. And without the flood lamps . . . I hated to admit, the tales of the hullen were starting to get to me. Leta's drawings were taking flight in my mind, and I could imagine the shadowy creatures trailing my every move.

"Right," I said with a quick glance behind me to ensure we were alone. "I'll tell Graymond to come out here himself. He *has* to see this." I pointed to the perfect circle.

While it wasn't the evidence of the Regency's involvement that I'd hoped to find, it was something for Leta's case. Something to plant doubt within the jury. Whatever the Regency had tried to cover up, I was afraid they were successful. There was nothing to suggest they were ever here.

We started back to Tavitch, my shoulders hunched. I kept expecting to see a glimpse of something move in my periphery. But there was no movement. No life. Which was worse.

"I'm more confused now than before," Narena said. The bird let out a few chirps from her bag.

I nodded. My thoughts were too muddied for speech.

Nothing of the town remained. Nothing to suggest that Leta was right about these edem creatures or that the princess was right about a Regency conspiracy. And yet the burn pattern indicated Leta hadn't started the fire.

As we walked, our footsteps disturbed the field of ash, leaving a trail behind like boots in the snow. Ours were the only visible footprints; no one else had been out here since the ash had settled from the air. The entire landscape was dead. How many people lay among these ashes? The ashes we breathed in with every breath.

My stomach twisted at the thought.

A breeze shifted the cinders ahead of us. It was the smallest movement, but with the landscape deathly still, any disturbance caught our attention.

"What's that?" Narena asked.

As we neared, the ash continued to shift and then rolled toward us.

"What the fu—" I started. Something was *under* the cinders. The movement wasn't due to the wind at all.

We staggered to a halt as a *thing* lifted upward. Where the gray dust clung to its body, I could make out expansive wings and horns arising from either side of its head like the branches of a tree. Its eyes were two blazing holes of sunlight. It let out a shriek and shook the ashes loose from its body. Once the ash tumbled free, the creature was no longer visible. And yet we could still hear its breathing and the click of claws as it stalked toward us.

"Cayder?" Narena's voice cracked.

Before I could answer, we heard the *thwamp* of two heavy wings. A cloud of gray surrounded us.

Narena screamed, and we both cowered to the ground. I waited for the talons to rake across our faces. Instead, we only felt the brush of air as the invisible creature soared overhead.

"Run!" Narena cried.

But I was too stunned to move.

The creature had left a perfect circle where it had been hiding beneath the ash. A circle the exact same size as the patch of grass Leta had been found unconscious in.

Leta was right.

The hullen were real.

# CHAPTER 19

# CAYDER

Narena sat opposite me on the trolley back to Downtown Kardelle, her arms wrapped around her bag as though it were a pillow. We were covered head to toe in ash from the plume the hullen's wings had created.

*The hullen.*

I still couldn't grasp that such creatures existed. I wasn't sure I ever would. And it now made sense why no one could provide proof. How could you provide physical evidence of something invisible?

Was it possible that Leta was also right about our mother? Had she been investigating these creatures for the Regency before she died? Had these creatures taken her life, as Leta suggested, and the Regency had covered it up?

"Are you all right?" I asked Narena. She hadn't said anything since we boarded the trolley. Ash was smudged on her cheeks like rouge.

"No," she said. "It's one thing to read about theories of edem creatures and another thing to be face-to-face with one." She shook her head, ash tumbling down her hair. "Are you?"

I'd never believed in any of Leta's theories. I'd always thought she was clinging to childish stories to avoid the reality we lived in—the reality of our mother gone and our family forever fractured. Her obsession with the veil never seemed healthy to me.

But now . . . now I knew she'd been right. There was more to the veil and edem.

I squeezed my eyes shut. How many times had I told her to stop with her foolish antics and beliefs and live in the real world? I *should* have been with her in Ferrington. I should have helped her investigate from the beginning. Maybe then she wouldn't be locked in Vardean.

Or maybe we'd be locked in a cell together.

I opened my eyes. "I am. We have proof that Leta was right. The hullen are real."

Narena placed her bag next to her, her body slowly coming back to life. "I hate to say it, Cayder, but we don't actually have any proof."

"Seriously?" I shook my head in disbelief; ash fell onto my shoulders. "We saw the hullen with our own eyes! Leta wasn't lying!"

"So what?" Narena asked, leaning forward. Some light had returned to her brown eyes. "What does that mean about the fire? You know we only have part of the story. That's not enough to write an article."

I tilted my head. "We're not writing an article, Narena. We're trying to free my sister from murder charges."

Narena grabbed my ash-covered hands in hers. "I'm sorry. You know I love Leta like my own sister, but she has a death echo. Unless we can explain an alternative theory, I'm afraid the jury will still find her guilty."

I was afraid of that too. "We don't have to prove she's innocent." I thought back to what Graymond had said about the prosecutor's burden of proof. "We just have to cast doubt. If I get up on the stand and say I saw these edem creatures, then hopefully that will make the jury question everything the prosecutor says. Especially if the Regency is covering up the hullen's existence."

She pulled back and grabbed her notebook. "What makes you think they are?"

I wanted to tell her about the princess, but I was worried word would get back to her journalist mother. Narena's mother had a habit of getting someone to tell the truth, whether they wanted to or not. With two of the princess's lawyers missing or dead, I couldn't risk Narena or her mother knowing what I knew.

"I'm not sure," I said. "But if we encountered the hullen after one trip to Ferrington, surely the Regency have as well."

Leta believed the hullen started the fire, but after seeing the creatures, I wasn't sure how. And the princess said it was the Regency. Perhaps the Regency had started the fire to rid Ferrington of the hullen? To protect the town, and the fire got out of hand? Was Leta merely their scapegoat for a horrific accident?

I closed my eyes again. My brain was working overtime to figure out how this was all connected.

"The hullen didn't attack us," I thought out loud. "Maybe they're not as dangerous as Leta believes."

It couldn't be a coincidence that Leta was the only person in the area who survived the fires. And the only living creature, aside from the hullen, had been that bird . . . If that really was Leta's bird, could it have survived because Leta was still holding it while the flames destroyed everything around them? Then what had protected them while everything else perished?

Everything but the hullen . . .

"*Edem be damned,*" I cursed. "The hullen weren't trying to hurt Leta! They were trying to protect her!"

"What?" Narena's eyes widened. "How do you know?"

"The circle of untouched grass was the same shape of the wingspan of the hullen. I think the creature protected her from the smoke and flames. How else could Leta and that bird have survived?"

"If you believe that bird truly is Leta's bird," Narena said, "and I'm not saying it's not, then why does she have the death echo?" Narena had found the bird a nice tree to live in in Tavitch.

"Maybe because she came in contact with the hullen?" I shook my head. "I don't know."

The hullen's existence didn't answer every question, but it filled in some of the blanks.

I couldn't stop now. I had to keep digging.

## CHAPTER 20

# CAYDER

I parted ways with Narena at Kardelle Junction. She'd promised to keep the presence of the hullen between us, for now. I couldn't risk our evidence leaking to the public during the discovery phase of Leta's trial, in case the prosecutor used it against us, claiming we were trying to create a biased jury. I would have to wait.

I arrived home before curfew, ashes still clinging to my clothes despite my trying to shake them loose on the porch.

"Cayder?" my father's voice boomed from somewhere inside the house. "Is that you?"

*Edem be damned.* What was he doing home this early? Or at all?

"Yes!" I called back, not sure who else he was expecting at this hour.

"Get in here!"

I took a deep breath and followed his voice into his office.

"Yes, Father?" I poked my head into the doorway but didn't cross the threshold.

His office overlooked the front garden and Mother's prized collection of blooming heart flowers. A crowded bookshelf lined one wall, and the opposite contained hundreds of newspaper clippings on reports of my father's cases. His victory wall from when he was a lawyer.

A solitary painting of Mother hung behind him, her smile radiant and glossy black hair a dark wave over her shoulder. A celestial globe made of brass hung from the ceiling. My eyes lingered on Ferrington—the easternmost point of Telene—and far from the veil. If the hullen were creatures made from edem, why didn't they exist all over Telene? Why only in Ferrington?

"What are you gawking at?" Father snapped. "Come in, boy."

I took the smallest step into the room.

"Where have you been?" he asked, leaning back in his chair and placing his clasped hands on the curve of his belly. "I've been looking for you."

"You have?" That was new. Father never cared where we were.

He took off his reading glasses and placed them on the desk. It was like looking into the future; we had the same dark hair and broad shoulders, but his were in a perpetual stoop.

"Leta's trial begins in two days," he said, as though that could possibly slip my mind. "I need you *here*, not off gallivanting with friends."

"I was helping Leta."

He leaned forward, placed his elbows on his desk. "And have you?"

I felt like I was in court. But I'd done nothing wrong.

"Have *you*?" I threw back at him.

He harrumphed. "This is the first time I've been outside Vardean since she was arrested. I've been searching for anything that will help her case."

"As have I." I approached the desk. "Do you know exactly what happened the night Mother died?" I nodded to the portrait behind him.

Father flinched as though he'd been slapped. We had an unspoken agreement never to mention Mother.

"What does that have to do with anything?" he asked.

"Leta was in Ferrington to find out the truth about her death," I replied. "Mother has everything to do with Leta's imprisonment."

"You know what happened," he said abruptly, placing his reading glasses back on his nose.

"I know what I was *told*." The truth could be a different story.

"You know all there is to know," he replied in exasperation.

"I don't know why she was in Ferrington that night. Or what she was doing for the Regency."

"Yes, you do," Father said. "She was gathering evidence for an edem-based crime. She was helping the court. She was doing her job."

"That's all?"

He lowered his thick dark eyebrows over his eyes. "Cayder, if you have something to say, just say it. I don't have time for this subterfuge."

"Fine," I said, squaring my shoulders. "Did Mother ever mention edem creatures called the hullen?"

My father groaned and placed his head in his hands. "Not you too."

"What if the Regency is covering up the truth out there?"

"Conspiracy theories will not be enough to save your sister," he said. "That's what got her into this mess in the first place. Is that what you've been working on?"

"I'm keeping an open mind."

He rolled his eyes. "I thought you were smarter than that, boy. I thought you were more like me."

"I'm nothing like you," I said bitterly. "I didn't abandon my family."

Father sat straighter in his chair, his face seething fury. "Abandon? I'm here, aren't I?"

"Now you are," I mumbled.

"I have done everything in my power to keep this family together since your mother died."

I threw my hands wide. "And how has that worked out for you? It's just you and me now, Father, and if we don't free Leta, it will only be you. Because trust me, I won't stay here in this house a moment longer than I have to. Leta is the only reason I'm still here. Leta is the only reason I still consider myself a Broduck. As far as I'm concerned, both my parents died seven years ago."

He wanted to blame me for the dissolution of our family; well, two could play the blame game.

"How dare you!" Father's chin wobbled as he pointed his finger at me. "I lost my wife that night. I do the best that I can!"

"It's not enough," I said. "Leta is in Vardean because she hates it here. She spent every night sneaking out to find some truth to why our mother never came home. If you were ever here, you would know that! And now you ask where *I've* been?" I laughed dryly. "I've been trying to save my sister from a life in prison because I know our father is useless!"

Father's nose flared as his face flushed, red spreading like a rash from his cheeks to his ears.

"Get out!" he roared. "Get out of my office!"

"Happily!" I slammed the door shut behind me.

I ran up the stairs to my room, my pulse pounding in my ears.

It was up to me. I would take the stand and expose what was happening in Ferrington, even if it meant taking the heat of the Regency.

I would do whatever it took to break Leta free.

———

The next morning, Graymond was barely through his office door when I launched at him.

"Leta is telling the truth!"

"What are you talking about?" He already sounded weary as he placed his bag on his desk, although he looked better than when I'd seen him on Tuesday. His dark skin was warm and his eyes clear.

"I went to Ferrington yesterday."

Graymond blinked slowly. "You visited a crime scene?"

"Yes—well, I—"

"Cayder." My name was a groan. "The prosecutor can use that

against us. You're Leta's brother. Whatever you uncovered there he can claim as evidence tampering."

"We should be claiming the same thing about the Regency! They're lying."

"About what?"

"The hullen," I said. "I saw the creature. They're real!"

"You did? What did it look like?"

"Well . . ." This was the difficult part. "It didn't really *look* like anything. It was invisible."

"An invisible creature?" he asked dubiously. "Then how did you see it?"

"There was this ash," I said, waving my hands, "all around it. It clung to its skin—or whatever it has for skin. I saw the outline of it. And then it disappeared into the sky."

Graymond did me the favor of not laughing in my face. "Did it look like this?" He opened Leta's file on his desk and showed me the drawing she'd made.

"Similar. Although the horns it had on either side of its face were taller and the wings less like a bat's and more like a bird's."

"I don't know what to tell you, son." He closed the file. "Your description doesn't match Leta's, and you have no proof. Just your testimony."

"You don't believe me."

He closed his eyes and exhaled slowly. "I believe you want to help your sister in any way possible, and that includes seeing something that might not be there."

"But it wasn't just me! My best friend, Narena, was with me."

"Narena?" he asked. "You know you can't speak about the

details of a case beyond Vardean's walls. I thought this apprenticeship was important to you. I thought the law was important to you."

Panic choked me. "It is! But finding out the truth is more important."

He ran a hand over his head, raking his nails through his cropped graying hair. "There are proper channels to uncover evidence, and sneaking into a crime scene is not one of them. And I need to warn you, Cayder, finding out the truth might not necessarily ensure Leta goes free. The legal system doesn't always favor the innocent."

"It should! Leta is telling the truth. That's what really matters, right? Surely you did some questionable things when you were younger to help your cases?" My breathing became increasingly rapid.

"Take a seat and a breath," he said. "I don't want you passing out on me."

I slumped onto my chair of boxes. "You're not throwing me off my sister's case?"

He pressed his lips into a tight line. "No. But we can't have any more secrets between us. No more excursions to crime scenes. Do we have a deal?" He held out his hand. My stomach dropped. I was already keeping another secret.

"Before I agree to that"—I grimaced—"I have one more confession to make."

Graymond eyed me wearily. "Go on."

"First, I need you to promise me that you won't tell anyone

else what I'm about to tell you. No reports to the prosecutor or the court about new evidence you've uncovered."

"*Cayder* . . ." This time my name was a growl. "I'm not promising you that. It's a part of my job to let the prosecutor know of new evidence. If I don't, the evidence will be thrown out of court."

I leaned back. "Then I can't shake your hand."

He pointed to the door, his features as serious as I'd ever seen them. "Then you can leave."

"*Then* you'll never know how the king died."

He snapped upright. "What do you know about that?"

"More than you, I'd wager. The princess and I had a little meeting on Friday. Just the two of us. She was in a very chatty mood."

Graymond laughed. "I should be angry, but somehow I'm proud. What did she tell you?"

"You have to promise me first," I said. "You can't tell the prosecutor anything."

He frowned. "Cayder—"

"Promise me you'll keep this between us, and I'll tell you."

"Fine," he said. "I promise, but no more secrets."

I shook his hand.

"Let's go see the princess. She can tell you herself."

## CHAPTER 21

# PRINCESS ELENORA

Once Elenora returned to her cell, she ate and drank everything she was given. She needed her strength if she wanted to survive this place and avenge her brother.

The superintendent would bring in her meals, dumping the bowl of soup through the bars in the cell as though it were trash, and she was forced to eat off the stone floor. Elenora was fairly certain Yarlyn was supposed to open the internal bars and place the food inside the cell, but any power she'd had as princess dissolved the moment her brother disappeared.

After a month of being locked inside Vardean, Elenora had learned her attorney couldn't help her—not against the Regency. She needed someone who wasn't bound by the rules of the court. Someone who wouldn't be required to report their findings during pretrial disclosure.

Last week, she'd overheard the prison guards talking about the new inmate on the top floor. A girl who'd been arrested for burning down the entire town of Ferrington.

Leta Broduck.

Elenora knew it couldn't be a coincidence that a sixteen-year-old girl torched the same town and on the same night the Regency had planned to destroy it. And while Elenora suspected the girl was innocent, there was little she could do about the matter.

Then she met Cayder Broduck.

And suddenly Vardean's walls didn't feel so impenetrable.

She needed his help, and in turn, she could help his sister go free. It was a gamble telling him the truth. And Elenora was not one to take gambles. As much as she longed for the world outside the castle isle, she had not fought for it. As much as she hated her mask, she had continued to wear it. Even when Elenora and Erimen had played games as children, she had played it safe. And Erimen always won.

Elenora hoped her gamble in letting Cayder in would pay off.

It was the only card she had left to play. And she would risk it all for her brother.

When she heard the key turning inside the external cell door, Elenora scrambled for her mask. She didn't want anyone inside the prison knowing her face. And after so many years of despising the mask, she now found it comforting. As though her mother was with her.

Elenora managed to have the mask attached by the time Cayder walked in, followed by Mr. Toyer. Her disappointed breath resonated in her ears.

*What's Mr. Toyer doing here?*

Had Cayder betrayed her? Didn't he realize that put Mr. Toyer in danger? He'd promised to keep this between them!

Was she so unpracticed in dealing with people other than her own staff? Had her judgment been clouded by the expectations of a princess, who was used to getting what she wanted? How did she know who to trust when her power and title had vanished along with her brother?

"Hello," Cayder said. She knew from the eagerness in his voice that he'd found something in Ferrington.

Mr. Toyer cast a dissatisfied look in his direction. "Don't speak to the princess so casually." He bowed his head in respect. "Your Highness."

Elenora didn't mind. She wanted Cayder to feel as though they were equals. She wanted him to trust her. But she would not speak to Mr. Toyer—she didn't want to be responsible for any further disappearances. She'd thought Cayder understood that.

Cayder approached, his hands gripping the bars. "Princess," he said. "I need you to tell Graymond what you told me."

Elenora's breath stuck in her chest like a wedge of ice.

He *had* betrayed her!

Hot fury melted the ice in her chest and scorched down to her fingertips. She spun on her heel and retreated to her bunk. She'd never been betrayed before. Aside from the Regency.

She couldn't trust Cayder. She couldn't trust anyone.

She'd stayed strong, thinking she had hope of escaping this cell, but that drained from her body like blood from a deep wound. Tears welled in her eyes and ran down her cheeks and into her mouth, clogging her breathing.

"Graymond can help us," Cayder said. "Can't you, Graymond? Promise her you won't tell the prosecutor the truth!"

Elenora could barely hear his response over her loud echoing gasps.

"I promise, Princess," Mr. Toyer said. "As your attorney, my allegiance is to you, and you alone." Elenora turned to see Mr. Toyer had placed his hand over his heart. "If you don't want me to speak of what I learn inside these walls, then I won't tell a soul. You, my client, are my number one priority."

She'd heard that from a lawyer before. And then they disappeared.

"Please, Princess," Cayder said. "I don't want to put anyone's life at risk, but we need your help."

"How many times do I have to tell you?" she said, her voice low and burning with betrayal. "The Regency will never allow me to set foot in a courtroom."

Mr. Toyer glanced at his apprentice. "What is she talking about?"

"My trial is cursed," she said. "Anyone who represents me disappears."

"I heard about your former attorneys," Mr. Toyer said. "But there are explanations to—"

"Of course there are," she said. "The Regency has an explanation for everything. With my brother gone, no one is around to question anything they say. No one can pull them into line."

She longed to be that person. But she couldn't do that from within her cell.

Mr. Toyer and Cayder exchanged a look.

"Please, Princess," Mr. Toyer said. "Let us help you."

She'd already said too much, but there was no going back. She still needed help if she ever wanted to be free.

"Okay," she said; her voice was ragged and tearstained. "I'll tell you what happened to my brother." She nodded to Cayder. "What happened the night he disappeared."

She hadn't revealed all the details. She'd needed Cayder to trust her first. She'd needed him to believe her.

She removed her mask and took in a deep breath.

Now she would tell him everything.

———

Erimen had been acting strange for the two weeks after their meeting with the Regency General. He was always busy. Running from one meeting to another. Never stopping. Never even pausing to check in with Elenora.

After their parents' deaths, Elenora and Erimen established a routine. At the end of every week, no matter what had transpired, they ate dinner together. Just the two of them. It was their way to check in with one another. To ensure that no matter the pressures from outside the castle, or inside, they were there for each other. And for the five years since the rebel attack in the Royal Gardens, they hadn't missed a single dinner.

Elenora looked forward to those evenings. She could take off her mask, both figuratively and literally, and be herself. She didn't have to pretend everything was all right. Not for Erimen. And no matter was too insignificant to discuss. Even if it was the fact that Elenora disliked the haircut the new stylist had given her.

They continued with their dinners together, as they had when their parents were alive.

"First and foremost, we are family," their father used to say. "The four of us. Then we are royals. Never forget it."

And Elenora didn't think Erimen had. Until the night before his disappearance.

Erimen didn't show up for dinner at their normal time, and she was forced to finish her meal on her own. The royal staff assured her that his meeting with the Regency had run late and that he would arrive home later that evening.

At midnight, with no Erimen in sight, Elenora decided to find out the truth for herself. She snuck out her window, climbing down the outside of the rocky castle, leaving her ghastly mask behind. While the interiors of the castle were beautiful polished stones, the outside was not much to look at—a sprawling building with four main turrets that covered nearly the entire island.

Once she landed on the pebbled beach that surrounded the castle, she hesitated. She wasn't sure where she was going or what she was planning to do, but she couldn't go to sleep without knowing Erimen was all right; she would wait for her brother's ship to arrive.

The flood lamps that surrounded the isle highlighted the silvery fish that skimmed by. The movement reminded her of edem shifting within a shadow, a sight she hadn't seen since the incident with the rebels.

Even so, the ocean calmed Elenora, reminding her that no matter how small the castle isle was, a big world lay beyond it. And one day, she would board a boat and cross the bay. One day, she would see the mainland again.

Elenora sat on the rocks, breathing in the fresh, salty air and awaiting Erimen's ship. She would force him to tell her what was going on. And ask why he was so distant of late.

After an hour of waiting, she saw a flame of red upon the water, burning in the moonlight—Erimen's hair. She was surprised to see he was not in the usual royal vessel, surrounded by the King's Guard. He was alone, in a small boat—nothing more than a dinghy, and with no attached flood lamp.

"Erimen!" Elenora cried. She waded out into the cool water to meet him. She climbed into the boat and threw her arms around his waist. "I was worried about you! You're all right!"

"Not really, Elle." He sagged against her.

"Eri! What's wrong? Where is your guard? Your ship?"

He coughed in response and slipped to the bottom of the boat. Elenora rowed the dinghy to shore. When they ran aground, she pulled Erimen onto the beach. The light of the flood lamps revealed a burn mark on his shirt.

When Elenora pulled back the charred shirt to examine the wound, there was no blood. And yet it looked like something had taken a bite out of Erimen's side.

"Oh!" Elenora cried. "What happened?"

Erimen's mouth opened and closed a few times before he said, "The Regency."

"The Regency did this to you?" She would've thought he was delirious, but the morbid expression on his face indicated he was telling the truth.

"I—I traveled to the Regency headquarters, but he . . ." The rest of his words were lost in a groan. Blood trickled from the sides of his mouth.

A white-hot fury like she'd never felt before blazed through every cell of her being.

"I'll get help." Elenora tried to stand, but her brother grabbed her wrist. He was surprisingly strong, considering his state.

"Elle," he whispered. "I'm going to die. I can feel it. I'm just happy I managed to make it back to you."

"No." Elenora's eyes flooded with tears. "You can't. You *won't*." Elenora had watched her parents die; she was not about to relive the experience with her brother. "I'm getting the doctor." But she didn't move, worried her brother would be gone by the time she returned. She didn't want to leave him alone in his final moments.

The castle loomed behind them, help so close, but unreachable.

Elenora saw a light appear out on the water, highlighting a large vessel. It was the Regency's ship. The flood lamp on the mast kept edem at bay while making them easy to spot out on the water.

Erimen let out a ragged cough. "I need you to listen, Elle. Will you—will you do that?"

She found herself nodding, although she didn't want to. She wanted to climb back up the lattice and into her bedroom. She wanted to cover her face with a blanket and forget this ever happened. But that wouldn't save Erimen.

"The Regency have been lying to us," he said. "You can't trust them." He gripped her hand in his, the light in his eyes dimming. "Ferrington." He coughed up more blood.

The wound on his side grew, his skin peeling away to dust like tissue paper too close to a flame.

He didn't have long. Elenora felt a pain in her side as though she herself were wounded.

"Shhh," Elenora said. "Save your strength. Tell me tomorrow."

He shook his head. "There isn't a tomorrow. You must stop them. They're going to burn down Ferrington during Edemmacht. You must . . ." His hand went limp in hers.

"No!" Elenora shook his shoulder, hoping her plea would be enough.

Then she realized she could do more than plead. And she had to act quickly, before the Regency reached the shore.

Erimen was too heavy to move, and time was running short.

When they were younger, the prince and princess would walk along the isle's rocky shoreline, and Erimen would challenge his sister to a stone-skipping contest. They would whip rocks into the water until their wrists ached. In the end, Erimen always won.

Still, over the years, Elenora had developed a good aim.

She picked up the nearest pebble and hurled it toward the flood lamp. It missed, and Elenora cursed her shaking hand.

"Stay with me, brother." She grabbed another pebble and targeted the lamp. This time she was rewarded with a shattering of glass.

The dark washed over them like a cool balm.

At first, Elenora didn't see anything. She thought the wavering light was the moonlight on the slick pebbles. But then the darkness moved.

She touched the edem and then placed her hands over Erimen's disintegrating wound.

"Heal him," she whispered urgently. "Undo his injury. Make him whole."

Erimen's eyes flicked open. "*No*—Elle." But he wasn't strong enough to stop her.

Edem spread across his chest and over his wound.

Hope sprang inside Elenora like a flower.

*This is going to work!*

She didn't think of the consequences of using edem. She didn't care. All that mattered was that Erimen lived. She would worry about everything else later.

"Stop," he whispered. He reached for Elenora, placing an edem-soaked hand on her neck.

She wouldn't—she couldn't be without her brother.

The Regency vessel had docked, and she could hear their thundering footsteps approaching and the flapping of their cloaks.

"Come on," she whispered. "Hurry up."

The edem spread up Erimen's chest and throat and over his head. For a moment, he was completely covered in darkness.

Elenora held her breath, waiting for the edem to retract and leave a healed Erimen behind.

"What have you done, Princess?" a man asked her, his tone low and even.

Elenora didn't even turn around. Let them arrest her.

But when the edem vanished back into the shadows, Erimen was gone.

# CHAPTER 22

## CAYDER

I watched Graymond's face as the princess told her story. His expression gave nothing away.

"You believe the Regency planned to burn down Ferrington for weeks?" he asked.

The princess nodded. "Whatever the Regency wanted to cover up out there was worth betraying the king."

"The hullen," I said with a nod.

"The *what*?" the princess asked.

"Creatures made of edem," I said.

Graymond paced up and down the cell. "You believe the Regency was keeping these creatures a secret? And they sacrificed an entire town and the king to keep that secret? *Why?*"

"I'm not sure," I admitted. "While the hullen didn't attack me, there has to be a reason the Regency want to keep their existence quiet."

Graymond rubbed his beard in thought. "That could be why they want Leta to take the fall."

"You believe me?" I asked, elated.

"Son," he said with a grim smile, "I don't believe you're a liar. I believe you saw something out there and something happened to your sister. That's worth investigating."

"How do we prove what they've done?" the princess asked. "My brother tried to expose the truth, and now he's gone. And I'm stuck in here. The Regency has too much power. We have to be careful."

"The princess believes the Regency silenced her former representation," I said. "That's why she didn't want you reporting your findings to the prosecutor. The Regency can't know we're onto them. It's too dangerous. For all of us."

The princess tucked a strand of blond hair back behind her ears. "They're keeping my presence here and my brother's disappearance a secret from the citizens of Telene for their own benefit. They want to control the nation. And I fear what other plans they might have. I have to get out of here."

"What do you want me to do?" Graymond asked.

"The Regency don't want me to have my day in court," she said. "I need you to use Leta's high-profile case to expose their involvement in my brother's disappearance and for covering up the fire. It's the only way I can get out of this cell!" Her eyes were bright, and her cheeks flushed pink. She looked much healthier than when I'd seen her in the infirmary.

Graymond continued pacing. "But how do we prove the Regency were the ones to start the fire? Leta was found in the middle of the crime scene with a death echo."

The princess lifted her blond hair off her shoulder to reveal her echo mark. "So was I, but I didn't kill my brother."

"But you *did* use edem," Graymond countered. "You were trying to heal him, although it didn't work."

"No," she said, and her brow crumpled. "Whatever they did to him while at the Regency headquarters couldn't be stopped by edem."

"So what, then?" I asked. "How do we prove invisible creatures exist?"

"You can't," Graymond replied with a shake of his head.

He was right. There was no way to prove to the jury that the hullen were real, short of bringing one into the courtroom.

"Actually," I said, "I don't think we have to."

He gave me a strange look.

"You said the burden of proof is on the prosecutor—they have to prove Leta is guilty beyond any reasonable doubt, right?" Graymond nodded warily. "Isn't it the same with the hullen? We don't have to prove they exist, but provide enough evidence to make the jury doubt that they *don't*."

Graymond narrowed his brown eyes at me, and I waited for him to dismiss my idea. "What did you have in mind?"

I stood tall, feeling a weight lift from my shoulders. "We bombard the jury with stories of the hullen. Detailed accounts from people who lived in Ferrington—"

"Isn't everyone dead?" the princess asked.

"Then we show them pictures, retell stories from books, *anything* to fill their heads with creatures of edem until they start fearing their own shadow." Just like I had in Ferrington before I saw the hullen for myself.

"Then what?" Graymond asked. "If we manage to convince the

jury that Leta isn't guilty, how does that implicate the Regency? How does that help the princess?"

"It won't," I agreed. "Not until we bring in our final witness. A witness who will tell the jury everything that the Regency has done. A witness who will tell the jury exactly what the Regency did to the king. A witness who no jury would ever doubt."

"Who's that?" the princess asked, her expression full of hope.

A slow smile spread across my face.

*"You."*

# CHAPTER 23

# LETA

Leta hadn't seen her brother all week, and today was the first day of her trial. Had he given up on her? Did he believe she was guilty?

When they were little, Leta had never kept any secrets from her brother. She hadn't felt the need. They usually wanted the same things and any tiffs were fleeting. But when their mother died and Cayder was sent away for a year, he came back different. Of course Cayder claimed it was Leta who had changed, and perhaps she had, but so had he. All he cared about was Vardean and the legal system. He believed that with their mother's killer behind bars, the Broduck family could move on.

He was wrong.

Trying to piece their family back together was like closing a wound with sticky tape. And Cayder and Leta were on two different sides, breaking the skin wide open as they moved in opposite directions. And their father? He didn't even factor into the equation. He used his job as an excuse to never be home.

Before her mother's death, Leta had been close with her father. He found her inquisitive nature charming and thought she would make a good lawyer one day. It was ironic that she was now the one inside a prison cell and Cayder longed to become the lawyer.

Leta was glad she would still have her chance to tell the truth and not be forced to plead guilty to a crime she didn't commit. Still, she wished Cayder believed her. If the jury found her not guilty and Cayder remained uncertain, it wouldn't be a victory. She knew he wanted to defend her, protect her, but *believing* her was a different story.

Cayder and Graymond came to collect Leta after breakfast. Cayder took one look at the ever-present guard in the corner and launched at Leta, wrapping his arms around her.

"I'm so, so sorry," he said.

He didn't need to say anything further. Leta broke down, her tears wetting his shoulder.

He believed her.

"How?" she asked, knowing he would understand what she meant.

"I saw them," he whispered. "The hullen." He looked to the guard again, then whispered furiously in her ear.

*"The king is dead. The princess is in Vardean for his murder. Ferrington is the link. The Regency are behind it all. They lit the fire. They killed all those people."*

Leta struggled to take it in. And yet everything Cayder said made sense. She *knew* the hullen were real!

"Are you ready, Leta?" Graymond stood in the doorway.

Leta ran over and embraced him. "Thank you, Uncle Graymond."

He smiled down at her, his eyes glassy. "I haven't done anything yet."

"You're here," she said.

"Your father would be here too, if he could." He nodded to her gloves. "You'll need to take those off."

Leta tucked her hands under her arms. "But—"

"We have nothing to hide, Leta," he said gently. "We need the jury to see that."

She glanced at her brother. Did he now believe the death of the bird caused her echo marks?

Cayder gave her a reassuring nod.

"Come on, little sis," he said. "We're getting you out of here."

———

The courtroom was buzzing with noise when Leta entered. The jury were up in the balcony, chatting among themselves as they waited for the judge. A hush fell upon the room as they spotted Leta and her counsel approaching the platform. Cayder stood on one side of her, and Graymond on the other.

Leta craned her neck to try to see the jury, but the seats were hidden behind an ornate iron balustrade.

"Their identities are concealed for their own protection," Graymond explained.

Fear spiked up her spine. "How will I know what to say to win them over?" she asked. How could she connect with a jury she couldn't see? How would she know if they were moving toward the correct verdict?

"You're telling them the truth, remember?" Graymond's forehead creased in uncertainty.

"Of course I am," she mumbled.

In addition to the stenographer from her last court appearance, there were three reporters sitting along the far wall. She recognized a woman with short black hair and golden skin as Mrs. Lunita, Narena's mother and a reporter from the *Telene Herald*. Leta had met her a few times at Narena's house. While Cayder wouldn't entertain any theories about edem and the veil, Narena had a more open mind.

If Mrs. Lunita recognized Leta, she didn't give anything away.

Cayder placed his hand on Leta's shoulder. "Everything is going to be fine. You're innocent."

"Yes." She couldn't bear to say anything more in case her voice faltered.

Two guards in full armor stood on either side of the table, as though they expected Leta to lash out or make a run for it.

She wished fleeing were an option.

A door banged shut behind them, and Leta turned.

Her father was here.

He nodded to her and took a seat at the back of the courthouse.

"I thought he wasn't allowed to be here?" Leta asked. A feeling of warmth spread through her chest.

"He can stay for opening statements only," Graymond said. "As a witness, he will have to leave before the prosecutor calls their first witness to the stand."

"All rise for the Honorable Judge Dancy," a courtroom clerk announced from underneath the balcony.

Judge Dancy moved swiftly into the room, the bottom of her cane clicking against the floor like the tick of a clock. Leta hoped that didn't signal that her time was almost up.

"Defense counsel and prosecutor, please sit," Judge Dancy said. Her brown skin reminded Leta of polished mahogany. Her gold jewelry glittered on her fingers, wrists and around her neck. She was far more glamorous than any judge Leta had ever seen, and she'd met quite a few over the years at her mother's parties.

Leta's stomach hollowed out at the thought of her mother. Had the Regency known about the hullen when they sent her to Ferrington? Was that why she was there that night? If that was the case, then the Regency were culpable in her mother's death. Was that why they wanted Leta to take the fall for the fires? Were they worried Leta had uncovered something to implicate them? Were they trying to discredit her?

Leta scrunched her hands into fists, allowing the pain of her nails biting into her palms to bring her back to the courtroom.

"Jury," Judge Dancy commanded, "stay standing."

Leta forced herself not to glance behind her. She didn't want to show her nerves, and she wouldn't be able to see their faces anyway.

The court clerk marched into the middle of the room. "Jury," he said loudly. "Do you solemnly swear on all that is good and light that you will listen to this case and render a true verdict and a fair sentence to this defendant?"

"We do," came a chorus of voices.

Judge Dancy nodded, brushing the top of her cane as she

would pat the feathers of a bird. "Please sit." She looked at Leta for the first time since she'd entered the room. "Today we begin the trial of the Regency and the nation of Telene versus Leta Broduck. Mr. Rolund"—she nodded to the slender prosecutor sitting at the table next to Leta's—"please present your opening remarks."

Mr. Rolund stood and turned to face the jury, his hand smoothing his white hair back from his forehead, his mustache flicking up at the corners as he glanced in Leta's direction. Cayder growled in response.

"He's just doing his job," Leta whispered.

"He's covering for the Regency," Cayder whispered back. "He's as bad as they are."

"Judge and jury," Mr. Rolund said, his voice projecting throughout the courtroom and quieting their whispers. "During this trial, you're going to hear about a girl who has disrespected the law since she was nine years old. Breaking curfew, dismantling floodlights and spreading lies against the Regency. She is a girl no one can control, not even her own family." Mr. Rolund smirked at Cayder, his mustache lifting higher on one side than the other. "She believes herself to be above the law and does whatever she pleases. She broke curfew to travel to the town of Ferrington to exact her revenge against the people who took her mother's life seven years earlier. While this crime is truly heinous, it was motivated by a simple act of revenge, and a simple verdict is all that I ask from you. If you need any proof of Ms. Broduck's guilt, I ask that you only look at her hands."

Leta heard the jury lean forward in their seats, looking over the balustrade to see what the prosecutor was referring to.

"Don't flinch," Graymond whispered to her. "They'll think you have something to hide."

She *did* have something to hide.

Leta sank her teeth into her bottom lip. She wanted so badly to conceal her hands, and herself, from view.

Cayder bumped her gently with his arm. Having him next to her gave her strength. It reminded her of all the times it was the two of them against the world. Like when they'd accidentally tracked mud all the way through the marble foyer hours before one of their mother's parties. Their mother, of course, had brushed it off. Their father, however, had ordered them to stay in their room and forbid them from joining the party.

Later that night, Cayder crept into Leta's room. He found her crying on her bed.

"We can still be a part of the party," he'd said. "Come on."

They tiptoed down the hallway and watched the party unfurl below them from their hiding spot on the balcony. Leta sketched the partygoers, trying to capture their likenesses and animated movements. Their mother was quick to spot them and had the kitchen staff send up some Delft deebule to enjoy while they watched. Many of their mother's friends were from work, and Leta loved catching snippets of conversations about the veil and edem and its time-altering powers.

Now she hated the Regency, and every time they were mentioned, it felt like tiny spikes flared through her veins.

Leta remained still, her echo-marked hands in full view of the jury. She didn't know yet if Graymond planned to use her story of the bird to explain away the marks.

"May the record reflect that Ms. Broduck's hands are covered in a death echo," Mr. Rolund said with a glance to the stenographer.

The stenographer's typing sounded like a gavel hitting the judge's podium, over and over and over.

*Guilty. Guilty. Guilty.*

But she couldn't think like that. Cayder said the princess would prove that Leta hadn't started the fires and the jury would forget all about her death echo.

Leta turned to look at her father, but his expression was unreadable. Was he questioning his decision to stand as one of her witnesses?

Graymond's opening statement was next. He placed his hand gently on Leta's shoulder before approaching the judge.

"Honorable Judge Dancy," he said with a nod up to the judge's podium. He turned to face the jury. *"Jury.* Ms. Leta Broduck and I appreciate your time in hearing this case." He straightened the lapels of his suit and stepped into the middle of the courtroom, his face tilted to the jury above. "Who is Leta Broduck? Over the course of the trial, you'll learn she is a bright, kind and artistic girl who tragically lost her mother at an impressionable age due to a mysterious edem accident. An accident that Leta hoped to uncover more about by traveling to the town of Ferrington. While she was there, the town was incinerated overnight. This girl"—Graymond pointed to Leta—"is lucky to be alive. And yet it's the prosecution's desire to paint her as a villain merely because she lived. I implore you, jury, keep an open mind, and look beyond the obvious." He gestured to her hands. "I implore you to listen to the evidence presented and realize the prosecution has no proof that Leta started this fire."

He clasped his hands close to his chest. "Am I trying to reduce the impact that these fires have had on the community and the families of those who lost their lives that night?" He shook his head. "Of course not. But we don't need another life lost, and that would be the result if Leta Broduck were sentenced to spend another day in Vardean. I ask the jury to find this sixteen-year-old girl, who was in the wrong place at the wrong time, not guilty."

He gave her a nod before taking his seat.

Leta understood the reason for repeating her age. She was young—she deserved another chance. If it had been any lesser crime, she'd be in Vardean Reform right now rather than facing a possible sentence of life in prison.

"Prosecutor," Judge Dancy said, her face stony, giving nothing away as to whether she was moved by Graymond's opening statement. "Call your first witness."

Leta turned to watch her father walk out of the courtroom. He didn't look back.

Her heart clenched, and she placed her hand over the sketch of the flower hidden inside her jumpsuit.

Mr. Rolund began his questioning by asking a Regency scientist, Dr. Estern, to the witness podium.

"Do you swear to tell the truth and nothing but the truth, in the king's name?" the courtroom clerk asked Dr. Estern.

"I do," she replied, then sat behind a podium to the side of the courtroom, below the judge's balcony.

Dr. Estern presented reports of the large shift in time that occurred in Ferrington the night of the fire. She showed coordinates of where the edem usage was detected and how this data was used to locate an unconscious Leta in the only part of Ferrington that remained.

Leta knew it looked bad—it had always looked bad. If she'd been part of the jury, she'd have believed herself guilty. She wished she could remember what happened the moment she tried to sacrifice the bird, but all that remained were shadows and the smell of smoke.

"Your witness, Counsel," Judge Dancy said once Mr. Rolund sat back down.

Graymond touched Leta's arm when he stood. He kept doing that. Was the action to make the jury see that she was not intimidating?

Leta laughed inwardly at the thought of anyone of her stature being intimidating. She barely came up to Graymond's shoulder.

Her brother gave her a reassuring smile, which Leta tried to return, but her head felt disconnected from her body, and she couldn't command her own facial muscles.

"Dr. Estern," Graymond said, "how many years have you worked for the Regency?"

"Objection," Mr. Rolund said, jumping up from his seat. "Relevance."

"It will become clear, Your Honor," Graymond promised.

"Proceed," Judge Dancy said. "Answer the question, Dr. Estern."

Dr. Estern wrung her hands; they were as white as freshly fallen snow. "Ten years," she answered.

"And in those ten years," Graymond said, "how many times has edem been used to create a fire?"

"I—I don't know every single case of edem usage," Dr. Estern said.

Graymond gave her a patient smile. "To the best of your knowledge, then," he said, "how many times have you known edem to generate a fire?"

Dr. Estern glanced at Mr. Rolund before replying. "Only once."

"One other time?" Graymond clarified.

She shook her head. "Only in this case."

"I see." Graymond nodded. "And how does someone start a fire with edem?"

"I don't know—I've not used edem before." Dr. Estern tapped her fingers agitatedly on the witness podium. "I could guess—"

"*Guess?*" Graymond raised an eyebrow. "You're the prosecution's expert witness on edem usage. I would hope that you would be able to provide more than a guess."

"Objection!" Mr. Rolund bounced out of his seat like a spring. "Badgering the witness."

Graymond hung his head. "I apologize, Dr. Estern. I merely wish to understand how the Regency knows the fire was started by Leta Broduck."

Cayder had gone ramrod straight. Leta could feel his excitement racing through him. Even though she knew he was worried for her, he was enjoying this. Enjoying seeing Graymond in action.

Dr. Estern cleared her throat. "It's my understanding that edem was used to start the fire by shifting multiple fires from different timelines and placing them into one area—*Ferrington*—to become a massive wildfire that spread through the region in mere moments."

"Hmm," Graymond said. "And how did you decide upon this . . . *theory*?"

Leta saw Cayder grin out of the corner of her eye. Graymond was subtly undermining this expert.

"When someone uses edem, they are displacing time," Dr. Estern said with a nod. "Past, present and future. The only way for a fire to be started by edem is to bring the flames from another timeline. Once the edem has fulfilled the person's desire, the timeline is restored. In this case, the fire would have returned to where it came from in the past or future."

"I see," Graymond said. "And did your readings from the edemmeter tell you this?"

Dr. Estern looked at her reports scattered across the witness podium, then said, "No. The edemmeter doesn't tell us what edem is used for, only where it occurs."

"Interesting." He tapped a finger to his chin. "So there's no way to know for certain that an influx in edem in the region of Ferrington that night was the cause of a fire?" Graymond asked.

Dr. Estern's cheeks flamed red. "No, but we can guess—"

"Thank you, Dr. Estern," Graymond said. "I have no further questions, Your Honor."

Graymond and Cayder exchanged a smile.

Leta wanted to feel hopeful, but she felt as though she was waiting for the rug to be pulled out from under her.

# CHAPTER 24

# CAYDER

I found it difficult to sit still while Graymond annihilated the prosecution. I wanted to leap from my seat and pump my fist, but I forced myself to sit quietly. Leta was surprisingly calm. She twitched every now and then; otherwise, she looked composed, but not callous.

Mr. Rolund called one of Leta's classmates to the witness stand next, but I didn't recognize him.

Leta bristled beside me.

"What's wrong?" I whispered.

Her large dark eyes found mine, but she didn't say anything.

"State your name for the court and your relationship to Ms. Broduck," Mr. Rolund ordered.

The boy looked younger than Leta, with greased-back black hair and a pinkish complexion. "Rener Wessex," he replied. "I'm in Leta's history class at Kardelle Academy."

"Mr. Wessex," Mr. Rolund said, walking the length of the

witness podium. "Can you please describe for the court your interactions with Ms. Broduck."

"She's a horrid shrew," Rener said.

"Objection, Your Honor." Graymond stood with a sigh. "This is opinion, not fact. This does not relate to the case at hand."

"Agreed," Judge Dancy said with a frown. "If you have a point, Mr. Rolund"—her eyes were narrowed—"I suggest you make it."

Mr. Rolund bowed his head toward the judge, but from my vantage point, I could see the sneer on his face. "Mr. Wessex," he started again, "can you please tell me what you overheard Ms. Broduck say in your history class?"

Rener glanced to Leta, then quickly away again, as though he was afraid of her. *He should be afraid of me. If I'm ever to see him outside this courtroom . . .*

"She said the Regency is a bunch of fools," Rener said with a scoff. "She said that she would do everything she could to uncover what they were hiding."

Mr. Rolund preened his mustache. "And what, Mr. Wessex, did Leta think the Regency was hiding?"

I shot Graymond a sidelong glance. Why would the prosecutor open this line of questioning? This played into our hands, not theirs.

"That there was an entire world on the other side of the veil," Rener said. "Where duplicates of ourselves carried out the opposite lives of the ones we've chosen. Our lives unlived."

Mr. Rolund raised an eyebrow toward the court. "She believes there are two of everyone?"

"Yes," Rener said, leaning forward eagerly. "She also said that the Regency is covering up a world where time runs in reverse and everyone walks backward."

Laughter erupted from the jury above.

*Edem be damned.*

Had she really told these absurd theories to anyone who would listen?

Mr. Rolund knew exactly what he was doing. He was discrediting Leta before we even uttered *the hullen.*

Graymond gave me a solemn, knowing look. *Patience,* it said.

But Leta flew to her feet. "I didn't say that!" she exclaimed. "I mean, I did, but that was a long time ago!"

I pulled on the sleeve of her gray jumpsuit to get her to sit.

"Enough, Ms. Broduck," Judge Dancy said, slamming her gavel onto the podium. "The defendant is not permitted to speak while a witness is on the stand, and you cannot address the jury directly."

Leta's display was only serving Mr. Rolund's claims that she could not be controlled. Which was exactly why he'd put Rener on the stand.

"No further questions, Your Honor," Mr. Rolund said, as though Leta had done enough damage herself.

I hated that he was right.

"Do you remember when Ms. Broduck said these things about the Regency?" Graymond asked when it was his turn to question the witness.

Rener glanced to Mr. Rolund. "I don't recall . . . not that long ago."

"Is that so?" Graymond asked. He pulled a piece of paper from Leta's file. "Permission to approach the witness, Your Honor?"

The judge nodded, her necklaces clinking together. "Permission granted."

Rener curled into himself as the much taller Graymond approached the bench. Graymond placed the piece of paper on the witness podium. "Can you please read from the top of this page?"

Rener's voice shook as he read. "Kardelle Academy, Senior History Class."

Graymond nodded. "The next two lines, please, Mr. Wessex."

"Leta Broduck," Rener said. "One hundred percent attendance." His lip curled in disgust.

I wasn't sure where Graymond was going with this, but I knew to trust him.

"And the last line?" Graymond prompted.

"Rener Wessex," Rener grumbled, his chin drooping to his chest. "Zero percent attendance."

Graymond let the information sink in, and I smiled at Leta. She didn't return my grin.

"And how," Graymond asked, "did you hear Leta mention this in a class you never attended?"

"I—I—" Rener pulled at the collar of his shirt. "It must have been another class."

Graymond handed over another piece of paper to Mr. Wessex. "Let the record show that I am now presenting both Ms. Broduck's and Mr. Wessex's schedules, and aside from history, they had no other common classes. Not since they were in middle school. If Ms. Broduck did indeed share her thoughts on the veil, it was approximately six years ago, when Leta was only ten years old." He smiled. "I'm sure you too believed in silly stories when you were young, am I right?"

"Someone else must have told me!" Rener said, clearly not wanting to be labeled a liar in front of the court.

"That, Mr. Wessex," Graymond said, a finger held to the brightly lit ceiling, "is hearsay, and I therefore ask the stenographer to expunge all mentions of Ms. Broduck's earlier beliefs from the record."

I sat back with a sigh. Graymond had done a great job at discrediting the witness. I doubted the jury would consider anything Rener had said as evidence.

I grinned at Mr. Rolund.

He hadn't seen anything yet.

———

"You did well," Graymond said at the end of the day when we returned to Leta's cell. She looked exhausted; meanwhile I was running on pure adrenaline. "The prosecutor did himself no favors with his witnesses. On Monday, we shall plant the seed of the hullen and make it grow."

Leta sank onto her bunk, bringing her knees up to her chest. "I'm sorry for my outburst earlier."

"That would be a first," I said, sitting beside her and nudging her with my elbow.

"Ha ha," she said dryly. "Rener and I have never gotten along. He's always made fun of me."

I swallowed down the guilt that I knew nothing about Leta's school life, who had bullied her or who were her friends. I'd been so focused on myself. And my own survival, believing she would always be by my side when I needed her. I'd been selfish.

"You did well," Graymond repeated with a nod. It was difficult to not feel confident with him in the room. He was always so assured of himself. It was contagious.

"How did you know about Rener not attending any of our classes together?" she asked. She was drawing in her sketchbook as we talked, something she said helped ground her and calm her mind.

"Both the prosecutor and I had to provide our witnesses as part of pretrial disclosure," Graymond explained. "I knew Rener Wessex was on the Regency's witness list, just as the prosecutor knows about Narena and your father taking the stand next week. I asked your school to send through every report they had and discovered you only had history together this year." Graymond smirked. "I suspected the prosecution was up to something."

"What about the princess?" Leta asked, her pencil pausing on the page. She was drawing a picture of the hullen again. The hairs stood on the back of my neck. "Isn't it dangerous to reveal your plan?"

"Pretrial disclosure was on Monday night," he replied. "I didn't find out about the princess and Ferrington until yesterday. New evidence is allowed to be admitted. The prosecutor might fight it, but I doubt the judge will agree when she discovers who our new witness is."

"See?" I said with a grin. "Everything's going to be fine."

"How about I leave you two for a moment?" Graymond said with a nod to the guard in the corner.

The guard grumbled but didn't argue.

Once Graymond left the cell, Leta flung her arms around my shoulders.

"Thank you, thank you, thank you!"

"Separate!" the guard ordered. "Now!"

I didn't want to get Leta in any more trouble, so I ducked out from her embrace and shifted along the bunk. She gave the guard a dirty look.

"Don't thank me yet," I said.

"I don't know how I could get through this without you. Because of you, I might actually get out of here."

I found it difficult to swallow. I couldn't shake the feeling that if I'd truly been a good brother to Leta, she wouldn't be here in the first place.

"You know Father would be more involved if he could," I said.

She raised an eyebrow. "Are you defending him?"

I laughed. "I suppose I am."

The smile disappeared from Leta's face as quickly as edem in the sunshine. "What do you think happened to Mother that day?" she asked. "Do you think the hullen were involved?"

"I don't know," I said. "They didn't attack me or Narena. I think they protected you from the fires."

I told her about what I'd seen out in Ferrington and the unburnt circle matching the wingspan of the invisible creature.

"That doesn't make sense," Leta disagreed. "Everything I've read and heard about the hullen paints them as destructive, dangerous creatures. And if they are related to edem, why are they so far away from the veil and nowhere else?"

I shrugged. It didn't make sense, but I knew what I saw.

"I bet Mother knew," she said, returning to her drawing. Her pencil spiraled around and around the empty holes of where their eyes would be.

"Then why didn't she say anything to us?"

"Maybe she didn't have the opportunity," Leta said, her face drawn. "What if the Regency silenced her like they silenced the king?"

I frowned. "You think they might have caused her death?"

"Don't you?" she asked.

I wasn't sure what I believed anymore. Ever since I started working at Vardean, my entire mindset had been reversed. I'd once wanted to be a prosecutor, interrogating people like Leta at Crown Court, and now I was on the other side, desperate to save an inmate's life.

Leta was the only real family I had left. And I had treated her as disposable, just like Father treated us both.

I grabbed her hands. She flinched, and I realized it was the first time I'd touched her skin without the barrier of her gloves. The gray death echo contrasted against her pale, freckly arms. I ran my hand over the mark of the bones. The skin felt no different to unmarked skin.

"How did this happen?" I asked.

She pulled her hands out from mine. "I told you," she said. "I killed that bird."

I shook my head. "You can tell me what really happened."

"Does it matter?" She shrugged. "I didn't start the fire; you know that."

"I want to know."

"No." She shifted away from me on the narrow bunk. "You don't want to know—you *have* to know. You've been like this since you came home from Vardean Reform. You have to know everything. *Where are you going, Leta? Why are you reading that mindless garbage, Leta?*" She put on a deep voice, imitating my tone, her face pinched haughtily. *"Why are you hanging out with those absurd conspiracy theorists, Leta?"* Her shoulders curled inward. "Why can't you accept me for who I am?"

I blinked at her. "Are you serious?" I waved my hands around us. "Because of your secrets, you're sitting in a prison cell and we're fighting for your freedom! You want me *not* to ask questions? Not to care?"

*"Care?"* She jumped up from the bunk, her sketches flying across the floor. The guard stepped toward us, but Leta glared at him and he stopped his approach.

"You left me alone with Father for a year!" she cried. "I didn't have anyone, so I made new friends."

"Friends like this informant you won't tell me about?" I said, seething with anger. "Are they the reason for that?" I pointed to her hands.

Leta stumbled backward. "Are you suggesting I killed my source—that's why I'm not telling you their name?"

"You killed someone." I hated myself as soon as I said it. But it was true. Despite my love for my sister, I still believed in evidence. And echo marks didn't lie, especially a death echo.

"Or something," she muttered.

"I don't think you killed that bird. I think Narena and I saw it." I swallowed hard. "Nothing survived out in Ferrington except for you and one bird."

"It must have been a different bird," she said, turning away from me. The pink flooding her cheeks gave her away.

I stood, hesitating before placing my hand on her shoulder. "I'm sorry you felt abandoned for all those years. But I'm here now."

She nodded but didn't meet my eye.

"I wish you trusted me," I said.

She huffed a quiet laugh. "I wish you trusted me too."

## CHAPTER 25

# JEY

The cell door opened on Saturday morning, catching Jey off guard. He'd rolled his inmate jumpsuit to his waist and was doing push-ups.

"Mr. Toyer!" Jey exclaimed. "A weekend visit? You should have sent word; I'm not prepared for visitors." He crossed his arms over his chest bashfully.

"Sit." Mr. Toyer jerked his chin to the table.

"What?" Jey sauntered over. "No hello?"

Mr. Toyer sighed. "I have some news."

Jey spun the chair around and sat on it backward. He pointed two fingers at him. "Shoot."

Mr. Toyer slid a piece of paper across the table but remained silent.

"I didn't bring my reading glasses," Jey whined.

"Just read it, Jey. Then sign below."

Jey swallowed sharply. This was serious.

# DEPARTMENT OF JUSTICE

## VARDEAN, TELENE
### *Criminal Record*

Inmate   #19550717

Age:   18

Criminal charges:   Using edem to murder
Dr. Bueter (father of the accused)

Secondary charges:   Stabbing of inmate,
petty theft

| Jury verdict: | N/A |
|---|---|
| Sentence: | Life in prison, no trial, no parole |

"Inmate 19550717?" Jey asked. "What? I'm just a number now? How insulting!"

"Do you understand what this means, Jey?" Mr. Toyer pointed to the paper. "You're going to spend your life here. As per the

Regency's request, the Crown Court believes you pose too much of a risk to society and has canceled your trial."

Jey tried not to let his relief show. "Give me a pen and show me where to sign."

"We can contest this, Jey," Mr. Toyer said. "Now's the time. Once this is signed, there's no going back."

"Contest it?" Jey asked. "Why? I already admitted to killing my father." He pointed to the skull on his bare chest.

Mr. Toyer nodded, but there was clearly something on the man's mind that he didn't—or couldn't—share.

"What will happen next?" Jey asked, genuinely interested.

"You'll stay here," Mr. Toyer said. He looked weary, as though he carried the weight of the nation on his broad shoulders. "After a few years, they may move you back down to another floor and grant you group mealtime privileges. Only on good behavior, of course."

Jey grinned. "Of course."

Mr. Toyer held out the pen. "After you sign this, my role as your public defender is over." The pen hovered between them. "Now is the time to tell me *anything* that you haven't already told me. Anything that I can take back to the judge to try and change your sentence or push for a trial."

Jey grabbed the pen from Mr. Toyer's hand and signed his name.

"Tell the superintendent that I like potatoes, don't eat meat and look forward to a nice long courtship."

Once Mr. Toyer was gone, Jey exhaled. He hadn't considered his trial would be canceled, but this worked well for him. He didn't want anyone looking into what happened the night his father died. That was why he'd insisted on pleading guilty. Not having a trial was easier.

That didn't mean Jey was ready to accept his fate. Once, he had been willing to sit in Vardean for as long as a judge determined. But now that he was here, his plans had changed. And that meant finding a way out of this cell.

Jey hadn't expected there to be so many guards on the top floor. That was foolish, really; it was where the most dangerous criminals were kept. Still, he hadn't counted on so many guards being posted outside one cell, the one with no windows. Jey hadn't decided yet if a collective group of guards should be known as a *thunder*—for the sound their boots made when they marched across the stone floor—or a *waddle*—for the way they followed each other around like geese. Regardless, their presence was making it difficult to conjure up an escape plan.

Most of the guards walked past Jey's cell without a second glance.

Aside from one.

She looked not much older than Jey and had bleached-white hair that curled against her brown skin, a small nose and large eyes. When she walked by, she would catch his eye and give him a nod. What she was nodding to him about, Jey wasn't sure. But he felt as though there was some understanding there. Some empathy. He would watch the guard join the others, and while everyone else stood still as a statue, she would shift from foot to foot or check her watch every few hours.

Since her initial nod to him, he'd tried a few times to engage with her.

On his second day on the top floor, he called out when she walked by.

"Hey!"

The guard had halted, looked at Jey and then continued walking. Not exactly the best start, but not the worst either.

Jey's girlfriend, Nettie, had taken a while to wear down. Most people found Jey's cockiness charming; at least his mother had. When Jey had first met Nettie, she had merely rolled her eyes at him.

Jey had to admit "Come here often?" wasn't the most original line for someone he saw every day on the trolley to school. But he thought she might laugh.

She didn't.

Her indifference to him, if not downright aversion, was what first intrigued him. Nettie never seemed to do or say what he expected, and Jey loved to be surprised. Each morning on the way to school, Jey would try again. Sometimes he would offer her a pickup line, other times he would say something completely random to see what her reaction would be. Would her pale skin flame with anger, or would she turn away, covering her face with a shield of hair so he couldn't see her grin?

He never expected his father to be the reason Nettie finally engaged with him—he supposed he should be thankful to him for that one kindness. If his father hadn't also been the cause of their split.

From his experience with Nettie, Jey knew it might take a while to wear down the guard's defenses.

This time, when Jey called out, she approached him.

"You know," the guard said with a tilt of her head, "you pestering me is going to get really old over the next forty years."

Jey mock frowned. "You think I'm only going to make it to my sixties?" He scoffed and puffed out his bare chest. "I find that highly insulting."

The guard studied the skull death echo with narrowed eyes. Jey felt an unusual wave of insecurity and quickly pulled up the top half of his jumpsuit to cover his markings.

Her mouth flicked downward. "What do you want?"

Jey willed his self-assuredness to return. He liked to think of it as a bottomless well that even Vardean couldn't deplete. "What's your name?" he asked.

"You want to know my name?" she replied.

He nodded. And she walked off.

"Wait!" Jey called out.

The guard rolled her shoulders, then walked back to his cell. "Look," she said. "This isn't social hour. I'm not supposed to talk to inmates."

"Then why are you?" He gave her his most alluring smile.

She laughed. "Put that away." She pointed to his mouth. "I've got a girlfriend."

"So do I," he said. "Or at least I did. Can't we be friends? Come on, I've got nothing else to do up here. Even my defense attorney is sick of me."

She flicked a white curl away from her mouth. "I can't imagine why."

He grinned. "I like you."

She shrugged. "I don't care."

"Humor me, please. Tell me who's in that cell you're all guarding around the clock. The one with no windows."

"Why should I?"

"Because you're bored too. You don't want to be here any more than I do."

She pursed her lips, and her eyes flashed. "You don't know anything about me."

Jey watched her storm off, noting the placement of the cell keys hanging from her belt.

He needed her to get closer next time. But how?

# CHAPTER 26

# LETA

The weekend passed slowly as Leta awaited her return to court. She missed her brother, and Graymond—his presence reminded her of a happier time when her life had not yet been tainted by grief and loss. When Graymond used to visit with his daughter and the whole world seemed full of possibilities. Back then, even stories of edem creatures seemed magical.

Leta filled the days with sketching everything she could remember of the world outside, in case she never got to see it again.

The second day of trial went much like the first. The prosecutor brought in witnesses to the stand to present evidence against Leta. Old friends, teachers and even the trolley driver who saw Leta embark on her trip to Ferrington that fateful day and said she had "death in her eyes and evil in her heart."

Witness after witness claimed Leta was stubborn, unruly and

dangerous. While Graymond would object to such comments, and thus they were stricken from the record, the jury could not unhear their words any more than a bell could be unrung.

The last of the prosecution's witnesses was the arresting Regency agent. Leta remembered the sandy-haired man with a narrow face and scraggly beard. His was the first face she'd seen after waking. He was the one who had roughly chained her death-echo-marked hands behind her back and told her she would rot in Vardean for the rest of her life for what she'd done. Leta had felt numb and hadn't said a word. Not until she arrived in an interrogation room.

"Agent Pharley," Mr. Rolund said to the man, "at this time, I would like you to read Ms. Broduck's original statement after her arrest."

Leta looked at her brother, but he stared straight ahead. Their words from Friday night still hung over their heads. Leta couldn't be too angry at him. She *had* lied to him about the death echo, after all.

To avoid her gaze, Cayder flipped through the files to find the transcript; his finger traced the words as Agent Pharley read aloud.

Leta Broduck Interrogation Transcript

---

AGENT PHARLEY: Ms. Broduck, I'm going to read you your rights. You must tell me if you understand them. If not, I'll explain them to you.

LETA BRODUCK: What happened?

AGENT PHARLEY: We'll get to that.

LETA BRODUCK: Why read me my rights? No one has told me what I've been arrested for!

AGENT PHARLEY: Leta Broduck, you have the right to remain silent. Anything you say here can and will be used against you in the court of law. You will be remanded in Vardean until your arraignment, at which time if you plead not guilty, you will be given a trial date. If you plead guilty, a judge will determine your sentence at a later date. You have the right to an attorney; if you cannot afford one, the Crown Court will appoint one for you. Do you understand these rights?

LETA BRODUCK: Yes, but I-

AGENT PHARLEY: Leta Broduck, can you explain your whereabouts last night? You live on the Sunshine Mile, correct?

LETA BRODUCK: Am I being arrested for breaking curfew?

AGENT PHARLEY: Don't be smart with me. You've been arrested because of what happened in Ferrington. And your hands.

LETA BRODUCK: I don't know what happened in Ferrington.

AGENT PHARLEY: The entire town of Ferrington, and most of its populace, was destroyed last night.

Why were you found in the middle of a burnt field, a death echo on your hands?

LETA BRODUCK: I-I don't know. I don't know how that happened.

AGENT PHARLEY: What were you doing in Ferrington?

(pause)

LETA BRODUCK: I was trying to find out the truth. I wanted to prove [inaudible]. I was there to provide a sacrifice. I was told that was all that was needed to conjure them.

AGENT PHARLEY: A sacrifice? You sacrificed the entire town?

LETA BRODUCK: No! I had a bird . . . I was planning to kill it to bring on the hullen.

AGENT PHARLEY: What is the hullen?

LETA BRODUCK: Creatures that want nothing but destruction.

(pause)

LETA BRODUCK: Is everyone really dead?

AGENT PHARLEY: All but a couple of lucky residents that lived on the outskirts of town. And you.

LETA BRODUCK: I'm so sorry! I didn't mean to hurt anyone.

AGENT PHARLEY: You admit to causing the fire?

LETA BRODUCK: I . . . I don't know. I just wanted the truth. But it's my fault. Because of me, everyone is dead.

[End of interrogation]

Leta felt the room's eyes weighing heavily on her shoulders. A few jury members had gasped when Leta claimed it was her fault. Even Narena's mother was shaking her head sadly.

Even though this was bad, she had to endure it. She had to make them see that *she* hadn't killed anyone in Ferrington. She wasn't dangerous.

"In her own words," the prosecutor said, "she admits fault. Don't listen to her lies now."

When it was Graymond's turn to cross-examine the witness, he picked up the copy of Leta's statement and approached Agent Pharley.

"Agent Pharley, what time did you find Ms. Broduck in the field in Ferrington?" Graymond asked.

"Before sunrise," Agent Pharley said. "Around five a.m."

Graymond nodded as though it was the most interesting fact he'd heard all day. "Was this before or after the fires had been put out?"

"Objection," Mr. Rolund said. "Relevance."

Graymond sent Judge Dancy a smile. "I promise there is a point to my questioning, Your Honor."

"Overruled." Judge Dancy nodded. "Continue, Counsel."

"Thank you," Graymond said.

Leta wasn't sure where he was going with this. She found herself leaning forward, holding on to his every word and every shifting expression on his face.

"The Regency didn't put out the fires." Agent Pharley scratched his neck. Leta noticed red blotches had appeared over his skin. Was he nervous? "The fires had returned to whatever timeline they came from hours before we found Leta Broduck."

"Interesting," Graymond said, turning his back to the judge to look up at the jury. "Tell me, then, how did the Regency know Ferrington had been ablaze?"

Agent Pharley considered Leta's statement as though he'd find the answers there. "I—we saw the smoke from a nearby town," he said.

"You saw smoke?" Graymond asked.

"Yes."

"And the closest town is?" Graymond prompted.

Agent Pharley looked at the statement again. "Ah . . ."

"Do you not remember the town you were stationed at only two weeks ago?"

"I remember," Agent Pharley said curtly. But clearly, he did not, as he didn't offer anything further.

"Answer the question, Agent Pharley," Judge Dancy said.

"Tavitch!" Mr. Rolund almost shouted.

Judge Dancy glared in Mr. Rolund's direction. "If you interfere again, Mr. Rolund, I will hold you in contempt of the Crown Court."

"Apologies, Your Honor."

But the damage had been done. Mr. Pharley now knew the answer to Graymond's question. Leta's nails broke against her skin, she'd been clenching her fists so tight.

"Right," Agent Pharley said with a nod. "The Regency was investigating an edem-based crime in the nearby town of Tavitch when we saw the smoke."

"Interesting," Graymond repeated, tapping a finger to his lip. "And how did you see smoke when it was nighttime?"

"What?" Agent Pharley shifted in his seat. "It wasn't night—it was morning . . . and we . . ."

"Stenographer," Graymond said, addressing the boy behind the typewriter. "Can you please repeat back to me what time Agent Pharley claimed to have found Leta Broduck in the burned-out field?"

The stenographer flipped through his notes frantically. "He said . . ." The boy's voice trembled—either with excitement or fear, Leta wasn't sure. *"Before sunrise. Around five a.m."*

"Thank you, son," Graymond said with a nod. "Do tell me, then, Agent Pharley. How did you see smoke from the nearby town of Tavitch, which is over four miles away, in the dark?"

"Well," Agent Pharley began. "You see, well—I . . . We saw the flames. Yes, the flames, not smoke."

"Stenographer," Graymond said. "Remind the court what Agent Pharley said about the fire when they arrived."

This time the stenographer's voice was firm when he answered, *"The fires had returned to whatever timeline they came from hours before we found Leta Broduck."*

"Interesting . . . If you did indeed see the flames, why did you not travel there immediately to put them out? Why arrive hours after the flames had destroyed Ferrington when Tavitch is only four miles away?"

"I—"

"And how did you know *when* the flames had vanished back to the past, or to the future, if you were not in Ferrington until five a.m.?"

"Well . . ." But he didn't offer an explanation.

"Which raises the question, Agent Pharley, what was the Regency doing in Ferrington before five a.m., if *not* to help the townsfolk and extinguish the flames?"

The roar of objections from Mr. Rolund and spluttering from Agent Pharley blurred into the background. Leta released a relieved sigh.

Cayder reached over and placed his hand on hers.

# CHAPTER 27

# CAYDER

I stayed in Graymond's office overnight; I was too excited to sleep. Today it was our turn to call upon our witnesses, which meant Narena and Father were to take the stand. And finally, the princess. Today we would seal Leta's fate.

Graymond had fallen asleep at his desk around four a.m. on top of his files, while I continued to revisit the questions for our witnesses. We had to continue to put the pressure on the prosecution. We'd begun to unravel the knotted truth, and now we had to lay it out for the jury.

We planned to have the princess fake a fainting spell while Kema was guarding her. I would intercept as Kema escorted the princess to the infirmary, and take the princess to the courtroom instead, where she would reveal what the Regency had done to her brother and the town of Ferrington.

Leta would go free, and the princess would be released to be crowned as the queen. And the Regency would be disbanded.

The entire nation was on the brink of permanent change. The

world would soon learn of the hullen's existence. How could I possibly sleep?

But I let Graymond rest while he could—it was the most sleep he'd had in nearly two weeks, since Jey's incarceration. We all needed to be at our best in court today.

---

The courtroom was buzzing with chatter when we entered the next morning. There had been a shift in atmosphere. What had once seemed a cut-and-dried case was unfolding very differently. And we had yet to play our winning card.

After Judge Dancy was announced and took her seat, she lifted up a piece of paper. "Before we begin today's proceedings," she said, "I have an announcement to make."

*This can't be good.*

I exchanged a look with Graymond. He shook his head; he didn't know what this was about.

"Mr. Toyer," Judge Dancy said.

Graymond rose. "Yes, Your Honor?"

"Your witness, Narena Lunita, did not present herself at registration this morning," Judge Dancy said. "She has been pulled from your witness list."

*What?*

Where was Narena? Was she all right?

I looked over to the media box and saw her mother was also absent. I felt like I was going to be sick.

Mr. Rolund smirked. *He* did this. But what exactly did he do? If he hurt Narena—

"Sit," Graymond said, his hand an anchor on my shoulder. I hadn't even realized I'd risen. "I'm sure they're both fine."

I wasn't. The two lawyers who had previously represented the princess were hardly "fine." I never should have gotten Narena involved. I never should have—

"Take a breath, son."

"Do you need a recess?" Judge Dancy asked. I was surprised to see concern pulling at her features.

"Please, Your Honor," he said.

"Twenty minutes," she granted.

I was out of my chair before she finished her sentence. I didn't care if my actions broke stupid court protocol. I needed to ensure Narena's well-being.

"Slow down!" Graymond said, running after me. "I'm not as young as I once was."

"If the Regency hurt Narena," I growled, "I'll kill them."

"Don't jump to conclusions. I'm sure there's a reasonable explanation."

I didn't reply. I couldn't think straight. All I could see was Narena lying lifeless on the stone steps of the library.

I ran into Graymond's office and headed straight for the phone. I held my breath as I dialed Narena's number. Graymond stood on the opposite side of his desk, his hands stuffed in his pockets. His usual proud posture looked stiff—too stiff.

*He's worried too.*

"Hello?" a voice answered on the other end. It was Mrs. Lunita. I swallowed in relief.

"Is Narena there?" I asked. "It's Cayder."

"Oh, Cayder," Mrs. Lunita said, her voice full of sorrow. My rib cage felt like it was cracking in two. "I'm so sorry, but she doesn't wish to speak with you."

"What?" I asked, exchanging a confused glance with Graymond. "So she's there? With you? She's all right?"

"Yes, she's here," Mrs. Lunita said. "I'm sorry she pulled out from the case. But she didn't want to lie. It's her future, you see. She wants to get into a good college. She wants—"

"Hang on," I interrupted. "What do you mean—lie?"

"About going to Ferrington with you," Mrs. Lunita said, her voice taking a harder tone. "I'm disappointed you asked her, but I understand you're under a lot of pressure. She wants to help your sister, but lying isn't the way to do it."

"I see." I hung up the phone.

"What is it, son?"

"Narena won't testify," I said. "I don't know how, but the Regency got to her. They're keeping her quiet."

His frown eased somewhat. "She's all right, then?"

I nodded. "We need to end this." I clenched my fists by my sides. "Today."

---

When we returned to court, I took the stand. We'd hoped to avoid using me as a witness, but without Narena, I was the only person who could testify to seeing the hullen.

Graymond thought Mr. Rolund might object, considering I'd

been in court when the other witnesses gave evidence, but the prosecutor merely laughed and said it was the defense's mistake to make.

I looked forward to proving Mr. Rolund wrong.

Sitting behind the witness podium and having the jury hover above you just out of sight was daunting. I could see why the other witnesses had buckled under the pressure. It felt like the entire court's eyes were on me. And they were.

But I would not falter like the others before me. The truth was a sword in my hand, and I was prepared to wield it. I wanted the Regency to come for me.

"Cayder Broduck," the court clerk said. "Do you solemnly swear on all that is good and light that you will tell the truth and only the truth?"

I swallowed roughly and held up my right hand. "I do."

Judge Dancy gestured to Graymond, her numerous gold bracelets clinking together. "Counsel, you may begin your questioning."

Graymond gave me a slight nod before approaching. "Cayder Broduck," he said. "Let's get the obvious out of the way, as I'm sure the prosecution will harp on about this: You are Leta Broduck's older brother, correct?"

"Yes," I said as confidently as I could. "I'm one year older than Leta."

"May I ask what your relationship is like with your sister?"

I glanced at Leta's heart-shaped face, and my chest grew tight.

*Be honest,* Graymond had told me before I returned to court. *Tell them the truth.*

"Not great," I admitted. "We were close as children, but we drifted apart when I was sent to Vardean Reform for a year."

A few jurors tutted in the crowd. Graymond and I had discussed letting Mr. Rolund reveal this bit of my past, as we knew he would.

*Better to get out in front of it,* Graymond had said. *It's nothing to be ashamed of.*

Once I might have been, but not anymore.

"You've used edem before?" Graymond asked now.

"Only once. I was ten, and my mother had recently passed away from an edem accident in Ferrington. She worked for the Regency. And she was—"

"Objection!" Mr. Rolund said. "Relevance."

Judge Dancy nodded to me. "I'm sorry to hear of your loss, Mr. Broduck, but answer only the questions asked."

"Of course, Your Honor." I was getting ahead of myself. The information was pressing against my chest, bursting to be free. I wanted to make this moment count and rectify all my past misdoings.

"Using edem landed you in Vardean Reform for a year?" Graymond asked.

"That's correct."

"Have you used edem since?"

I didn't hesitate in responding. "I have not. And I will not."

"Have you ever known your sister to use edem?" Graymond asked.

I stared down Mr. Rolund. "No."

"Were you with your sister, the defendant, in Ferrington on the night in question?"

"No," I said. "I was in my home on the Sunshine Mile."

"Have you ever been to Ferrington?" he asked.

Now was my chance. "Yes. I visited last Wednesday to try to find out what happened to my sister. I visited with a friend, Narena, who was meant to be a witness today, but she . . . is unable to." I glared at Mr. Rolund, but he didn't flinch. I was sure I could see a smile under his white mustache.

"Did you find anything of note in Ferrington?" Graymond asked.

"Objection!" Mr. Rolund said. "Leading the witness."

"Overruled," Judge Dancy said. "Mr. Broduck, you may answer the question."

I nodded in thanks. "I saw the hullen—creatures made of edem. Creatures that the Regency have failed to report to the citizens of Telene but are very much real."

I expected a gasp from the crowd, but there was nothing but silence.

"Your Honor," Graymond addressed Judge Dancy. "May I show something to the jury?"

"You may," she replied.

The clerk rolled in a corkboard at Graymond's request, and he started pinning up pieces of paper until every inch of the surface was covered.

"Honorable Judge and jury," Graymond said, his arms spread wide. "These are hundreds of letters from people who lived in Ferrington over the past twenty years. They are all reports to newspapers claiming to have seen or heard something that could not be explained. They called these creatures the hullen—Delft for 'the living dark.' These letters prove that Ms. Broduck, and indeed her brother, are not the only ones to have seen or heard something unusual in Ferrington."

Graymond turned his attention back to me. "Cayder, did you know of or believe in the hullen before you visited Ferrington?"

I shook my head. "No, I'd never even heard the word until my sister was arrested. And I didn't believe in them until one was staring me in the face."

Graymond pulled down the letters and pinned up new pieces of paper. Once the image was complete, the hullen stared back at us.

"Do you recognize this image?" Graymond said.

"Yes," I said. "That is the drawing my sister did after visiting Ferrington. And it holds a striking resemblance to what I saw out there. That is the hullen."

The shadowy creature with large wings and horns had taken center stage in the courtroom. I heard a few people gasp in response.

*How does the truth taste?* I thought, grinning at Mr. Rolund.

We were just getting started.

## CHAPTER 28

# CAYDER

Mr. Rolund rolled up his sleeves as he approached me on the witness podium. The eager glint in his eyes concerned me, as did the twitch of his mustache, as though he was fighting back a smile. I wanted to wipe that smirk permanently off his face.

"Cayder Broduck," he said, "is it true that you would do or say anything to help your sister go free?"

I glanced at Leta. Of course I would, but I couldn't play into the prosecutor's hands.

"Remember," he said. "You're under oath."

I squared my shoulders. "I would help my sister in any way I could, but I would not lie."

"No?" Mr. Rolund asked.

I leaned forward. "No. The hullen are real. They protected my sister from the fire in Ferrington; that's why she's still alive."

Mr. Rolund snorted. "I'm not asking about those silly creatures your sister talks about. I'm asking you if you would lie to help your sister."

"Objection," Graymond said. "Asked and answered."

"Sustained," Judge Dancy said. "Ask a new question, Mr. Rolund. Or release the witness."

Mr. Rolund nodded. "My next question is," he said, "have you ever lied before?"

I huffed a laugh. "Everyone has told a lie at least once in their life."

"You admit you're a liar, then?" Mr. Rolund raised an eyebrow.

"No," I said, staring up at the hidden jury. "I admit that I might have told a harmless lie or two, but I'm not lying about the hullen. And I'm not lying about my sister's innocence."

"You've never lied to someone to get your way?" Mr. Rolund asked.

I shrugged. "Not that I can think of."

"Request to approach the witness, Your Honor," he said.

"You may," Judge Dancy replied, gesturing below her.

Mr. Rolund handed over a piece of paper. I swallowed sharply when I realized what it was.

"Can you please read this letter to the court?" Mr. Rolund asked.

I took a deep breath, let it out through my nose and read the letter aloud.

*Dear Alain,*

*It's my pleasure to welcome Cayder as an apprentice at the State Library over the summer before he begins his final year at school. I'm sure he will learn a great deal by my side that will aid him in his endeavors to study law.*

*I do hope you will accept our next dinner invitation. It's been far too long.*

*Sincerely,*
*Laino Lunita*

Where did he get this letter from?

"Hmm," Mr. Rolund said. "That's interesting, as you haven't been at the State Library for the summer, have you?"

"No, but I—"

"Did your father know you changed your mind?" he asked.

"No. But it was—"

"You lied," he interrupted. "You lied to your father so that you could spend the summer at Vardean, working alongside a defense attorney." He swung around to point at Graymond. "Is that true?"

I raised my face to the ceiling and shut my eyes for a brief moment.

"Yes," I said. "That's true."

Mr. Rolund grinned. "You made sure you were here for the summer so that when your sister was arrested, you could ensure that she would go free."

"Objection," Graymond said. "Opinion, not fact."

"I'll allow it," Judge Dancy said, although she didn't look pleased about it; her brows were pinched together. "Answer the question, Mr. Broduck."

"That's ridiculous!" I spluttered.

"Mr. Broduck," Judge Dancy said, "keep your voice down."

"How could I help my sister when I didn't even know she was going to be arrested? I'm just a high school student! Not a criminal mastermind!"

"Strike that from the record," Mr. Rolund said to the stenographer. "I didn't ask a question."

I gritted my teeth. *That ass!*

"No further questions," Mr. Rolund stated.

I stomped down from the witness podium and slumped next to Leta. She gave me a sad smile.

We'd been played.

"Take a breath," Graymond whispered. "He's trying to undermine your testimony. Don't let him win."

I couldn't meet Leta's eye. I'd failed her.

———

Our father was next. He looked infuriated for even having to be there, although he was wearing his best suit. The one he wore to Mother's funeral. It didn't fit anymore; the buttons wouldn't fasten over his belly.

Graymond began by asking about Leta's childhood and temperament. Father told the court about how Leta used to collect flowers from the garden and place them in every room of the house. She would rescue any beetles she found on the petals to release back outside. For a man who mostly communicated through grunts and withering stares when at home, he managed to weave together a picture of a sensitive and sweet girl with an inquisitive mind.

"Just like my wife," he finished by saying.

I looked over at Leta, and tears were quietly running down her cheeks. We'd never seen this side of our father.

When it was the prosecutor's turn, Mr. Rolund straightened his tie and approached Father.

"Judge Alain Broduck," Mr. Rolund said. "Are you surprised to find your children have lied, deceived the court and broken the law?"

My father glared at Mr. Rolund. "My children are teenagers. Am I surprised they have lied to me? No. Do I think they broke the law and are deceiving the court? Also, no."

"And yet your daughter has a death echo on her hands." Mr. Rolund approached the corkboard and replaced the picture of the hullen with a sketch of Leta's echo mark. "Do you deny this evidence?"

Father cleared his throat. "I cannot deny it, no."

"Then you must admit that your daughter used edem and therefore broke the law," Mr. Rolund said. "And not just any edem usage: edem used to kill."

Father grumbled, "I admit that's what it looks like."

"Do you believe in the hullen?" Mr. Rolund asked as though it was the most ridiculous idea imaginable.

"I believe there are things we don't know about edem," Father said. "My wife and daughter are not alone in their desire to know and understand the truth to the veil."

That was unexpected. Father had never entertained Leta's theories before. Was he lying now, or had he been lying to Leta for years when she approached him with her theories?

"Speaking of your wife, Maretta Broduck," Mr. Rolund said, "she died seven years ago in Ferrington, is that correct?"

My father's face flushed red. "Yes."

"Your daughter claims that she was out there trying to find out what really happened to Mrs. Broduck that night," he said. "But does she know the truth?"

Leta and I exchanged a glance. *Truth about what?*

"You'll have to be clearer in your questioning," Father said, sounding very much like he was the judge of this court.

"Does your daughter, or your son, know that you too have broken the law?"

Father shook his head. "I have *never* used edem, if that is what you're implying."

"I'm not. I'm *implying*"—a sly smile stretched his mousy mustache—"that you have used your position as judge to break the very laws you claim to uphold."

Mr. Rolund turned to watch our reaction. I wasn't sure what game he was playing, but I wasn't going to give him the satisfaction.

"I don't know what you're referring to," Father said.

"Let me be clearer," Mr. Rolund replied. "It is illegal to visit an inmate unless you are their legal representation, correct?"

"I have not visited my daughter," Father replied. "As much as it has pained me to stay away, I have."

And I believed him.

Leta's breath stuttered in her chest. I wanted to place my arm around her shoulder. And for the first time in many years, I wanted to embrace Father too.

"I know you have," Mr. Rolund said. "But that is not the visit I'm referring to."

"Get to the point," Judge Dancy said. "The court grows impatient."

"Yes, Your Honor." Mr. Rolund nodded. "My question is, did you or did you not pay a visit to an inmate seven years ago?"

"Edem be damned," Graymond muttered under his breath. But I was surprised he didn't look shocked; he looked upset. Upset that this information got out. Which meant he knew about it.

Father didn't reply, crossing his arms over his chest. The red flush had spread down his neck.

"Remember that you're under oath," Mr. Rolund said.

Father let out a grunt. "I did," he admitted. "I needed to face the man who had taken my wife away from me and my children."

"You used your position as judge to speak with the man who was then on trial for your wife's murder. But that wasn't all, was it?"

How could Mr. Rolund know this? Father would have been removed from the bench had this information been widely known by the court.

Father mumbled something.

"Speak up for the court, Judge Broduck," Judge Dancy said, her tone unforgiving.

"I wanted to know what happened that night in Ferrington," Father said, his hands clasped on the witness podium as though he was begging for compassion. "I wanted to know about my wife's last moments."

I glanced at Leta. They weren't so different, after all.

"You forced him to change his plea," Mr. Rolund said. "You threatened him. You made him plead guilty."

"He killed my wife, damn it!" Father roared. "He deserved to rot in this place!"

The entire courtroom went silent.

"You broke the law," Mr. Rolund said. "You made sure the man who killed your wife would not go free."

"Yes," Father admitted, hanging his head, his breathing labored. "Yes, that's true."

Mr. Rolund nodded sagely. "I understand what a tremendous loss it must have been for your entire family. And how Mrs. Broduck's tragic death turned a once-law-abiding family into serial lawbreakers and edem criminals."

"Objection, Your Honor," Graymond said, his voice weaker and more feeble than I'd ever heard. "Speculation."

"Speculation?" Mr. Rolund raised a white eyebrow. "Leta Broduck is in this courtroom for using edem, her father has admitted to interfering with a trial, and Cayder Broduck lived at Vardean Reform for a year. These are facts, not speculations!"

I couldn't catch my breath. My mind spun.

"Sustained," Judge Dancy said.

Mr. Rolund shrugged. "I have only one final question, Judge Broduck. And that is, how did you get access to your wife's killer?"

Father placed his head in his hands. "Does it matter? It's not relevant to this case."

"I think the jury should be the judge of that," Mr. Rolund said with a nod to the balcony.

I could see a few people gripping the balustrades, leaning over to better hear every word.

Our case was hanging in the balance, and I felt Father's next words would tip the scale.

"Let me rephrase," Mr. Rolund said. "Who is the person who provided you with access to this inmate, allowing you to break the law?"

Father sucked in a breath. "It was my fault. I told him I just wanted to see his face. He didn't know that I—"

"Answer the question," Judge Dancy ordered. It wasn't lost on me that she didn't use Father's official title.

"Let me make this really simple for you," Mr. Rolund said, a sick gleam in his eye. "Is the person who aided your breaking the law in this very room?"

Father tilted his head back and closed his eyes. "Yes." It was as though the word pained him, pulled from his rib cage.

"Good." Mr. Rolund grinned. "And can you point this person out for the jury?"

Father raised a shaking hand. He wouldn't open his eyes, as though he couldn't bear to witness what he was about to do.

The jury gasped.

"Let the record show," Mr. Rolund said, "that Judge Alain Broduck is pointing to Mr. Graymond Toyer."

# CHAPTER 29

# LETA

Everything happened quickly after that. Leta felt like she couldn't keep her head above water. Shouts and insults were flung around her, and she was trapped in the center.

Leta's father was forced to stand down as a witness and judge. He was ordered to leave Vardean and await a disciplinary hearing to determine if he should be stripped of his judgeship. And Graymond was dismissed from Leta's case for aiding in the breaking of the law. He could be disbarred, depending on his own disciplinary hearing. Which left Judge Dancy with only one option.

Declare a mistrial.

Leta was escorted to her cell while Cayder and Graymond bickered back and forth. She wasn't listening to anything they were saying. All she could think about was her father. How he'd been so distraught over his wife's death that he had broken the law to ensure the killer was put behind bars. And now, because of Leta, his secret was exposed to the world, risking his entire future as a judge—the only thing he really cared about.

She understood why he always shut her down and turned her away when she started talking about theories of the veil. He didn't want Leta to allow her grief to cloud her judgment. He wanted Leta to let her mother go. To move on. To live her life.

Leta had destroyed everything.

"We'll get another lawyer," Cayder was saying. "We were winning. The prosecutor knew that, that's why he brought up everything about our mother."

"Trials are not a game," Graymond said. His handsome face looked haunted, his lips dry and pale against his brown skin. "There is no score. Not until the jury makes their final decision."

Leta realized at some point they'd returned to her cell, although she couldn't remember the exact moment. The patches in her memory reminded her of waking in the field in Ferrington, the rest of the night a dark haze.

"All the evidence we presented is no longer admissible because of me," Graymond said. "The court believes I have a bias in this case. Therefore, none of the evidence we've collected in my time can be used again. I'll send word back to the office. You'll have to start from scratch with a new lawyer."

Leta's drawings, Cayder's testimony, all of it. Gone.

"We still have the princess," Cayder said. He'd been tugging on his dark hair, making it stick up in all different directions.

"This time you'd have to put the princess's name on the pretrial witness disclosure list," Graymond said. "The Regency will ensure she never takes the stand."

"What, then?" Cayder asked. "What do we do?" Her brother's face was drawn, his dark brows anchored together, his movements frenetic.

Leta picked up a pencil, desperate to stop her mind from spiraling. But nothing came to her. Her pencil wouldn't move across the page. She couldn't even control her own art anymore.

"Nothing," Leta said quietly. She couldn't go on. She couldn't continue to destroy her family because she didn't know when to quit.

They turned to her. Cayder blinked, as though he'd forgotten she was even in the cell with them.

"We do nothing," she clarified. "I've ruined too many people's lives. It doesn't matter that I didn't start the fire. Father will most likely lose his job over this. Graymond, you might be disbarred. I'm so sorry." She stared down at her echo-marked hands. "Whose life will I destroy next?"

"You're kidding." Cayder grabbed her shoulder. "*Your* life will be destroyed if we give up."

"Maybe it should be," she muttered, mostly to herself. She pulled away from her brother and sank down onto her bunk. She was tired. So, so tired. Tired of pretending she wasn't terrified. Tired of pretending she was strong.

Tired of lying.

"Leta," Graymond said in that reassuring deep voice of his. "You did not do this. Your father and I made a mistake many years ago. A mistake we thought was long buried and long forgotten. We are the ones who should be sorry. This never should have impacted your case."

"It was a mistake that wouldn't have come to light without me!" she said.

"How did Mr. Rolund find out?" Cayder asked. Every time he said the prosecutor's name, he looked like he was ready for a fight.

Graymond shook his head. "I don't know. No one else was there. Unless a guard saw us? But how could they know what was discussed inside that cell? And why didn't this come to light sooner?"

"Does it matter?" Leta asked. "My case is over. All the evidence, gone. Please just leave me alone." She closed her eyes. "I want to sleep."

She felt the bunk shift as Cayder sat beside her. "I'm not leaving you, Let. This isn't over. Not now. Not ever."

She wanted to tell him that her life had ended before the night of the fires. The night she got the death echo. But she couldn't tell him the truth.

Because then he really would give up on her. And she didn't really want to be alone.

# CHAPTER 30

# PRINCESS ELENORA

On Wednesday afternoon, Princess Elenora prepared for her moment in court. She'd never much thought about the legal process; it was her brother's job to set the laws based on advice from the Regency. Elenora's job had been ensuring humanitarian efforts. Ensuring the people were happy. Her schedule had been packed with meetings and delegations and galas. She used to daydream about spare time. About what hobbies she would explore if she could. She would daydream about having moments to herself, for herself.

But now that Elenora had each and every day on her own, she hated it. She wanted someone to share time with. She was desperate for conversation. She imagined her soul withering like the dried husks of an old torlu tree. If someone were to cut her open, she would be desiccated inside.

To pass the time, Elenora invented games to play. Each day, she would count the screams and curses from the lower levels, or the times she heard the *click click click* of the elevator chain. The next day, she would hope to beat those numbers.

Erimen had always played games with her. As children, they spent their winters around the fireplace, playing late into the night while their parents attended to royal business on the mainland. Sometimes they would tell each other wild tales of the world beyond the castle isle: people who wore their clothes inside out on Wednesdays or ate dinner for breakfast and breakfast for dinner. Just because they could.

Their stories grew more fanciful in each telling, until the mainland, which was less than an hour's boat ride away, became a fantastical place that might as well have been as foreign as living on the moon.

Elenora let out a sigh. She missed her brother so much. The only way to ease her pain was her plan for retribution. To see the mighty Regency fall. She looked forward to taking the stand in front of a judge, jury and the media. Let them all see her face. The Regency couldn't hide any longer, and neither would she.

She had changed out of her infirmary gown back into the billowy black-and-white dress that she had been arrested in. She placed her mask over her face and curled a gray scarf around her neck like a snake—a piece of material she'd ripped from one of her skirts to cover her echo mark.

She wanted to look regal. She needed to look authoritarian. She was still the princess, after all.

The cell door unlocked, and Elenora quickly raked her fingers through her blond hair to detangle it. She wished she had one of her other dresses to wear for this special occasion, not one that had collected grime and dirt over a month in a prison cell.

Instead of the young guard Elenora was expecting, Cayder entered the cell.

"Cayder!" Elenora cried, rushing to the bars between them. "I thought Kema was escorting me to the courtroom?"

He was looking at the filthy floor.

"How is the case going?" she asked.

When he finally looked up, Elenora gasped at his shattered expression.

"What is it?"

His hair was in disarray and his eyes were bloodshot.

"Princess," he said. "I'm so sorry, but our plan failed."

Elenora felt like she'd swallowed a stone. "What's happened?" Had Mr. Toyer been hurt? She *knew* she should've kept her mouth shut!

"Leta's trial has been canceled," he said.

"No!" She slumped against the bars. "Where's Mr. Toyer?" she asked, removing her mask.

"He's been barred from any cases until after his disciplinary hearing. He can't represent you anymore. He's been asked to leave Vardean."

She was relieved Mr. Toyer would be safe. He seemed like a good man. But how would she get out of this cell now?

"What will happen to your sister?" Elenora asked.

Cayder shook his head. "Graymond is going to ask another lawyer to step in, but we can't have you testify, not without pretrial disclosure. But I won't give up. I'll find a way to free you both."

She could see the love he had for his sister on his face. She felt the same way about her brother. The two of them against the world.

"How can I help?" she asked.

He glanced up and smiled.

"The princess of Telene wants to help me," he said. "How did I get so lucky?"

"Call me Elle," she said. "Erimen was the only person who did, and now . . . *Well*, I'd like someone to know me for me."

He stepped closer to the bars, and she followed suit.

"If only we could find my brother," she said. "Then he could tell the court exactly what the Regency did to him and their involvement in the Ferrington fire."

"Why do you believe he's still alive?" Cayder asked. "What proof do you have?"

"The way it happened," she said. "No one just disappears like that. The Regency did something to him. I don't know what it was, but he's not gone. I can still feel his presence."

Cayder smiled. "I feel that way about my mother. Seven years on, and she's still with me."

He didn't believe her, and the thought stung.

Well, she would just have to prove it to him.

"I need to get out of here," she said. She gave him a grim smile. "I feel like I'm disappearing from the world. Just like Erimen did."

"You're not," he said. "I'm here. And you're not going anywhere."

She gave him a wry smile. "That's what I'm afraid of."

"Poor choice of words." He clenched his jaw, the muscles flicking. "I don't know what else to do," he admitted. "You were our key to proving the Regency started the fires in Ferrington."

"We'll figure something out," she said, her hands resting on the bars between them.

Cayder glanced up shyly before slowly placing his hands over the top of hers. A bolt of warmth spread down their joined fingers and throughout her body. She leaned forward, wanting to be closer. She rested her forehead on the cool bars. He mirrored her.

"How do we get you out of here?"

"I don't know," she admitted. She didn't want to break the spell, the held breath between them, the racing of their hearts. But this was not real. These bars were real. This prison was real.

"Break me free," she said.

"I'll try," he whispered back.

There was something so intimate about his breath crossing her exposed skin. Goose bumps prickled along her arms, and the hairs stood up on the back of her neck. Did he feel it too?

He carefully reached out his hand through the bars. "May I?" he asked.

She nodded. And his fingertips skimmed her cheek lightly, as though he was scared she would break. Tiny sparks of warmth bloomed wherever his fingers met her skin.

"Princess," he murmured.

"Elle," she corrected.

He chuckled breathlessly. "I promise to get you out of here."

The key in the lock twisted, and they pulled apart, the spell broken. Elenora reached for her mask and quickly placed it over her face.

"Time's up," the superintendent said, her expression fierce.

Elenora scowled at the woman. She'd been unnecessarily cruel to her since her arrival in Vardean.

"I'll see you tomorrow," Cayder promised.

"No, you won't," the superintendent said.

Cayder turned to her. "Graymond said he would send another lawyer and that I could finish my apprenticeship with them. He said I could stay—"

"You can't."

"*What?* I—" Cayder began.

Yarlyn cut him off again with a wave of her hand. "All pending trials have been canceled, as per the new Regency law."

"I'm sorry, but *what?*" Cayder spluttered. He glanced at Elenora.

She had feared this would happen. In her brother's absence, the Regency could do whatever they pleased.

"Because of your sister's crime," Yarlyn explained, "the Regency have decided to increase the punishment to ensure a tragedy such as Ferrington cannot happen again. Any edem-based fatalities will automatically incur a sentence of life in prison, no trial needed. Only smaller edem infractions will go to court."

Cayder's mouth opened and closed. "You're saying my sister has already been sentenced? Without a jury's verdict?"

Yarlyn nodded. "Her sentence is life in Vardean." She nodded to Elenora and held out a piece of paper through the bars.

Elenora read through the document.

# DEPARTMENT OF JUSTICE

## VARDEAN, TELENE
### *Criminal Record*

---

Inmate   #19710801

Age:   17

Criminal charges:   Using edem to kill King

Erimen

Secondary charges:

| | |
|---|---|
| **Jury verdict:** | N/A |
| **Sentence:** | Life in prison, no trial, no parole |

"You're not letting me have a trial?" Elenora asked. She had worried the Regency would do something like this but had not thought it could happen so soon.

"You can't do that!" Cayder said, his face reddening. "That's against the law! Everyone has a right to a fair trial."

"The law has changed since the Regency came into power." Yarlyn shrugged as though it didn't bother her either way.

Elenora could hardly breathe; her breath rasped in the mask.

*This can't be.*

*This can't be.*

"The king would never stand for this!" Elenora said, her hands fisted by her sides. "He believed in justice. He believed that everyone had the right to tell their story. He wanted what was best for the citizens of Telene."

Yarlyn considered the princess for a moment. "Perhaps you should have thought of that before you killed him."

"I didn't!" Elenora cried.

Yarlyn waved Elenora away. "Cayder, you must leave this cell at once. You don't represent the princess anymore. You're not allowed to visit this inmate. In fact, without Graymond, you can't be here at all."

Cayder's brows were furrowed, his eyes an amber blaze. "No. This isn't right. Even you know that, Yarlyn."

"I know the law is the law," she replied. "And I am to uphold my part in the system."

Elenora could do nothing as the guards led Cayder from her cell.

And just like that, Elenora's plans for revenge slipped through her fingers.

# CHAPTER 31

# CAYDER

I was numb. This couldn't be happening. The Regency had taken control, just as Elenora—*Elle*—had warned me. Both my father and Graymond weren't allowed to return to Vardean until after their disciplinary hearings. And my sister was stuck in this place without the option for a retrial, or even an appeal.

I would never understand why the Regency had burned Ferrington to the ground. Why they had kept the hullen a secret. Or why they had blamed my sister for everything that had happened.

I felt the pressure of the stone walls pressing in against me, as though I too were a prisoner of this place. I needed to get out of here while I still could.

For the first time in my life, Vardean was the last place I wanted to be.

———

As soon as I returned home, I headed toward my father's office. I could hear the loud, angry clacking of the keys of his typewriter.

"Why didn't you tell me?" I asked, storming straight into the room.

Father didn't look up from his work. "Go away, boy."

"No," I said. "I won't. I won't hide from the truth. Not like you have."

He pulled off his glasses and looked up, his face full of disdain. "You kids have been hiding the truth from me. If you had just—"

"Just what?" I clenched my teeth. "Pretended Mother didn't die? Pretended like our lives were fine without her? That we didn't lose you that night too? That our family isn't in pieces?"

Father shook his head, his skin pale, dark circles under his eyes, his breathing labored. Had he always looked this unwell? Or was I only now noticing?

"I did the best that I could," he said. "You kids seem to think it was just you who lost the most important person in your lives. But I lost her too."

"And because of this family's obsession with secrets and lies, now Leta will never be free."

He looked like I'd slapped him. "What are you talking about?"

"The Regency," I seethed. "They've changed the law. Anyone who's arrested for an edem-based fatality is immediately sentenced to life in Vardean. Leta won't get another trial."

I expected Father to slam his fist on the table, to rise up and fight alongside me. But he wilted into his chair.

"Then there is nothing we can do."

"Nothing?" I asked. "Your only daughter is trapped in that place for a crime she didn't commit! And you want to give up?"

He leveled his dark eyes on mine. "I'm likely to lose my judgeship. I begged you to stay away from Vardean. I begged you both to let go of your mother's death. Because I wanted you to live your lives. I didn't want you caged by your grief like I am!" His low voice transformed into a roar.

"Your anger is misplaced, Father," I said. "You should be angry at the Regency for covering up Mother's death, not at me and Leta for wanting to know the truth."

Father shook his head again. "It doesn't matter what happened to your mother that night," he said. "The result is the same."

"But what about justice?" If the Regency or the hullen had killed Mother, then the man Father forced to plead guilty for her death was innocent.

Father huffed a laugh. "Justice is an illusion. A mask we wear over our grief. Take off the mask, and the pain is visible for everyone to see."

I gripped Father's desk to prevent myself from sinking to the floor. "You're a judge. You can't honestly believe that." I'd built the last seven years around the thought that justice was the only way to move on from the tragedy of losing Mother.

Father ran his hands down his face, and I realized he was crying. I'd never seen him shed a tear, not once.

"Life will go on," he said. "We will learn to live with your sister in Vardean, just as we've learned to deal with your mother's death."

"I—" But I couldn't speak.

He had truly given up on Leta.

My bones felt hollowed out. My muscles as though they were made of stone. I could barely raise my head to say, "You're wrong."

Father leaned forward, his expression softening. "No, Cayder, I'm not. I spend my days in the courtroom. I spend my life around people who have lost everything. And I'm telling you, the only way to move on is to let go." He closed his eyes for a moment. "It's the only way to survive. Now it's time for you to let go too."

I stumbled back. As much as I didn't want to give up on Leta, I knew some of what Father was saying to be true. Vardean wasn't the sanctuary I'd imagined it to be since I left the reform school. It didn't represent justice and peace. It was a twisted institution that didn't know the difference between innocence and guilt. And now, with the Regency in control, Vardean stood for something far more sinister. A veil of lies.

I stomped up the stairs to my room and ripped the Vardean posters and schematics from my walls. I didn't want a reminder of the place that had taken my family from me. It was a place where those in power could do exactly as they wished, without any consequences. My father, my sister and Graymond had all paid the price for wanting to find the truth.

And the Regency would do anything to ensure it stayed hidden.

Without a fair trial, Leta and Elle would spend their lives locked away for crimes they didn't commit. I felt so completely helpless, as though I too were shackled in Vardean.

I could barely take a breath.

What would I do now? How could I live in a world without my sister? While we had grown apart in the past few years, she'd always been there, and I'd thought she always would be. What else could I do? Without Father, without Graymond, I was powerless.

I was an arrogant boy who had waded into an ocean of monsters.

And I'd been eaten alive.

# CHAPTER 32

# CAYDER

I sat in my chair, staring at the blank walls for the rest of the night. I couldn't think of how to help Leta. I couldn't even get myself to shift out the of chair.

On Thursday morning, a knock came at the door.

"Cayder." It was Narena. "Can I come in?"

She opened the door when I didn't reply. She was carrying a silver platter of hotcakes piled high with torlu berries and cream, and a glass of milk on the side. "Your favorite." She smiled tentatively.

When I remained silent, she said, "I didn't make them, if that's what you're worried about."

She placed the tray on the bedside table. "I'm so sorry, Cayder." She sat on the edge of my bed. "I heard about the new law. It's all over the news. And I'm sorry I wasn't there to help. I'm sorry—"

"Why weren't you?" I twisted to face her. "No one took my testimony seriously because I'm Leta's brother. We needed someone impartial. We needed you—*I* needed you."

Tears filled Narena's eyes, and her amber skin flushed red. "I was scared! A Regency agent came to my house and told me that if I testified, my mother would disappear, and we both know that's not an empty threat."

"If you'd told me," I said, "Graymond could have informed the judge the Regency was involved in witness tampering."

"I had no proof! Would you risk the safety of your family?"

I turned away. "My family is gone now."

Narena shook her head. "It's not over."

"It *is*." I groaned. "What else can I do? No trials. No appeals. It's done. Leta will spend the remainder of her life in prison because of me."

Narena shook her head in confusion. "Because of you?"

"Because I failed her!"

Narena knelt beside my chair, forcing me to look into her eyes. "You didn't fail, Cayder. You're not responsible for what happened to your sister. You did your best, and Leta knows that."

"That doesn't change the outcome."

"I know. What can I do?"

"Have you told your mother about the hullen?" I asked.

She shook her head, her long dark hair whipping around her face. "No. You told me not to."

"Would she believe you if you did?" I asked. "Maybe she can write an article from an anonymous source?"

"Newspapers have already written such reports and testimonials over the years," Narena said with a shrug. "They're always debunked by a Regency expert."

She was right. We'd used such reports as evidence in Leta's

trial—evidence that could never be used again, even if retrials were allowed.

"The princess is the only person who can change the law," I said. "She's the only one who has the power to undo what the Regency has done."

"Surely the Regency can't change laws like"—she snapped her fingers—"that."

"They can if they're in charge." I frowned. "There's nothing we can do."

"You're going to give up? That's not like you."

I scoffed. "You gave up before I did. You knew you couldn't fight the Regency while I was too stubborn to admit I was out of my depth. But not anymore. I know exactly where I stand."

Narena gave me a small smile. "Your stubbornness is one of your best qualities."

I didn't laugh. "It means I delay the inevitable." I leaned back in my chair and continued to stare out the window. "I'm sorry, Narena. I've got no fight left in me."

———

Narena stayed until close to curfew. Nothing she said could change my mind. When I couldn't fall asleep, I headed across the hall to Leta's bedroom and opened the door. I was surprised to find her room swathed in darkness; her room's permalamp was missing a bulb. I chuckled and sat on the edge of Leta's bed.

Mr. Rolund was right: We didn't control Leta. We never could. Her unruliness and inquisitiveness were a part of who she was.

I watched edem flow through the shadows all around me. It

was too easy to access edem inside your own home, away from the Regency's watchful eye. I was tempted to reach out for it, to command the magic to do my bidding. To change my fate. Leta's fate. Elle's fate.

But I would only end up in a cell myself.

Edem wasn't the solution. It never had been.

I left Leta's bedroom, shutting the door behind me.

---

I awoke the next morning to someone yelling my name.

"Cayder!" the voice called from outside. "Cayder! Let me in!"

I dreaded shaking the sleep from my bones. In my dreams, I'd been blissfully unaware of the reality that now came crashing down upon me.

"Cayder!" the voice insisted. "If you don't come down, I'm coming up."

I was too sluggish to move. Soon Kema's face peered through the third-story window.

*"What in the veil?"* I reached to open the window.

"Thank you," Kema said, tumbling into my room. She pushed herself up onto her feet. Her brown skin was slick with sweat, and her white locks were damp. It looked like she'd run all the way from Downtown Kardelle.

"If you're here to ask me to come back to Vardean," I said, "you're wasting your time. Even if I could, I'm not going back."

Kema leaned against the windowsill, catching her breath. "You need to," she panted.

"As I said—"

She grabbed my shoulders, her eyes wide. "Listen to me, Cayder. Your sister was poisoned last night. You *need* to come back."

All the air left me in a rush. "Is she all right? When did this happen? *How*—" I jumped to my feet, swayed and then fell back into the chair. I hadn't eaten or drunk anything for two days.

"She's alive," Kema said, answering the most important question first. "But unwell. Something was slipped into her dinner last night. I was on duty when she started being sick. She's in the infirmary under observation."

I was throwing on clothes before Kema had finished speaking. "Who did this?" I bared my teeth.

Kema shook her head. "We don't know. The guard who gave her the food has disappeared."

"The Regency." I clenched my hands to stop from punching something. "They're trying to silence her."

Kema shook her head. "What are you talking about?"

"I'll tell you everything on the way," I said. "Come on."

———

I gave Kema a rundown of everything that had happened as we journeyed across to Vardean on the gondola. I needed someone to trust while Graymond and my father were expelled from the prison. And Kema and I had been close once.

The crack in the sky behind Vardean looked like a pulsing, angry vein. Hatred for the Regency pumped through my blood, demanding revenge. First they framed my sister; now they were trying to take her life.

Kema's brows rose higher and higher the more I told her. "Dad never said anything about this to me."

"He couldn't," I said. "Even without client confidentiality, he didn't want you involved. It was safer that way." I was surprised the Regency had allowed me to live after what I'd said in court.

"What are you going to do?" she asked.

"I have to get Leta out of there." I glared at the building that rose out of the ocean like a tentacle from some monstrous sea creature, ready to latch on and never let go. I couldn't believe I had once enjoyed living there. I couldn't believe I'd wanted Vardean to be my life.

"I don't know, Cayder," Kema said. "Leta's safer in the infirmary than back in her cell. Whoever got to her the first time is likely to try again."

"That's not what I meant," I said, tearing my eyes from Vardean. "I'm not going to break Leta out of the infirmary." I squared my shoulders.

"I'm going to break her out of prison."

# CHAPTER 33

# LETA

Leta now knew what dying felt like.

Your pulse raced and then slowed. You felt every heartbeat, as though your body was counting down until the last, making each *thump* count. And although you were so thirsty, you could not keep down a single sip of water, as your body tried in vain to expel the poison. Your body flushed hot and then cold and colder still, until your teeth chattered and your bones shook. And then . . . nothing. A numbness washed over you like a wave from the ocean, carrying you out further from the shore. Further from your body. Further from life.

Leta had never thought much about her own death. She'd been too concerned with the details of her mother's.

What had her mother thought before she died? Did she have time to think of her children? Had she been scared?

Now Leta knew the unfortunate truth.

Dying was terrifying.

Somehow, Leta woke. She wasn't surrounded by darkness, or the other side of the veil—which she'd once considered some kind of heaven. And her mother wasn't by her side.

Leta wasn't dead.

A doctor loomed over her, pressing a cup of liquid to her mouth. She had freckled brown skin and a mop of amber curls.

"You need to drink," the doctor said, her voice like ice on a humid summer's day.

Leta wanted to sit upright, but every single muscle in her body screamed at the thought of the slightest movement.

Stillness was the only comfort right now. The blanket against her skin felt like sandpaper, and the light above her bed burned her eyes.

"Where am I?" she rasped out, her jaw aching as she spoke.

"The infirmary," the doctor said. "Don't fret, dear. You're going to be all right."

"What happened?"

The doctor's eyes darted away. "You ate something bad."

Leta thought back to the dinner she had. She couldn't remember anything tasting strange.

The doctor patted her hand. "You're going to be all right."

She'd already said that, which made Leta question whether she was, in fact, going to be all right.

"Where is she?" a voice growled.

*Cayder!*

Leta tried to sit up, but her body wouldn't cooperate. It was like living in a dream—a nightmare.

"What are you doing in here?" the doctor asked.

"That's my sister!"

Leta couldn't see him. Where was he?

"It's all right," another voice said. It was the guard who had restrained Cayder back when Leta was first brought into Vardean. "I'll stay with him."

Cayder's concerned face appeared above Leta, and she was awash with relief.

"How are you feeling?" he asked. She'd never seen her brother so frazzled. His hair was a mess, and his skin was white as bone. He had dark circles under his eyes as though he hadn't slept in days. And she was pretty sure he was wearing a jacket over his pajamas.

"I'm alive," she said. That was all she could commit to at this point. Her throat felt like burning coals every time she swallowed.

Cayder spun to the doctor. "Who did this?" he demanded. "Where's Yarlyn? I want to speak with her. Now!"

"I'll see if I can find her for you," the doctor said.

Once the doctor was gone, Cayder drew close. "I'm getting you out of here." His amber eyes were intense.

Leta groaned in reply.

"What hurts?" His eyes darted around her.

"Everything," she admitted.

"Cayder," the guard said. "She needs to rest. We can't do this now."

"We have to, Kema," Cayder said. "You said so yourself, we

can't let her go back to her cell. It's too dangerous. You managed to get me in this time, but people are going to realize I shouldn't be here."

*Kema?* Uncle Graymond's daughter?

It had been so many years since she'd last seen the petite girl, but beneath the uniform and the bleached locks, Leta could see her old friend.

"Do what?" Leta asked. She wanted to close her eyes against the bright light and sleep.

Cayder's thick brows furrowed together, and he got that particular look in his eye when he was thinking something through.

"Do *what?*" Leta repeated.

She felt like she was back in the courtroom, where everyone was discussing her fate, as though her opinion on the subject didn't matter. That was one of the reasons Leta loved art. She could control it. And it never controlled her.

"I'm breaking you out of here," Cayder said, his voice low and urgent.

Leta laughed, and it felt like she had swallowed tacks. "Be serious."

"I am serious." He grabbed her hand. "The Regency tried to have you killed. They poisoned you. Apparently spending your life in Vardean isn't enough."

"No," Leta said, sitting up slightly and ignoring the feeling of her muscles being ripped from the bone. "You're not going to do that."

Cayder blinked. "You want to stay in prison?"

"Of course I don't!" Leta replied. "But I don't want you ending up in here too."

"Do you think you can stand?" Cayder asked, ignoring her.

"They're not going to let you walk me out of here!" Leta said in exasperation, her voice barely above a rasp. "Kema? Some help please?"

"Leta's right," Kema said.

Cayder shot her a dirty look. "I thought you were on my side."

"I am," she replied. "But we need to think this through. We need to form a plan. We can't barge our way through security. Not when Leta can hardly talk, let alone stand."

"When Leta is better," Cayder said, "she'll be moved back to her cell. What do we do then?"

Kema tapped a finger to her lip. "We unlock the cell door." She made it sound so simple. "I happen to know a guard who has a set of keys to her cell." She grinned, her whole face lighting up.

Leta was surprised when Cayder disagreed with her. "I don't want you involved, Kema. You'll lose your job."

She shrugged; her white hair bounced. "I don't like it much anyway."

"Really?" he said. "Then why do you still work here after two years?"

She shook his comment off. "I want to do what's right. *This* is right. My father would say the same."

Cayder studied her for a moment before a smile curled the edges of his mouth. "Okay, so what's the plan?"

Kema paced around Leta's bed. "It's not going to be easy to break out of here. And even then, where will you go? You'll have to live a life on the run. The Regency won't just give up. Not with the information you have."

Cayder was quiet for a moment. Leta wanted to shake her brother. He wasn't thinking clearly. He was acting impulsively. That wasn't like him.

"There's only one person who can make everything right," Cayder said. "The princess. If we break her out of Vardean as well, she can tell everyone what the Regency did to her brother. She can get them ousted from the government and pardon Leta."

"You've both lost it," Leta said, finding her voice. "No one has ever broken out of Vardean. I don't want either of you arrested." She closed her eyes and let out a heavy breath. "Too many people have suffered because of me."

But they weren't listening to her. It reminded Leta of when they were kids and Kema and Cayder would leave her out of their game. It was never intentional, but they had always been closer, and Leta was often left on the outside looking in.

"One problem." Kema raised a finger. "I don't have the key for the princess's cell. Only Yarlyn does."

"Could you get it off her?" Cayder asked.

"Not easily," Kema admitted. "I'm no thief, after all."

"Neither am I," Cayder said. "You know who is a thief, though? A thief who might help us?"

Kema and Cayder grinned at each other.

"Who?" Leta asked. "What are you both smiling about?"

"We're getting you out of here, Leta." Cayder patted her leg. "It's time to visit my favorite client."

# CHAPTER 34

# CAYDER

I had to be careful with how I approached Jey about my plan. I couldn't have him selling me out to one of the guards in exchange for something he wanted. I still wasn't sure what happened the night his father died. That made him unpredictable, and dangerous.

Kema went to the guard lounge and changed into her uniform to "escort" me to the top floor.

"How do we make sure Jey doesn't give the plan away?" I asked as the elevator rose. "He claims he doesn't care about being in Vardean. How can we make sure he helps us?"

"No one *wants* to be in Vardean," Kema said. "Aside from you, Boy Wonder."

"Not anymore," I muttered darkly.

"We have to figure out what he wants," she said. "Everyone wants something in this place, even if it's not freedom."

"Could we get him out of solitary?"

Kema chewed on her bottom lip. "I don't have that power, but there has to be something he wants from the outside. A letter from a friend? Something we could smuggle in?"

I nodded. "I'll see what I can work out."

Kema gave me her cell key and wandered off to distract the other guards gathered around the princess's cell. I quickly unlocked the door and slipped inside.

Jey was doing push-ups.

"Nine hundred and ninety-nine." He did one more push-up. "One thousand." He winked. "Come for the show, mate?"

I rolled my eyes. I'd forgotten how annoying he could be. "I've come to see how you're doing."

Jey pushed up to his feet. He'd unzipped his prison uniform to show off his echo marks. "It's hot in here."

"Is that a problem?" I asked. "Perhaps I could get you a fan or something."

He cocked an eyebrow and slicked a hand through his black hair. "What? You're going to sit by my bedside and fan me?" He sat down on the chair and drummed his hands on the table. "What's new? Where's Mr. Toyer? I thought he said he doesn't represent me anymore."

"Shhh," I said, gesturing to his hands. "Can you be quiet for a second?"

He leaned across the table as though he was about to whisper. "Why?" he asked at normal volume.

I glanced through the bars to the landing, but no one was looking in our direction. Not yet. I needed to be quick. I wasn't supposed to be in Vardean anymore, let alone on the top floor.

"That's right. Graymond doesn't represent you anymore."

"And what? You do?" he asked with a smirk.

"No," I ground out. "No one represents *anyone* anymore. No trials. No appeals. Nothing."

I expected some smart-ass response, but he looked taken aback. "What? For everyone?"

"Yes. It's a new Regency law. Anyway, that's not why I'm here."

He narrowed his eyes. "Then why are you?"

"I—I was worried about you."

Jey tilted his head back and laughed. "You're a terrible liar."

"If you want my help, you have to be quiet!" I whispered.

His jaw snapped shut. "How can *you* help *me*?"

"Actually," I said, "I need your help. And in return, I'll give you whatever you want. Better meals. A letter from a loved one—"

"What do you know about the people I love?" His expression was serious, which was unusual.

"I know you didn't love your father, that's for sure," I snapped before I could stop myself.

His brown eyes flashed dark. "You don't know *anything*."

I hadn't come here to argue with Jey. I needed him on my side. "You're right. I don't know anything about you other than what you've told me and Graymond. But I'm here, willing to offer you a deal."

Jey leaned back in his chair and crossed his arms behind his head, the picture of ease. "What is it that you want from me? Aside from my glorious company?"

I refused to take the bait. "I want you to steal something."

"I'm sorry, what?" He shook his head. "I must have misheard you, as I thought you said you wanted me to commit a crime."

I took the seat opposite him. "Jey, I need your help."

"I'm stuck in this cell," he replied, matching my serious tone. "What can I possibly steal that's of any use to you?"

"A key," I said. "The superintendent's key, to be exact."

Jey propped his elbows on the table and rested his chin on his hands. "And why would I do such a dangerous thing? I'd like to get out of solitary one day and live the good life back on the eightieth floor."

I rubbed the back of my neck as I ran through all the things Kema and I could offer him, which weren't many.

"Why do you want her key, anyway?" Jey asked. "It only opens that one cell . . . *Ohhhhh.*" He snapped his fingers. "You want access to whoever that secret prisoner is, don't you?"

"Yes." That was a good enough reason. "I need to speak with them about something."

"No deal," he said with a shrug. "There's nothing you can give me that I want."

"Surely there's something I can arrange to make your life sentence easier?"

"I highly doubt that."

"You like working out, don't you?"

Jey flexed his biceps. "Yes. And thanks for noticing."

I clenched my teeth to stop myself from growling at him. "What if I could arrange some exercise equipment?"

He cocked his head, interested. "Do you have that power?"

No. But Kema could sneak something in here.

"Would that be something you'd like?"

"Why are you so interested in talking to that inmate?" Jey asked.

"I can't tell you that."

He pushed back from the chair. "Then I can't help you."

"Why do you care?" I asked as he retreated to his bunk. "You get something you want, and I get something I need."

"Because," he said, "if I'm going to help you, risking my release from solitary, I need more info. You know gossip is currency in this place, right?"

"So?"

"So I know your sister is locked up here," he said, jerking his thumb toward Leta's cell. "Why are you stealing a key to speak with this mysterious prisoner when you could be stealing a key to speak to your own sister?"

"My sister is none of your business."

I hated that Leta was just another piece of gossip traded for sport.

"And she's not in her cell," I said. "She's in the infirmary."

"I see," he said. "The whisper network is a little quieter up here on the top floor. What happened?"

"Are you going to help me or not?"

"Not," he said with a nod. "I don't need exercise equipment that badly. As you can see, I'm doing well enough without it." He grinned slyly.

I nearly stormed out then and there, but Jey was my only chance. Leta would be back in her cell in a few days, maybe less. I didn't have time to think of another plan.

"Get me that key," I said. "And I'll give you whatever you want."

Jey thought it over for a moment, then nodded at my hand. "A trade," he said. "A key for a key."

"You want me to give you the key to your cell?" I asked. "Why?"

"I thought you were smart, mate." He stood up from his bunk and approached me slowly. Step by step. "I want out."

"But . . ." He'd wanted to plead guilty for his father's death. He'd wanted to be in Vardean. Why did he change his mind?

"Leave your key with me, and I'll get you the other one." He shook his head. "Why do you care about the other inmate over your own sister?"

I couldn't let him know this was all a plan to help Leta go free, in case he decided to turn me in to Yarlyn.

"You don't understand anything about family," I said. "You killed your own father."

He locked eyes with me, and something flashed that wasn't cool indifference. "A key for a key," he repeated.

As long as I got Leta out of here, what did it matter if Jey escaped?

"Fine."

Jey held out his hand, expectantly.

"Nice try," I said. "You get me Yarlyn's key, *then* I'll give you this key."

"You swear?"

"On my sister's life."

"Okay, then," he said. "What's your plan? I can't exactly waltz up to Yarlyn. My charm only gets me so far."

"I was hoping you might have a suggestion."

"Stealing involves a deft touch," he said. "And a distraction."

"What kind of distraction?" I asked.

Jey shrugged. "No one pays much attention to me. I was trying to work on one of the guards up here, but I couldn't get her close enough to steal her keys."

I paced along the length of the cell. The only time I'd seen Yarlyn open a cell door was when the princess had fallen ill. But Yarlyn was unlikely to concern herself with Jey's well-being. She would only care if it was someone important or innocent.

*Someone like me.*

But how could I put myself in danger? There weren't any weapons, or anything sharp even, in Vardean. We were checked for contraband items every time we walked through the gate.

"How did you get that knife?" I asked. "The one you used to injure that inmate?"

"From someone who works in the kitchen. His name is Ryge. Nice guy," he said with a nod. "If you give him something of value, he'll hook you up with whatever you want."

"What's valuable to Ryge?"

"Not necessarily *for* Ryge; he'll do a trade with another inmate. Ryge is the middleman."

"Right. And what do other inmates need?"

Jey scratched his chin in thought. "Alcohol, tobacco, magazines, newspapers—"

"Newspapers?" I asked. "You're kidding."

"Think about it," he said. "You're locked in here for years, with only the meals to indicate time passing." He pointed to the light prism above us. "You have no contact with the outside world. No friends to write to. No family can visit. Newspapers give you an insight into the world outside. It helps pass the time."

"An insight into a world that is corrupt," I said, smiling.

Jey furrowed his brow. "Why are you grinning at me like a fool?"

"Because," I said, "I know how to provide a distraction *and* deliver something of value."

"How's that?"

"A newspaper article. Providing something better than gossip. The truth."

"What are you talking about?"

"Don't worry about it. You just get me a knife. Deal?" I held out my hand.

He shook my hand without hesitation. "Deal."

# CHAPTER 35

## CAYDER

I intercepted Narena on the stairs to the State Library as she headed home for the day.

"Narena!" I called out.

"Cayder?" She turned, surprise etched in her features. "What are you doing here?"

"I need your help."

Her face lit up. "I knew you wouldn't give up! What can I do?"

I didn't think she was going to like what I had to say next. "I need an article exposing the Regency, their involvement in the king's death, and the existence of the hullen."

"Oh no." She started walking down the stairs, her long black hair creating a curtain between us. "Cayder, I can't! My mother will lose her job—or worse! I can't risk having her involved."

"Your mother doesn't have to know."

She halted. "What do you mean?"

"*You* can write the article," I said. "Sneak into the *Telene Herald* tonight and after tomorrow's newspaper is printed, swap out the front plate with the article and do the smallest print run you can. I'll then smuggle those newspapers into Vardean to distribute during mealtimes, when the inmates outnumber the guards."

"Why?" she asked, frowning. "How will this help Leta?"

I told her about my plan to break Leta out of Vardean, along with the princess.

Narena stared at me for a long moment, not blinking. "That's not funny, Cayder. That's breaking the law."

"What is the law but what the Regency decides?" I asked. "Last week, it was law that everyone deserved a fair trial. This week anyone who's suspected is immediately sentenced. All I'm doing is helping innocent people go free. That is what the legal system should be upholding. That is what *I* believe the law to be. I thought you'd agree."

Narena pressed a finger to her lips, glancing around the stairs. "Someone might overhear you."

She was right. It was too dangerous to be talking about the Regency when anyone could overhear us.

We headed to the Belch Echoes—we both ordered water this time—and climbed the stairs to the top floor. It was a bustling Friday night, and the music was loud enough to conceal our discussion.

"What if it was your mother stuck in Vardean for the rest of her life for a crime she didn't commit?" I asked. "Or your father? What would you do?"

Narena clasped her hands. "Anything."

I smiled ruefully. "Then you know why I'm doing this."

"I'm worried, Cayder," she said. "If you're right, then the

Regency will stop at nothing to keep their secret quiet. I don't want you to get caught in their crosshairs."

"It's too late for that. The only way to get out of this mess is to expose the Regency for who they really are."

"And what's that?"

"Liars," I said. "Greedy, power-hungry liars."

She nodded but didn't look convinced.

"What is it?" I asked.

"We still don't know why the Regency is willing to go to such drastic measures to cover up the existence of the hullen. It concerns me."

"You saw the hullen with your own eyes," I reminded her. "That's what really matters."

"I suppose so," she said.

"Your mother will be safe," I assured her. "Hundreds of people work at the *Telene Herald*. No one will know you were involved. Just make sure no one sees you."

She nodded. "If it will help Leta . . ."

"Thank you, Narena."

"Just tell me what you want it to say, and I'll have it ready by tomorrow morning."

———

Narena was true to her word. Overnight, she snuck out and used her mother's key to get into the *Telene Herald*. She wrote an article exposing the Regency for hiding the existence of the hullen and tampering with evidence to convict innocent people. The language in the article was explosive and was sure to elicit a heated response in inmates who'd been locked in Vardean for years. She also included Leta's sketch of the hullen on the front page. With the article printed in the *Telene Herald*, no one would question its credibility.

I ripped out the pages from one of my law books and folded copies of the newspaper inside. They would hardly look out of place for an apprentice lawyer.

Now it was time to put my plan into motion. But first, I had someone to visit.

A CLOSED sign hung on the door to the Edem Legal Aid office. But even on a Saturday morning, I knew better.

"Graymond!" I rapped on the door. "Let me in!"

I heard footsteps before the door opened.

I nearly recoiled in shock.

I'd never seen Graymond out of his perfectly tailored blue suits; his white T-shirt was ratty and his pants were ill-fitting. His salt-and-pepper beard was unkempt, and his brown skin had lost some of its warmth.

"Cayder?" His eyes were red and hooded as he took me in. "What are you doing here?"

"I wanted to see how you were."

Graymond moved to the side and allowed me in.

While the office had never been well maintained, it looked like a tornado had swept through all the files.

"I'm looking for a loophole," he said, gesturing to the mess. "Something we can use to discredit the Regency."

We weren't so different in our thinking. As much as I wanted to confide in Graymond, telling him about my plan to break Leta and Elenora free, I didn't want him getting in more trouble because of my family. I had to keep another secret. Tell another lie.

"Did you find anything?"

Graymond ran his hands down his face with a sigh. "Without a ruling monarch, the Regency are in control of Telene's legal system. There's nothing we can do."

"I'm sorry." I hated thinking that he might lose the job he'd dedicated his life to.

"You're sorry?" he asked. "I'm the one who should be sorry. I never should have taken on Leta's case. I should have realized the dangers of the prosecution uncovering the truth."

"You were trying to help my father," I said. "You didn't know what was going to happen."

He let out a labored breath. "I am a man of the law. I never should have let him into that cell in the first place."

"Is that why you had a falling-out with him all those years ago?" I asked.

"Yes. I told your father to admit what he'd done, but he refused—even though he knew I was right."

"It's not your fault."

"I'm so sorry I failed your sister," Graymond said. "And you. I've only ever wanted to protect your family."

I swallowed down a lump in my throat. "I know, Uncle Graymond. I know."

He looked at my bag and my suit. "Where are you off to?" He shook his head. "Don't answer that. I know exactly where you're going."

I hoped he couldn't also tell what I was planning.

"I need to see her," I said. "The Regency tried to have her killed."

Graymond swore. "We need to get her out of there."

"We will." I was already working on it.

"Is there anything I can do to help?" he asked.

"There's one thing," I said. "I need a token to get back in."

"They took mine," he said, a shadow crossing his face. "But Olin has one for when he assists me."

Speaking of Olin. "How is everyone?"

"I gave them all paid leave," he said with a shrug. "We have no trials to work on." He rummaged through a drawer in Olin's desk. "*Ah!*"

He pulled out the red token and pressed it into my hand. "Stay strong, son. Have faith."

I used to have faith. Faith in the justice system. In Vardean. In trials.

But that faith had failed me.

"Thank you, Uncle Graymond."

Now I had to take matters into my own hands.

### Step One: Get a Knife

---

When I met up with Kema at the security checkpoint, she searched my bag, as she had on my first day at Vardean, and I handed over Olin's token.

"Any updates?" I whispered as she leaned in to check my jacket pockets.

"She's still in the infirmary," Kema whispered back, not halting her movements. "She's doing much better. Yarlyn plans to move her to her cell on Monday."

I had two days to figure out the rest of my plan.

Kema was chewing on her bottom lip.

"What is it?" I asked.

"The Regency have agents on the top floor now," she said. "They're guarding the princess."

"Shit."

"My thoughts exactly."

"What do we do?"

She nodded to some prison employees approaching. "Meet me in the foyer before you head home for the day. We'll talk then."

I headed to Graymond's office to keep out of sight. I didn't want Yarlyn to know I was here. While I desperately wanted to visit Leta and see how she was recovering, I had to focus on the escape plan.

I pulled the scrunched-up poster of Vardean from my bag and flattened it as best I could on Graymond's desk and labeled the important parts of the prison.

There was only one way in and out of Vardean, and that was via the gondola. And the only way to get to the gondola was via the foyer's front doors. And there was a guard on each side of the gate—most likely to become a Regency agent in the next few days. There had to be another way.

Elle and Leta were both on the top floor. Could we break the glass ceiling and escape that way? I didn't know how thick the glass was, but I had to imagine it wouldn't shatter easily. And if

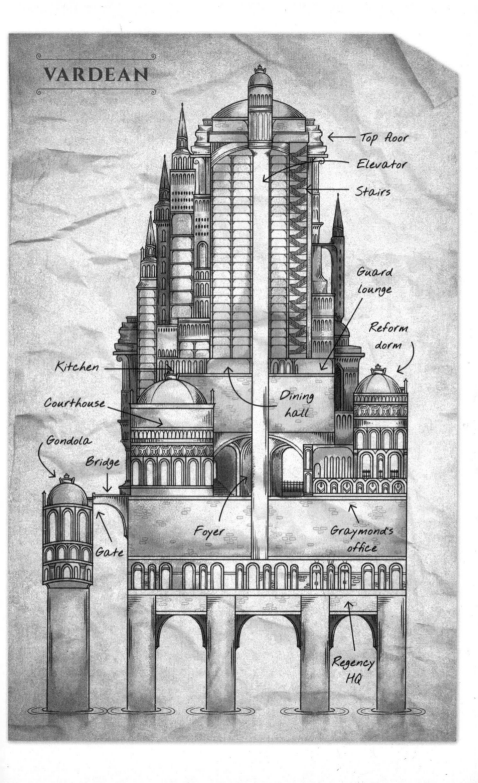

VARDEAN

Top floor

Elevator

Stairs

Guard lounge

Reform dorm

Kitchen

Courthouse

Dining hall

Gondola

Bridge

Foyer

Graymond's office

Gate

Regency HQ

we did break it, we'd be arrested by one of the Regency agents before we could go free.

While there were slits in the rock in each cell to allow for some airflow, they weren't large enough to squeeze through or push any kind of excavation weapon in from the outside. And knives and forks would do nothing against the dense stone walls.

The laundry was washed on the ground floor, behind the courthouses. Meals were prepared in the kitchen, on level one. Only food and cleaning supplies were brought into Vardean, which were transported via gondola on Mondays. That would be the best time to escape, as the glass gondolas would be full of empty crates and boxes to hide in once they had been unpacked.

And yet we still needed to walk out the front door and along the bridge to the gondola station. Only a guard or an employee could leave without any trouble. Even with Kema on our side, she couldn't escort three criminals outside of Vardean without being detained.

Which left only one option. Disguise Elle and Leta as prison guards.

# CHAPTER 36

# JEY

Cayder's guard friend visited Jey before lunch on Saturday. She was carrying a towel and sporting a pissed-off expression.

"Here," she said, shoving the towel through the bars and flicking her white curls back from her face. "Take better care of it, or you won't get another replacement." She stormed off before any of the newly placed Regency agents could question her actions.

Jey appreciated her performance. It reminded him of his days on the stage. A successful act was all about commitment.

He picked up the towel and walked to the far corner of his cell before unrolling it. Inside were newspapers with an article exposing the Regency. Jey grinned. He had to give it to Cayder; it wasn't such a terrible plan. In fact, Jey wished it had been his idea to discredit the Regency and his father's legacy. Inside the wad of papers was a note.

*Dear Mr. Ryge,*

*Please arrange for a sharp knife to be delivered at your earliest convenience. For your troubles, I provide the following newspaper articles. Please distribute these to the inmates at the food hall on Monday night.*

*Thanking you for your time and assistance,*
*Jey Bueter*

Jey couldn't help but laugh. It was so formal and *polite*. If Cayder had known Ryge, he would have realized how ridiculous this letter was—something Jey would never write. He hoped Ryge wouldn't question it.

When Jey's lunch tray arrived, he forced himself to eat the food even though his stomach felt as though he'd swallowed rocks. He hadn't felt this ill since his father died and the days after.

Eight weeks on, and Jey still wasn't sure how to process his father's death. He'd always hoped he'd have more time—hoped that eventually his father would learn to care for him. But after two years of living together, they'd grown no closer, and Jey still didn't understand what made his father tick.

For his mother, family had been everything. She'd instilled that notion into Jey ever since he was a child. Being together, sharing their lives, that was what mattered. Everything else was secondary.

His father, however, saw things differently. All that mattered was the Regency and the work they did. All that mattered was Telene. His father had this sense of purpose and impossible level of ambition that prevented him from living in the moment and seeing what he had in front of him.

Jey supposed, for a man so obsessed with time-altering magic, it made sense that he would never be living in the present and would forever be looking forward, or back.

And that had been his undoing.

Once Jey had swallowed the final mouthful of vegetable stew, he placed the newspapers underneath the upturned bowl. The bowl being turned upside down would signal to the dishwasher that a deal was to be made. They would then speak to Ryge and organize the drop-off. Jey placed the silver cloche on top to conceal the smuggled papers.

The rest of the day moved painfully slowly. Jey hated not knowing what time it was. He tried napping, but any noise woke him and made him think of his father.

His father had despised noise. He needed complete silence to work. On the rare occasions that his father was home, Jey would tiptoe around the house—desperate to earn his approval. So much so, Jey became a specter in his own home, too scared to make a noise and be noticed by a man who clearly wanted him gone.

Now that the moment to flee Vardean was upon him, Jey grew nervous. And he wasn't the nervous type. Nerves hindered your thoughts and actions. He'd learned that from his drama teacher.

He had to remain confident. Calm. But as the minutes ticked by, his resolve began to shake and shatter.

His thoughts swirled so loudly in his head, he almost missed the sound of the food slot opening for his evening meal.

Jey made himself count to ten before getting off the bunk. He felt the guard's eyes on him as she walked away. Every action from here on out mattered more than the past eighteen years combined. He couldn't screw this up.

As Jey approached the tray, he reminded himself that it might take Ryge longer to arrange a weapon or that the flipped bowl might have been missed by a new dishwasher and the newspapers might now be mush in a tub of soapy water. Many things could have gone wrong.

Jey believed in positive thinking, but this was too important. He needed to set expectations. If he didn't receive the knife today, there would be another day.

Jey *had* planned to stay in Vardean as punishment for his father's death, but his plans had changed mere days into his incarceration, and he'd been plotting how to escape since. Now that Cayder had dangled the literal key to his freedom in front of him, he would not let it go. After all, he shared his father's tenacity, perhaps their only shared trait.

He removed the silver cloche from the tray. Underneath sat a large piece of fowl.

That was it. No vegetables. No bread. Nothing.

Jey cursed. How many times did he have to tell the kitchen he didn't eat meat? Then it dawned on him that there was also no knife. He let out a frustrated breath. Still, that didn't mean that the contraband was uncovered.

He sat with his back against the bars. He wasn't hungry, and he certainly wasn't going to eat the fowl.

Jey had lifted the tray, prepared to shove the plate back through the food slot, when he noticed something. The skin of the fowl had been cooked in a peculiar way. A large blackened circle with two smaller circles and a curved line. Jey rotated the plate.

The burns formed a smiley face.

It had to be a message from Ryge, but what was the message? That the knife was on the way? Why hadn't he given him anything else to accompany his meal? Why no potatoes or vegetables?

Jey smiled down at the crispy fowl skin in understanding.

He never would have paid attention to the fowl if there had been other food with it. Which could only mean—

He ripped the fowl breast in half. Inside, there was a flash of silver.

A knife.

# CHAPTER 37

# CAYDER

### *Step Two: Obtain the Disguises*

Later on Saturday night, I met Kema in the foyer. Her usual neat white curls were in disarray as though she'd been tugging at them. Her back was ramrod straight, and her eyes darted around the room until she fixed upon me.

"Follow me." She led the way through the back hallways of the courtroom till we reached the guard lounge.

Kema used her key to unlock the door. Inside wasn't anything elaborate. The circular room was surrounded by lockers with a few banged-up tables and chairs arranged in the middle. The furniture looked like it'd been around for almost as long as Vardean had. Luckily, the room was empty.

"Would you like something to eat?" Kema bounced on the balls of her feet. She looked as nervous as I felt.

"I don't think I can stomach anything right now."

She grimaced. "I haven't eaten anything all day."

We sat around one of the small tables. "Has the eagle landed in the hutch?" I asked, wanting to remain vague in case another guard walked in.

"Huh?"

"You know . . ." I waved my hands around.

"Oh!" she said. "Yes, but we've got to work on your code. Eagles don't live in hutches. You're thinking of rabbits."

"Of course."

"And there's no one else in here," she said.

"Another good point." I grinned sheepishly. We weren't off to a good start.

"What's the plan, then, Boy Wonder? Jey is going to get the knife and then what? Take you hostage?"

I nodded. "Something like that. We need Yarlyn to get close enough to Jey that he can steal the key."

"Can we trust him?"

"I hope so." Jey changing his mind about wanting to be in Vardean was concerning, but I didn't have time to question his motives. Leta would be returned to her cell on Monday.

"And then?" Kema asked.

"We need to disguise Leta and the princess as guards." I gestured around the room. "I'm hoping you can help me with that."

"That, Boy Wonder, I can." She leaped from the table and started rummaging through a hamper. "These uniforms need to be cleaned by the laundry. We're not allowed to wear our uniforms outside Vardean." She pulled out a few different sizes. "These should fit Leta and the princess. You should wear one as well so no one questions why you're still here."

I nodded. "I'll smuggle the uniform in under my clothes, but how will we get the uniforms to the others?"

"Do you have a bag?" she asked.

I handed over my satchel, and she pulled out all my books and placed the folded uniforms inside. "Bring the bag to the top floor on Monday and then leave the rest to me."

"Kema—wait," I said. "I appreciate everything you've done for me and Leta, but you don't have to do this. I know we were friends as kids, but that doesn't mean you have to risk your job, your freedom, for us. Unless this is revenge against the Regency because of what they did to your father?"

She took in a deep breath and exhaled slowly. "Did I ever tell you why I started working here?"

"Because of Graymond?" I guessed.

She shook her head, her lips pressed together. "A friend of mine was arrested."

"Oh."

"The only way I could visit her was to work here."

"Is she still here? Or has she been released?"

Kema rubbed the bridge of her nose, reminding me of her father. "She lasted two years in this place," she said, closing her eyes. "She didn't want to spend her life in here. And she was refused parole."

I didn't push for more details. "I'm so sorry, Kema."

She opened her eyes. "So am I."

"Why did you stay here?" I asked. "After she passed away?"

Kema swallowed roughly. "I hadn't paid my penance."

"I don't understand."

"Do you remember the incident near the Royal Gardens five years ago?" She hunched forward like a broken doll.

"The explosion that killed the king and queen?" Elle's parents. Killed in an instant. All because rebels wanted to prove that edem could be used in everyday life. That balance was needed, not rigid restrictions. The rebels believed small amounts would keep people happy. They said it would help Telene become a more stable nation.

It did the opposite. After the explosion, sentencing for edem crimes was even more severe.

Kema bit her lip and nodded.

"Was your friend a part of the protest?" The trial had been the largest case in Crown Court history. It was all over the newspapers for months.

"Yes." Kema hung her head. "But she wasn't alone." When she raised her head, a tear slipped down her cheek.

I leaned forward. "Are you saying that you . . . ?"

She wrung her hands. When she placed them on the table, I realized she'd been wiping makeup from her skin. Across her hands was a network of gray lines, as through someone had taken a hammer to her skin, shattering it into pieces like the edem balloon had shattered the cobblestones on the street that day.

"I was one of the rebels," she said. "But I managed to get away while the Regency arrested the others."

I glanced at the death echo marking her hands. "How did you get this job?"

"My father," she said with a nod. "And waterproof makeup."
She made to hide her hands under the table, but I gripped on to
them.

"Graymond knows what you did?"

She nodded.

I remembered Graymond talking about second chances and
not being punished for one mistake. I thought he was referring to
Jey, but had he been talking about Kema all along?

"Kema—you don't have to spend your life working here
because you weren't arrested. You're allowed to move on."

"I know," she said. "It's not that. I want to spend my time
here to help people who weren't as lucky as me. People who were
caught. They need someone to look out for them." She smiled.
"Like your sister. Like you."

"Now you want to throw it all away?" I asked. "You know
Vardean will never let you work here if they realize you helped me."

"I don't want to, not when the Regency is in charge. My plan
was flawed," she admitted. "If innocent people are getting locked
in here without the chance for a trial, then what can I possibly
do to help them? How can I ensure they survive this horrid place
when people like Leta are being poisoned?"

I understood her anger, but I wasn't sure Graymond would
agree. "What would your father say if he knew you were helping me?"

She smirked. "He'd tell me to screw my head on right. But
secretly, he'd be happy." She shrugged. "Someone has to fix
what's going on in here."

"Elle," I said. "I mean, the princess. She's the only one who has the power to rectify what's broken."

"You get this little dimple right"—she poked the side of my face—"*there* whenever you talk about the princess. You like her."

My cheeks heated. "It doesn't matter what I feel. What matters is we get her and my sister out of here."

"Agreed. I'll see you on Monday," she said. "Try to get some rest before then."

I nodded, but I didn't plan to rest. I needed to memorize the prison's layout so nothing could derail my plans.

There was no room for error. Either we all got out, or we died trying.

It was time for:

### Step Three: Steal Yarlyn's Key

# CHAPTER 38

# PRINCESS ELENORA

Elenora sat in her black-and-white dress on her cell bunk, her mask on her face, still as a statue.

*This is all I'll ever be,* she thought. *A figurehead.*

Powerless. Trapped. Alone.

Over the past few days, she'd allowed herself to consider a different future. One where she wasn't stranded on the castle isle. One where she wasn't "the princess." But Elle. And she wasn't alone.

But that was over. She would never be anything but what she was. What fate had determined for her. What the Regency had decided she would be.

And she would never see Cayder again.

The emptiness in Elenora's heart had been patched together piece by piece with Cayder's visits. Elenora knew she would never be whole, that she would feel the agony of her brother's loss every day, like she felt the agony of her parents' deaths. But as time went by, that pain would lessen and other distractions would push to the forefront, and everything else to the background.

Cayder was such a distraction.

Now the Regency had also taken him away.

Yarlyn had continued to bring Elenora her daily meals, but the superintendent's anger at the princess had seemed to wane. On Saturday evening, Yarlyn unlocked the internal barred door and carefully placed the tray inside the cell. Elenora wasn't sure what had changed. Still, she did not move. She would not eat. She would not drink.

Elenora willed herself away from her body, her cell, her life.

That night, Elenora faded in and out of consciousness. Still, she always woke to find herself on her bunk. Stuck in Vardean.

By Sunday, Elenora started to hallucinate from lack of water.

She saw her brother, his red hair perfectly coiffed, wearing his regal gray suit with gleaming brass buttons down the front.

"Erimen!" Elenora whispered. "You're here!"

She expected him to walk forward and embrace her. But he shook his head sadly.

"Is this what our parents raised you to be?" he asked, a sneer upon his face.

"No!" Elenora said. "I'm not a criminal. I didn't hurt you. I was trying to—"

"That's not what I meant," he snapped. That was when Elenora should have realized she was imagining Erimen, for her brother would have never raised his voice at her. "You have given up. You're a coward."

"No," Elenora repeated. But she knew his words to be true.

She *had* given up. She had placed her fate in the hands of others. As she always had. That was the life of a princess. Your life was not your own. It belonged to the people.

"I'm sorry," she whispered. Tears rolled down her cheeks; her breath was hoarse inside her mask.

Erimen knelt before her. "Don't be sorry. *Get up.* And get out of here."

"How?" she asked. "No one is here to help me."

"Help yourself," Erimen said, his gray eyes blazing. "Do whatever it takes. Make our parents proud."

Elenora reached for her brother and fell forward on the cell stones. The fall snapped her out of her daze.

Her brother wasn't here to help. No one was.

Elenora ripped off her mask and crawled toward the internal doors. She took a long drink from the cup of water and chewed on the stale roll from last night's dinner.

She couldn't give up. Not now. Not ever.

The Regency couldn't hide in the lower levels of Vardean forever.

The princess of Telene was coming for them.

# CHAPTER 39

## LETA

It wasn't until Monday morning that Leta gained enough strength to stand on her own. Whoever had tried to poison her knew their stuff.

*Or not,* she thought. For she was still alive.

*Take that, Regency assholes.*

Cayder had vowed to get her out of Vardean, but she wasn't sure what he had planned. He hadn't come to visit her since Friday, and now that Leta could eat and drink, and stand, on her own, the doctor had discharged her back to her cell.

Leta didn't want to return to the top floor. She'd heard the whisperings around the infirmary that the Regency had sent their own agents. She was safer down here, but the doctors needed her bed. Someone was always getting into a scuffle during mealtimes.

When the moment came to return to her cell, Leta was surprised to see Kema pull back the curtains.

"Time to go home," Kema said cheerily.

Leta pushed herself up from her bed. "Must I?" she asked wearily. She still wasn't back to her normal strength.

"You must!" Kema said. She winked, then stooped to place her shoulder under Leta's arm to ensure she didn't fall. Kema was a much taller girl, and Leta was pretty sure Kema could carry her, if she needed to.

"What's going on?" she asked as Kema led her to the elevator. Another guard joined them, and Kema shook her head slightly.

They couldn't talk. Not here.

Once they reached the top floor, Regency agents swarmed them, their gray cloaks trailing behind them like a silver stream.

Leta couldn't catch her breath. Had one of these agents poisoned her? As soon as she was alone in her cell, how would she be safe?

"It's okay," Kema whispered. Leta knew Kema could feel her trembling. "I'm going to be up here the entire time. No one is going to hurt you."

Leta wanted to believe that. She pulled the thin material of her infirmary gown around herself, hating feeling so exposed.

Leta waited for an agent to lunge at her. Plunge a knife into her chest. She waited for a blow to strike her across the temple. She waited for hands to cover her throat. She waited for the end.

"Almost there," Kema said, her voice soothing. Kema unlocked her cell, and Leta jumped inside like a frightened rabbit.

"Here," Kema said. "Your clothes."

Leta took the bundle of material.

"Don't change until tonight. I have a feeling it's going to be a chilly evening." Kema winked. "You'll know when the time is right."

After Kema left, Leta unrolled the clothes. She was surprised to find a guard uniform and not an inmate jumpsuit.

She ran her hand along the Vardean emblem on the peaked cap.

"What are you up to, Cayder?" she whispered.

# CHAPTER 40

# JEY

Jey's dinner was pushed through the food slot, signaling the beginning of the end. Monday night, time to put on the performance of a lifetime.

Jey took a bite out of the bread roll, because he wasn't about to let that go to waste, then pulled the knife from inside his jumpsuit. He twirled it in his hand, counting the seconds until he heard the clang of the elevator door closing and the *click click click* of the chain.

He began to count as the elevator rose.

*One. Two. Three. Four.*

It could be a guard escorting a prisoner . . . Or it could be Cayder.

Jey continued until he counted to four hundred—the top floor.

"Here goes everything," Jey whispered.

Shortly after the elevator stopped and the metal door screeched open, Cayder's dark coif was visible as he walked around the landing toward Jey's cell. Cayder paused outside the bars but kept his eyes firmly straight ahead. Even though Cayder didn't look in his direction, Jey could feel the electricity snapping between them.

This was it.

Jey fisted the knife in his hand. He was ready.

"Hey, you," a voice called out from down the landing. A Regency agent who wore his cloak as though it were lined with real silver approached. "What are you doing here, kid?"

Cayder shrugged theatrically. "I want to see my sister. She just left the infirmary."

The agent threw his head back and laughed, as though it was the most preposterous thing he'd ever heard. "Her trial is over. No visitors on the top floor. Now, leave!"

"Fine," Cayder grumbled. *"Oh!"* He pointed at his shoe dramatically. "My shoelace is undone. How annoying!"

Jey had to clench his jaw to stop from groaning in response. Cayder was a terrible actor. He never would've made it on the streets. Nothing about Cayder was subtle.

Cayder placed his bag on the ground and started undoing an already-tied lace. Jey mentally cursed. If you were going to con someone, you had to complete the required prep. Cayder should've untied his laces *before* he'd come up here. Jey hoped this plan wouldn't fall apart based on Cayder's poor acting.

By the time Jey reached the bars, Cayder was only halfway through tying his shoelace as though he were three years old and had yet to figure out the method.

Jey grabbed Cayder by the collar and jerked him backward into the bars.

"Oomph!" Cayder cried as his head clanged into the metal wall.

Jey wouldn't allow Cayder's terrible acting to ruin this opportunity. The boy had to feel some pain.

"Don't move!" Jey yelled so the Regency agents farther down the landing could hear. "Or I'll slit your throat." He pressed the knife against Cayder's neck—his Adam's apple bobbed; he was probably worried Jey might actually draw blood.

*Good.* Real fear would help sell this.

The agents sprang into action; four surrounded Jey's cell.

"Please don't kill me!" Cayder said, his voice meek.

"Let the boy go," one agent demanded.

"Or what?" Jey cackled. "You already have me on the top floor. What else can you do to me?"

"We can do many things," she replied, "to make your life more miserable. Just try us." Her bright blue eyes were like lightning in a storm, her nose proud, and grin severe.

Jey pointed with his free hand to the knife against Cayder's throat. "*Details*, please."

Cayder whimpered. "Don't let him hurt me!"

"Shut up!" Jey spat. "Let the adults talk."

Jey pressed the knife a little more into his neck without splitting the skin, and Cayder was quickly silenced.

"What do you want?" the agent asked.

Jey was tempted to reveal exactly what he wanted, but that would give away the entire plan. If Jey wanted to escape, he needed to do it without anyone knowing. He needed Yarlyn. He needed her key.

Which meant he needed to put on a show.

"First of all," Jey said. "No more fowl. *Seriously.* How many times do I have to inform Yarlyn that I don't eat meat? Frankly, it's inconsiderate."

"Are you serious?" the agent asked. "You're making food demands?"

"No," Jey said. "I'd also like a pillow." He rolled his head from side to side, careful not to prick Cayder with the knife. Well, not *too* careful. "I have a sensitive neck."

"This is a joke," another Regency agent grumbled.

"You should try sleeping in here," Jey said. "You'll find it's no joke."

The agents looked at Jey as though he'd lost his mind.

"If we organize these two things," the first agent asked, "you'll let this boy go?"

Jey could see the tension in Cayder's posture, which had nothing to do with a knife being held to his throat. They needed more than that.

"Did I say I was finished?" Jey tsked. "That's the first two items on my list. *Boy,*" he said to Cayder, "retrieve the list from my left pocket." Cayder reached down with shaking fingers— perhaps Jey was playing this part a little too well. Cayder was scared of him.

Cayder pulled out a scroll of toilet paper and unrolled it.

Unlike Cayder, Jey had prepared himself for this moment. Props were vital to a believable performance.

"There's still ninety-eight demands to go," Jey said.

"What did you write with?" one of the agents asked in horror.

"What do you think?" Jey grinned wickedly. He wasn't about to tell them that the brown color was thanks to gravy.

"Help!" Cayder yelled, dropping the list. "Please!"

Cayder's cries had drawn interest from the inmates on the levels below. They began hollering and cheering. The wave of noise passed down level by level. While they couldn't see what was going on at the top floor, they were encouraged by the racket. Plus, it was something to do. *Anything* to ease the boredom. The inmates began to stamp their feet and bang against the bars.

It didn't take long before the elevator rose once more; this time the superintendent was among her guards. Her short silver hair fell in sheets around her sharp jaw, and her brown eyes glittered in the dark. A small smile whispered across her face as she approached. Jey could tell she lived for moments like this.

Well, so did he.

"Mr. Bueter," the superintendent said with a nod. "Good evening."

"Superintendent Yarlyn," Jey said, knife still at Cayder's throat. "Evening to you as well."

"What's that?" She eyed the toilet paper on the floor.

"His list of demands," the woman with the vibrant blue eyes said.

"Let the boy go," Yarlyn said. "And I'll make sure your demands are met."

"How do I know you won't just flush my important document down the toilet?"

Yarlyn didn't flinch. "You have my word."

"*Ahhh.* Does any sweeter relationship than a prisoner and their superintendent exist?" he mused.

Yarlyn snatched the strip of toilet paper from the ground.

*Close, but not close enough,* he thought.

He watched Yarlyn read through his scribblings, waiting until she got to the last item.

"Freedom?" she read out loud. "You want me to release you?"

Jey nodded. "After careful consideration, I've decided that prison life isn't a good fit for me."

Yarlyn kept her composure, which Jey had to give her credit for. "Just so that I'm clear," she said. "You'll only let Cayder go if we release you from Vardean?"

"Yes," Jey said solemnly. "Now, make it snappy, as I'd like to be home in time for supper."

Jey pictured the face of his girlfriend, Nettie, when he thought of the word *home.* She was his home. Without his mother and father, she was all he had left. He needed to see her, at least one more time.

"Help me!" Cayder said to Yarlyn. "Do *something!*"

As the additional guards surrounded him, Jey said, "Come any closer, and I'll end him!"

"Okay, okay," Yarlyn said, her palms up. "Let's slow down for a moment. Regency agents—" She nodded to those who had gathered. "Take a step back. We don't want any bloodshed."

Jey could tell from the look on a few of the agents' faces that they would have been more than happy to watch Cayder bleed. But this was Yarlyn's prison. For now.

"Open the cell door!" Yarlyn commanded.

Kema stepped forward and opened the door, giving Jey a wide berth so he could walk through.

Jey kept the knife at Cayder's throat as they inched along the bars and out the open door.

"Now," Yarlyn said, her hand out. "Give me the knife."

Jey let out a real laugh. "You're kidding, right? This"—he nodded his head to Cayder—"is my leverage. And I'm not letting go of it until I smell fresh air."

"All right," Yarlyn said. "We'll follow you down to the station. No sudden movements."

Cayder let out a ridiculous whimper, and Jey was tempted to kick him in the shins.

"Sounds fair to me," Jey said. He pretended not to notice the knowing look exchanged between a guard and Yarlyn. They weren't letting Jey anywhere near a gondola.

Which was fine by him. He had other plans to see to.

As Jey and Cayder shuffled toward the elevator, Jey shifted the knife farther away from Cayder's neck. Yarlyn took that as a slipup and pounced.

She dove toward Jey, shoving him to the side. Jey thudded to the ground, close to the edge of the landing. The knife fell to the floor below. He heard the distant *plink* as it hit the rock floor down on the ground level.

He twisted to face Yarlyn. She was standing over him, her face exultant.

She was still too far away. He swept her leg from under her.

Yarlyn crumpled to the ground, and Jey launched onto her back, reaching for her belt and the key.

The other guards, and agents, sprang at him. Jey was yanked backward by one Regency agent, while another threw a punch, connecting with Jey's face.

His vision blurred as tears sprang to his eyes, but he could still see Cayder—or rather, two Cayders. Both of them smiled.

Jey pulled away, desperately scrabbling for Cayder.

"You filthy little son of a—" He spat into Cayder's face.

In the chaos, no one heard the sound of something small and metal hitting the ground.

The agents piled on Jey once more, tugging his hands behind his back and shackling them together.

As Jey was pushed onto the grimy floor by the superintendent, he saw Cayder pick up the key that he'd spat at him.

Jey grinned a bloody grin.

# CHAPTER 41

# CAYDER

*Step Four: Set the Princess Free*

While Yarlyn and the Regency agents detained Jey, Kema sidled in behind me. She took my satchel off my shoulder, grabbed the key from my outstretched hand and slipped away from the group.

"I demand retribution!" I said, rubbing at my neck where Jey had nicked it. He'd played his part a little too well. I was relieved he was detained.

But a promise was a promise. I'd give him his key before we escaped.

"Retribution?" Jey side-eyed me. "I'm already locked up in here!"

He kicked one of the Regency agents loose, and then Jey flipped onto his back.

"Pin him down!" Yarlyn roared.

I risked looking over my shoulder.

Two guards exited the princess's cell. *Kema and Elle.*

I swallowed down my exultation when I caught a flash of Elle's smile before I turned back to the fray.

"How am I meant to eat?" Jey asked, jerking at his binds.

"You should've thought of that before," the superintendent said. Not a single hair on her head had shifted out of place in the scuffle.

One of the Regency agents shoved the toilet paper into Jey's mouth. "Eat this!"

Kema and Elle joined us quietly. I held out my hand behind my back, and Kema placed the key into my palm.

"I'm sorry," I said to Yarlyn, stepping in close behind her and hooking her key onto her belt. "I should've been more careful up here."

"You shouldn't even be here," she replied. "How many times do I have to tell you to leave? I have half a mind to lock *you* in a cell, for your own protection, if nothing else."

I tensed. She wouldn't, would she?

"I'll escort him out of here," Kema said. She placed a hand on my shoulder. "I'll make sure he's on the next gondola home."

Yarlyn glanced at Kema, looking right by Elenora, who stood beside me, her cap pulled down to cover her face—a face that few people in this prison had even seen.

"Fine." Yarlyn looked annoyed and exhausted. "I don't want any more trouble tonight, *clear?*"

I nodded. "No more trouble from me."

"Get back to your posts," Yarlyn said to her guards. "And lock this kid with a death wish away."

My stomach clenched, thinking I was about to be hauled off my feet, but she was referring to Jey. While he was pushed back into his cell, his face contorted with fury. If I hadn't known any better, I'd have thought he hated me.

Perhaps he did.

"What are you waiting for?" Yarlyn asked Kema. "Get Cayder out of here."

Kema opened her mouth to reply, but she was cut off by a Regency agent bellowing from down the landing.

"The inmate is gone!" The agent was outside the princess's cell.

We followed Yarlyn as she investigated the agent's claims. "What?" the superintendent demanded. "How is that possible?" She reached for her key on her belt to find it was right where she'd left it. Kema and I exchanged a look.

"No," Yarlyn said, mostly to herself. "I locked the internal door before I left her dinner. I *always* lock the door. Check the other cells!"

Kema ran to Leta's cell, and I saw a glimpse of Leta's round face through the bars. "Leta Broduck," she shouted back to Yarlyn. "Still here, ma'am."

"Jey Bueter is right where we left him," an agent with bright blue eyes said.

"Good," Yarlyn said with a nod.

One of the Regency agents closed in on Yarlyn, a menacing look upon his severe features. His black brows were like thick gashes across his pale face, his nose sharp like a knife. "Where is she?" he asked.

Yarlyn glanced at the silver-cloaked agents that had surrounded her. For the first time, I saw fear flicker behind her careful facade. "I don't know. I lock the cell every time I leave food in there. No one else has been allowed to visit since last Tuesday. No one else has a key."

"Find her," the Regency agent said with a jerk of his proud chin. "Or you're out of a job."

I hoped that was the worst outcome. Yarlyn wasn't the nicest person in the world, but I didn't want to unleash the fury of the Regency upon her. We all knew what they were willing to do.

Yarlyn cocked her head to the side and inched closer. They would have been nose-to-nose if Yarlyn had been a head or so taller. "You'd like that, wouldn't you? Then you could take over my prison. Are you sure *you* didn't free her?"

"We don't have time for this," the agent replied. "Find the prin—the inmate, or else."

The man started to walk away and nearly ran into Elenora, the very inmate he was looking for.

Elenora ducked her head. "Apologies, sir."

I held my breath, but he merely waved her apology away. "Find her! Now!"

Yarlyn turned to address her guards. "Sweep the prison. But be discreet, we don't want to cause a scene; you know how the inmates can get if they smell trouble. Kema, you stay up here. The rest of you, go!"

Some guards took to the stairs; others headed toward the elevator.

"What do we do now?" Elenora asked; her face radiated hope.

"Step five," I said. "Free Leta."

# CHAPTER 42

# LETA

Leta had pulled on her uniform when Kema had come by to check that she was still locked in her cell.

*Now,* Kema had mouthed.

The uniform was too tight around her hips and bust and pooled around her ankles, but she didn't care.

She was getting out of Vardean.

But first she had to wait for the guards to clear the top floor, per the superintendent's instructions. Leta climbed on her bunk and covered herself with a sheet, in case any guards or Regency agents checked in on her.

After what felt like hours but was likely only minutes, her cell door was unlocked.

"Cayder!" Leta jumped up from her bunk and threw her arms around her brother. "You're here!"

"I promised you I'd get you out of here."

"That you did."

"No Broduck left behind," he said with a grin.

Tears flooded her vision. "Thank you."

Behind Cayder stood another guard with a long blond plait, a satchel on her shoulder.

"Princess?" Leta asked.

She nodded. "I'm so sorry about what happened to you."

"And I'm sorry to hear about the king. I always liked him."

The princess closed her eyes for a moment, as though the mention of her brother was physically painful.

"What's the plan?" Leta asked Cayder.

"We need to stay up here for the moment," he said. "But first I need to give this key to Jey Bueter."

"Bueter?" The princess flinched. "As in Dr. Bueter? Why is he here?"

"Jey killed his father almost two months ago," Cayder said. "He helped us get Yarlyn's key, and I promised I'd give him his cell key in return."

"Are you sure?" the princess asked, frowning.

Cayder shrugged. "As sure as I can be trusting a criminal."

He left the cell, and Leta stared after her brother, confused. Cayder must be mistaken . . .

"What?" she heard a voice ask her brother from down the landing. "You're going to leave me like this?"

Leta inched closer to the voice.

"I have your key," Cayder replied to the unseen inmate. "That was the deal."

"How can I escape with my hands tied behind my back?"

Cayder shrugged. "That's not my problem."

"Wait!" Leta cried as Cayder moved to throw the key through the bars.

She rushed to the cell and peered in. A tall boy lay on his stomach, his hands shackled behind his back. He'd rolled to face Cayder, his lip split and bloodied. His eyes flicked over to hers.

"Jey?" Leta asked. Her heart thudded in her chest.

*How? Why?*

Cayder exchanged a glance between the two of them. "You know each other?"

Jey's grin stretched like a lazy cat in the summer sun. "Why do you think I'm here, mate?"

Cayder shook his head. "I don't understand."

"What are you doing here, Jey?" Leta demanded.

Jey shrugged awkwardly from the floor. "Surprise?"

"Surprise that you're locked up in Vardean too?" Leta cocked her head. "And what are they?" She pointed to the echo marks across his arms. "What in burning shadows is going on?"

"I can explain," Jey said.

"Please do," Cayder said. "And start with how you know my sister."

"Well, this is awkward," Jey said, squirming on the floor. "This wasn't quite how I imagined being officially introduced to my girlfriend's brother."

"Your *what?*" Cayder spun to Leta.

Leta stared down at her hands, the echo marks covered by the stolen guard gloves.

"I'm so sorry, Cayder," she said. "I should have told you the truth." She tucked her hands under her arms.

"What truth?" Cayder asked. "What are you talking about?"

Leta closed her eyes as though she couldn't face her brother when he heard all the secrets she'd been keeping:

Why she didn't tell him her informant's name. Why she claimed the bird's death had caused the death echo. Why she had headed to Ferrington in the first place.

She had killed Dr. Bueter. She had killed Jey's father.

# CHAPTER 43

# JEY

Seeing Leta again brought all those memories back. The good, the bad and the devastating.

Before Jey moved into his father's house, down the street from Broduck Manor, he'd heard about the tragedy that had befallen the Broduck family. Jey was a year above Cayder and two years above Leta at Kardelle Academy, and gossip spread around the school grounds like a virus. Most students gave the Broduck siblings a wide berth.

Jey would often see Leta walking the campus between the art and science buildings, some kind of paint smudged on her cheek or splattered on her hands. Her brother, on the other hand, was at the top of every class and the head of the Legal Studies Club— and spent lunchtimes running mock trials. He never saw Cayder on the trolley to school, as the older Broduck would arrive an hour before classes began for extra study. Jey always thought the boy tried far too hard.

Jey had attempted to strike up conversations with Leta for

weeks on the trolley ride to school. It wasn't until he mentioned his father was the Regency General that he finally gained Leta's attention. He'd mentioned in passing that his father was meeting with the king, a humble brag to try to break down her walls. He thought the comment might pique Leta's interest, as many people idolized the royal family—especially the handsome king—but it was his father that sparked her interest.

"Perhaps your father knew my mother?" She'd turned to him then, her dark eyes alight. It was the first time she'd looked at him for any length of time, and Jey felt his pulse race under her gaze. He wasn't used to someone paying such close attention to what he said. Not since his mother passed. A sad fact he knew he had in common with Leta.

But Jey couldn't walk up and ask his father about Maretta Broduck—for it would require his father to actually acknowledge his existence. The only other option was to sneak into his father's office and see what information he could find to relay to Leta.

"I propose a date," Jey said. "In return for information."

"That's bribery," Leta replied, although a smile played on her face. Jey couldn't help but stare at the bow in the middle of her top lip, this perfect curve.

Jey shook his head. "I like to think of it as an additional incentive."

"And what are the other incentives?" she asked, curious.

He puffed his chest out. "Why, me, of course."

Leta laughed, and Jey took note that her nose crinkled in a way that made him want to kiss her.

When she finally agreed to go for ice cream and a walk along the Kardelle Cliffs, she'd asked him to call her Nettie.

"It was my mother's nickname for me," she admitted with a shrug. "She used to call me 'my Lettie,' which later became Nettie. I like the idea of hearing the name again." Her smile faded.

Jey knew it was likely that Leta was using him for information on the Regency, but he thought it was a harmless curiosity. And he didn't mind being used, not if it meant spending more time with her.

Each morning, Jey would tell Leta some new piece of information about the veil as they journeyed to school. Leta would listen and smile and occasionally laugh. He loved the sound of her laugh. He hadn't heard carefree laughter in so long. Certainly not in the house of Dr. Bueter.

As time went on, they stopped talking about the Regency and Jey's father. Instead, they talked about how they dealt with the passing of their mothers and how they'd felt like different people since their deaths. Leta had found a way to cope with the grief by throwing herself into researching the veil—following in her mother's footsteps. She claimed that the result of her investigations would alter her life, and that of countless others. "My father will have to listen to me when the truth is laid out before him."

Jey couldn't understand why Leta's father, and brother, had distanced themselves from her, but he knew he wasn't the person to give advice about family dynamics.

In talking with Leta, Jey realized he hadn't dealt with his grief at all. He'd buried his feelings deep down and tried to survive the nonexistent relationship with his father.

"Don't be one of those people who hates their life but doesn't have the courage to change it," Leta would say.

Jey hadn't thought he was unhappy until Leta spelled it out so clearly. And he didn't want to be caught in the web of his father's indifference forever.

For their six-month anniversary, Jey asked Leta over to his house for dinner. His father was working late that night— according to the cook, Riva—and Jey took the opportunity to invite Leta over. It was the first time he'd invited someone inside his father's house.

Jey had given Riva the night off and prepared a native Meiyra dish of ginger-and-pepper rice and pickled torlu berries. His mother used to cook the dish for his birthday, and the smell of sweet and savory spices in the air made Jey feel as though she were in the house with him.

Leta had brought a fresh batch of crispy fried deebule for dessert, a dish her mother used to make for special occasions.

"And every second Sunday," Leta said with a laugh.

After eating, Leta had excused herself to the bathroom.

While she was away, Jey planned to tell her that he loved her. He wanted to declare his love in a way that could never be forgotten, but he wasn't sure how.

His plans were interrupted by the arrival of his father.

"Dad!" Jey exclaimed in surprise when his father passed by the dining room. "You're home."

Dr. Bueter cast a brief look in Jey's direction.

"Jey," he said in that distant way of his. "Hello."

If he noticed the flowers and candles on the table, he made

no comment. Jey was sure his father couldn't care less about his private life.

"What are you doing in here?" he heard his father ask from farther down the corridor.

Jey followed his father's voice into his office. Leta was standing behind the desk, papers in her hands.

"Where are your reports on the night Maretta Broduck died?" Leta asked, two bright splotches appearing high on her freckled cheeks.

Why was she in his father's office? Had their relationship been a ruse to get here? What information was she after?

The questions fell heavily on Jey's shoulders. Had she ever cared for him at all?

"Who are you?" his father asked. Jey was used to his father's detached stare, but this expression was different. His blue eyes burned with anger.

"Her daughter!" Leta jutted out her chin. "Why is there no report of edem usage that night from the edemmeter?"

"That is confidential. You can't be in here. Jey," he said without a glance at his son, "get her out of here."

Leta held out pages of graphs and maps. "Why are you tracking the movement of edem creatures? I thought they were just a myth?"

Dr. Bueter moved to snatch the reports from her hands, but Leta ran around the desk, out of his reach.

"Give those back to me," he snarled.

Over the two years Jey had lived under his father's roof, he'd learned his father had two default settings: annoyed and disinterested. Most of the time, he alternated between both when in Jey's presence.

This version of his father, with red flushing up his pale skin and the wide flaring of his nostrils, was unfamiliar to Jey. Whatever walls kept him distanced from his son had evaporated, like a momentary breakdown of the permacloud. His father's attention was clear and sharp.

"Leta meant no harm," Jey said, unsure how to deal with his father now that he had finally gained his attention. "She's interested in the veil. She doesn't mean—"

"Give me those files, Jey, or so help me . . ." But he didn't finish the threat.

While Jey didn't care what his father thought of him, he realized he did want his father's approval. He would never be able to introduce Leta to his mother, and no amount of cooking could ever make up for her absence.

His father was all he had left. And he wanted him to like Leta. He wanted him to care.

"Leta?" Jey held out his hand to her. "The documents."

"No." Leta moved toward the doorway. "I need to know the truth. Tell me what's going on in Ferrington. Was my mother investigating these edem creatures?"

"It's none of your business," his father seethed.

"My mother died out there." Leta held the pieces of paper close to her chest. "It *is* my business. My father, Alain Broduck, is the senior district judge," she said. "I'm sure he'll be interested to find out the Regency have no reports of edem usage on the night his wife died."

Dr. Bueter narrowed his eyes. "Are you threatening me?"

"Come on, Nettie," Jey said, hoping the nickname would snap her out of her fury. "Let's get out of here." But she wouldn't even look at him.

"If you don't tell me the truth," Leta said, "I'll find out myself. I'll go to Ferrington and uncover what the Regency is hiding, and there's nothing you can do about it!"

"You!" he said, looking at Jey properly for the first time in months. "You brought this spy into my home. Was this your idea?"

Jey burst out laughing. "My idea to what? Make you notice me? Make you care about me? Yeah, *Dad*," he said sarcastically. "You got me. I've been working the long con for the past two years."

"This is no joking matter," he said, pointing to Leta. "That girl is trouble. She could ruin everything I've built."

It wasn't lost on Jey that this was the longest conversation he'd ever had with his father.

"That's all that matters to you, isn't it?" Jey said. "Your work. The Regency. The veil. You worry so much about Telene's destruction that you don't see the world under your own roof imploding!"

"All I see is two spoiled children," he said. "Leta Broduck, correct?" He didn't wait for Leta's response. "Your father will be very disappointed to find out who you've become."

"My father cares about the truth!" Leta said, waving the documents in the air.

Dr. Bueter picked up the phone. "Either you hand over the documents, or I call my agents. You decide your future . . ."

"You can't stop me," Leta said.

"Your choice." His father shrugged, then picked up the phone and dialed a number. "Yes, it's me," he said to the person at the other end. "I need to report an edem crime committed by an intruder in my house."

"No!" Jey launched toward his father. "Leave her alone!"

His father pushed him away, and Jey stumbled backward and slammed into a bookshelf. A paperweight toppled from the shelf and struck Jey on the temple. He slumped to the floor.

"Jey!" Leta crouched by his side. "Are you all right?"

Jey's tongue felt heavy in his mouth. He couldn't move. He felt something hot trickle down his forehead, painting his vision red.

"Get up!" Leta pulled on his hand. *"Please!"*

But he couldn't. He couldn't move his arms. He could barely lift his eyelids as blood pooled across his brow.

"I'm sorry, Jey," his father said. "I can't risk it." He pressed the phone to his ear. "Yes, I'm still here . . . Yes, at the house. Come quickly. There's been an incident. My son has—"

That was when the lights went out.

Leta had grabbed a poker from the fireplace and smashed it into the office's permalamp. Jey could see edem shift in the shadows, whispering like someone lurking in a dark alleyway, beckoning.

While Jey ignored the edem, Leta did not.

"Stop him," she commanded, edem slithering up her arm like a black snake. "Make him stop!"

Edem poured like a wave toward Dr. Bueter, washing over him. When it fell away, Dr. Bueter dropped the telephone. His hand, which had been clutching the phone, had withered to skin and bone. The muscle wasted away. Seconds later, so did his skin.

Jey thought perhaps he was imagining things. His father's mouth was open mid-scream. Chunks of hair and flesh peeled away like petals in the wind. His muscles shriveled like burning paper. Finally, his father's eyes popped like overripe torlu berries.

The skeleton of his father fell forward, and Jey only just managed to roll out of the way. As the bones hit the floor, they shattered into pieces.

Jey blinked at the scene before him, waiting to wake up. But this was real.

Leta screamed over and over again.

Jey managed to push himself up using the side of the desk. He lumbered over to Leta, his head feeling as though it had cracked in two.

"What have I done?" Leta asked. She was staring at her hands; they were marked with bones as though her skin had peeled away like his father's.

*A death echo.*

Leta buckled to her knees and began sobbing.

"It's okay, Leta," he said. "It's okay." He put his arms around her, and she cried into his shoulder.

"I just wanted him to stop. I didn't mean to—I thought that if—" The rest of her words were lost to her tears. Leta had always seemed so strong, and her sorrow felt like a dagger to the chest.

"You didn't have a choice," he said. "It was your life or his."

His father never would have allowed Leta to leave. Even

though his father was rarely around, Jey immediately felt his absence.

*You have no one now,* he thought.

Only that wasn't true. He had Leta.

They clung to each other, unable to move. Unable to accept their new reality. But Jey knew they couldn't stay huddled together for long.

"We have to get out of here," he said. *"Now."*

"What are you talking about?" Her skin was the color of snow, her eyes dark and wild, her hair sticking up in all directions.

"We have to get out of here before the Regency arrives."

Jey knew that they would follow up on the call. It wouldn't be long before they uncovered what remained of his father and discovered Leta's echo-marked hands.

"I'll explain what happened," she said. "I'll—"

"Be arrested," Jey said curtly.

Her chin drooped. "It's what I deserve."

"It was an accident," he said.

"I killed him. I don't know how you can even look at me right now."

Although she had taken his father away from him, his only remaining family in Telene, he wasn't angry. He was merely sad and exhausted.

Jey gently lifted her chin with his hand. "Easily. I love you."

It was far from how he planned to tell her, with edem swirling around them and his father's skeleton lying close by, but he knew it to be true.

Did that mean his father deserved to die? *No,* Jey thought, but he couldn't stand the idea of Leta spending her life in Vardean because his father couldn't be reasoned with.

"Don't say that," she said.

"Why?" he asked. "Because you don't feel the same way?" He hadn't thought about that. And now wasn't the time to worry about bruised egos.

"Because it makes me feel worse!" she cried. "I killed the father of the boy I love."

Jey held her tighter.

"Come on," he said, pulling her to her feet. "We have to get out of here."

There would be time to explain everything he hadn't told her about his father and their relationship.

First, they needed to run.

———

When they found an abandoned development site north of the Unbent River, they finally slowed.

"You should head home," he said. "Make sure you talk to your brother or father. You need an alibi for tonight. I can stay here while we figure out what to do next."

She closed her eyes, and tears fell down her reddened cheeks. "How can I explain this?" she asked, holding up her hands.

"Maybe it will fade?" Jey suggested, knowing perfectly well that death echoes never faded.

She nodded but didn't say anything.

Jey hated seeing her this way. All the fire and fight in her had been extinguished in one moment, like a cloud covering the sun.

"They don't even know we're dating," she said.

"Good. Then there's no reason the Regency will ever connect the crime back to you."

"And what will you do?" Her brown eyes focused on anything but Jey's.

"I can't go back to the house," he said. "Riva knows I was home, and my father mentioned me on the phone. It's not safe."

Leta sat on the edge of the concrete foundation and looked out over the brown water. "Now you can't do anything. Because of me."

Jey sat next to her and placed his arm around her. "We're not locked in a cell, Nettie. I take that as a win."

She twisted to face him, her eyes full of unshed tears. "How can you be so relaxed about all this? I killed your father!"

Jey knew he had a habit of deflecting with humor and bravado; it was the way he coped with sadness. It had been that way since the death of his mother.

He took Leta's heart-shaped face in his hands. "I *hate* that this has happened to you. And I don't want you to think I don't care; I do. But I don't know how to grieve a man I never really knew. It's like reading a new scene for a play. I know the emotion I should feel, but the emotion is not mine."

"You're allowed to grieve," Leta said. "He was still your father. And you're allowed to hate me."

"Never," he whispered.

And he meant it.

Over the next few weeks, Jey traveled to the market and stole food, while Leta returned home and pretended that everything was normal. She visited as much as possible.

"You stole a fowl?" Leta asked when she arrived a week before his arrest. "You don't eat meat."

"Correct," Jey said with a nod to his feathered friend. "Nibbles and I have come to an understanding that she is the provider of this household and will gift me eggs."

"Nibbles?" Leta smiled. It wasn't her normal smile, the one that lit her eyes, but he would take whatever he could get.

"Beware." Jey stuck a finger in his mouth. "She bites."

Leta dumped a basket of fresh deebule on the crude table Jey had set up by the water bank. It was made from chipboard and a few planes of wood. "Do *I* not provide for this household?"

"Hmmhmm," Jey mumbled as he stuffed his face with the delicious fried pastries.

"My grandmother's recipe," Leta said. "Mother used to make them for me and Cayder every Edemmacht."

"The day commemorating Delften arrival in Telene?" Jey asked.

"Their arrival in Ferrington, to be precise."

Leta had that faraway look in her eye that made Jey nervous. Her face took on that distant expression anytime Jey mentioned his father. While they tried not to talk about it, it was difficult when Jey was living in a half-built house on the Unbent River because of what happened that night.

He held out a fluffy deebule. "Hungry?"

She shook her head and sat at the table. "Not really."

Leta never seemed hungry anymore. He wished he knew how to make it all better.

"I was thinking I'd go out there," Leta said, staring into the murky river instead of looking at Jey. She did that when she knew he wasn't going to like what she had to say.

"Go where?" he asked, licking the sugar from his fingers.

"Ferrington."

He set down the half-eaten deebule. "Are you joking? You know Regency agents are crawling all over Ferrington because of those stories."

"What if they're not stories?" Leta asked, finally looking at him.

Jey glanced at the gloves Leta had taken to wearing. "It's too dangerous."

"My mother died out there!" Her eyes flashed, and Jey almost smiled because her fire had returned. "I need to find out the truth to that night. It's all I have left!"

"It's too dangerous, Nettie. The Regency will be looking for my father's killer, and if you show up in the town with a death echo, they're bound to figure out what happened."

She jutted out her chin. "Not if I'm careful."

"No." Jey stood up, brushing the sugar from his mouth. "You can't." He wasn't used to being serious and stern, but Leta had to understand that everything they were doing was for her own protection.

She stood as well, and while she was a few heads shorter than Jey, she was much more intimidating. "You can't tell me what to do."

He laughed humorlessly. "Of course I know that. You're Leta Broduck."

She wrapped her arms around him, and he bent down to kiss her. Even with everything that had happened, he still felt the same electricity run through his body whenever they touched, like the buzz of a ripe torlu berry hitting your tongue.

When they finally pulled apart, he said, "Just promise me you won't do anything foolish."

She nodded and pressed a quick kiss to his lips. "Promise."

Jey pulled her close and rested his head on top of hers. He was glad she didn't make him promise the same thing. For he knew he might have to do the one thing Leta would never forgive him for.

He would have to turn himself in for his father's murder.

# CHAPTER 44

## CAYDER

The truth felt like the stone walls of Vardean had collapsed in on me. Leta stayed uncharacteristically quiet while Jey explained what really happened to his father.

That was the reason she had the death echo—nothing to do with Ferrington or the hullen.

"Why didn't you tell me?" I asked. Why didn't *Leta* tell me?

"Tell you what?" Jey lifted a brow. He'd managed to pull himself up into a sitting position. "That I'm innocent, and your sister killed my father?" He scoffed. "I came to Vardean so she would be safe." He jerked his chin at my sister. "Next thing I know, Leta's thrown in here for the fires in Ferrington."

"That's why you didn't want to go to trial," I said. "You didn't want people to figure out the truth about your father's death."

He nodded. "I took the fall so Leta didn't have to."

"I didn't tell you to do that!" Leta snapped. "You were supposed to be hiding out at the Unbent River until we figured out what to do; instead you turned yourself in for *my* crime. Without telling me?"

"You gave me no choice," Jey said.

"No choice?" Leta roared.

"Shhh," I said. "Keep your voice down."

But I might as well have been invisible; Jey's gaze was locked on my sister's face. "Every night you visited, you slipped further and further away from me. You wouldn't let go of the idea of what was in Ferrington."

"That's where you were sneaking out to?" I asked Leta. "Jey was your source?"

Leta shook her head. "Dr. Bueter was my source." She closed her eyes. "Now you know why I couldn't tell you."

"I wasn't planning to turn myself in," Jey said. "But with you so determined to go to Ferrington, I thought it was the only way to ensure your safety. No one would look at you when I was locked in here."

"What about your echo mark?" I asked him.

"It's just a tattoo," he said. "If you're looking for some street cred for fighting as part of the Brotherhood of the Veil, there's an artist who can re-create echo marks—or even a death echo—for a price." He let out a humorless laugh. "Mr. Toyer was right; I didn't kill my father. I just wanted to *look* like I did."

"And that inmate you stabbed?" I asked.

Jey shrugged. "I wanted to be closer to Leta. I thought it would be easier to free her." He gestured to the key in my hand. "You never told me you wanted to break her free, so I was planning to tonight."

My head spun.

"Leta?" I asked. "Why didn't you tell me what really happened?"

She threw her hands in the air. "I didn't want you to look at me the way you are now!"

"And how's that?" I asked.

"Like a killer!"

I carefully placed my hands on my sister's. "I don't think you're a killer."

"You don't?"

"No," I said. "I wish you had trusted me with the truth, but I understand why you didn't." Before I started working at Vardean, I might not have understood what led someone to break the law, but now I did. And if Jey forgave my sister and had given up his freedom to protect her, who was I to question that?

"So," Jey asked, "are you going to let me out of here, or what?"

I unlocked the cell door and released his shackled hands.

Once he was on his feet, he glanced awkwardly at Leta. She kept her hands tucked close to her sides. I was sure it wasn't the loving reunion that Jey had planned.

"Come on," I said to Jey. "Let's get the others."

———

Kema was pacing Leta's cell when we rejoined her, and Elle was sitting on Leta's bunk. She jumped to her feet when we entered.

"What?" Kema asked, seeing Jey. "Are we breaking everyone free now?"

"Only the handsome inmates," Jey replied with a grin. He glanced at Elle. "Who's this? Another guard on our side?"

"Elenora," she said, holding out her hand.

"The princess?" He almost choked on the word. I'd never seen uncertainty cross Jey's face before. She nodded, and he shrugged and shook her hand. "Nice to have you on board this escape train, Princess. I'm Jey Bueter."

Elenora's smile faded. "Cayder said you killed your father?"

Jey glanced at Leta. "It's a long story."

"Then the Regency General is still alive?" she asked.

"No," Leta said flatly. "He died almost two months ago. He disintegrated in front of our eyes."

"Just like my brother," Elenora murmured.

I started shedding my outerwear to reveal my prison uniform underneath. "Girls, you may want to turn around."

"Or not," Jey said to Leta. I was happy to see my sister roll her eyes.

I stripped down, handed over the uniform for Jey to wear and dressed back in my normal clothes. I hoped our new addition to our crew wasn't going to be our undoing.

After we'd changed, I placed Jey's and Leta's inmate uniforms under Leta's sheet so it looked like she was sleeping.

"What now?" Elle asked, her eyes sparkling with hope.

"We wait," I said.

"For what?" Jey asked. "An open invitation? I doubt that's coming, mate."

Before I could reply, an alarm sounded through the building.

*"Vardean is in lockdown,"* an amplified voice wailed. *"Everyone sit on your bunks with your hands visible until further notice."*

*"That,"* I said, "was what we were waiting for."

We walked out onto the landing. Below us, a fight had broken out in the dining hall and spilled onto the ground floor. We leaned over the barricade to see dozens of Regency agents clashing with fifty or so inmates.

"Step six." I smiled. "Inspire chaos."

"What did you do?" Leta whispered.

Below was a swirl of silver cloaks as the Regency agents attempted to tackle inmates to the ground.

"I told them the truth," I said. "With Narena's help."

"She's all right?" Leta asked.

"She is. She's sorry she couldn't make your trial." I shook my head. "There's so much to fill you in on."

And there was still so much I needed to know about her and Jey, but first, we needed to get out of here.

"We should avoid the elevator," Kema said, gesturing toward the stairs at the back of the building. "I don't want to descend into that." She nodded to the throng of angry inmates below.

We walked down two by two; Elle stayed close beside me.

"Are you okay?" I asked her.

She nodded. "I will be."

"Let me take that," I said, grabbing my satchel from her shoulder.

"I can carry it," she said. "I'm not some useless doll, you know."

I grinned. "I know." The satchel was heavy. "What's in here?"

There had been only three uniforms inside, which were now being worn by Leta, Jey and Elle.

"My mask," she said, her cheeks reddening. "I couldn't leave it behind. It's one of the few things I have left from my mother."

I patted the bag. "I'll take care of it."

As we descended, the stairwell increased with guards and agents trying to tame the angry horde.

"What are you doing?" one guard yelled at Elle.

She flinched back. "I'm sorry?"

"Spread out," the guard said. "You two—" He pointed to Leta and Jey. "Take floor three. You—" He gestured to the princess and Kema. "Take floor fifteen and you take fourteen. *You*—" He took in my blazer and suit pants. "Stay out of the way."

When no one moved, the guard shouted, *"Now!"*

———

Perhaps chaos was not the best plan after all. Guards and Regency agents were everywhere.

Each time a Regency agent passed, Elenora flinched.

"It's okay," I whispered. "We have to play along for the time being. Let them think we're helping."

Elenora nodded, pulling her cap lower.

We had to wait for the commotion to settle on level one before we could venture to the foyer below. In the meantime, Elenora pretended to check the locks and looked into the cells to make sure no one else was hiding inside, and I tried to stay out of the way.

"Cayder Broduck?" a man called out from one of the cells as we passed by.

I halted, not recognizing the voice. I peered into the cell.

A middle-aged man with skin the pallor and texture of spoiled milk sat upon his bunk. His hair was long but with exposed patches of scaly scalp.

"Cayder?" Elenora whispered, pulling on my sleeve. "What's wrong?"

"It *is* you!" The man leaped up. "You look so much like your father when he was young. I knew it had to be you."

My breath short-circuited in my lungs. "*Who* are you?"

"I don't expect you to know me." The man hung his head. "My name is Hubare Carnright."

Shock shuddered up my spine. I stumbled backward.

"Then you do know who I am," he said, shame flooding his voice.

I barely registered his last words, or that Elenora clutched my arm, a question in her eyes.

I was no longer in Vardean; I was back at Broduck Manor, and I was ten years old.

My father was telling me that my mother would never come home from her latest Regency trip.

"Why?" I'd asked him, not understanding. Had she been delayed? Did she need to stay in Ferrington longer?

My father had said two words: "Hubare Carnright."

The name had haunted me ever since.

At first, I'd thought this man had kidnapped our mother and

held her captive. I would ask my father when he would release her back to us. It wasn't until I was older that I understood the truth.

"Cayder?" Elenora asked. "What is it?"

But I couldn't speak.

Over the years, I'd imagined the many things I would say—or yell—at Hubare Carnright if I were ever face-to-face with him.

*You destroyed my life!*

*You ruined my family!*

*You should never go free!*

*You should feel the pain that I feel every day!*

But now, faced with the man who had caused the accident that had killed my mother, I couldn't find the words.

Like Father had said, I'd never been at peace. I hadn't felt justice had been served. I hadn't spoken of my anger because it would be admitting that I hadn't—and couldn't—move on from my mother's death. Whatever happened that night, it was likely an accident. And this man would pay forevermore. Over the past three weeks, I'd realized people made mistakes. People acted selfishly or recklessly or desperately or naively, but that didn't mean they were monsters who should be locked up for life. I understood that this man's fate could have been my own.

While it didn't lessen the pain of losing my mother, it did ease my anger.

"I'm sorry," Hubare said. "The man said he'd shorten my sentence if I told him what happened that day your father visited my cell." He laughed humorlessly. "I should have known he was lying. Everyone at the Regency lies."

I stepped up to the bars. "What man?" I asked.

"He didn't tell me his name," Hubare said. "But he was pale and had a white mustache."

*Mr. Rolund.*

So that was how the prosecutor found out about Father breaking the law. Mr. Rolund must have looked into Father's past, including any cases he was involved with, in hopes of uncovering something to discredit him.

"I'm sorry," Hubare said again. "I ruined your life twice. First your mother's accident, and now this. Please know one thing." Hubare twisted his hands together. "She was not in pain when she passed. It happened so quickly. One moment she was there, and the next, she disappeared."

My mother didn't disappear. She was swept into a ravine. We buried her body.

"What are you talking about?" I asked. I gripped the bars between us. "What happened to her?"

Hubare swallowed audibly. "The weapon I was testing malfunctioned, and she was caught in the line of fire. It was a tragic accident."

Elenora approached the bars, her eyes fierce. "What weapon?"

"The ones powered by edem," Hubare said. "We were testing them out at the base in Ferrington."

*Ferrington.*

My heart thudded to a stop, and Elenora gasped.

"That's what they're covering up out there!" she said breathlessly. "Weapons!"

"You're not a farmer?" I asked Hubare.

The man shook his head. "I worked for the Regency, like your
mother."

We had to get out of Vardean. *Now*. The world needed to know
what the Regency were up to.

Although he didn't ask for it, I said, "I forgive you." Then kept
on walking.

# CHAPTER 45

# JEY

Jey did his best impersonation of a guard, shaking cell doors and checking locks to play the part.

"How did you convince the Regency that you killed your father?" Leta asked quietly as they walked the landing.

"It was simple." Jey tapped his heart. "No one questions your confession when you have an echo mark."

Leta looked at her gloved hands. "Thank you," she said.

"You're not mad at me?"

"Of course I am!" Leta exclaimed. "But I know your heart was in the right place. Still, you should have told me what you planned. This entire time I thought you were back at the Unbent River with that fowl of yours."

"If I'd told you," he said, "you would have stopped me."

She poked him in the chest. "With good reason. And yet I ended up in here anyway. Don't you think that's what the universe wanted?"

"No. And I don't care about the universe. I care about you."

"It would be easier if you didn't," she muttered.

"For whom?" he asked.

"For both of us."

"Well," he said, "I'm sorry, but I don't do things the easy way." He waved his hands. "Let the record show that Jey is gesturing to the prison around him."

Leta laughed, and Jey joined in. It felt good. Being together. Laughing. Freedom would come soon enough.

"I missed you," she whispered.

He didn't look at her but said, "And I, you."

---

After the inmates were subdued, Jey and Leta headed down to the ground level. They couldn't see Cayder, Kema or the princess, so they took the elevator.

As the elevator lowered into the section of rock between the prison sector and foyer, Jey took the opportunity to pull Leta toward him. He tangled his hands in her short brown hair, and she tilted her head back to kiss him. She eased into his embrace as though she were sighing.

He kissed her fiercely, pouring every pained moment over the last three weeks into the kiss, knowing that their time together would be brief.

He was going to make it count.

But all too quickly, the elevator moved out of the rock and into the foyer.

Leta grinned, straightening her uniform. "I hope you don't greet all your prison colleagues that way."

He snickered. "Not a chance."

The elevator pulled to a stop.

"We'll continue that conversation later," he promised her.

She nodded. "You better."

The foyer was fairly empty; most workers had gone home. The only people in the room were six Regency agents guarding the door to the gondola bridge.

Jey cursed under his breath.

A flush of anger flooded his body. Of course they wouldn't allow anyone to leave; Vardean was still in lockdown.

Jey approached the agents as he did everything in life. With swagger. "Hello, friends," he said. "Any updates? I'd like to be home before midnight." He winked. "I have a friend coming over, if you know what I mean."

The Regency agents weren't like prison guards, and it wasn't merely their fancy uniforms and silvery cloaks. It was their manner. They were more statues than people. They didn't even blink at Jey.

"Oh." Jey frowned. "Do you really not know what I mean?" He yanked at his collar. "Well, that's awkward. Let me explain. When you're in love, although it doesn't necessarily *have* to be love, two consenting people can—"

One of the agents marched forward, his cloak flapping behind him like wings. He was tall and narrow, and looking into his deep-set eyes was like staring into the veil itself. They contrasted with his ashen skin and slicked-back fair ponytail. "No one is to enter or leave Vardean until the inmate is captured."

Jey gestured to the quiet foyer around him. "What inmate?" Sometimes it was best to play dumb.

"If you don't know," the agent grumbled, "then you don't have clearance. Wait for the announcement."

Jey glanced at Leta. They couldn't wait for an announcement that would never come.

"What if she . . . ?" Jey grimaced, realizing he may have already given to much away. "I mean, they, already escaped?"

The agent narrowed his eyes. "No one leaves until after the announcement."

"Got it," Jey said. He pointed at the agent. "We'll wait . . . for that, then."

He nodded to Leta, and they headed back toward the elevator.

"What do we do now?" Leta whispered.

The Regency agents were watching their every move. The elevator started rising before they could climb back in. When it descended again, Cayder, Kema and the princess were inside.

"Buddy!" Jey said loudly, clapping Cayder on the back. "What are you still doing here? Vardean closed to employees almost two hours ago. It's nearly curfew!"

Cayder glanced around Jey to the wall of Regency agents by the exit. Luckily, the kid was bright.

"I know!" Cayder said as loudly. "I lost track of time. What should I do?"

"Let's head to the guard lounge," Kema offered with a reassuring nod. "You can wait there until dawn."

They followed Kema down the brightly lit hallways toward the lounge. They weren't the only ones there; many guards had chosen the same spot to wait out the lockdown. A few were playing cards around tattered old tables. Others were chatting by the lockers.

Kema nodded toward a corner. They gathered in a circle as far away from the rest of the guards as they could.

Cayder filled them in on what he'd uncovered from Hubare.

"My brother was going to visit Ferrington," the princess said. "He was going to tour all the major regions. He would have uncovered what they were doing out there."

"You think they burned down their own base to make sure no one found out about it?" Leta asked.

"The timing lines up," Cayder said. "But what are these edem weapons?"

They all looked at Jey. "Don't ask me. My father never shared any of his plans with me. I could barely get a hello out of the man, let alone his plans for world domination."

"They must have created the weapons to destroy the hullen," Leta said. "That's why they set up the base all the way out there."

"Maybe," Cayder replied, but Jey could tell he didn't agree with his sister.

"What do we do now?" Leta asked.

"We wait it out," Kema said. "Just like the agents suggested."

Jey held up a finger. "One problem. They're never going to find the missing inmate. Because—" He nodded to the princess. "And soon they'll figure out we're missing too."

"The agents will have to give up sometime," Cayder said.

If the Regency agents were anything like his father, Jey doubted that. "Or perhaps they'll start searching employees, including guards."

"What do you think, Kema?" Cayder asked.

Kema grimaced. "I've never been in this situation. There's a reason no one escapes Vardean."

"Then what?" Jey said, pulling at the too-short sleeves of his uniform. "Let's pack it in and return to our cells like good little inmates?" He shook his head. "I don't think so. We've come this far."

"It's not far enough," Cayder muttered.

Leta reached out and grabbed her brother's hand. "This isn't your fault."

Cayder raised a dark brow. "Isn't it?"

"All right, all right," Jey said. "Enough with the pity party. We need a plan."

"I'm all ears," Cayder said.

"I never would have said such a nasty thing"—Jey shrugged—"but I guess your ears are a little bigger compared to your—"

"*Jey.*" Leta jabbed him in the ribs with her elbow. "Stop it."

"Sorry," Jey said. "Force of habit."

"Being a smart-ass?" Cayder threw back.

"Boys! Boys!" Kema scolded. "Now is not the time for a pissing contest. You're each as annoying as the other. Thus, you both win. Congratulations," she said drolly. "Now we need a new plan."

"Eventually, they'll have to let employees go home, right?" Leta asked. "And what happens tomorrow when the lawyers and judges try to come to work?"

"Trials are on hold," the princess said, her voice quiet. "Maybe no one will come. Or go."

No one had a response to that.

"The Regency are in control," she continued, eyes distant. "The only way out is *through* them."

"You're kidding?" Jey asked. "We can't take on that many guards. I mean, I'm good in a tussle, but that's beyond even my capabilities."

"There has to be another way," Cayder said.

Jey crossed his arms. "Just because you want there to be doesn't mean there *will* be." Optimism would only get you so far.

"What if I feign illness?" Leta suggested. She did look a little paler than usual. "Say I need to see a doctor?"

"They'll take you to the infirmary," Kema said. "And the doctors are bound to recognize you after your time there."

Leta chewed on her bottom lip. "Good point," she said. "You grew up studying this place, Cayder. Isn't there anything we can do? Anywhere else we can go?"

Studying Vardean was a strange pastime, even for a kid like Cayder. But Jey bit his tongue. Now was not the time to point that out.

"Vardean Reform will also be in lockdown, like the rest of the building," Cayder said. "There's nothing we can do."

"That's not true," the princess said.

"What do you mean?" Cayder asked. His face had this ridiculous expression every time he looked at the princess. But Jey couldn't begrudge him too much, for he knew he sported one similar when he looked at Leta. Like she was the sun in the sky.

"Vardean is in lockdown because of me," she said. "No one knows Leta and Jey have also escaped." She glanced at the floor, her face twisting as though she'd tasted something sour. "The lockdown will end if they get what they want, and you'll go free. It's the only way."

She glanced at Cayder.

"I have to turn myself in."

# CHAPTER 46

# CAYDER

No!" I shouted. Elenora was *not* giving up! I wouldn't let her.

"Shhh," Kema admonished, her eyes fierce.

A few guards looked over, and Kema tilted her head back and laughed boisterously.

"Sorry, Cayder," she said, "but I win this round. Better luck next time!"

The other guards returned to playing cards or talking among themselves, not caring enough to see what game Kema was referring to or that none of us were holding cards. I blew out a breath.

"I wish we could turn *you* in instead," Jey muttered.

"Funny," I shot back.

"It's the only way," Elenora said. "They need someone to lock up. We have to give them what they want. We have to give them a princess."

"I need you," I replied. "I mean *we* all do. How can we reveal the truth about the king without you? The truth about their weapons? How can we overthrow the Regency?"

She smiled sadly. "It's our only option."

"What about me?" Leta said. "Not that I don't appreciate your sacrifice, Princess, but how can I ever live a normal life if you don't pardon me?"

Even if we managed to escape, we would all have to live our lives on the run, forever looking over our shoulders, worrying about the day we would be caught by the Regency.

"I don't know," she replied. "But we have to try." She wouldn't look at me, her gaze fixed to the floor. She knew this meant game over. She would never be free, and we would have to abandon any hope of our lives returning to normal.

"Hey," I said, lifting Elle's chin. She took in a shuddering breath. "We're not giving up."

She placed her hand over mine and gently pushed me away. "Please, please let me go. I need to do this. For my brother."

"Don't you want the Regency to pay for what they've done?" I asked.

"I do," she said, her eyes turning steely. "And they will. Trust me."

"I'm afraid the princess is right," Kema said solemnly. "It would be one thing if it was only Yarlyn in charge. But with the Regency determined to keep the princess locked up, there's no way they'll let us through the front door. Not until the princess is found."

"We tried," Jey said, clapping me on the back. "It was a good plan, mate. As good as any."

Easy for him to say; he wouldn't be the one left behind.

"How are you going to explain where you got your uniform from?" Kema asked, one brow raised. "Or how you escaped?"

"I'll tell them the superintendent helped me," she said with a shrug. "There's already dissension in the ranks. The Regency will be happy to blame this on Yarlyn. They'll be able to use this to oust her."

"That could work," Kema agreed reluctantly.

"I'll come back for you," I said, ducking my head to look Elenora in the eyes. "I promise, Elle."

She glanced away. "I'm so sorry, Cayder. I have to do what I can."

"No," I said. "I'm sorry."

I *would* come back for her. Even if I had to hand-deliver a newspaper to every single person in Telene. They would hear about Elenora and her brother. They would know what really happened here.

"You should come with me," Elenora said, tears lining her voice. "You can make a run for it during the commotion of my arrest."

Leta touched Elenora's arm. "Thank you."

Elenora turned, hiding her face from me.

I could barely take in a full breath; my chest ached. As much as I didn't want to see the moment she was detained, I didn't want her to be alone. We walked slowly back to the foyer, peering around the corridor to see if the Regency agents were still lining the exit.

"*Edem be damned,*" I cursed. Didn't we deserve some bit of luck?

"It's time," Elenora said.

"Did you want your mask back?" I asked, remembering it was still in my satchel.

She shook her head and smiled sadly. "You keep it."

No one knew what else to say. I couldn't trust my own voice, so I nodded.

"One last thing . . ." Elenora said. She rose up onto her toes and pressed her lips to mine. I felt a spark ignite between us. My heart hammered, and warmth flooded my body. When she pulled back, she whispered into my ear. "Please remember that I'm sorry. But this is the only way. I have to take matters into my own hands."

Before I could respond, she walked into the center of the foyer.

"I like your girlfriend," Jey said. "She's doing the right thing."

"She's not my girlfriend." But I was too tired to put much energy behind the denial.

Elenora stood before the Regency agents, and I felt like I'd swallowed hot coals. The burn traveled down my chest and into my stomach.

The burning turned to flames when Elenora started gesturing in our direction.

"What is she doing?" Kema asked.

I caught a snippet of her conversation. ". . . the one with the short brown hair," she said. "Check the boy's bag. He has the princess's mask."

It took me a moment to understand. Elenora *hadn't* turned herself in; she'd turned Leta in—using the fact that no one knew her face against us. She was claiming that Leta was the unmasked princess!

Elenora wasn't sorry that my plan failed; she was sorry because of what she was about to do.

Betray us all.

"No," I said, shaking my head in disbelief. *"No!"*

The Regency wouldn't believe a lie like that. They had no proof that Leta was—

"Oh shit," Jey said as the Regency agents rushed toward us. Elenora gave me a long apologetic look. But she didn't run for the front door; she headed to the elevator.

*What is she doing?*

"Run!" Kema cried. "Now!"

As we headed back down the corridor toward the guard lounge, I saw the elevator descend rather than rise.

The princess was heading to the Regency headquarters.

But why? She'd never escape that way.

Unless . . .

She never planned to escape.

How could I have missed it? She never said she wanted to escape Vardean. She had only ever said she wanted to escape her cell and make the Regency pay for her brother's disappearance.

She wanted revenge. And she was heading to the Regency headquarters to get it.

"I take that back," Jey said as we ran. "Your girlfriend is a horrible person."

"She's not my girlfriend!" I snapped. This time I meant it.

I'd been so fooled by her beauty, I'd missed her true intentions.

But what did she think she'd find down in the Regency head-quarters? She'd been so convinced her brother was still alive; had she pinned her hopes on finding him down there? Surely she wouldn't be so foolish.

The sound of the cloaks flapping behind us sounded like the beat of a drum that grew louder and louder as they gained.

"Maybe we should stop and explain," Leta said, breathing hard. "I'm not the princess, after all."

"You're still an escaped inmate!" I said between pants. "And I *do* have the princess's mask in my bag."

Leta huffed. "Good point."

We circled back to the guard lounge but ran past the door.

"Stop!" an agent yelled from behind us. "There's nowhere to run!"

"What do we do?" Leta cried.

"Break the lights?" Jey suggested, pointing above us. I noticed he was the least out of breath, and although we had more pressing concerns, it irked me. "Use edem to escape?"

"That's illegal!" Kema said. She was keeping pace with Jey, stride for stride.

"I'm pretty sure we passed illegal a few hours back when we broke out of our cells," Jey offered.

"Or when we got arrested," Leta countered.

We spun around another corner and almost ran headfirst into Yarlyn.

"What's going on?" she asked.

"Princess," Jey said with a huff, keeping his cap low so she didn't recognize him. "She's in the foyer."

"Then why are you running in the opposite direction?"

Jey shrugged, and we sprinted off.

"Stop them!" an agent yelled to Yarlyn. "The princess is among them!"

We twisted down another corridor. A few more right turns, and we'd end up back at the foyer. Every corridor led to the foyer. The agents were right. There was no way out.

"Any ideas?" My legs were beginning to tire.

"We take the stairs," Kema suggested.

"To where?" Jey asked. "The prison sector? No, thank you."

"I hate to admit it," I said, "but I agree with Jey."

I knew the schematic of Vardean as well as the corridors of Broduck Manor. Going up wasn't a way out.

"I have a plan," Kema said. "But you're not going to like it."

"It's a plan," I said. "I already like it."

"Then follow me."

# CHAPTER 47

# LETA

Leta wanted to slow everything down. She wanted to hold on to her brother, to Jey and to Kema, before this all ended horribly. A sinking feeling built within her, as though the world was shifting under her feet and she was scrambling to remain standing.

She wished she had her pencils. She wished she could slow down time in the only legal way she knew how. But she couldn't draw her way out of this mess.

Kema was fast, no doubt a part of her guard training, and Leta struggled to keep up. They heard the constant *thump thump thump* of the Regency agents behind them, but so far they'd managed to elude them.

*Because the Regency knows there's no way out,* Leta thought bitterly. *They're in no rush. We're like trapped rats. They're enjoying this.*

"I thought we agreed there's no point in going back up," Jey said as they took the stairs two at a time. Or at least Jey did with his long legs; Leta stumbled behind him, her hand clutched in his.

"Trust me," Kema said.

Once they reached the ground floor of the prison sector, Kema slowed to a walk. Guards were everywhere.

"Don't look suspicious." Kema nodded in acknowledgment to a few guards.

Leta wasn't sure how that was possible. Her face and back were slick with sweat, and she could hardly suck in a breath. If her prison uniform wasn't tight before, it was painted on now.

"Just breathe, Nettie," Jey said.

She smiled at him. The nickname reminded her of her mother and how she used to throw a thick blanket over the permalamp and allow the coolness of shadows to wash over Leta's face. When Jey used that name, she felt her mother walk alongside her like her own shadow.

Cayder had said their mother hadn't died in a landslide, but during an accident at the Regency base in Ferrington. Leta knew that couldn't be the full story. She didn't trust Hubare any more than the Regency General. They all kept secrets. They all told lies. And Leta knew, in her gut, that her mother's death was no accident. And her gut hadn't been wrong so far.

Kema led them to the dining hall and blocked the door behind them with a chair. Newspaper articles on the veil and Leta's sketches of the hullen were littered across the floor.

"You did this?" Leta asked her brother.

"With some help from Narena." Cayder smiled, although

there was no humor behind his eyes. The betrayal of the princess had destroyed a part of him—even though they had known each other for only a short while, she had meant something to him. And Cayder didn't often let people in.

"Can't say I have much of an appetite," Jey commented, sticking his finger in an abandoned bowl of orange soup. "What are we doing here?"

Kema leaned up against the brick wall. "Remember I said you weren't going to like the plan?" she asked. They all nodded. "The only other way out of here is through the waste chute."

"The waste chute?" Leta asked. "As in . . ."

"Old runoff water from the kitchen, food scraps, you name it." Kema nodded.

Jey cocked an eyebrow, his handsome face flirting with the idea. "I'm in."

But Cayder was shaking his head. "We're two hundred feet above sea level. The impact will likely kill us."

"I know," Kema said. "I'm not suggesting we jump into the ocean from the chute's exit; I'm suggesting we use the chute to get to the outside of the building, then climb down toward the Regency headquarters."

"You want to travel *into* the belly of the beast?" Jey scoffed. "I'd like to retract my previous agreement, thank you very much."

"The headquarters is fifty levels down, and there's a bridge leading out to the veil," Kema said. "Jumping into the water won't kill us from there."

"I'd rather take my chances with the agents," Jey said. "I don't want to get *that* close to the veil. We have no idea what will happen."

"We don't," Cayder agreed. "But we *do* know what will happen if we're captured. We've been down that road before. It's a good plan, Kema."

Leta had to admit the idea of seeing the veil up close intrigued her. She was her mother's daughter, after all.

"We don't have another option, do we?" Leta asked.

"No, we don't," Cayder said. "And I know the schematics to this place inside and out."

"Then we do it," Leta said. "We have to."

Jey stood up and pressed a kiss to her temple. "We've got this. You go where I go. One step at a time."

She nodded, knowing there was no way she could have the same kind of reach that Jey would.

"This way, then," Kema said, sliding over the top of the serving counter toward the kitchen.

"Wait!" Leta exclaimed. She picked up one of the newspapers from the floor. "Does anyone have a pencil?"

"Nettie," Jey said gently. "Now's not the time to draw my portrait."

She pushed him away with a laugh. "I want to write to Father." She nodded to Cayder. "To say goodbye."

"Don't think like that," Cayder said. His brows furrowing. "We need to—"

"Even if we make it," Leta interrupted, "we can't go home. Not without the pardon from the princess."

Leta hadn't been close to her father in years, but he was still her father.

"Here." Kema held a pencil out. "I have one."

Leta grabbed it and started writing down her swirling thoughts. All the things she wished she had said to her father in the years since her mother died. How she knew their distance wasn't his fault. They had all reacted to grief in their own ways.

When she was finished, she wiped the tears with the back of her hands.

"Cayder?" Leta held out a piece of paper.

The page hung in the air.

"I don't know what I'd say," he admitted.

"Tell him whatever you feel like," she said.

"But be quick." Jey nodded to the dining room door.

Cayder wrote something short and left it on the counter.

"My turn," Kema said, reaching for the pencil.

"No," Cayder said to her. "You should stay here."

She placed her hand on her hip. "Are you serious?"

Cayder nodded. "No one knows you helped us. Those Regency agents don't know who you are. You could still get out of this unscathed."

"I thought we'd already talked about this."

"That was different. I thought we could all be pardoned once the princess"—he winced—"overthrew the Regency."

"Cayder's right," Leta agreed. "You haven't done anything wrong."

Kema pulled back her sleeve and scrubbed at her arm, revealing an echo mark on her forearm. "Haven't I?"

There was so much Leta didn't know about her old friend. She hoped there would be time to ask the questions buzzing around in her mind.

"Think about Graymond," Cayder said. "He would hate to lose you. And what about your girlfriend?"

She laughed. "I'm not lost. I'm doing the right thing. For everyone."

"Fine," Cayder said. "But don't blame me if you regret your actions."

She tapped his nose. "I haven't yet, Boy Wonder."

They joined Kema on the other side of the serving counter.

"Where's the waste chute?" Leta asked.

Kema beckoned them over to a cupboard. Behind the door lay a tunnel small enough for a person to squeeze through. The opening seemed to head straight down and into the dark. The rancid smell made Leta want to hurl. It wasn't long ago that she'd been poisoned, and her stomach still ached.

"I don't know that I'll fit in there," Jey said, a look of concern crossing his face. "I might be too broad."

"There's only one way to find out!" Kema said, far too cheerily.

Jey bent down to inspect the tunnel. When he retracted his hands, they were covered in brown sludge.

"Lovely," Jey muttered, wiping them on his gray guard pants.

"You're welcome to stay behind," Cayder said, and Jey grunted. "I'll go first."

"Be my guest." Jey gestured to the chute's opening.

Cayder squatted down and peered into the dark.

"Wish me luck."

# CHAPTER 48

# CAYDER

*Step Seven: Escape via the Waste Chute*

My plan was unraveling. And there wasn't anything I could do to stop it.

"Well?" Jey asked. "What are you waiting for?"

I wasn't much narrower than the width of the chute, so I pulled off my jacket and shoes. I looked into the hole, and it appeared to tunnel straight down. Edem shimmered within the shadows.

Was that a safer way out?

I didn't think so. Leta had merely tried to stop Dr. Bueter from calling the Regency, and he'd ended up dead. It was too much of a risk.

Leta, Jey and Kema loomed anxiously over me.

"I'm going now," I said, mostly to force myself to follow through.

I wiggled closer to the edge of the chute, my legs dangling into the unknown.

"Do you need a nudge?" Jey asked helpfully.

"No," I said. "I got this."

I closed my eyes and then pushed off.

I didn't plan on screaming.

The drop was steep, almost vertical. I bellowed as I plummeted. Some disgusting-smelling sludge flicked up onto the side of my face. I didn't want to think about what it was. I just wanted it to be over.

I tried to slow myself down by pressing my feet to the sides of the metal chute, but it resulted in more gunk being whipped into my face. As the liquid slushed around me, I felt like I was drowning in a whirlpool of mud.

Leta must have followed me next. Her shrieks echoed above me.

My heart hammered in my ears. My breath stuck in my throat. Just when I wasn't sure if it would ever end, the chute began to level out. And I could see moonlight ahead.

I was approaching the exit too fast.

I desperately flung my hands out to find purchase.

*No. No. No. I'm going to go over the edge. And I'm too high up!*

If I didn't die from the impact of hitting the water, I'd shatter all my bones.

"Come on," I urged myself. "Slow down."

My socked feet slipped against the liquid that lined the metal. I couldn't get any traction.

I wondered if it would be better to hit the ocean in a ball? Or should I try diving in? There had to be a reason people dove in with their hands first. I'd shatter my fingers, wrists and arms, but maybe I'd survive.

*Maybe.*

I was so close to freedom. Freedom for Leta. Freedom for us all.

*Maybe* wasn't good enough—I had to figure this out.

I twisted onto my side and braced my feet and hands against the wall. My shoulders jarred into the metal, and my feet dented into the chute.

Like a piece of bread lodged in a windpipe, I came to a stop.

I scooted toward the opening; once my feet dangled free into the open air, I paused.

"Cayder!" Leta screamed. "Get out of the way."

*Burning shadows!* She was hurtling toward me and would no doubt push me right off the edge.

"Twist onto your side!" I yelled up the tunnel. I couldn't make out anything in the darkness.

I could feel rather than see as Leta stopped inches before colliding with me, a wave of sludge rolling over my head.

"Sorry!" Leta cried.

I coughed up gunk from my lungs. "It's okay."

We shouted the message of how to slow down to the others. Still, I wanted to get out of the chute in case they were unable to stop.

From the prison schematics, I knew the chute opening was flat against the external stone wall, so I twisted onto my stomach and eased backward over the lip. I could feel the chill of the cool summer night air on my soaked pants as I felt around for a foothold. Once I found purchase on the edge of a stone, I lowered myself out of the chute, holding on to the bottom edge for support.

I took a deep breath and reached out with one hand to grip on to another stone, and then pushed away from the chute's opening.

The veil crackled behind me. I'd never been so close; the hairs on the back of my neck stood on end. The longer I stared into the black, the harder it became to see anything outside of it. It drew me in, willing me to give up the light and enter the dark. Forever.

Alongside the one main crack of the veil were smaller cracks that I'd never noticed before. They snapped like lightning. Where the veil met the ocean, it burrowed down, the water circling around the dark abyss.

"Cayder?" Leta asked, her pale foot dangling out from the chute. "Help?"

I blinked, turning away from the veil, and guided Leta onto the stone edge beside me. Her hair was plastered against her fair skin; streaks of grime ran down her rounded cheeks. She was shaking.

"You're all right," I said.

Her trembling intensified, and I realized she was laughing.

"If that hadn't been completely terrifying," she said, "it would have been fun!"

Kema was next to climb out of the tunnel. She grinned. "Well, wasn't that an experience?"

"One I'd never like to relive," I said.

Kema easily swung her way out of the chute and onto the stone wall, almost as though she defied gravity. I was sure I hadn't been as graceful.

Jey was last to arrive, and I was surprised he didn't have any snippy remarks. His face had paled, and his arrogant smirk was nowhere to be found.

"What now?" Leta asked, worrying her lip in between her teeth.

Kema pointed to a narrow metal bridge suspended over the ocean that connected the side of Vardean out to the veil. "That's where the Regency monitors the veil."

Did they also test weapons at the headquarters? Or only out at the Ferrington base, where no one knew what they were up to? Did the princess head down to the headquarters to get her hands on the weapons as proof or for revenge? Who was she hoping to hold accountable when the Regency General was already dead?

He'd turned to dust a week before her brother had disappeared. Her brother that she had hoped was still alive . . .

Waves crashed against the pillars of Vardean.

"Jey?" Leta asked. "Want to lead the way?"

He nodded, still unnerved by the waste chute. He reached out for a stone below him and shifted his weight easily from one stone to the next.

"You go." I nodded to Leta. "I'm right behind you."

She set her jaw and followed Jey.

"You all right?" Kema asked me.

"I swallowed some sludge," I said. "But I'm alive."

She nodded. Her white hair was tainted an off-yellow color

from the muck, but otherwise, she looked the least ruffled. I wished I had her nerves.

I took off after Leta, placing my feet where she placed hers. Kema followed close behind.

We moved bit by bit, stone by stone, working our way down and across to the bridge below. The veil continued to buzz and crackle behind us. It felt like a shadow looming over our shoulders, whispering in our ears. But there were so many voices whispering, you couldn't make out the words.

"Do you feel that?" I asked.

Leta nodded. "I felt something similar in Ferrington before I passed out. Let's just hope the hullen aren't around."

Unlike Leta, I wasn't sure the hullen were dangerous, and yet clearly the Regency wanted to keep their existence a secret. Why?

The humid night made my shirt and hands slick with sweat, threatening my hold on the rocks.

"How is everyone?" I asked when we were halfway toward the bridge.

"Just peachy," Leta said.

"We can take a breather," I proposed.

"Great idea," Jey muttered. "Why not have a picnic up here while we're at it?"

I glared at him. Why did he have to make everything so difficult?

"As soon as we're on the bridge, we need to jump into the ocean," Kema said helpfully. "We can't risk being seen by the Regency. They work all hours of the day and night."

Leta groaned. "I'm already aching from head to toe."

"We only have to swim around to the station platform," I said. "Then we can climb up and onto the next gondola."

"If the gondola is even running," Leta said. "Surely they shut it down when Vardean went into lockdown?"

*Good point.* "Then we rest for a bit and swim back to the mainland."

"Do you have any idea how many miles that is, mate?" Jey asked.

I sagged against the rock wall. "I don't know, okay? Swimming was never a part of my plan. I'm adjusting as we go along."

"We swim to the nearest boat in the harbor," Kema suggested. "We're in guard uniforms; we can say our boat sank or something."

*Or something.*

She was guessing. We all were. We weren't criminal masterminds, no matter what portrait the Regency painted of us.

"One step at a time," I said. "Get to the landing, then jump into the water. We'll find a boat from there."

In the darkness, a boat would be easy to spot. They were required to have a flood lamp installed on top of their mast, to keep edem at bay.

Occasionally, I saw edem moving in the shadows against the rock wall, but I ignored it. As far as I was concerned, edem was as dangerous as the Regency. And far more unpredictable.

I wanted to get away from the veil as quickly as possible. Something about its presence was magnetic. I was afraid that I wasn't strong-willed enough to resist its call.

But what was it trying to tell me? Was it merely trying to draw me in so I would never see daylight again?

I thought about the hullen and how they supposedly had come from the veil. How they had seemingly protected Leta from the fires in Ferrington. If they weren't dangerous, then why had the Regency built their weapons to destroy them?

Hanging hundreds of feet above the swirling ocean was not the place for such questions.

The veil crackled, and lightning forked through the sky. Only this time, the lightning was bright white.

"Oh shit," I said.

Rain streamed from the sky like a curtain. I blinked back the water, desperate to wipe at my face, but I didn't dare risk letting go of the rock.

"Be careful!" I shouted over the roar of the rain. "The stones will be slippery now." One wrong move, and we were done.

"Perfect," Leta remarked. "At least it will wash the stink from our hair and clothes."

"Always a silver lining!" Kema said cheerily. She tilted her head back and opened her mouth to drink some water.

"We're almost there," Jey called to us. He'd pulled away from the group as we struggled to keep up.

"Finally," Leta muttered.

I gave her a small smile, but she cursed in response. It took me a moment to realize why.

Her foot had slipped across the surface of the stone, not catching the edge of the foothold. She rocked backward to prevent herself from falling forward, but she overcompensated, leaning too far back.

She teetered and I reached for her, her name a cry upon my lips.

But I was too late.

She lost her grip and fell backward toward the crashing waves below.

# CHAPTER 49

# CAYDER

Leta plummeted toward the ocean. Her mouth was open in mid-scream, and yet no sound came out.

"Leta!" I cried.

I'd failed her.

All I'd wanted to do was protect my sister. To free her from Vardean. To allow her to live a normal life. A life of freedom.

But it was over now. As soon as she hit the ocean, she would be gone forever.

There wasn't time to seek out edem. There wasn't time to change the past, present or future. There was only time to watch Leta fall into the waves and the rocks waiting below.

I couldn't hear anything but my sister's voice when she was four years old. Telling me we would be together forever. Us against the world.

I had closed my eyes, not wanting to see the moment she was taken from me, when I heard another clap of thunder.

Instinctively, my eyes snapped open. This time, it wasn't the storm.

I gasped at the sight before me, nearly losing my own grip of the stone wall.

The hullen.

But not the creature I'd glimpsed in Ferrington. Not the outline of some kind of beast. This creature was unmistakable and terrifying. Its horns rising three feet on either side of its head, its wings expansive and feathery. Its eyes like the glint of silver in moonlight. I shuddered as it drew nearer, the rain dripping off its beating wings.

*"Burning shadows,"* Kema remarked.

Another fork of bright white lightning tore across the sky. The light illuminated the creature's outline and Leta dangling from its taloned feet.

"Leta!" I cried with relief.

Her eyes were wide and mouth open, but she was alive. Thanks to the hullen.

The hullen offered Leta to us from its talons. Jey grabbed Leta's arm and pulled her onto the stone wall beside him. The hullen flapped its wings, hovering in front of us for a moment.

"Thank you," I whispered.

The hullen turned to take flight, returning back through the veil to whatever was on the other side.

I understood now, the veil was a doorway to another world, a world where the hullen lived and breathed.

"Are you all right?" I asked Leta.

"I'm fine." Her voice was light and breathless. She touched her shoulder where the hullen had grabbed her. "It saved me."

"The hullen protected you," I said, stating the obvious. "Twice."

The creature had saved Leta when she'd been in need both here and in Ferrington. Leta hadn't used edem to bring the hullen to her; the hullen had sensed her fear as she fell. Her pain.

Something tugged at the back of my mind, begging me to listen.

I couldn't ignore the truth laid out in front of me. Not only were the hullen *not* dangerous, but they protected people. Then why were they only in Ferrington? Why weren't they helping people all over Telene?

Something must have drawn them out there. Something that generated a lot of pain. Something that called to them louder than anything else.

*The Regency's weapons.* It had to be!

Leta had said the hullen were known for breaking into homes in Ferrington, searching for something. What if they were searching for the Regency base? Searching to destroy it? To end the pain the weapons caused and *could* cause?

The hullen came from the same world as edem; it wasn't a stretch to believe they could see the past, present *and* future. Which meant the future the hullen could sense was worrisome enough for them to cross through the veil and try to stop it.

We had to figure out what the Regency was up to.

———

By the time we reached the bridge, my fingertips and palms were red raw. My feet weren't in much better shape, my socks in tatters.

But we'd made it. We were alive. The storm had passed, and all that remained was a light mist.

Jey was the first to make it down to the landing. He held out his hand to help Leta down. Kema and I jumped down beside them.

The bridge leading out from the veil down to Vardean was closed off by large wooden double doors.

While my original plan had been to jump straight into the ocean, I was now drawn in a different direction.

"Where are you going?" Kema asked as I opened the doors.

"To unmask the Regency," I said. "And uncover the truth."

The Regency headquarters was a brightly lit room where machinery buzzed and whined. A towering bronze celestial globe sat in the center. The globe spun, two rings shifting across its surface. It occasionally stopped moving when the two rings intersected.

The edemmeter.

Standing beside the globe was the princess. She held up a strange-looking gun that contained a glass tube of swirling dark shadows.

*Edem.*

She pointed the barrel of the gun at a tall man with blond hair and a silver Regency cape.

Both the man and the princess turned as I opened the doors.

"Father?" Jey asked.

The Regency General, Dr. Bueter, was very much alive.

# CHAPTER 50

# PRINCESS ELENORA

Elenora hadn't planned on betraying Cayder. He had been kind to her, and she had often thought about pressing her lips to his. To inhale his sigh, and he inhale hers. She imagined them walking hand in hand along the castle isle. She imagined falling asleep to the sound of his breathing and waking to his beautiful smile.

But that future was elusive. And Elenora had more pressing concerns.

Elenora knew the Regency General was alive the moment Cayder told her that Jey had killed him almost two months ago. That was impossible, of course, for the Regency General had arrested her on the beach a week later. How could a dead man still be leading the Regency?

As much as she hated Dr. Bueter, she was thrilled to realize he was still alive, because that meant her brother was too.

While Cayder and Kema had been focused on getting Yarlyn's

key during Jey's distraction, Elenora had her sights set on stealing an agent's key to the Regency headquarters.

She had planned to part ways with the others, but when she saw the agents in the foyer, she realized she couldn't access the headquarters without attracting attention. She needed a diversion. And she'd promised herself, and the memory of her brother, that she would find a way out. Whatever the cost.

Unfortunately, that cost was betraying Cayder and his friends.

Elenora had locked eyes with Cayder the moment she placed the Regency key into the elevator and pushed the lever down. She wanted to say so much. Most of all, she wanted to apologize. But Cayder and the others only cared about freedom. Elenora wanted more than that. She wanted to hold the Regency General accountable.

Most of all, she wanted her brother back. And she knew Cayder didn't believe her brother could still be alive. She needed to do this herself. For once, she wasn't going to be told where to go, what to do or what to wear.

Elenora's fate was in her own hands for the first time in her entire life, and it was thrilling.

As the elevator descended into the rock below, Elenora ran through her situation.

She was dressed in a guard uniform, but guards weren't permitted down in the headquarters. She would be captured as soon as they saw her. She looked around the elevator for something that could be used as a weapon, but of course, there was nothing.

As the elevator descended lower, the light above flickered, inviting edem inside.

Elenora grinned and placed her hand into the shadow.

"Disguise me," she commanded.

Edem coiled around her hands, across her chest, and rolled down her back, transforming into a long silver Regency cloak.

"Thank you," she whispered into the dark.

———

When the elevator stopped, Elenora stepped into a corridor that tunneled underneath Vardean. She took a deep breath, steadying her nerves. She had never done anything like this. She had never done anything unexpected. Every moment of every day had been planned for her. But now she was taking back control.

Even with her agent uniform, Elenora had to tread carefully. She followed the flickering light bulbs that lined the rocky ceiling. The Regency didn't seem to care about the lights down here; edem came and went as the lights flashed on and off.

She knew she was close to the headquarters as the buzz and whine of machinery echoed down the tunnel.

*This is it. I'm coming for you, General.*

Elenora stepped into a large room with a bronze globe spinning in the center. She knew from her meetings with the Regency General that this was the edemmeter. A dozen or so agents were examining the globe where two rings had collided.

"Edem was used in Vardean, General," one of the agents said.

No one had even turned to look at her, the flap of her cloak behind her marking her as one of their own.

"How?" Dr. Bueter asked, approaching the edemmeter.

Elenora glanced around the room. This was her moment. She would find out what really happened to her brother. And she would bring him back.

"The glass prism has been shattered!" Elenora declared.

That attracted everyone's attention.

Dr. Bueter turned to her. "What did you say?" he asked, speaking in that low and slow way of his.

"That's why I came down here, General," Elenora said, hoping he wouldn't recognize *her* voice. "The inmates are using edem to escape! We need everyone's help upstairs!"

"That's impossible." Dr. Bueter shook his head.

"I'm afraid not," one of the agents said. "The edemmeter doesn't lie."

Elenora fought back a grin. She was using his own trusted equipment against him.

"Go, then." He waved to the Regency agents. "Do what you must to contain the situation."

The agents each grabbed a weapon from the wall and headed down the corridor. Elenora stood off to the side as they left.

The anger bubbled inside her, dark and bitter. This man had taken her brother from her, and yet he walked around the room as though he owned it. As though *he* were the king.

*This is what he wanted all along,* she realized. *Power.*

She watched him use his equipment, hoping he would reveal how he'd come back from the dead, and how Elenora could perform the same process on her brother.

After a while, she realized she would have to force the truth from the general's lips. Time was running out. The agents would soon return after finding the prism still in one piece.

Elenora grabbed a weapon from the wall. She watched the swirling darkness in a glass chamber above the trigger.

Was this the same kind of weapon used on her brother?

"Not joining your agents, Dr. Bueter?" she asked.

Dr. Bueter flinched; he had been so focused on his work, he hadn't realized she had stayed behind and had been watching him this entire time.

"Why are you still here?" he asked.

Elenora lifted the gun. "To avenge my brother."

She pulled the trigger. A small black flame shot out of the gun's barrel. It hit the table beside the general, which disintegrated into a cloud of dust.

"Burning shadows," Elenora gasped. "What is this thing?"

Dr. Bueter put his hands up in surrender. "Who are you? What do you want?"

Elenora advanced and backed Dr. Bueter into a corner. "You don't recognize me?" she asked.

His eyes roamed her face, and Elenora enjoyed his confusion. "No. Should I?"

"You *should* bow," she said. "While I haven't been crowned yet in my brother's absence, I am unofficially your queen."

Dr. Bueter's mouth dropped open. "Princess Elenora?"

"Are you that surprised to see me?" she asked. "You locked me up in here after that day on the beach. Did you expect I wouldn't fight back?"

"Put the gun down, Princess," he said. For the first time, she felt like he was taking her seriously.

"No," she replied. "Not until you tell me what you did to my brother."

Dr. Bueter nodded to the gun in her hands. "I think you've already figured that out."

"Where is he?" She glanced around the room as though her brother might be locked down here.

"He's dead," Dr. Bueter said. "For all intents and purposes."

"So were you." Elenora stepped closer. "And yet here you stand."

"That's different."

"How?" she urged.

Surely her brother could be brought back the same way?

"Tell me!" she demanded.

Before he could reply, the door to the bridge outside opened and Cayder walked inside.

# CHAPTER 51

# JEY

Jey wondered if he'd slipped while climbing and hit his head on a rock. He swayed, catching himself on the side of the building.

It couldn't be his father. His father was dead.

Jey had seen his father's body disintegrate and the death echo appear on Leta's hands. And he'd been arrested for the crime the moment he confessed.

If his father was alive, why hadn't anyone told him? Why was he in Vardean at all?

His father was the reason they were all here. And yet he was standing as though it was another day at the office. Albeit a very strange office, with a furious princess holding a gun to his head.

Leta made a strange, strangled sound beside him. Jey glanced down at her. Her breath was coming in shudders, like the night she'd thought she'd killed his father.

"What are you doing here?" the princess asked.

"Really?" Jey replied. "That's your first question?"

"Jey," his father said, "stay calm so she doesn't attack."

"Calm?" Jey snorted. "You were dead. And now you're not."

His father held up his hands. "I can explain."

"You better," he said.

"I don't care about your explanations." The princess butted the nuzzle of the weapon against Jey's father's chest. "I care about my brother. Bring him back. *Now*."

"I can't," his father replied. "That's not how this works."

"This?" The princess fired the gun at one of the electrical panels on the wall. It disintegrated under the black flame.

"Stop!" Dr. Bueter cried. "Please, don't destroy everything I've created."

"Why shouldn't I?" the princess asked. "You destroyed everything I care about."

"It was an accident!" Dr. Bueter said. "I didn't know what your brother looked like, like I didn't know your face. When he broke into the Regency headquarters, I thought it was espionage. I ordered my agents to shoot him. I didn't realize who he was until it was too late. Tell her, Jey. Tell her I'm not a cruel man."

*Cruel? No.* But he wasn't a kind man either.

Jey approached his father cautiously, even though it was the princess who held the gun.

"Did you know I was in prison?" Jey asked. "For your murder?"

His father's eyes went wide. "The Regency doesn't control Vardean; the monarchy does."

"That monarchy?" Jey gestured to the gun-wielding princess.

"You mean the princess who has been locked up for almost two months?"

"Let's go, Jey," Leta said from the doorway. She hadn't stepped into the headquarters. She was looking at his father as though he were a ghost.

"I agree," Kema said. "Let's get out of here while we still can."

"Not until I have my answers," Jey replied.

He expected Cayder to argue with him, but he simply nodded. Finally, they were on the same page.

"Answer the question, Father," Jey said. "Did you know Leta and I were in prison?"

His father sighed. "Yes, Jey. I did know. But I couldn't do anything about it."

Jey should have been surprised, but he wasn't. At this point, he would have been more surprised if his father had done something in his son's best interests, as opposed to the Regency's.

"You didn't want anyone to know you weren't really dead," the princess said. "Why is that?"

Jey liked this side of the princess; it almost made him forget about her betraying them. *Almost.*

"Because he didn't want anyone to know about his base in Ferrington, isn't that right?" Cayder asked. "You didn't want anyone to know about your weapons, about the pain and destruction you plan to cause."

"You don't know anything," Jey's father said.

The princess raised the gun to meet his eyes. "Then explain. How did you come back?"

Jey's father nodded to the gun in Elenora's hand. "Squeeze the trigger."

His father had lost his mind. He wanted the princess to shoot him?

"Shoot the panel again." His father motioned to where the panel had disintegrated.

Elenora narrowed her slate-gray eyes before pulling the trigger. The obsidian flame blazed in an arc toward the panel, and rather than further destroying the equipment, the panel pieced itself back together from dust.

"Edem," Jey's father said, "is the manipulation of time. Harnessing edem's power allows us to unmake something and then bring it back."

"Harnessing?" Cayder asked. "You mean *weaponizing*."

"It depends on how it's used," Jey's father said. "I was nothing but bones thanks to her." His blue eyes slid over to Leta, and she shrunk back. "My team were able to reach me in time and undo the damage, thanks to what *you* call a weapon."

"You shot my brother," the princess said. "It *is* a weapon. Bring him back now!"

Jey's father shook his head. "That's not how it works. You need something to undo—some remains. Your brother has gone to the other side."

"What other side?" Jey asked.

That familiar look of frustration crossed his father's face. "As I said, edem is the manipulation of time. When you use edem, you take something from the past or future. When your desire is fulfilled, the object returns to its timeline. The world on the other side"—he nodded to the crackling veil—"is where something goes when it's been displaced by time. A holding station, if you will."

He gestured to Elenora's agency outfit. "I suppose *you* were the one who used edem earlier?"

The princess nodded, the gun's barrel not wavering.

"Where do you think the clothes you were wearing beforehand are right now?" Jey's father raised a fair eyebrow.

Leta took in a shuddering breath beside Jey. "You're saying that if someone dies from edem, they're transported to the other side of the veil?" she asked, exchanging a look with Cayder.

"Yes," he said bluntly.

"What about my brother?" the princess asked. "Where is he?"

"I don't know," he admitted. "Somewhere on the other side."

"You don't care," she replied.

She was right. Jey's father didn't care about anything other than the Regency. He didn't even care enough to reveal to his own son that he was still alive or to free Leta from the guilt she held over his death.

All of this was his father's fault.

"Why?" Jey asked. "What is so important that you had to keep being alive a secret?"

Jey knew no answer his father gave would ever be good enough. And yet he still wanted to know. He wanted to hear the last excuse his father would make, before he moved on. *Really* moved on.

No more acting.

"Telene has been on the verge of destruction for years," Jey's father said. "And not because of the veil, because of our king."

Jey thought the princess was going to shoot his father there and then, but she didn't.

"Our war is not with the world beyond the veil," he continued. "It's not a war with edem or the hullen. It's here. Within our own world, just beyond Telene's shores. And I needed to gain the upper hand."

# CHAPTER 52

# CAYDER

Unlike Jey, I was not surprised to find the general alive.

Now I understood why the princess had reacted the way she had when I'd first told her about the Regency General's death. I thought she had been questioning our faith in Jey, but she had questioned the general's death altogether. And when we found out about the weapons in Ferrington, she had been hopeful, not concerned. Hopeful that her brother was still alive, like the general was.

"You want to wage war on the other nations?" I asked. That was what this was all about?

World domination, as Jey had joked.

"I want to force the other nations to reopen the borders," the general said. "Without trade, Telene will not survive the next decade."

"You obliterated our main source of trade in Ferrington," Leta said. "With your edem weapon!"

After seeing the weapon in action, it was clear what had been the cause of the inferno in Ferrington. It wasn't a fire at all, but a black blaze. A weapon that turned life into dust.

"An unfortunate accident," the general said. "We were working on a new weapon, one with a greater reach." He shrugged as though three hundred lives hadn't been lost that day. "Not all experiments go to plan."

I didn't believe him. He could have undone the damage if he wanted, and yet he hadn't. "I think your experiment went exactly to plan. You *wanted* to wipe out the entire town, and the hullen along with it. But you didn't know that the hullen were impervious to your weapon. Why would edem hurt the hullen when they come from the same place?"

The general narrowed his eyes at me. "Cayder Broduck, correct?" He laughed. "I should have realized the weapon's creator would have an intelligent son."

I glanced at Leta in shock.

*No.* Our mother never would have created something so destructive. Our mother was kind. Caring. She didn't create weapons. She didn't hurt people.

The general nodded at my realization. "She was the best of us. I was sorry when she passed. We tried to bring her back, but there was nothing left of her."

I grabbed the gun from the princess and pressed it into the general's chest.

"Cayder, no!" Leta pulled on my arm.

"What did you do to her?" I snarled.

"Nothing!" He held up his hands in surrender. "She was testing out a new weapon. She was a scientist. Accidents happen. We all know the risks."

I was getting sick of hearing about "accidents."

"Let's see if you can come back to life twice," I said, my finger on the trigger.

"Come on, Cayder," Kema said. "This isn't what we came here for. This isn't you. Let him go."

That was what my father said. *The only way to move on is to let go.* Let Mother go.

Grief had tied me to my anger, and my anger fed into my grief. Shooting the general wouldn't bring our mother back.

I handed the weapon over to the princess.

Unlike Elenora, I wasn't here for revenge. Kema was right; I was here to free my sister.

"Let's go," I said, grabbing Leta's hand.

But it was too late.

Half a dozen agents entered the headquarters. The agents brandished edem-fueled weapons; they pointed one at each of us.

"Took you long enough," the general said, pushing the gun in Elenora's hand away.

The general had been stalling, telling us what we wanted to hear so Elenora wouldn't shoot.

"Apologies, General," one agent remarked. "The prism has not been shattered. It was a ruse."

"Clearly." The general gestured to us. "Now arrest these intruders."

"No!" the princess said, pointing the weapon back at the general. "Take a step toward any of us, and I'll kill your leader."

"Please, Princess," the general said with an exhausted sigh. "You know that if you shoot me, it's not the end. My team can bring me back. But they won't do the same for you and your friends."

"Maybe not." She shouldered the weight of the gun. "Still, I bet this hurts." She pulled the trigger.

The small black flame shot out and hit the general's chest. The black fire scorched away the general's uniform and burrowed through skin and muscle and bone. The general screamed as the fire tore into him.

He sagged to the floor, his hand pressed to the hole in his chest.

"Arrest them!" he ordered.

One agent shot toward us, and I ducked down behind the globe, pulling Leta along with me. The princess shot back, disintegrating a stone wall. A gray haze filled the air.

"Stop shooting!" the general cried. "You'll destroy everything!"

An agent knocked the princess in the side with the butt of his gun. She dropped like a stone, and he pulled the weapon from her grasp.

"We have to get out of here," I said to Leta.

She nodded. "To the ocean."

I shook my head. "New plan."

Now we knew the veil held an entire world behind it. A world with creatures that wanted to protect, not kill. A world where Mother was possibly still alive.

*No.* I didn't want to escape Vardean. I didn't want to jump into the ocean and hope that we could find a boat to take us to shore.

I wanted to go through the veil.

# CHAPTER 53

## CAYDER

*Step Eight: Escape Through the Veil*

We had one last chance for freedom.

And now I understood what that meant.

Freedom wasn't justice. It wasn't peace. It was fighting for what was right. Fighting for the truth. And I wouldn't give up. Not until my last breath.

An agent appeared out of the smoky haze, his gun raised. He swung the weapon at me, and I ducked out of the way. Another agent appeared and tackled Leta to the ground, the muzzle of his gun pressing against her temple.

"Go!" she screamed.

There was only one way out of here.

I ran down the bridge, out across the ocean and toward the veil, although every cell in my body told me to stop. A buzzing sound filled my head as I approached the black crack in the sky. Even louder was my breath.

I couldn't hear if anyone was following me, and I didn't turn around to check.

The closer I got to the veil, the dimmer the floodlights became. No light shone onto the veil itself; that would prevent the Regency from carrying out their tests. By the time I reached the edge of the bridge, I could see edem swirling all around me.

I stuck both hands into the darkness.

"Bring me the hullen," I ordered.

Seven years had passed since I'd used edem, and I'd forgotten the way it felt.

The shadows rolled over my fingers and writhed around my arms. The feeling was cool and warm at the same time, as though all sensation was muted. I held my hands up in front of my face to check that my arms were still there.

A sense of peace washed over me. A sense of control. That everything would be all right.

That I was protected.

The constant hum of the veil behind me was silenced.

I turned around slowly.

Behind me stood the hullen. I stepped away from the veil and allowed the creature to climb onto the bridge. Another stood close behind. They both opened their mouths of pitch-black and screeched into the night.

I clasped my hands over my ears, certain my eardrums were about to burst.

The hullen took flight and charged toward the Regency agents.

The agents stopped fighting and stared at the vengeance heading their way.

One hullen picked up the agent that had Leta pinned to

the ground in its talons and threw him off the cliff. The man screamed as he fell to the water below.

The agents fired at the hullen, but the black flames danced across the creatures' wings, creating no impact. The hullen charged again, knocking the agents into the wall.

Kema clocked an agent in the chin and stole his gun. She shot at a man who had Jey cornered. The man fell to the floor.

The hullen let out a screech, then returned back through the veil.

"Come on!" I yelled to the others.

They bolted down the bridge toward me.

Something warm crept along my back, heating either side of my shoulder blades. It felt like the warmth of smoke blown against my skin. I pulled my shirt off one shoulder and glimpsed a gray pattern of feathery wings trailing down my back.

An echo mark of the hullen.

Kema was the first to reach me. "Nice work, Boy Wonder." She grinned, and I smiled back.

Jey and Leta arrived hand in hand.

"Agreed," Jey said. "You saved our skin back there. I owe you one."

Leta released Jey and threw her arms around my neck. "Thank you, Cayder."

"We're not out of here yet."

The princess was the last to reach us. She was covered in ashes from the destruction she'd caused.

"I'm sorry, Cayder," she said. She nodded at each of us. "I'm sorry to all of you. I should have told you what I was planning. I should have trusted you."

"We wouldn't have helped," Jey offered with a sly grin.

"I know."

The princess had been selfish, and while I hadn't forgiven her for her betrayal, I understood her reasoning. She would do anything for her brother. As I would do anything for Leta. And without the princess, we never would have uncovered the truth.

My mother had died from edem, which meant that she was on the other side of the veil. Along with the king.

"You're not going to like what I suggest next," I said.

Leta glanced over her shoulder to what remained of the headquarters. "Anything to get us out of here. The Regency are sure to rebuild."

She was right. With their edem-fueled weapons, they could easily undo all the damage we'd created. We needed a more permanent solution. We needed the king.

I gestured to the veil. "We go through. To find Mother. And your brother." I nodded to the princess.

The princess blinked. "Really? I can come with you?"

"I promised I'd get you out of here." That promise felt like it belonged to someone else. Someone who believed that if you had faith in the justice system, good prevailed. But I wasn't that boy anymore. Sometimes you needed to fight for freedom.

Her expression softened. "Thank you, Cayder."

I nodded, not ready to accept her apology. Not yet. Her betrayal still blistered inside my chest like a wound from an edem weapon. And while I wasn't sure I could stop the spread, the princess didn't deserve to be locked up in Vardean. I wasn't sure anyone did.

"What about the Regency General?" Kema asked. "He'll be on the other side."

"Then we'll take him down there too," the princess said.

We all glanced at Jey, and he shrugged. "I agree with Warrior Princess."

Kema laughed. "You know I'm in."

That left one person. The reason we were all here.

"Ready?" I asked my sister.

She placed her free hand in mine. "Ready."

"No time like the present," Jey agreed.

"What do you think is on the other side, aside from the hullen?" Leta asked. "What do you think is going to happen next?"

I gazed into the darkness of the veil. It called to me. Beckoned me closer. The whispers increased, and I was sure I could hear my mother's voice.

"I don't know," I admitted. "But whatever it is, we'll face it together."

We launched off the bridge and into the sky.

KEEP READING FOR MORE
FROM ASTRID SCHOLTE

"This riveting YA thriller . . . is among the most exciting stuff being put out
in the genre right now." —*Entertainment Weekly*

# THE VANISHING DEEP

Bestselling author of *Four Dead Queens*

## ASTRID SCHOLTE

# CHAPTER ONE

## TEMPEST

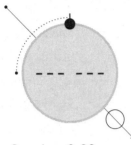

Sunday, 8:00 a.m.

I DIDN'T WANT to resurrect my sister because I loved her.

I didn't want one final goodbye, to whisper words left unsaid or clear my conscience of any slights between us. I didn't want to hear her voice say my name, *Tempe*, one last time.

I wanted to soothe the anger that scorched through me. An anger that had a life of its own, taking hold within me, propelling me to action—even on the days when I was exhausted from the early-morning dive, even when I'd had enough of this scrappy life.

I wanted to drown memories of her long dark hair, curling in the water as she dove deeper ahead of me, always knowing where to search next. I wanted to extinguish memories of her dancer limbs twirling above her head as storms raged nearby. I wanted to forget her now-silenced bell-like voice once and for all.

As much as the thought of her name angered me, the thought of never hearing it again angered me even more.

Her name had begun to fade in the two years since her death, like the last rumble of thunder in a storm. In the beginning, friends—all Elysea's—would say *your sister*, as if saying her name would send a fresh wave of tears down my already flushed cheeks. Then, as days turned into weeks, her name was said soft and tentative, signaling to me that it was time to start moving on. To get out of bed, to live my life.

When weeks turned into months, people stopped speaking about her altogether. As though she never existed.

Then I'd heard something that changed how I felt about her, transforming my grief to anger.

So now I *needed* to hear her voice one last time. I needed the truth. And for that, I needed to resurrect her.

Neither of us could rest until then.

The boat shifted with the waves; I adjusted my footing so I didn't fall into the sea. The *Sunrise* had been my parents' transportation to work. Small, but swift. The shell-colored deck was triangular, with two "wings" underneath the stern of the boat, which hooked down and into the water to keep balance at high speeds. A cramped cabin was suspended below, its belly dipping into the sea like an overfed familfish.

I gazed at the deep blue waters. From above, you could see a slight turbulence beneath—a hint of something other than sand, salt and sea.

A sunken city—one that I had scavenged for years, and from which I had never returned empty-handed. My deeply tanned olive skin spoke of the years I'd spent on and under the water, searching for scraps.

Today would be my last dive here. Elysea had found this site when I was twelve years old, and after five years, I knew every twist and turn of the labyrinth of steel, glass and stone. There was only one room left untouched. And I wasn't leaving until I explored it. After that, I would need to find a new dive site and hope it hadn't already been ravaged like so many sunken cities in this section of the sea.

I tightened the straps of my flippers, made from blunted blades of Old World knives. The rusty, thin metal sheets shrieked as I flexed my foot to test the movement.

"Oh, shut up," I said. The flippers were my mother's, and I couldn't afford new ones. I wouldn't waste Notes on anything other than reviving my sister, or topping off my breather.

*One last dive,* I thought as I put the breathing tube in my mouth and pulled the pliable transparent dome over my head. As I clipped it onto the neck of my diving skin, the dome inflated.

*One final goodbye.* Another memory to shelve, another link to Elysea forever severed. The thought should've brought a wave of sadness, but I felt only cold, steely determination. Soon I, too, could forget Elysea's name.

I took a shallow breath to check the gas levels of the small cylinder attached to my belt.

My breather beeped twice.

*Oxygen low.*

I yanked the dome off and spat out my breather. Aside from food, diving gas was the most expensive commodity. It allowed us to search for relics from the Old World—for anything useful in the new one. My dive finds barely covered the costs of living on the Equinox Reef and what was left went toward my sister's resurrection. I was hoping I could unearth something from the remaining room to fund topping off my breather and allow me time to locate a new ruin, without having to dip into my savings.

I placed the breather back in my mouth and pulled the dome over my face. The levels would have to be enough.

I rattled some black stones with iridescent blue spirals in my palm, like miniature swirling galaxies. I dropped one into the ocean, saying a prayer to the Gods below, to allow me to enter their world, their sacred sanctuary—and survive it. It was a childish habit. When Elysea and I were young, we'd thought it was the will of the Gods below who took souls from boats in a storm and the air from the lungs of divers. We didn't realize it was simply chance, bad luck or unskilled diving. The perils of our world.

Together, we'd learned to conquer the ocean. Or so I'd thought. Until Elysea had drowned, almost exactly two years ago.

Before I allowed any further doubt to muddy my mind, I grabbed my oilskin bag, clipped it to my diving belt and tilted backward off the boat.

The water was cold, but only my fingertips were cool, the

rest of my body protected by my diving skin—a material made of thin, rubbery blue plates stitched together like fish scales, which I always wore under my clothes. I kicked my weighted metal flippers, which coaxed me downward.

*Take shallow, steady breaths.* I couldn't help but hear my sister's voice in my head. She'd taught me how to dive, after all.

"The free fall is easy," she would say. "Save your air for the return trip. When you'll need it. Just follow me into the dark, Tempe." She never called me by my full name—Tempest—saying it was too harsh for her little sister. "Temp*ee* sounds sweeter," she'd said.

I could barely remember the little girl I'd once been.

A plume of bright light shone from the corner of my eye—my map to the world below. I kicked toward it as I fell. Before long, my vision was illuminated by shades of blue, purple and pink, dotted along shafts of rusted metal. Since the Great Waves around five hundred years ago, bioluminescent coral had grown along the city ruins, lighting the way toward the ocean floor, like Old World lights on cobbled streets, or the stars in the night sky. A sunken constellation.

The sight never failed to take my breath away. And even though the building was long dead, it glowed with life. It was beautiful.

I followed the path downward.

When I passed a red-brown metal turret, I took a slight turn to the left. Rusticles, like fossilized seaweed, dripped from every edge. The holes that were once doorways and windows into a lively world were now the soulless eyes of a watchful, watery tomb.

A lost city. A drowned society. The perfect harvest.

My breather beeped again. I took shallower breaths, hoping the Gods were in favor of my presence. Many divers had searched for the Gods below. A temple, a shrine, a palace. *Anything*. But they'd remained undiscovered. It gave naysayers ammunition to doubt the deities' existence.

But in a world made almost entirely of water, we needed our guides. The Old World believed in the Gods above and followed the stars to journey across the land. But with hardly any land remaining, it was pointless to look to the sky. The water was our master.

I wished we'd begun with the lower levels of the building when we'd initially discovered this site. But it had been my first dive. Elysea had wanted to start closer to the surface, even though I'd argued that I was ready. She'd only been two years older than me, but after our parents' deaths, she'd acted more like my guardian than my sister. Back then, I'd barely fit into my mom's abandoned flippers.

"You'll grow into them," Elysea had said, fastening them as tight as she could around my then-small feet. "It's better that they're big so you can use them for longer."

I hadn't argued, excited to be included on the dive.

After five years, I was now one of the best divers on our home of the Equinox. While other kids went to school, sailed with their parents, swam with their friends, danced with their siblings, I dove. And dove and dove.

There was nothing on the surface for me now.

I dove deeper, keeping my breaths shallow to save gas.

As much as I missed diving with Elysea, I liked being by myself. With nothing but the waters to guide me, the Gods below protecting me, and the quiet to soothe my restless mind. My anger.

Elysea had been lucky to find this ruin. It must've broken free from a larger cluster of buildings during the Great Waves. Most sunken cities were overcrowded with divers, and few relics were left to be found. Not this building. This ruin was all mine.

The dive site was located close to the isle of Palindromena, and most divers steered clear of the brutal waves that crashed against the jagged coast. Too many people drowned there. Plus, those who lived on the Equinox were superstitious. The island was cloaked in mystery and tainted by death.

But I wasn't afraid of Palindromena. The facility had always been a specter in my life, but never touched me directly, like a looming shadow.

When I reached the ocean floor, I darted through a knocked-out window. Coral had grown around the frame, lighting the entrance. Many people believed the Gods below were to thank for the coral that had appeared in the years since the Great Waves, showing the way to sunken treasures. Without the

Gods, and their coral, the Old World would've been lost to the ocean.

My breather let out another warning beep. I had to be quick.

The building's ground floor had been a row of tiny shops, all interconnected. More coral bloomed inside, illuminating the rooms. The first shop was some kind of eatery. Tables tipped upside down, slivers of ceramic plates and glass cups were now debris in the water.

I rushed through the room, keeping my eye out for anything I might've missed. Anything *valuable*. Old cups were interesting, but not worth many Notes. I needed something useful for more diving gas and to fund Elysea's resurrection.

Down here, skeletons were as common as the yellow familfish that traveled in schools of hundreds up near the Equinox. Coral had grown in the gaps of disintegrated bone, piecing together the skeletons and fortifying them from further decomposition. They floated through doorways and rooms as though they continued to live and breathe, while their flesh and muscle had long peeled away.

I was twelve when I first saw a glowing patchwork skeleton, providing fuel for a week's worth of nightmares. Now they were friends. I'd given them names, backgrounds, personalities. It made it less creepy. *Slightly.*

I'd never made friends easily, but down here, the skeletons didn't have a choice.

I nodded to Adrei. His red-and-pink calcified skull rested on the café counter, his bony hand beside his face as though

I'd caught him deep in thought. On the ocean floor, there was little movement, no currents or fish to disturb him. As I swam by, my flippers rippled through the water and his luminous fingers rattled, as if to say hello.

I continued on to the next room.

"Hey, Celci," I said to a skeleton stuck floating between two corridors. I'd named her after my old aunt, who'd passed away from crystal lung when I was a child. I still remembered her teeth too large for her face, like this skeleton. I gently nudged Celci as I passed, moving her into the next room to be with Adrei. Even the dead shouldn't be alone.

The shop next door had been a bookstore; I passed without a second look. The room had been sealed before I'd forced open the door. While I'd managed to salvage some books, the rest had quickly broken down and clouded the room. The books I'd already retrieved weren't worth much; as soon as they were brought to the surface, the pages began to decompose in the humid salty air. Perhaps it would've been better to leave them down here, their words trapped within the pages, their untold stories safe.

So much of our history had disappeared. Most of the tales of the Old Gods had been forgotten, giving rise to the New Gods. People believed the Old Gods had turned away from us and our selfishness and didn't warn us of the impending waves.

When the Great Waves hit, people struggled to hold on to their faith.

It wasn't until the coral began blooming that people believed we weren't alone. We hadn't been abandoned by the Gods after all. Like the stars in the sky, the coral would guide us to supplies submerged below.

We could survive this new world with the remnants of the past.

My mom had believed in the Gods below, but my father hadn't. Did Dad's lack of faith cause their deaths? Did he misread the churning waters and darkening skies that became the vicious storm that destroyed their boat? But then, Elysea—

My breather let off a few frantic shrieks. *I hear you,* I thought. *But I'm not done yet.*

I arrived at the last untouched room and jimmied the door open with my diving pliers. I held my breath, not only to save diving gas but in anticipation. But I couldn't see anything inside. I snapped off a piece of coral from the door frame and swam into the room.

I let out a disappointed breath.

Bits of once-colorful material hung in threads from rusted poles, fallen from the ceiling.

A clothing shop.

I'd hoped the room, located at the back of the building, had been protected from the impact of the waves, like the bookshop had, but the shop's window faced an internal courtyard. And the glass was long gone.

I shifted old bits of clothing around in hopes of finding jewelry, trinkets, *anything*. But the Great Waves had drained all life from this room.

My breather started beeping more insistently. I had minutes left and I still needed to start my staggered ascent to avoid decompression sickness. I was going to have to buy more diving gas and hope it didn't take too long to find another dive site.

Then something caught my eye. Something nestled within a patch of bright pink coral. Something green. A rare color, certainly down here.

I swam through the shop's missing window and glanced up. Part of the building had collapsed onto itself, sealing the courtyard within. No wonder I'd never seen it.

But that wasn't what had caught my attention.

I swam forward, my heart beating in time with the increasing beeps of my breather. *It can't be. It can't be.*

When my fingertips touched the waxy green surface, I took in a dangerously deep breath. My breather started wailing, but it barely registered.

It was a plant. A *plant*! Thank the Gods below!

My breaths came in gasps now. A plant would be worth hundreds, thousands, of Notes.

I would be ready. Ready to go to Palindromena. At last, ready to say a final goodbye to Elysea.

My hands hovered over the plant, scared it would disintegrate at my touch.

How was this possible? Sure, some divers found plants, but most were a kind of seaweed. This was different. Seaweed couldn't grow down here in the dark. This was a land plant. And somehow it had survived.

I pushed debris away from the plant. Something had fallen on top of it and covered most of the foliage. Something organic, from the soft and granular feel of the debris. A tree! It must've fallen in the waves and protected the plant from decomposing.

I took in an excited breath, only to come up short. The breather's beeping had turned into a constant shriek.

I was out of air.

I shoved my fingers into the soil and dug around for the roots. *There.* I gave the plant a gentle tug, and it came up easily. A few leaves and branches snapped off. If I could get this plant to the surface intact, it would be a miracle.

A burn began to build in my chest as I pulled a transparent sleeve from my bag and wrapped it around the roots. Heat seared through me, shooting down my veins and bubbling at my lips.

*Air. I need air.*

I wouldn't be able to make it back through the shops and to the surface. I needed a quicker way out.

I glanced up. It was my only chance.

Tucking the plant under my arm, I kicked my flippers. Hard. The burn began to flame in my muscles.

*Surface. Now.*

I swam upward, reaching the blockage that had sealed in the courtyard. It was a section of plaster knocked askew from a nearby wall. I shoved the plaster with my shoulder, hoping it would give way and lead me up and into the light.

This building had been good to me. Surely it wouldn't let me down. Not now.

The breather stopped beeping, no longer needing to warn me. I was either dead or at the surface. Still, I had time. Years of diving experience had expanded my lungs. I held the small amount of oxygen in my chest. I had a few minutes left.

The plaster began to break free as I rammed into it, fragile from the hundreds of years of being submerged. I tore at the wall until I saw the glimmer of the sun. The surface!

I swam through the opening, but there wasn't time for a steady ascent. When I made it to the surface, I would have to take a recompression pill to neutralize the bubbles that were currently forming in my muscles and bloodstream. But that was the least of my problems.

The small amount of oxygen in my lungs was gone. My lungs were done. My legs were done.

I thought of Elysea. This was how she'd felt in her final moments. All around her, blue. All around me, blue. The burn. The ache. The terror.

But no one would find me down here. There was no one left *to* find me. I should've stayed down with Adrei. I didn't want to die alone, like my sister had.

I kicked and kicked, but the light seemed too far away. I heaved for another breath, but there was nothing left. I spat out the breather inside my dome, defeated.

This was it, my last moments. I thought of Mom and Dad.

And Elysea—even after everything she'd done. I hoped I would see them again, in whatever happens after death.

As my vision dimmed, my stubborn lungs tried one last time, heaving in a breath.

Air! I almost choked on it. Of course! A small amount of air had been used to inflate the dome.

My lungs expanded in relief. And the breath of oxygen was gone.

But it was enough.

I pushed for the surface.

TURN THE PAGE
FOR AN EXCERPT FROM

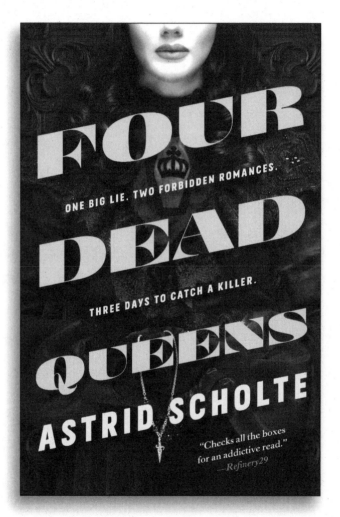

# *Keralie*

The morning sun caught the palace's golden dome, flooding the Concord with light. While everyone halted their business and glanced up—as though it were a sign from the four queens themselves—we perched overhead like sea vultures, ready to swoop in and pick them apart.

"Who shall we choose today?" Mackiel asked. He was leaning against a large screen atop a building that displayed the latest Queenly Reports. He looked like a charming, well-dressed young man from Toria. At least, that was what he *looked* like.

"Choices, choices," I said with a grin.

He moved to drape his arm heavily around my shoulder. "Who do you feel like being today? A sweet young girl? A damsel in distress? A reluctant seductress?" He puckered his lips at me.

I laughed and pushed him away. "I'll be whatever makes us the most money." I usually picked my targets, but Mackiel had been in a good mood this morning, and I didn't want to tip the boat. He submerged easily into darkness these days, and I'd have done anything to keep him in the light.

I shrugged. "You choose."

He raised his dark eyebrows before tilting his bowler hat to further survey the crowd. The line of kohl around his lids made his deep-set blue eyes stand out all the more. Nothing escaped his scrutiny. A familiar smirk played at his lips.

The crisp Concord air was clean, unlike the acrid tang of seaweed, fish and rotted wood that pervaded our home down on Toria's harbor. It was Quadara's capital and the most expensive city to live in, as it shared boundaries with Toria, Eonia and Ludia. Archia was the only region separated from the mainland.

The stores on the ground level sold a variety of approved goods, including Eonist medicines, the latest Ludist fashions and toys, and fresh Archian produce and cured meat—all collated and distributed by Torian traders. Squeals of children, the murmur of business and sighs of queenly gossip bounced between the glass storefronts.

Behind the buildings rose an opaque golden dome, encapsulating the palace and concealing the confidential dealings within. The palace entrance was an old stone building called the House of Concord.

As Mackiel searched for a target, he held his middle finger to his lips—an insult to the queens hiding inside their golden dome. When he caught my eye, he tapped his lip and grinned.

"Him," he said, his gaze landing on the back of a dark figure who descended the stairs from the House of Concord into the crowded main square. "Get me his comm case."

The target was clearly Eonist. While we Torians were bundled

2

up in layers to ward off the biting chill, he wore a tight-fitting black dermasuit over his skin, an Eonist fabric made of millions of microorganisms that maintained body temperature with their secretions. Gross, but handy in the depths of winter.

"A messenger?" I flashed Mackiel a hard look. The delivery would be of high importance if the messenger was coming from the House of Concord, the only place where Torians, Eonists, Archians and Ludists conducted business together.

Mackiel scratched at his neck with ring-covered fingers, a nervous habit. "Not up for the challenge?"

I scoffed. "Of course I am." I was his best dipper, slipping in and out of pockets with a feather-light touch.

"And remember—"

"Get in quick. Get out quicker."

He grabbed my arm before I could slip off the roof. His eyes were serious; it had been months since he'd looked at me that way—as though he cared. I almost laughed, but it lodged somewhere between my chest and throat.

"Don't get caught," he said.

I grinned at his concern. "When have I ever?" I climbed down from the rooftop and into the crowd.

I hadn't gotten far when an old man stopped abruptly in front of me and raised his hand to press four fingers to his lips in respect for the queens—the *proper* greeting, as opposed to Mackiel's middle-fingered version. I dug in my heels. My spiked soles gripped the well-worn cobblestones. I halted in time, my cheek brushing the back of his shoulders.

*Dammit!* What was it about the palace that inspired such slack-jawed stupidity? It wasn't like you could see anything through the

3

golden glass. And even if you could, so what? The queens didn't care about us. And certainly not someone like me.

I slapped the cane from the old man's hand. He stumbled to the side.

He turned, his face pinched in annoyance.

"Sorry!" I said. I fluttered my lashes at him from under my large-brimmed hat. "The crowd pushed in on me."

His expression softened. "No worries, my dear." He tipped his head. "Enjoy your day."

I gave him an innocent smile before slipping his silver pocket watch into a fold in my skirt. That would teach him.

I stood on my toes to find my target. *There.* He didn't look much older than me—eighteen, perhaps. His suit clung like a second skin—from his fingertips to his neck, covering his torso, legs and even his feet. While I wrestled with corsets and stiff skirts each and every day, I couldn't imagine his outfit would be any easier to dress in.

Still, I envied the material and the freedom of movement it allowed. Like him, my muscles were defined from constantly running, jumping and climbing. While it was not unusual for a Torian to be fit and trim, my muscles weren't from sailing back and forth to Archia, or from unloading heavy goods at the docks. I'd long been entangled within the darker side of Toria. Hidden beneath my modest layers and pinching corsets, no one knew of my wickedness. My work.

The messenger hesitated at the bottom of the House of Concord stairs, rearranging something in his bag. Now was my chance. That old man had given me inspiration.

4

I dashed toward the polished slate stairs, fixing my eyes on the palace with my best imitation of awe—or rather slack-jawed stupidity—on my face, my four fingers nearing my lips. Approaching the messenger, I snagged my toe in a gap between two tiles and pitched forward like a rag doll. Inelegant, but it would do the job. I'd learned the hard way that any pretense could easily be spotted. And I was nothing if not committed.

"Ah!" I cried as I crashed into the boy. The rotten part of me enjoyed the thwack as he hit the stones. I landed on top of him, my hands moving to his bag.

The messenger recovered quickly, pushing me away, his right hand tightly twisted around the bag. Perhaps this wasn't his first encounter with Mackiel's dippers. I stopped myself from shooting Mackiel a glare, knowing he'd be watching eagerly from the rooftop.

He was always watching.

Changing tactics, I rolled, purposely skinning my knee on the stone ground. I whimpered like the innocent Torian girl I pretended to be. I lifted my head to show my face from under my hat to take him in.

He had that Eonist look, evenly spaced eyes, full lips, high defined cheekbones and a proud jaw. The look they were engineered for. Curls of black hair framed his tan face. His skin was delicate, but hardy. Not at all like my pale creamy skin, which flaked and chapped in the winter wind and burned in the blistering summer sun. His eyes were on me. They were light, almost colorless, not the standard Eonist brown, which guarded against the sun's glare. Did it help him see in the dark?

"Are you all right?" he asked, his face giving nothing away.

Eonists' expressions were generally frozen, like the majority of their quadrant.

I nodded. "I'm so, so sorry."

"That's okay," he said, but his hand was still at his bag; I wasn't done with this charade just yet.

He glanced at my black boot, which had scuffed where my toe had caught between the stones, then to my knee cradled in my hands. "You're bleeding," he said in surprise. He did indeed think this was a ploy for his belongings.

I looked at my white skirt. A blotch of red had spread through my undergarments and was blooming across my knee.

"Oh my!" I swooned a little. I looked up into the bright sun until tears prickled behind my eyes, then turned back to him.

"Here." He grabbed a handkerchief from his bag and handed it to me.

I bit my lip to hide a grin. "I wasn't watching where I was going. I was distracted by the palace."

The messenger's strange pale eyes flicked to the golden dome behind us. His face betrayed no emotion. "It's beautiful," he said. "The way the sun illuminates the dome, it's as though it were alive."

I frowned. Eonists didn't appreciate beauty. It wasn't something they valued, which was ironic, considering how generically attractive they all were.

I bunched the hem of my skirt in my hands and began pulling it up over my knee.

"What are you doing?" he asked.

I swallowed down a laugh. "I was checking to see how bad it is." I pretended I only then remembered where he was from.

"Oh!" I rearranged my skirt to cover my legs. "How inappropriate of me." Intimacy was as foreign as emotions in Eonia.

"That's all right." But he turned his face away.

"Can you help me up?" I asked. "I think I've twisted my ankle."

He held out his hands awkwardly before deciding it was safer to grip my covered elbows. I leaned heavily against him, to ensure he didn't feel any shift in weight as I slipped a hand inside his bag. My fingers grasped something cool and smooth, about the size of my palm. The comm case. I slid it out and into a hidden pocket in my skirt. As soon as he had me on my feet, he released me as though he'd touched a month-old fish.

"Do you think you can walk?" he asked.

I nodded but swayed side to side. Novice dippers gave themselves away by dropping the act too soon after retrieving their prize. And my knee *did* hurt.

"I don't think so." My voice was light and breathy.

"Where can I take you?"

"Over there." I pointed to an empty chair and table in front of a café.

He held on to my elbow as he guided me over, using his broad shoulders to navigate the crowd. I fell into the chair and pressed the handkerchief to my knee. "Thank you." I tipped my head down, hoping he'd leave.

"Will you be okay?" he asked. "You're not alone, are you?"

I knew Mackiel would be watching from somewhere close by.

"No, I'm not alone." I put some indignation into my voice. "I'm with my father. He's doing business over there." I waved a hand vaguely at the surrounding shops.

The messenger crouched to look under the brim of my hat. I

flinched. There was something unsettling about his eyes up close. Almost like mirrors. Yet, under his gaze, I felt like the girl I was pretending to be. A girl who spent her day at the Concord with her family to enjoy the spoils of the other quadrants. A girl whose family was whole. A girl who hadn't shattered her happiness.

That moment passed.

Something flickered behind his expression. "Are you sure?" he asked. Was that real concern?

The cool of the metal case pressed against my leg, and Mackiel's hot gaze was on my back.

*Get in quick. Get out quicker.*

I had to disengage. "I need to rest for a bit. I'll be fine."

"Well, then," he said, glancing behind him to the House of Concord, his hand on his bag. As a messenger, his tardiness wouldn't be tolerated. "If you'll be all right . . ." He waited for me to refute him. I might have oversold my fragility.

"Yes. I'll be fine here. Promise."

He gave me a stiff Eonist nod, then said, "May the queens forever rule the day. Together, yet apart." The standard exchange of interquadrant goodwill. He turned to leave.

"Together, yet apart," I recited back to him. Before he had taken a step, I was up off the chair and among the crowd.

I clutched the comm case in my hand as I ran.

## ACKNOWLEDGMENTS

I wrote three different manuscripts before settling on *League of Liars* as my third book. After *Four Dead Queens* was published, I was much more aware that I wasn't just writing for me. Readers have expectations, and you've all been so incredibly supportive since my debut novel in 2019. I wanted to prove that your support was not in vain and return the favor in some way. And the only way I know how is to write a story worthy of your time. I hope *League of Liars* was that book for you!

First of all, I want to thank my mum and dad. When I was a teenager, Dad used to say that I'd make a good lawyer, as I was good at arguing my case. Instead, I decided to work in the film and TV industry and become an author. But I know he's just as proud. And without Mum's patience while I rambled on about my books, *League of Liars* would probably remain unfinished, and I would definitely be a nervous wreck.

Which brings me to Andrew. If it weren't for you, this book

100 percent wouldn't exist. You continue to be my anchor in the storm, and I promise to dedicate another book to you, one that hopefully doesn't release during a pandemic and will have a much easier publishing journey. Love you.

To my friends and family, who are always so encouraging, I will never not be surprised (and elated!) that you actually read my books. In particular, the TC girls, Katya, Ella, Jess and Shannon—thank you for being your awesome selves.

I'm so lucky to have such talented author friends. Huge thanks to Mel, Sabina Khan and Adalyn Grace for their friendship and wise words. Amie Kaufman, Marie Lu, C. S. Pacat, Sarah Glenn Marsh and Stephanie Garber, I admire your work so much and I'm so lucky to know you!

Without Penguin Teen, there would be no *Four Dead Queens*, *The Vanishing Deep* or *League of Liars*. Thank you to my editor, Stacey Barney, for helping me make this book much more than I ever could have imagined it could be; Theresa Evangelista for creating the incredible cover, which made me squeal (something I rarely do); Felicity Vallence for her marketing wonder powers; and Jennifer Klonsky and the entire Penguin team for their belief in me. A huge thank-you to Hillary Jacobson for coming on this journey with me and to my agent, Sarah Landis, for jumping in with such enthusiasm for this story and my writing.

And lastly, but importantly, I want to thank you. Without you, there wouldn't be a second book, or a third, or hopefully a fourth in my publishing career. I cannot thank you enough. I truly hope this book helped you escape the world we currently live in. It can be a difficult place at times, but I believe the best is just around the corner. We will have in-person events again. We will share in the joy of stories together. I look forward to seeing you there.

And that is no lie.